Dark Feathered Hearts
by
John Guy Collick

The final volume of The Book of the Colossus

Published by John Guy Collick

John Guy Collick asserts his moral right to be identified as the author of this book.

ISBN: 978-0-9954673-2-3

At the end of time all directions are given in relation to the body of God. His head lies to the north, and his feet point south.

And I recall when as a child
I felt your hand take mine
To lift me up from squalid wood and iron
To guide me over nickel floors,
Past cobalt walls
To point through crystal at an empty sky
And fill my head with dreams.
But most of all you taught me how to hate
The loving lies that said I'd found a home
In your cruel dark-feathered heart.

Odilon - Abigail Fabrice

Neke the Abhuman squatted in the middle of the lead map. He placed the storm lantern down, took the needle from behind his ear and traced the fractal marking the network of halls around the wreckage of the Whispering House. Something was wrong but he didn't know what. It nipped at the edge of his thoughts - a shadow scampering out of sight whenever he tried to pin the bastard down. To be fair it was the first time they'd attempted to pluck a building out of reality from eleven thousand leagues away, but King Max had been in mortal danger, leaving them no choice. After the destruction of the AntiHelix he'd ended up trapped in the emperor's mansion deep inside the Ear Canal and if they hadn't rescued him the Great Task would have finished in a heap of rubble at the feet of the giants Ombratulla, Belsalice and Ruth.

Aeons ago the Abhumans had lived in the centre of the left forearm of God - that immense mannequin tumbling through a void long emptied of stars and planets. Bereft of light and hope, they'd scavenged deep within the interstices of a being so vast that a single cell measured three miles across - each one a maze of wood, canvas and iron. At the point of despair - when they'd realised their race would perish before the deity woke, stood and walked through the portal into the next cosmos - the Brittle Hag came to them. The alien, atoning for her own people's self-centred cruelty, plucked them out of the abyss and stewarded them into awareness. She gifted them with a starship that contained its own universe, and charged them with a doom upon which the fate of every living and unborn human depended.

The Machine Men who'd built the heart and mind of God had created eight giants, each one an aspect of the sleeping god's soul, and sent them out into the realms of man to learn about the creatures they were destined to carry into the new universe. But traitors slew the titan Bassandis in the battle for Metacarpi, and only a fragment of his consciousness survived, locked inside Max Ocel's dreams. Neke and his people promised the Brittle Hag they would take the raggedy Time Scavenger back to the Head so the dead giant could be rebuilt.

If only it were so easy. The titan's sisters declared war on mankind and laid waste to the Empire of the Ear. King Max and Queen Abby were wilful children driven by their own passions, thinking that whatever they cast their eyes on in the moment was the most important thing in the whole of creation. They'd forced Neke to imprison them once for their own safety and he was seriously tempted to do it again.

And now this.

Claws ticked on metal and Neke glanced over his shoulder to see Goma and Hama hovering at the edge of the map. They'd alerted him to the anomaly as soon as they'd captured the Whispering House, but he was damned if he was going to show any gratitude. They lacked discipline, their definitions were inadequate, and they relied on naïve axioms. In Neke's opinion innate talent was worse than laziness.

"Have you found the source?" clicked Hama.

Neke tapped the needle against the lead. Taking too long to answer would only feed their arrogance.

"Not yet."

"I have a stupid notion, and one not worthy to trouble friends with, but in my foolishness it struck me that here the folds in space-time are out of alignment," ventured Goma, gesturing at a point on the sheet twenty yards away. Neke seethed, stood up and loped over the white-dusted metal. His companion crossed his claws across his chest and bowed. The leader of the Abhumans, knowing full well the upstart was about to prove what an atrocious show off he really was, looked down at the diagram. After staring at the complex pattern for several minutes he placed his paws flat on the floor to stop himself falling over. He was supposed to be seeing a schematic of the interior of the spaceship about seven hundred miles away, but none of it made sense. Walls, corridors and rooms couldn't curl up in a spiral like that - could they?

"Does that mean what I think it means?"

Hama nodded.

"Something is trying to get in from outside."

"Outside where?"

"Outside everything."

CHAPTER ONE

When Crysanthe ran she was back in the forests north of House Uella, crushing the black glass-sharded leaves under her bare feet, the wind freezing her face as she listened for the crystal drones. This starship was so dangerous with its infinite spaces. Her dreams and memories fell too easily between her and the endless walls of rusted iron.

Somewhere to her left a twelve-foot-tall witch powered along a gantry in her exoskeleton, Selva Selvaggia riding piggy-back on Nem and holding the rifles so Crysanthe could run free. She leapt across a trench, scanning the shadows ahead for her quarry. The vault angled into the darkness. She spotted fresh clumps of rust snatched out of the floor. *Close. It came this way.* She should be terrified, having glimpsed the monster fleeing the settlement, but the precise discipline of the hunt filled her with joy. *I can still do this. I can still chase my own perfection.*

"Crys!"

She lifted her hand without breaking stride and caught the rifle, letting the momentum of its drop give her a boost as she sprinted towards the ragged hole in the wall ahead. Nem and Selva disappeared into the jumble of tunnels piercing the mile-thick bulkhead above, seeking to flank the beast.

Except the Abhumans had changed the internal configuration again. Instead of sloping up towards the next vault the corridor stretched down to an expanse of wooden planks thrown across a twisted frame. The fools kept reaching deep into the Body of God, looking to rescue those who dwelt in the shadowy interstices of the colossus. But the aeons had stripped those hidden night-refugees of their humanity - warping them into creatures driven by hunger and hatred - and now one of them was loose in the ship. Crysanthe froze, scanning for movement or any thickening of the darkness that might mark an enemy, rapid tactical diagrams clattering through her mind. She'd lose time - just seconds but enough. Their quarry had fled at speed. Selva and Nem would catch up easily and she knew they'd have little trouble overcoming it but she still wanted to be there when it happened.

She slung the rifle and hopped from plate to plate, sensing the shifting floor, sticking her arms out for balance as if trying to fly. A sheet of battered copper canted downward. She spotted a clear passageway half a dozen yards below so instead of jumping for the next foothold she let herself drop through a tangle of corroded cables.

Crysanthe landed at the edge of a soft fan of light spreading towards her from another archway a quarter of a mile ahead. She couldn't see what lay beyond, but there was no mistaking the sound of tearing skin and fur. The fierce disciplines in her head told her to wait for the others to arrive, but she didn't want to lose the thread of her childhood memories. She stalked through the opening into a domed hall so high it had its own cloud layer drifting half a mile below the cleated fish-scale ceiling.

It was at least as big as Nem, though now it squatted on the edge of a square pool so its boulder-sized knees flanked a head like melted plastic. Long ropy locks as thick as Crysanthe's thumb plastered wet skin the colour of crude oil. It held half an Abhuman in its fist and tore at the corpse's neck with black teeth, mumbling to itself around the gobbets of meat. If its expression was anything to go by it wasn't enjoying the meal. As she watched it let the body drop and reached forward to scoop up water. It spat it out and, to her astonishment, started to cry, rocking back and forth on its heels as it keened to itself. Tears glistened on eyes that looked like sacs of congealed blood.

Crysanthe hesitated before bringing the rifle to her shoulder. Maybe the creature was intelligent after all, but it'd attacked the settlement as soon as Neke and his friends had plucked it from deep inside the Spinal Cord and for all she knew the idiot Abhumans had pulled more of these things into the ship. She aimed for the base of the creature's neck and fired, hoping for a clean execution.

It must have heard her, jerking round so the bullet clipped its shoulder. She shot it again, but the beast was hideously fast, ripping the rifle out of her hands. She jumped away but fell sprawling. It grabbed her leg, splattering her with grey blood from the new wound in its face, and swung her across the floor like a mop, claws tearing at her before letting go. Crysanthe hurtled over the uneven plates on her back. A splash and she was looking up at the ceiling through rust-clouded water. The bastard had tossed her into the pool and she was trapped.

She stayed submerged for as long as she could, waiting for a shadow to appear at the edge or slip in beside her. When she broke the surface her attacker still squatted at the far end. It chewed at the Abhuman corpse, watching her, oblivious to the pale threads running from the gashes on its shoulder and cheek. Shreds of oily skin hung down from its eye socket. Crysanthe realised it was either scared of the water, or just waiting for her to tire and drown. Tactics formed and reformed in her head as she riffled through a thousand battles and firefights. Her leg ached and a dark cloud gathered around her thigh. The pool stank of formaldehyde and stale iron, making her eyes water. Anger grew - at her own stupidity and the mutant that gnawed away at the carcass, staring at her as if it was her fault the Abhumans were inedible.

She hunted for inspiration. She didn't think she'd been badly injured, but was losing blood. Selva and Nem could be anywhere in this shifting labyrinth. No point waiting any longer. Crysanthe had no illusions about bargaining with the monster, especially after the carnage in the settlement. Three dead before they'd chased it into the depths of the ship. Once it'd given up on its meal she'd be next.

She risked a glance down and spotted a faint circle of light in the pool wall. The creature bent its head over its food, lost in misery for a second. Crysanthe hyperventilated and sank beneath the surface. A tube spiralled away, wide enough for her to fit. Through the acrid fuzz she saw rungs along the bottom and felt the current pushing her forwards. She grabbed one and hauled herself along. *One hundred and twenty yards in my lungs, then I die.* She counted them out in arm swings. When she hit ninety, long past the point of no return, the tube looped upwards for a short distance. Round grills set in the roof let her press her face against the metal and take in more air. Interlocked cogwheels as big as houses arched into the lightless void on all sides. It was so tempting just to lie there, cling to the bars and let the intricate patterns whirl her exhausted thoughts away, but even now the monster might be swimming after her.

At another hundred and thirty-five yards the pipe broke open into a channel that curved into a mist-filled hall. Crysanthe dragged herself half out of the water, almost blind with suffocation. During the last few moments of life she could have sworn the tunnel's walls had turned to glass, and smeared faces with open mouths had tracked her convulsive scramble. She didn't recognise any of them. The air roaring back into her lungs was sharp with ammonia but she no longer cared. She rolled onto her hands and knees and stood up.

The claw marks on her thigh looked ugly, but at least the bleeding had stopped and she guessed that the chemicals in the water had pickled any bacteria from the monster's talons, but she didn't have any weapons and was lost. She left the stream and limped towards the wall rearing up into the mist half a mile away. Dark shapes suggested doors or holes. Crysanthe had a rough map in her head from the distances and directions she'd travelled so far, and reckoned she knew the rough orientation of the settlement and the centre of the ship – unless Neke and his friends decided to twist everything around again and snatch more demons from inside God's torso.

A corrugated steel plate fell into the room with a crash and the creature stepped through, blood eyes staring into hers with relentless hatred. Crysanthe turned and sprinted back towards the pipe. A futile move. Even if she swam back against that current she'd just end up in the pool again. Her injured leg gave and she stumbled. Feet slapped the ground behind her and she dropped sideways into a reverse roll. Cloth ripped and pain drew train tracks down her back. When she came back up the creature was pacing slowly round her, chuckling to itself. It held bloody shreds of battle canvas in its fist. Crysanthe started to jog backwards. The beast cocked its head and grinned with long black teeth before loping in pursuit. It wasn't even trying.

"You shut us down in the darkness, you skin people oh so bright beneath your lovely skies. You buried us among the filth and the poison and the old machines and the chemicals." Its voice was achingly beautiful - the seductive contralto of a trained opera singer.

"We're going to save you, save you all," said Crysanthe. "This ship carries part of God's mind. Once he's awake he'll take us all through the God Door and you'll walk across fields and beaches under new suns."

"Liar."

Its arm lunged out further than was decent and hooked another rent across her stomach. More blood welled between the ripped webbing. The creature licked its finger and grimaced.

"Tainted flesh and foul water."

The mist grew thicker and Crysanthe found it hard to focus on her enemy. She was shaking badly now, trying to keep her thoughts together against the exhaustion and pain. In this fog she'd have little forewarning before the next attack.

It jumped for her, talons held high. A metal claw grabbed her round the waist and threw her backwards. She hit the floor, smacking the back of her skull against the thick rust. She had a confused impression of machine arms and black oil twisting over each other in a tangled mess. Something shrieked and there was a sound like a chicken leg being wrenched from a carcass.

Nem held the beast's head in both hands. She turned it this way and that before tossing it to one side and slapping the palms of her metal hands together as if wiping off the dirt.

"I hate monsters. They're all ungrateful shits."

As Crysanthe clambered to her feet Selva jumped down from her perch on the witch's shoulders and sprinted towards her. She ran her hands over Crysanthe's leg, stomach and back before teasing her hair apart and hissing at what she found. Clearly satisfied that her lover wasn't going to die immediately she pushed her exquisite face into Crysanthe's, pale blue eyes burning, and shouted.

"You fucking *idiot!* You almost got yourself killed."

For a second Crysanthe was too stunned to respond. Without thinking she became General Uella again, facing down breath-taking impudence from one of her very own Companions. She instinctively went to slap the girl, hard, but Selva caught her arm and pushed it away. Once upon a time she'd have broken the neck of anyone who dared to treat her like this, but now all she could do was stand open-mouthed and trembling. Unbelievably her eyes filled with tears. Selva stalked back to where Nem was poking at the corpse with a metal-spined foot and pretending to be deaf.

Crysanthe rode on Nem's back while the girl walked beside. She'd calmed down enough to stare at the top of her partner's exquisitely tattooed skull and worry. *You are my anchor in the storm of this universe.* The general had been completely alone, abandoned to die, face smashed in and body full of alien parasites. When all had been lost, calm, knowing Selva Selvaggia stepped out of the shadows and reawakened a love so fragile and terrified she'd thought it gone forever. The Companion from Splenius never got angry. She might get tight round the mouth once in a while, or let a flash of irritation show in those stunning eyes, but it rarely lasted. Crysanthe had never seen her rage like this. Had she really been so stupid in chasing after the monster without waiting? Did she deserve such contempt? She was a warrior for God's sake, they both were. *If I lose you I lose everything.*

"This is the third time we've had intruders in the ship." said Selva, as calm as you please, though the muscles still bunched in her jaw. Crysanthe longed to reach out to touch her, even though her sudden sense of vulnerability made her angry and ashamed.

"The ship is snatching chunks out of the depths of

God's body," answered Nem.

"It's the Abhumans," said the general. "Tell them they've got to stop trying to save monsters."

The witch gave a deranged chuckle.

"The scallywags won't listen to me."

Crysanthe opened her eyes again to find herself snoring into the back of Nem's enormous head. The woman smelt of sandalwood. She sat up, leaving a patch of drool in the witch's hair, and saw they'd returned to the Abhuman settlement. Most of the creatures had gathered around the map room. The rest looked down at her from the balconies and holes in the walls of a wide shaft that stretched upwards for two miles. Crysanthe stepped gingerly down, refusing Selva's hand, and limped into the hall. Max Ocel, Abby Fabrice and Nem's sister Ioam stood beside three shrouded corpses at the edge of the lead chart. Neke and five other Abhumans huddled over the frosted metal, scratching signs with bright pins.

"What was it?" asked Max, staring at her injuries. Abby whistled.

"You look like you've been pissed on by a giant."

Crysanthe ignored her.

"It was human," said Selva, stepping into the room behind her. "All the creatures in the depths are human. The long wait has transformed them in the same way it changed the Abhumans."

"It spoke to me. I think it was just hungry and thirsty, and lonely too," added Crysanthe.

"So you killed it," said Abby.

Max rolled his eyes and pointed at the corpses. Abby shrugged and sniffed. Crysanthe hoped sheer exhaustion would keep her own rising anger at bay. She'd had enough run-ins with Abby Fabrice to know that the only way she'd ever get any peace was by murdering the insufferable shit.

"What if there's more?" asked Ioam.

Neke broke away from the other Abhumans and loped towards them, clicking his claws and tongue.

"There will be no more from that region. We have closed access. Those creatures are too far gone to be brought out of the darkness," translated Abby.

"You've got to stop this," Crysanthe said to the creature. It looked at her with billiard ball eyes filled with her own haggard and bloody reflection. She tried to become General Uella, wincing as she pulled her shoulders back. At least Neke had the grace to hunch down a bit in awe.

"Stop yanking places out of the body of God. You know our mission is too important to run these risks. We've no idea what's hiding in there."

"No. We want to bring people into the light, as the Brittle Hag did to us, so they too can walk beneath new suns."

"Unleashing monsters into the ship threatens everything." She sensed the humans stiffen at her tone of voice but Neke just stared back in what looked like the Abhuman equivalent of placid interest.

"They're not monsters," clicked the creature. Max swore.

"I am King Max. I order you to stop," he shouted.

"Nice one," said Abby.

This was getting nowhere.

"The centre of the ship is stable," ventured Neke. "Where this realm intersects with the old universe you will be safe."

"If you discount all the giants and villains waiting for us back there," said Abby.

Crysanthe turned to Selva. The girl looked as calm and attentive as ever. It threw her for a moment and she couldn't shake from her mind the desperate fury she'd seen in the woman's eyes a few hours ago.

"We'll move back to our old quarters."
Selva nodded.
"As you wish."

It was at times like these that Crysanthe really wished she'd kept a few of the crushed suns inside her to mend her injuries. She sat naked on the bed in their cabin while Selva sewed up the gashes in her thigh and stomach, occasionally letting her feelings be known with a sudden yank of the needle. Crysanthe suffered in silence, refusing to be drawn. At length the girl leaned forwards and bit off the end of the thread. She stared silently at the wound for a while before dipping down to plant a soft kiss between her patient's legs. But when she looked up her face was hard and her eyes filled with tears.

"I thought I'd lost you."

"I'm General Crysanthe Uella, Commander of the Dogs. We are the Athanatoi of the Empire of the Ear, remember? One slobbering demon pulled out of God's guts isn't going to kill me," she answered, though underneath the bluster she suddenly felt ashamed. She reached forward and lifted the girl's chin with her finger.

"I'm sorry."

"Don't go into the ship anymore. You don't need to."

Selva really was upset. She'd never known her Companion like this before and it shocked her. The girl took her hand and pressed it to her own cheek as if she held the most precious thing in the universe.

"Why?"

"I've seen what it does to you. Whenever we enter those infinite spaces, those halls and corridors and mazes, you're happier than I've ever seen you before and the further you go, the worse it gets. It's as if you want to run away from us all, from me, lose yourself among all that iron and steel and emptiness."

Crysanthe let her hand drop. Was it true? The Brittle Hag's ship did fascinate her. On the outside it looked like a crude metal disc with a single letterbox window, but the interior spiralled out into an infinite universe far beyond their own threadbare reality. The Abhumans lived in this trans-dimensional realm, endlessly mapping its configuration on a lead sheet grown to half a mile on each side. They used their knowledge to snatch lumps out of the body of God and store them in the immense halls, vaults, pits and caverns - to what purpose? No-one could get a sensible explanation out of them, not even Nem who, of all of them, was closest to these infuriating creatures. They were looking for something, but they didn't seem to know what.

Anyone with half a brain would have avoided the vessel all together. It was a never-ending chaos and now its inhabitants were cheerfully adding monsters to the mix in the crazed belief it was their duty to rescue mankind's cast-offs. But it was also the only ship fast and tough enough to carry its passengers to the other side of the Head so they could enter the western ear and finally make contact with Theuderic and his Machine Men. They had no choice but to travel in it and hope Neke and his friends didn't end up turning the whole thing inside out along the way.

Yet that wasn't why Crysanthe had been spending ever more time inside the vessel, journeying further and further with the others, or once or twice on her own. The immensity of this realm that existed - where? - fascinated her. There was always another hall, another corridor, another door to step through, each bigger than the last until she stood at the edge of rooms as big as worlds where clouds threaded between mountains of scrap. Today, when she'd chased the beast, it had felt so natural to be there, the walls blurring into an abstract canvas on which she could paint her memories and her longing.

Chasing crystal drones through the forests of Catagen.

She'd been a warrior and a scion of one of the greatest houses of Long Lock. All gone. She'd briefly been Empress of the Ear. All gone. The Empire itself was now a federation with Thin Hans of Splenius and her brother Bauto leading the interim government and the Companions acting as a transitional administration. The crushed stars left behind after the siege of the AntiHelix - the intelligent microscopic suns that had powered the armies of Ombratulla, Belsalice and Ruth - went back to their own time having discovered what horrors they'd been party to, vowing never to return. Once they'd filled her own mind with their helpful chatter, now it was silent. Everything had fallen away - home, titles, family, triumphs and honours. Was that why the ship called to her? Did its abstract emptiness and dancing shadows echo the naked cipher Crysanthe Uella had become? She looked into Selva's eyes. The girl watched her closely, trying to guess her thoughts.

"Even if the empire has gone and you're empress no more, we will still have to treat with Theuderic, or whoever or whatever stands between us and the God Door," said Selva. "You must do it. We can't lose you."

"Why me?" asked Crysanthe, genuinely puzzled.

"You are Crysanthe Uella. You are the best of us."

She was about to give a sarcastic answer but saw the message in the girl's eyes, remembered the desperate fear and anger in her lover's face when Nem rescued her from the monster, and relented. She teased the girl up into her embrace without thinking and yelped in pain. In the end they had to make love at arms' length so as not to tear any stitches, laughing at the frustration of it. Long afterwards Crysanthe, forgiven, kissed the sleeping girl on the top of the head and gave her a silent promise not to disappear into the ship. Yet in her dreams, she raced barefoot and alone over iron bridges and along cliffs that angled out over continents of metal plating and shattered glass, an entire universe of nothing calling to her.

CHAPTER TWO

MAX STOOD AT the window watching God's skin roll beneath the ship. Even though the Abhumans had taken over the navigation of the vessel with their insane mathematics he wanted to feel as if he still had some semblance of control. They drifted over the boundary between the Sternocleidomastoid and the Omohyoid muscles. To the north God's jaw formed a cliff eighteen thousand miles high. This craft could have reached the other side of the Head in a day or two, but there were too many unknowns, too many uncertainties ahead. Neke and Nem said they were approaching something - a fundamental rift in space-time that lay between them and the west. Max could sense it in the air, a tightening of reality that made his teeth ache and crammed him further into himself.

He was exhausted, spending as much time awake as possible. He didn't want to dream in case he returned to the garden marking the boundary between his mind and the deity's. Max was terrified he'd alert Belsalice and Ombratulla and through him they'd find his daughter and the fragment of Bassandis, or Ihanna the Machine Man would learn that the giant's soul was inside his unborn child's head and it was Abby, not he, who needed to be torn apart to rebuild God. They should never have joined the expedition. In the last night in Splenius he'd had the choice of running away from all this and living out the rest of his days with Abby in some far-flung realm - down by the feet perhaps, or beyond. But the ghost of his bastard of a father pushed him on - *stone duty* - and Abby agreed. God only knew what demented self-destructive urge she chased. He fumed, fingers tightening around the dead ball of the control stick. Cretins, both of them. What kind of responsible parents would they make if and when Rebecca ever turned up?

"Max?"

He jumped. Ihanna the Machine Man stood at the entrance to the cockpit, watching him with her prison-window eyes, a shard of exactness in the light from the corridor. *Act normal.* It was so hard with the aching fatigue clutching at the edge of his mind. Whatever happened he didn't want her inside his head. The second he stepped back into the garden he'd no doubt she'd be there, and if Rebecca turned up to say hello she and her mother were doomed. But perhaps Ihanna had already visited. Anselm found no problem entering Max's thoughts to have a rummage around when the fancy took him.

She stood beside him on steel pinion legs and looked out at the night landscape. As they'd ascended the side of the Neck, following the curve towards the Thyroid, the lights below had faded away. Unlike the radiant chaos of the Abdomen, God's throat was an empty wilderness lit by the occasional glowing mist or single light amid thousands of miles of nothing. Whoever or whatever built the colossal fabric of the Anterior Triangle were long gone - more empires and kingdoms crumbling under the weight of a million years of the Great Task.

"An ancient realm," murmured Ihanna.

Two beacons hundreds of leagues apart drifted beneath the spacecraft. Max wondered if anybody still lived there and, if so, what they had become. Far to the south a single arc of purple lightning illuminated the arches of a broken viaduct seventy miles high.

"Has Bassandis contacted you since we left the Anti-Helix?"

Max kept his eyes fixed on a guttering flame on a mountain side as it crawled towards them.

"No."

The last time he spoke with the giant was in a gazebo spun from black diamond in a garden inside his daughter's mind. He'd told no-one but Abby.

"I can't enter the Mind. Belsalice and Ombratulla are watching and we Machine Men don't have minds capable of protecting us like you God Talkers. We always interfaced directly with God's soul, and that means we're exposed."

"Can they harm you?"

"Once I would have said no," answered Ihanna. Thankfully she kept her gaze on the landscape outside. Right now he felt as if he had a map of Rebecca's whereabouts tattooed across his face for all to see.

"But with these alien powers they brought out of deep time - the science and the energies of all those crushed suns," continued Ihanna. "God knows what they're capable of now."

A long silence fell between them. Max hunted for an excuse to leave that wouldn't look too obvious. As always the first thing he wanted to do after talking with the Machine Man was find Abby to make sure she was still alive - a stupid anxiety, but he'd already thought he'd lost her twice and couldn't go through that again.

"Why are they filled with such unrelenting hate?"

The question took him by surprise. Ihanna was as still and precise as ever, but he could have sworn he detected a desperate sadness behind her diffident tone.

"Because we killed Bassandis, and Ruth egged them

on to vengeance?" he suggested.

"The murder of their brother was a crime, but not one that warranted the slaughter and enslavement of thousands, or this urge to turn God against his makers. If Ombratulla and Belsalice can feel such loathing, and be so cruel in executing revenge, something is fundamentally wrong with the mind of God. It's flawed somehow, and we Machine Men have failed."

Max had no answer.

"I only hope Lord Theuderic can bring them back," finished Ihanna, speaking to no-one in particular. Max sensed a chance to slip away but as he turned to go Ioam and Nem came into the cabin. Thankfully the mad sister had taken off her exoskeleton and put some clothes on. Her outfit had been created by Thin Hans' favourite designer. She wore striped stockings, a leather miniskirt, rubber bodice and blue ruff, and her hair fountained up above her head in a three foot pony tail.

"We know what's ahead," said Ioam.

"A symmetry line," added Nem.

Max had no idea what she was talking about.

"The bones of force that hold God together are mirrored along a central axis. We're about to pass through it," explained the more stable witch.

"And?"

Max noticed Ihanna watching Ioam intently. This didn't sound promising.

"We might get turned inside out, or scrunched up very very very *very* small," Nem circled her finger and thumb and peeped at him through the hole. "Or we could just explode. Maybe the western side of God is made of antimatter and the symmetry line keeps us apart for a reason."

"If it extends through the whole body why didn't we come across it at the Umbilical Ocean?" asked Max.

"Either Leontine kept her Steel Sphere east of the boundary, or you did pass through it but her world protected you," said Ioam.

"Are we safer here or back in the Abhumans' universe?"

"Mr Furry told me to tell you all to stay here," said Nem.

A hand slipped into Max's and with a jolt of panic he saw Abby beside him, chewing the inside of her cheek and squinting at the jumbled chaos of God's throat.

"We're not stopping," she asked. "Are we?"

"Not unless we're planning on giving up," said Ioam. "I'm guessing there's no other way of getting to Theuderic except through the other ear."

Ihanna nodded.

"If you humans want to prepare yourselves I'll stand watch here. As far as I know Machine Men can pass between the two sides of God's body without injury. I doubt it will harm you, but it might not be pleasant."

As far as you know? Max assumed Ihanna was as all-knowing and wise as Anselm had appeared to be, and in constant contact with the Kingdom of the Machine Men deep inside the Heart and Head. Yet she talked like an exile, as if her understanding of her own people came from memories and part-remembered folk tales.

"If we carry on at this speed we'll hit the symmetry line in about an hour," Ioam was saying. She jerked her thumb over her shoulder. "We'll sit in our bower with pillows over our heads. I suggest you do whatever might bring you comfort."

They left the cabin but Max chased after Ioam, catching up with her at the entrance to her room. The ceilings in the ship's hub were too low for the sisters so she sat on a leather scatter cushion and worked at the nape of her neck with fingers as long as Max's forearm, wincing with relief.

"I want to get Bassandis back into my own mind," he said after checking to make sure Ihanna still stood sentinel on the bridge.

"How are you going to do that? You haven't a clue where he is." The fingers stopped kneading. "Have you?"

She glanced in the direction of the control room.

"You don't trust the machines. Can't say I blame you. I've had enough of creatures we make only to have them rebel against us. All creations chafe against their creators, why should these be any different? They may claim to serve mankind, but do they really?"

She waggled her head from side to side and her vertebrae cracked like snapping branches.

"If Bassandis goes back inside your mind what's to stop them killing you to get him out?" Her eyes narrowed. "So the only reason you'd want that is to protect someone else. Abigail."

She spotted his alarm.

"We're God Talkers, Max. We look after each other. That clockwork bitch can drop dead. But Abby's not one of us so how come Bassandis is inside her?"

"He isn't, he's hiding in our baby's head."

"Fuck me." Ioam put her long white hands to her piranha mouth.

"It's worse than that," said Max. She'd guessed enough for him to realise there was no going back, so as quickly and as softly as he could he explained about Rebecca, how she was conceived in the next universe and filled with energies from that reality.

"She's the new power in God's mind. She pulled Abby in to save me when Ombratulla and Belsalice tried to capture me. Bassandis is in her garden, but if the Machine Men find out they'll kill Abby and Rebecca to extract him. If I can get him back into my mind they'll be safe."

Ioam stared at Max in silence. She was terrifying with her blazing almond eyes and shark's teeth grin, and she'd toyed with the idea of killing him once or twice, but he reckoned he'd been through enough with her by now to trust her not to betray him to Ihanna.

"Come to get stuff ready," Nem announced, squeezing in through the hatchway.

"What's the Machine Man doing?" asked Ioam.

"Staring out of the window mumbling to herself."

Ioam told her sister to shut the door.

"Bassandis is inside Max's baby's head and he wants to take him out so Ihanna and her friends don't kill Abby or the bairn."

So much for confidences. Ioam caught Max's expression.

"Calm down, it's Nem. She's a God Talker. I'd trust her with my life and so should you." A thought struck her. "Bassandis can come and stay in my mind palace. I owe nothing to the future and everything I ever loved has gone except Nem. Perhaps Sorameistre waits from me in the west but I think she'll be as cruel and indifferent as the others."

"Why doesn't he live in my whirly sphere house?" asked Nem.

"No," said Ioam. "Absolutely not. He's been traumatised enough already."

Nem sniffed and started to bundle up cushions and random pieces of bric-a-brac.

"You'd really take Bassandis into your head?" asked Max, trying not to sound too desperate. Ioam nodded.

"The problem's getting him from Rebecca's garden to your palace," continued Max. "He'll have to traverse the Mind. Belsalice and Ombratulla will be looking out for him."

Nem lifted her sharp bladed face to the ceiling and

sniffed again.

"We're here. Better get ready."

Max went to find Abby. She was prepping herself for the encounter with the symmetry line by stretching - though he couldn't see how that would help if reality itself was about to flip. He guessed it was yet another diversion to fill her mind. The interior of the Brittle Hag's ship drove her crazy with boredom. She got some solace from adventuring in the trans-dimensional realms, but Max understood the real reason for her long periods of truculent brooding. She was supposed to be pregnant - eleven months gone, but the only signs of a child were random visions and an increase in bloody-mindedness.

Abby sat cross-legged on the bed and poked for the umpteenth time at her abdomen with her finger. Such a look of woe crossed her face that it broke Max's heart. He shuffled beside her and enfolded her in his arms. She clung to him as if he was about to be torn away.

"Ioam will take Bassandis into her mind, if we can get him there. That'll mean you and Rebecca will be out of danger."

She snorted into his chest.

"We're about to fly through a rent in space-time in a starship full of monsters, towards a showdown with three mad giants. I've got this thing inside me doing God knows what."

He took her face in his hands.

"It's our child."

"Yeah, right. You've spoken to her, visited her mind garden or whatever it's called. I met her once in a dream."

"Surgeon Tali showed us on her scanners." A nub of flesh no bigger than a finger nail. He guessed it was a foetus and the doctor had assured him everything appeared normal, if you discounted the vision of the four-year-old from a new universe playing a children's game with a titan in a suit. Abby pressed her face against his neck.

"I don't know Max. I don't know what to think anymore. I feel as if we're just bobbing along like corks to our own destruction."

It started in his feet. Abby gave a muffled shriek. Max recognised the sensation immediately - it was exactly the same as when the Brittle Hag forced her way through the hull of Leontine's ship in her distortion sphere, pulling Max after her. Someone was simultaneously scraping every millimetre of his skin with a razor blade. It passed over his body in an unbearable loop while the fabric of the ship boomed and rang like a steel plate flexed to the limits of endurance. As the symmetry line sliced through his eyeballs he had a brief vision of chaos, as if the entire universe had been flayed and nailed to a spinning infinite-dimension grid. He heard Nem give a whoop of fear and delight like a child tipping over the brow of a roller-coaster. With a final ear-splitting chime the spacecraft broke free and silence poured through the corridors. Abby peeled her sweat-soaked face away from his shirt, panting hard. Ioam leaned against the door, eyes showing white around their irises.

"You OK?"

Max nodded.

"Nem wants to do it again," said the witch. "I said no."

When they'd untangled themselves and got used to the idea they were still alive, and the ship intact, Max led the others to the cabin where Ihanna stood as precise as ever, looking out over the nightscape. If the transition had affected her in any way she didn't show it. She nodded into the distance.

"There."

A red light winked at the base of a mountain range built out of jumbled cubes. It just looked like another random spark to Max.

"What about it?"

"It's a beacon. It's repeating a pattern with enough variation to suggest intelligence behind it. It started shortly after we crossed the symmetry line."

"An SOS or fuck-off?" asked Abby.

"I don't know," answered the Machine Man.

"Worth investigating?" Max's gaze met Abby's. *A distraction from your unhappiness?*

Crysanthe and Selva came into the cabin, holding hands in a white-knuckled grip. Selva appeared as composed as ever but the general had a wild look about her.

"We should carry on and not waste any more time," she managed to say.

That was enough for Abby.

"I think we should definitely go and check it out."

Before the shouting started Ihanna spoke up.

"We've no idea what lies before us. If there are living creatures here they can give us valuable intelligence. Besides, we have a duty to help whatever is there if they're in need."

"Do we?" asked Ioam. "Since when?"

In the end they outvoted Crysanthe. As the Brittle Hag's vessel approached the mountain range Max saw a tower in the centre of a cluster of domes that looked part-melted. The scattered radiance from the emergency beacon fell across a net of blue-black cables, as if someone had knitted baskets from a giant's hair, turned them upside down and kicked them out of shape. At first he thought they'd suffered an attack but quickly realised they'd been built that way. Smeared yellow and purple ovals might have been windows, but otherwise the station looked deserted. Certain angles and shapes in the complex tugged at his mind, awaking vague memories he couldn't place.

"I think it's Black Rose," said Ihanna.

The memory of Odilon bursting into a fountain of tattered soot filled Max's thoughts with howling panic. He made for the controls so he could angle the craft over the mountains and hit maximum speed before any of those dark-feathered bastards came after them, but Abby grabbed his arm. What was she doing?

"You're joking," he said. "One of those creatures slaughtered the Philosophers. Anselm barely overcame him - there might be hundreds in there."

"That was Odilon," said Abby. "He's dead."

He'd seen that face before - the mix of desperate longing and total loathing at the thought of meeting a creature who'd betrayed her entire childhood. Odilon had dangled vile lies and promises of salvation with his alien deity in front of her, claiming he did it out of love.

"And who's to say they aren't all against us?" he asked.

"There's no reason to assume that every Black Rose has turned on humanity," said Ihanna. "There's nothing stopping them from destroying our god and condemning mankind to the eternal night. If they were united they would have done so aeons ago. It sounds as if your enemy was a rogue agent."

"He spoke of others," said Abby.

"If you're worried, I'll enter the structure alone. You can take this vessel to a safe distance."

"We need you to guide us to Theuderic. I forbid it." said Crysanthe. Abby snorted and muttered something abusive.

Max felt fur on his arm and saw that Neke and a couple of other Abhumans had floated silently in. The creature had a cut on the side of his bread-loaf head, no doubt from the earthquakes caused by the symmetry line.

"It's abandoned," he clicked. "We had a look."

"You've already been inside?" asked Max after a few seconds silence.

"We wanted to test our ability to reach out into this universe after we passed through the rift. No problems at all."

"You created a portal into a Black Rose base and went and had a sniff around?"

By now he'd realised that Abhumans had difficulty reading tone of voice and tended to take everything he said at face value. He guessed Neke wore the equivalent of a chirpy grin, which made him look like a cross between a slavering wolf-hound and a giant spider.

"Show us," said Abby, treading on Max's foot in case he made the mistake of telling her she had to stay behind.

Neke led them into the trans-real dimensions of the ship. Whatever they'd passed through had shaken the internal layout like puzzle pieces in a tin, and nothing was the same as before. The passageway from the hub turned into a maze of narrow wooden-slatted corridors followed by ravines that fell into darkness, spanned by arched bridges of woven copper. Once in a while the Abhumans paused, listening, and Max heard the distant sound of metal, stone, wood and ceramics breaking apart and re-assembling in titanic shapes as the effect of the symmetry line continued to ripple outward through eternity. When they reached the settlement, now resting on a perfectly circular plateau three miles across, Max found the entire adult population crammed into the map hall scribbling away on their hands and knees. At the far end, a dozen creatures unrolled a two-yard wide bale of lead while four more carefully soldered its long edge to the chart.

They're updating their maps.

After Ioam pulled her clothes off and clambered back into her exoskeleton the Abhumans took them another half mile to a wall filled with odd-angled doorways and vents. After apparently picking one out at random they led the party along a sloping passageway that snaked back and forwards through what looked like solid mahogany. It eventually changed into a brittle, greasy plastic weave - a smaller version of the citadel's outer walls. A hundred yards from the exit, in a steady draft of acid-tainted mist flowing up the tunnel from the dark violet-lit space beyond, they checked their weapons and Crysanthe told them they'd execute something called bounding overwatch.

"Bollocks to that," said Abby, pushing past her. Max hurried to keep up, the general's curses ringing in his ears and the ground under his feet vibrating as Nem followed. He stepped out onto a cracked concrete floor beneath a domed space criss-crossed with an immense tangle of cables, each as thick as his body. His first guess was that it was wreckage, but a closer look revealed impossible complexity. It reminded him of the four-dimensional map Pell had used to navigate their way out of Interosseus. Maybe this was a bigger version. It looped and writhed in knots, spirals and curlicues, stretching into the half dozen tunnels leading to the rest of the base.

Neke scampered down a curving passageway with Abby and Nem while Crysanthe and Selva followed on behind, sighting down their rifles as they jogged soundlessly through the shadows. Max ran to catch up. He prayed the Abhuman was right, and the Black Rose station really was abandoned.

CHAPTER THREE

AFTER A HUNDRED yards the corridor turned into a tube, the flat concrete floor replaced by the same undulating weave as the walls and ceiling. The pipe filled up with clutter. At first a few machines lay scattered here and there - dark metalled boxes with indicators, switches and dials, clusters of tubes banded with copper and spheres of midnight-blue glass. Max threaded his way between, following a curve to find the others standing in front of a wall of artefacts and crates blocking the bottom half of the passageway. Above their heads the cats' cradle webbing disappeared into the purple gloom, shimmering like a network of blood vessels filled with indigo oil.

"Warehouse? Supply depot?" asked Abby. Nem plunged her metal hand into a box lid and wrenched it open. Books and papers spilled out - paperbacks, leather volumes, sheaves of manuscript tied with string, ring-bound manuals with plastic pages grown yellow at the edges. While Abby and Ioam leafed through a couple Max read the spines - *Blackmail or War? The Current Great Illusion, You and the Refugee, Must War Spread?* Earnest self-help masking tendentious, patronising rubbish. They had all the hallmarks of his father's Department of Social Wisdom and every other petty dictator's bureaucracy besides. Crysanthe clearly thought the same. She showed one to Selva, who shook her head with a laugh before the general tossed it back onto the heap. More crates yielded bales of wool and corroded tins of an unidentifiable meat. *Rations and supplies.* For who? Max doubted the Black Roses needed any of this - had they abandoned this facility so that others could take it over and use it as a way station?

Nem powered over the wall, returning a few minutes later to tell them that the stacks stretched as far as she could see. If they were going any further they'd have to scramble along the tops of the boxes. Max spotted movement in the web above but when he sighted along his carbine, heart smacking against the chrome stock, he saw three Abhumans scrambling through the cables on all fours like tree cats. They dropped down and one by one half-carried, half-led the humans up to join Nem. Ihanna sprang from lid to lid on her needle legs at breakneck speed.

"Still think this is Black Rose?" asked Max.

She gestured at the web above their heads.

"That has their signature, but I don't understand why they were stockpiling all this."

Crysanthe asked Neke again if he was sure the station was abandoned. Despite his cheery nod she told Selva and Nem to guard their rear.

"Max, Ioam and Ihanna, come with me. I'll run point, you take flank."

Abby gave her a *what about me?* look. Crysanthe looked her up and down and shrugged.

"Do what you want."

The general set off along the passageway. Max had to clamp Abby's arms to her sides, and by the time she'd calmed down the other three were twenty yards ahead. He sprinted after them, stumbling and barking his shins on the edge of mothballed machines coated in concrete dust.

After half an hour's exhausting scramble, made worse by the cheerful ease with which the Abhumans tripped through the web overhead, the boxes stopped at a junction. Two refuse-choked corridors led away to Max's right but the one ahead was clear. It was much smaller than the main conduit and looked designed for foot traffic. The shining cradle ended at the wall above the entrance. Crysanthe crept forward, Abby stalking her shadow to make a point. Max followed, but after a dozen paces he trod on something soft. One of the occupants must have left a rug or blanket on the floor - a ragged heap the colour of black onyx. Puzzled, he prodded it with his gun. The material looked paper thin and petalled. *Seething petals.* He remembered his hands sinking into the boiling mass of Odilon's Black Rose body as he fought with the traitor on a chain two miles above Metacarpi. He jumped back, stomach churning in disgust, ready to empty his magazine into the tattered mass just as Abby yelled out.

"MAX! GET IN HERE!"

He sprinted after her. The tunnel opened onto a domed junction. Machines rested against the walls, lights shining on a few consoles. The rest of the group gathered in front of a translucent teardrop hanging from a sheath of twisted cables like a giant's earring. It was as if the unholy engines had brought Max's memories to life, for inside stood Odilon the Watcher, his hands pressed against the curving wall. Without thinking Max shouldered his gun and fired half a dozen rounds at the Black Rose. Although the creature winced away from the impacts the bullets didn't even mark the pod's surface. Crysanthe kicked his elbow. His arm went dead, and he dropped the weapon. Ioam hoisted him up by the collar so he had to balance on tiptoes. He heard Abby's frantic swearing and saw that the sorceress had his partner in the same grip on the other side. Nem powered into the room, kicking up a clatter of sparks with her steel feet. Selva straddled her shoulders.

"Selva. Cover those two idiots," the general told her.

The girl jumped down and levelled her carbine at Max's head. Her ice eyes glittered and Max realised the bitch would have few qualms about pulling the trigger if her lover so ordered it. He tried to paint a semblance of reason on his face.

"Ioam, it's OK."

"Better be," she said, letting him drop. Even so she kept her right hand clamped over his shoulders, fingers on either side of his neck and nails poised over his heart.

"This creature killed Bassandis, and slaughtered countless others including the Philosophers working with the Steel Queen." said Max, as slowly as he could manage. Odilon's penny-coloured gaze bored into his eyes. *But you died. You fell into a raw wormhole. Nothing survives that.*

"Go on," said Selva, her gun never wavering.

"This is Odilon the Watcher, my father's best friend. The two of them found Bassandis in the Wasteland, but my father didn't know what he was. The Black Rose fooled him into thinking he'd discovered a weapon to defend the city. They imprisoned the titan, and when Alaric turned up with the fleet they set Bassandis loose so the ships would destroy him. Odilon killed my father, and before that he murdered my mother when I was two years old."

"So this is the total bastard," said Ioam. "Obliterate it."

"How?" asked Abby. That brought Max up short. Underneath the defeatism and contempt in her voice he detected an odd hunger. Did she want to keep this monster alive? Did she still have feelings for it, after all its betrayal, all that had happened?

"We came across him again in the Steel Queen's sphere. He told us that Leontine was building a wormhole to bypass the God Door using the Philosophers to run the equations she needed. He wants to stop humanity getting into the next universe, so after trying to destroy part of God's mind he slew the Philosophers and wrecked the Queen's experiment, destroying her kingdom in the process. He tried to kill me, but Anselm fought with him and they both fell into the rift."

"Max. I don't think that's Odilon."

Abby's comment silenced everyone in the room. Max pushed Ioam's hand away and took a few steps towards the pod. Abby joined him. Selva paced alongside, rifle still pointing at his temple, angled so the bullet would pass through both their heads.

"They're shape changers, remember? We saw Odilon transform into different people in Anselm's city."

Was she right? God, but it did look like the treacherous shit - those copper eyes and that rubber-mask face throwing your feelings back at you even as he wormed under your skin.

"Odilon couldn't have survived that wormhole," he said. But even if this wasn't Odilon, the Black Roses were dangerous and powerful, and their motives growing darker as the last night fell.

"Leave it," he decided. "If it's trapped it can stay there."

The creature's mouth moved, though the translucent crystal blocked all sound.

"...and imprisoned me." said Ihanna. She studied the being's face. "Your god is in great danger. Set me free and I will intercede on your behalf with my god," the Machine Man lip-read.

"Yeah right," muttered Abby.

"Why have you taken that form?" asked Max.

"He can't hear us," said Ioam. Nem walked up to the pendant and tapped the surface with her claw. It rang out like a cymbal.

"When Anselm first met Odilon he spoke with him in my mind garden, trapping him under a glass," Max explained to Ihanna. "The Black Rose was terrified. Can you control the creature if we release him?"

He expected Abby to have a fit … but was that the start of a grin on her face? It looked frightful. God only knew what she was planning if she got near the alien.

"Maybe Max is right," said Selva. "If we can't destroy it and it's trapped we should leave. It's too risky to mess with."

"I want to know what happened to the other Black Roses," said Ihanna. Max told her about the one he'd stepped on, and Nem dragged the corpse in like a discarded rug leaving a sooty trail behind her. Memories of the struggle on the iron link washed over him, making the room sway. The witch held up a cluster of three yellow boxes with a tube running through their centres.

"Found this underneath. Looks like it's still working."

Ihanna took the device and pointed it at the imprisoned Black Rose. It stepped back from the glass with its hands up.

So now we have something you fear, thought Max.

"Basilius did this," the creature said through Ihanna. "He killed Tanieates and imprisoned me."

The Machine Man turned to the others.

"If we're going to talk properly with this creature, we'll have to let him out. Finding out why the Black Roses are turning against mankind could be just as important as restoring God's mind."

"We saw Odilon tear apart two dozen people," said Max. "Even Anselm struggled to contain it."

Ihanna faced him and her bland, inhuman expression unnerved him.

"I have this." She held up the weapon.

"OK, let's do it," declared Crysanthe in a tone Max had come to recognise as her imperial commander voice. It always yanked a wire inside his head, making him pull his shoulders up a fraction. Abby just rolled her eyes.

Under Nem's direction the Abhumans swarmed over the cable, tracking it back to one of the machines humming against the wall. The Black Rose, speaking through Ihanna, coached them through half a dozen steps Max didn't understand until the weave started to unravel and the crystal dropped end over end to the floor, the alien remaining upright throughout the whole descent. When it touched the concrete its walls dissolved like ice in a furnace, leaving a ring of hissing steam and the cold taint of chlorine in the air.

The Black Rose stepped towards them. Max fought the urge to run screaming over the crates, desperately telling himself this wasn't Odilon returned from the dead, intent on ripping him apart to get at God's mind.

"My name is Ramul," said the Black Rose.

"Why do you look like that?" asked Abby. Ioam had let her go as well and she walked towards the alien who gave her a kind smile.

"I did it for you, Abigail Fabrice, to show you a face I know you love."

Abby lifted her gun and emptied it into the creature. Max hit Selva as hard as he could on the elbow before she could shoot, snatched the carbine and reversed it to point at her. The woman's expression didn't change but he barely had time to duck as her roundhouse kick scraped the top of his head. He hopped out of range only to thump the back of his skull against the muzzle of Crysanthe's weapon.

"Stop now or I will blow your brains through your face." Even with Abby's shrieking curses filling the room the woman's soft command paralysed him. Selva retrieved her rifle with a moue of amusement. He turned to see Abby pinned to the ceiling by the Abhumans who clearly thought they were protecting her. Ramul, unhurt, looked around with baffled interest. Max remembered Abby shooting Odilon just after he'd killed his father, to the same effect.

"Max, please give me one good reason not to execute the insufferable idiot," said Crysanthe wearily. Ramul peered up at Max's partner, who still struggled and shouted in the middle of a cluster of grey limbs.

"I'm sorry Abby, I didn't mean to upset you."

The Black Rose burst into a cloud of petals. Nem clanged back in alarm as the other humans dropped into combat crouches. Only Ihanna stood as precise as a footman, pinion legs side by side and hands clasped at her waist. The whirling chaos clumped together with a gentle thud to form a new body. It still looked like Odilon - bald and copper eyed, but this time it was a young woman with long, pointed features.

"I didn't realise that Odilon would inspire so much hate."

"Odilon imprisoned Bassandis and tried to destroy the Steel Queen. He lied to me and Abby."

"I was unaware," came the alien's answer. "Odilon is one of the utter enemies of man, and they dwell far away from me and my fellows. While many are content to let their thoughts float through the Black Rose weave, the utter enemies have withdrawn into their own fortresses and battle stations and shielded their intentions and ideas. We only see the effects of their actions and from this we understand they are implacably opposed to mankind entering the next cosmos."

Max had a bunch of questions to ask but first he had to deal with Abby. After he'd told her to behave in half a dozen different ways and volume levels she finally gave in, dropping down with the Abhumans who immediately formed a wall in front of her. She folded her arms and stared at Ramul from under her red thicket, murder written all over her face.

"Why do you call them 'utter enemies'?" asked Ihanna.

"Because they are neither true enemies nor indifferent enemies."

"How many enemies do we have?" said Ioam. "And are there indifferent, true and utter friends?"

Ramul nodded.

"I am an utter friend."

Abby spat on the floor.

Max was suddenly aware that they were standing in a bubble of light in an infinity of darkness, like plastic figures in a snow globe floating over a cold ocean.

"You spoke of battle stations," said Crysanthe, lowering her gun. "Are these Black Roses coming to attack?"

"No, they won't."

"How can you be so sure? And why would we trust you?" asked Max. He waited for the creature to elaborate but no further explanation came. There was little point in pushing. Even if an armada was descending on them from the depths of empty space what they could do about it?

"What happened here?" asked Ihanna. Max noticed she'd moved to within a few paces of Ramul and hoped she could handle the prisoner if it turned nasty.

"There were six of us here, one from each faction. We don't fight beyond the limits of our god, but Basilius - another utter enemy - broke the code. He attacked by stealth and in the battle only he and I survived. I imprisoned myself in the pod for protection, and Basilius fled. I think - I hope - he's returned to our deity."

"If you can't see Odilon's thoughts why did you turn

into him for my benefit?" asked Abby.

"Odilon loved you, and that love continued to ripple through the weave long after he and his friends closed themselves off. I thought it would help if I became the ideal Odilon, as he should have been."

Abby swallowed. Her eyes glistened for a second and Max noticed the tendons flicker in her throat. He knew what she was battling against, and for her sake the last thing he wanted was for her to react.

"Kill it or leave it here," he said to Ihanna. "I don't trust a word these bastards say."

Ioam nodded in agreement.

"All monsters are ungrateful shits," added Nem helpfully.

"No," said Crysanthe. "We have to treat with these creatures. She may be the only link we have with the Black Rose God."

"You must come with us and speak with Theuderic," Ihanna announced to Ramul.

"You're making a colossal mistake," warned Max. "It's already trying to get inside our heads with its charades."

"We can deal with it," said Selva, giving him a look that made him feel like an idiot peasant leaning over a fence.

"It would be better for me to return to my God and plead on your behalf."

"No, I need you to talk to the Lord of the Machine Men first," said Ihanna. "Will that be a problem?"

She unclasped her hands and took a step towards the alien. Perhaps the others didn't see the threat, but Max remembered Anselm blossoming into a lethal cage, Odilon hammering against the razor-thin bars in his attempt to escape. Ramul gave Ihanna a bow.

"Not at all."

On Max's insistence, the Abhumans built a cell for the Black Rose - a steel cube with a single window made from transparent onyx a foot thick. Selva was appalled at this treatment of an envoy from the aliens, but there was no way he was going to let the creature roam free and thankfully Crysanthe sided with him. The box sat on the floor of a room in the ship twenty leagues from the settlement, surrounded by white plastic walls that rose four miles to a cloud bank that shed an endless drizzle.

Max and Abby stood side by side watching Ramul, who waited unmoving in the centre of her prison. Max guessed it wouldn't take much effort for her to break out, and he sensed she tolerated imprisonment for her own reasons. Politeness? He didn't think so. He was looking at cunning and deceit warped into alien shapes, forged in this thing they called the weave - millions upon millions of minds dividing themselves into factions and counter-factions. *Utter enemies, true enemies, indifferent enemies, indifferent friends, true friends, utter friends. And we thought all we needed to do was build a puppet.* He had so many questions, but all Ramul's answers had been as vague and evasive as expected. She wouldn't even tell them why the station was full of crates stuffed with food, clothes and all manner of bizarre and pointless clutter.

"I can't get him out of my head," said Abby, snapping him out of his thoughts. Her hair had collapsed in the damp and she looked like a ginger rat.

"This isn't Odilon."

He put his arm round her shoulders – feeling tendons like stone ridges.

"How do we know he isn't out there, or in her - part of some group consciousness - watching me through her eyes?"

She rubbed her stomach again.

"That's why I hate him. He won't leave me alone. He's

still in here as well," she tapped her own temple. "With all his loving lies."

Four Abhumans had taken it on themselves to stand guard over the alien. They looked a sorry bunch, squatting down in the rain and amusing themselves by scratching mathematical diagrams on the floor with their claws, their fur plastered against their pot-bellied bodies and scrawny limbs. One of them, Goma, loped over and clicked at Abby.

"Go and get dry and warm for baby's sake."

She sniffed and wiped the water from her face.

"Rebecca's not even in this reality. I doubt she's going to catch cold."

Max let it pass but led her back to their room in the centre of the ship, and once they'd dried off he called Ioam and Nem over.

"If we take Bassandis out of your baby's head she's no longer under threat, and neither are you," said Ioam.

"What about you though?" asked Abby. The witch snorted.

"I dare any of those pointy-toed buggers to try and open my brain."

Abby looked at Max.

"So how do we do this?"

Max turned to Ioam and Nem.

"When's the last time you entered God's mind?"

"Not since we left the Whispering House. Even if the giants can't see into our heads we didn't want to risk alerting them. They know where your mind garden is, but not my palace or her, er ..." she hunted for a suitable word, "... playground." She nodded at her sister, who gave Max a cheery grin filled with razor fangs.

"You can enter whenever you like? You can control it? Can you teach me?"

Max had struggled to return to his garden. It always

seemed a hit and miss affair. Surgeon Weep got him inside, as had Anselm. Once or twice he'd returned when he'd been desperate and Abby had knocked him out, an experience he didn't particularly want to repeat. Like the sisters he'd avoided trying to go back, fearing the titans or Ihanna would follow him into the mind of God and learn about Rebecca. But if he wanted to track down Bassandis he'd no other choice.

"Shall we try now?"

Ioam and Nem held hands, and both reached out to Max. He hesitated for a fearful second but realised that with two twelve-foot-high sorceresses by his side he was as safe as he'd ever be.

"First sign of danger and we're out," said Nem, sounding remarkably normal for once. Giant spider hands enfolded his. He closed his eyes and in a second the floor fell from under his feet. He could have sworn he heard Abby call his name.

He walked inside his mind garden. It looked small and cold and empty. A white iron table stood in the centre. He approached it and ran his fingers over the lacework. Rust peeked through the enamel which had yellowed and started to peel. One of the chairs lay on its side. He picked it up - a strange wave of unhappiness passing through him. *Bassandis and Rebecca have gone. There's only me.*

"Is this it?"

Ioam and Nem stood behind him, looking around with barely concealed disbelief. He didn't care for the look of distaste on Ioam's face and Nem seemed to have been hit with a fit of the giggles. He bristled. This was the inside of his head. It might not be much, but he could do without the sneers. Next they'd be running their fingers over the furniture and tutting at what they found.

"Why? What's it supposed to be like?"

"You didn't find out you were a God Talker until a

couple of years ago, did you? Even so, is this the best you could do? No wonder Bassandis and your daughter buggered off."

"Hello?" said Nem, looking beyond the clapboard boundary. In his embarrassment and anger he'd forgotten about the black walls fencing in his mind, erected by Ombratulla and Belsalice shortly after the Abby storm rescued him. They ran across the domed hills, rising up to the burning sky. With a churning surge of dream fear he saw what looked like huge faces peering down at them over the tops of the barriers. For a second he thought they were the giantesses themselves, but soon realised they were the dark sentinels that wandered the soul of God like errant dreams.

"We should leave. There's nothing here."

Ioam took his hand.

"Poor Max," a man's voice said, and he opened his eyes to find himself back in the cabin with Abby and the witches. They looked down at him with expressions of curious pity and all he wanted them to do was go away and leave him alone.

CHAPTER FOUR

THE MORNING AFTER they'd departed the Black Rose station Crysanthe cornered Abby just inside the corridor leading beyond the hull of the Brittle Hag's ship. The woman stared up at her with that oh-so-familiar expression of childish defiance. It was all she could do not to smack the idiot hard. It'd be interesting to see how far Abby thought she could defend herself. Crysanthe had seen her fight - dirty, fast and effective but all over the place. Snapping that scrawny neck might take a bit longer but God it would be so, so satisfying. Selva had warned her this was a bad idea, and she was beginning to suspect the Companion was right. She summoned every discipline she had and assumed the mantle of General Uella. Abby looked her up and down.

"What?"

"I don't care if you hate me, but your constant infantile disobedience puts everyone in danger."

"You pompous bitch," laughed Abby.

"I want a truce."

The woman scratched the inside of her ear, squinting with concentration, before tapping Crysanthe on the breast plate.

"Fuck off."

She turned to go. Crysanthe grabbed her arm. Abby instantly ducked under but the general was ready. Using the inside of the woman's elbow as a fulcrum she threw her on her back. Abby lashed out with a foot, hooking it behind Crysanthe's ankle so she thumped down on one knee.

"Come on then, you arrogant cunt," said Abby, hopping onto the balls of her feet, weaving her fists side to side like a boxer. Crysanthe, furious at her own lack of self-control, rose to her feet. She forced the expression of loathing and irritation from her face.

"Why? Why do you do this? We're trying to save humanity. Every single person on this ship is essential for this. And yet you persist in behaving like an obnoxious fourteen year old desperate to prove something. Do you really detest me that much?"

Abby dropped her hands and chewed the inside of her cheek. She put her head to one side and pursed her lips. Crysanthe saw a thoughtfulness that looked completely out of place on that pouting brat face.

"Power."

"What?"

"I don't hate you. It's nothing personal. I hate power. The power of lords over commoners, men over women, the strong over the weak. It turns you all into cruel, vicious bastards. What did you do when you were Madam Commander Death-fuck or whatever you called yourself? Slaughtered thousands, tossed a raped teenager into a vacuum, sent battleships to wipe out a city you'd never heard of."

It was pathetic - the chafing of a truculent child against its schoolmaster, spouting all the tired old rubbish about injustice and tyranny.

"Without order and discipline we are nothing. How else can we achieve the perfection we strive for?"

Crysanthe cursed herself for even engaging in an argument with this wretched woman. Once she would have killed her on the spot.

"Bullshit. Look where it's got us. We stand at the end of billions and billions of years of order and discipline and power and I haven't seen much perfection to show for it."

Enough - it was time to get this encounter back on track and close it down.

"Stop defying me at every single turn. If I represent evil incarnate fine. I understand. But we have a mission to finish and you're pregnant with Max's child. We can't protect it and the future of everyone else if we're all dead thanks to your wilful recklessness."

For a few seconds fury shone in Abby's eyes and Crysanthe girded herself, realising this time the fight would be for real. The other woman rubbed her stomach and suddenly looked very small and sad. Her shoulders slumped and she kicked at the rusting wall. *Got you.* Abby sniffed, shook herself and gave Crysanthe another defiant glare. But there was something in those striking green eyes, a flicker of helplessness and confusion the woman clearly struggled to mask. She suddenly felt embarrassed, as if she'd intruded on a grief she didn't know how to console.

"I'm not going to give you any more orders," she said. "But the battle against tyranny is over. Look at us. What power do any of us have anymore? Stop putting yourself and the rest of us in danger."

Abby conceded her a laugh and to Crysanthe's surprise stuck her hand out. She braced her feet against the floor just in case, but the shake was genuine, if perfunctory. The woman gave the wall one last kick and sloped off towards the Abhuman settlement, hands in pockets and head down. Crysanthe found herself staring after the dwindling figure, snapping out of her reverie only when Selva threaded her arm around her waist.

"How'd it go?"

"How do you think?"

"You're both still alive."

Selva reached up and gave her a lingering kiss. There was something knowing in the touch of those lips.

"There's a link between Abby and the Black Roses," said the girl. "A powerful bond we can use to our advantage if and when we have to ask them for help."

"Will it come to that?"

Crysanthe studied her lover closely. She'd be shifting and re-shifting pieces across that thousand-squared chess board in her mind.

"Maybe Ramul is right and our only hope is in sending a delegation to the God of the Black Roses, casting ourselves at the mercy of the aliens," said Selva. "This talk of utter enemies and utter friends suggests the aliens are taking a close interest in the affairs of man - perhaps too close."

"Could you stand before such creatures and speak for humanity?"

Crysanthe hoped the Companion would say yes, but she knew what the answer was - the Empress of the Ear would have to plead for clemency, no-one else. *I ruled for just ten days.* Selva was the master diplomat, not her. The girl read her mind.

"I can't do it. At the very end we won't need diplomats with fine words and cunning stratagems if we have to beg an alien god to carry us in its arms into the new universe."

She kissed Crysanthe again, but it was no comfort.

"We'll reach the western singularity soon. Come and see."

The starship rose over a line of mountains built from tumbled metal cylinders and Crysanthe found herself looking down at a wash of pale blue spread out across the universe ahead of her. It faded to white in the distance. Beyond that a fine thread of mercury silver stretching from north to south marked where the land petered out after a light year to reveal the naked singularity. Directly below her the surface of the Skin sloped down in a ragged ocean of broken shapes, silhouetted against the atmosphere. The shining air revealed, for the first time, the outline of thousands upon thousands of delicate structures. Spires, clusters of aerials, towers suspended in nets of cables and chains slung from arches that lofted for miles into the night - God's neck was suddenly encased in a vast necklace of invention. Most of the buildings and machines had no discernible purpose - but once she thought she spotted a cluster of rocket ships, their hulls half-finished and left to decay. Not one light shone among this wreckage of centuries.

They'd all gathered in the control room, standing almost cheek to cheek with Ioam and Nem bending over them like parents herding children through a museum. Crysanthe found her elbow resting on Neke's head, and to her irritation Abby elbowed between her and Selva to get a better view. That ridiculous hair tickled her face.

"What're those?" asked Max.

"Ye Gods," murmured Ioam.

As they descended she realised they were floating towards a forest of hands spread out in terraced rows, wrists buried in the surface and fingers and thumbs spread upwards at the empty sky. There must have been thousands, each identical and fashioned from black metal and lustrous stone. They grew larger and larger until, in silent fear, they found themselves flying between fingers a hundred miles high. The giants themselves could have stood on the tips and seemed no bigger than fleas. Neke reached across and took the control stick from Max, twitching it from side to side, clearly compensating for twists in space-time caused by those vast sculptures.

"Idols? Works of art?" asked Abby.

"Perhaps they were templates," said Selva. "For God's hands, left by the original designers." Crysanthe glanced across at Ihanna but if the Machine Man knew the answer she wasn't going to share it. She turned her attention to the realm beyond the body and tried to make out any signs of civilisation. They were still too high up and all she could see were the usual muddy reds and browns of crumbled planet dust, rucked up here and there into mountain ranges that looked like nothing more than wrinkles in blood-stained linen. If they waited for night-fall, when the energies in the air faded, they would probably spot the lights from the cities, nations and empires on this side but Crysanthe had spent too long in the darkness and was impatient to reach the Ear. She sensed that the others felt the same. Abby jiggled from foot to foot.

"We'll follow the Sternocleidomastoid muscle to the Styloid and then head for the Lobe," said Crysanthe. "We'll take up position a thousand miles out so we can get an idea what's there before we approach the Meatus."

She caught Selva's eye. The girl winked and gave her a happy grin.

"Maybe Thin Hans has a twin."

Crysanthe doubted it. Thin Hans the dancing pervert with his harlequin clothes, lecherous drawl and wicked-ly cunning mind had to be a one-off. After taking over the commonwealth he'd suggested compulsory weekly orgies for all civil servants and she didn't think he'd been joking.

The first shock came when they saw the western ear was incomplete. Immense shelves and gantries reached down from the rim to the singularity, encasing the Helix in a lattice of scaffolding rendered into grey fur by the distance. The building platforms rose out of the atmosphere to disappear into the shadows just below the Meatus. It seemed as if someone had fashioned a staircase leading up to God's mind, but as they took it in turns to try and make out details through high-powered binoculars they realised that each step was big enough to hold a continent. Crysanthe searched for any rivers of light reaching up to the Ear Canal. Even in the twilight days of the Empire of the Ear the endless traffic and commerce between the AntiHelix and the Nine Kingdoms had marked a radiant tattoo across the upper neck as thousands upon thousands of transports, warships and flyers journeyed to and from the centre of power. Here she saw only the shadowed mass of the lower skull and edge of the jaw. If there was communication between those stacked worlds she couldn't see any evidence. Ioam spoke for all of them.

"It's dead. There's nobody here."

"Perhaps they've all gone into the Body now the Great Task is finished," suggested Max.

"Does that look finished to you?" asked Abby, nodding towards the gantries and machines canted against the Occipital bone where it fanned out below the ear.

"Alaric said God was finished and ready to wake up," said Max, fixing Crysanthe with his grey eyes. Dogged courage bubbled under the man's permanent expression of perplexed fear.

"The Machine Men told us it was time," said Selva. In the silence that followed Ihanna stared past them all at the incomprehensible vastness of the Head, lofting up into the night like a wall splitting the universe in half.

"We're not going to discover anything by dicking around out here," said Abby eventually. "Why don't we have a look?"

She glanced up at Crysanthe, who found herself nodding.

"Take us in."

The lowest step stretched fifteen thousand miles from north to south - a wasteland littered with scrap, machines, empty buildings and fragments of scaffolding. Some lay in neat stacks long rusted into mountain ranges tens of miles high. Other sections looked as if they'd tumbled from the Ear. The Meatus was twenty thousand leagues above the atmosphere and though all they saw was endless darkness, Crysanthe sensed the tension and hunger in the room. This was a race with the giantesses, but they had no understanding of the end game or any idea how quickly Ombratulla, Belsalice and Ruth would reach the centre of the Head. The titans planned on forming the Mind, but for that they needed the Giants of the West. And how would Theuderic react to a new giant, built by alien technology and filled with the soul of a woman driven insane by grief and revenge? Crysanthe had no intention of letting them blunder into an unknown situation without adequate intelligence, and to her relief even Abby seemed to concede the need for caution. Who or what still lived on these planet-sized steps? People? Monsters? Defences with machine minds addled into senility by the endless centuries? It was maddening to have to pick their way across these desolate platforms at a crawl when they could have been at the entrance to the Meatus in hours, but she refused to take any more risks.

The next level looked like a child's play pit filled with sand and dotted with an endless network of lakes and rivers. Still no signs of life. Surely this was once home to kingdoms, perhaps even another empire, but if any civilisation had existed it was long buried in the sand, or scoured away by the thin winds kicking up dust devils out of the pale grey desert. Max told Neke to take the ship down, as puzzled by the absence of people as she, but when they dropped close to the surface they saw the hills of fused glass and sour rainbows filling the lagoons.

War, ancient and dreadful.

The third and fourth steps lay well above the atmosphere and were nothing more than chaotic scrap yards covered in yet more machines, and endless landscapes of iron, cloth, plastic and wood. On the fifth Crysanthe noticed a cascade of mist flowing over the lip, illuminated by lights shimmering green and blue in the space beyond. The first sign of life, and when they rose over the edge the streaming vapour became an atmosphere clamped to the final platforms by force fields. Banks of spotlights, beacons, neon guidance grids, warning torches and vented machine exhausts dappled the fog, flickering as shadows moved between them with constant mechanical precision. Ihanna unfolded her arms, gaze fixed on the landscape.

"Machine Men," she said. "Talking to each other in light."

"What are they saying?" asked Crysanthe.

"They're looking for a giant. A woman. She passed through here a few days ago, and now they're hunting for her."

"Ombratulla? Belsalice? Ruth?"

"Sorameistre?" whispered Ioam. In the faint light from the window the witch's face looked like a cruel idol cast in porcelain.

"They're not saying."

"I think we have company," said Max. Three craft shaped like crossbow quarrels rose up through the fog, chemical rockets flaring from their tails.

"They're Machine Men," confirmed Ihanna. "Though I don't recognise the design."

"When's the last time you visited Theuderic?" asked Abby.

The silence lasted a few seconds too long.

"About seven hundred years ago. Things have

changed."

The Machine Man noticed the others staring at her.

"Ambassadors work remotely. We walk among you, observe and file our reports. Maybe they get read. Perhaps they don't. Our world is made of concentric rings. Theuderic sits in the middle. I and my kind live in the outer ring. Between him and me lie a thousand circles," she turned to look out of the window. "A thousand gates and a thousand doorkeepers."

Crysanthe was tempted to take the ship back out into the darkness and wait until they figured out exactly what they were up against. She'd stupidly assumed that Ihanna was their ticket into the presence of the Lord of the Machine Men. Now it turned out that the creature was almost as much a stranger as they were. There'd often been rumours that the beings living deep in the Mind had turned their backs on humanity, looking inward as they tried to tame the energies powering God's dreams. She'd put most of the whispers down to the paranoia of her own increasingly self-absorbed world, but from what Ihanna was saying it sounded as if Theuderic's kingdom was as arcane and alien as that of the Black Roses.

Too late. The squadron shone lights at the Brittle Hag's ship and Ihanna told them they were being politely invited to follow the craft up to the next level. They could easily have outrun the fliers, but in the end they were all too hungry to learn what had happened.

More fog covered the next plateau but the lights had congealed into a complex in the centre of the six-thousand-mile-wide plain. As they approached it resolved itself into a couple of hundred brightly lit squares filled with busy motion. They landed in the middle of a field of polished copper fringed with intricate towers of machinery that looked semi-organic. Their fronds waved and flickered in the mist, performing delicate tasks the purpose of which Crysanthe could only guess at.

"To begin with Ihanna, myself and Selva Selvaggia will speak with the Machine Men."

Abby and Max exchanged glances and the woman looked as if she was gearing herself up to object.

"We're expendable. You're not," Crysanthe added.

"What about the Black Rose?" asked Max. Crysanthe had noticed that both he and Abby refused to use the alien's name.

"Let's find out what the situation is first," Selva replied. "If the Machine Men have lost control of the Mind it might not be a good idea to let Ramul see the chaos."

When Crysanthe first decided to abdicate as empress and journey to the west she'd planned to leave all traces of her former life behind. In the aftermath of the war against the sisters, with her family and home gone, the collection of perfections built up over the years looked like so many trinkets and scraps of nothing. Lost in her wooden belief in duty, discipline and cruelty she'd kidded herself that all her paintings, sculptures, books, artefacts, wardrobes, wines and essences symbolised the ideal she'd yearned for, and that her purpose in this universe was to preserve and clarify all the beauties of a billion centuries, whatever it took. In a cloud of self-hatred she'd almost taken a flamethrower to it all but Selva persuaded her to gift the treasures to her Companions. She'd even handed out seven gorgeous battle-plastic breastplates to Thin Hans for his daughters, causing him to burst into tears in front of everyone and sob over his undying dedication to her for two hours.

In the end Selva helped her pack a couple of trunks with clothes and treasures the girl had chosen - not the most exquisite, but certainly the most practical. Now that she was about to stand before Theuderic, Lord of the Machine Men, she was grateful to her lover who picked out a long dress of a black corundum mesh threaded with white gold and a three-foot-high mantilla carved from the crest of an ancient chalicothere. It was designed to intimidate, and she wore a viciously sharp unsheathed dagger at her waist. Selva donned a cobalt blue uniform - an emblem of her own understated but razor-fine efficiency.

The God Talkers returned to wait in the Abhuman settlement while Ihanna, Crysanthe and Selva disembarked, the ramp snapping closed like a pair of iron jaws behind them. They found themselves in a sea of white mist that stopped abruptly a few feet overhead. Whirling beacons and dancing chains of lights came and went in the darkness above the fog, their rhythm occasionally broken by the passage of colossal machines that revealed nothing but their spiny silhouettes. The cold air stabbed her nose and throat and carried the harsh after-taste of ammonia.

No-one had come to meet them, and Crysanthe didn't know whether to read this as an insult or not. Before she could ask, Ihanna strode ahead, gesturing for the two humans to follow. After half an hour she spotted more Machine Men, three standing facing in their direction while the fourth sat at a large wooden table, hands folded patiently over each other like a commander about to begin an interrogation. He stood up as they approached while the others rotated on the spot, their eyes never leaving the general and her lover. All four creatures looked virtually identical - pinion legs, heads made from the finest papier-mâché under which tiny cogs and levers endlessly flickered.

"I am Crysanthe Uella, representing the Commonwealth of the Ear. I'm here to speak with Lord Theuderic about the giants of the mind and the last remnant of Bassandis. We also have with us a Black Rose, one Ramul, who calls herself a friend of man."

"I am Tephroseris," the creature gestured for Crysanthe to sit. Selva took up position behind, a hand resting on her shoulder. The scuffed table looked like it had been hurriedly carried here from a kitchen, and a jug of water and half a dozen glasses sat in the centre. Tephroseris poured two out and passed them over. As agreed Crysanthe waited until Selva had sipped hers before drinking. Sterile and tasteless. The silence and the bland looks were unnerving, and she guessed that entire conversations were rattling back and forth between Ihanna and the others. Her suspicions were confirmed when Tephroseris answered the question she hadn't yet asked.

"The giants Belsalice and Ombratulla arrived in the kingdom of Theuderic, along with Ragaleis who was sick and a creature they claimed was a fourth giant - but who clearly wasn't. At first Lord Theuderic was happy to welcome them and we guided the titans into the Chamber of the Mind so they could wait for the arrival of their sisters and brothers from the west. But when Ombratulla and Belsalice entered they released an unknown, alien virus into our systems. It cast us out and sealed the chamber. This was four days ago. Since then Ombratulla has emerged. We tried to speak with her but she ignored our attempts and flew into the west. We presume she is looking for her siblings."

Tephroseris's casual description of the rout of the Machine Men, in the same clipped sing-song voice as Ihanna's, was deeply unsettling.

"You're completely cut off from the giants?" she asked. Tephroseris opened his hands as if conceding a trivial point in an argument.

"Can't you contact them in the Mind itself?"

All five Machine Men stood or sat immobile, prison-window eyes looking into nothing. A colossal machine drifted across the distant lights like a whale.

"God's dreams are full of new monsters and defences, some of which are specifically aimed at Machine Men. We tried to approach the titans but we've lost over a hundred - their own minds emptied by an unknown power. Whatever technology the giants have access to appears to have infiltrated the substrate of God's soul, allowing Ombratulla and Belsalice to manipulate the parameters of His thoughts so they can find and destroy us if we enter. They also attempted to turn our own servant machines against us, but we have created barriers to prevent this happening."

Tephroseris leaned back in his chair and looked directly into Crysanthe's eyes.

"If you can help us undo the terrible damage caused by your Empire of the Ear then we would be very grateful."

Another silence.

"He is coming," said the Machine Man.

CHAPTER FIVE

MAX AND ABBY found Ioam sitting on the edge of the new plateau inside the Brittle Hag's ship, dangling her feet over a sheer drop that fell for three miles to a floor covered in what looked like thousands of house-sized dice with the spots rubbed off. Something in the set of her shoulders made Max hesitate. He was about to suggest to Abby that they go back to the settlement when the witch sighed, a long murmuring sound that stopped him in his tracks.

"Max? What is it?" she asked, without looking round.

"I thought we could try and contact Rebecca once more before we meet Theuderic - this time from your mind palace."

"You want to invite her into my head?" asked Ioam, standing up to face them.

"If we can," said Abby. She was gripping Max's hand so hard it hurt. She held her other up to the sorceress.

"Don't know how this will work," said Ioam, taking their fingers in hers. "But we can try. We might want to sit down."

They shuffled into a loose circle. The God Talker pursed her demon mouth.

"If we do this I want you to promise me that you'll flee as far away from this place as possible - from giants and empires and Abhumans - and go and find a quiet little corner to live out the rest of your days. Let me and Nem deal with this mess."

Hearing his own thoughts spoken aloud in that terrifying, resonant voice stunned Max. He looked across at Abby who stared back with such an expression of desperate love and longing he was tempted to up and take her with him right now.

"I promise," he said.

"They're all treacherous, every last one," observed Ioam to no-one in particular. She closed her eyes. Max followed and a second later came the all-too familiar sensation of the ground disappearing.

A pale blue ceiling rested on arches built with columns teased from crystal. Max looked down and saw his reflection in black and white tiles polished to mirror perfection. And the books. Hundreds, no thousands, no millions - in piles, on stands, whirling away on shelves that had their own gantries and staircases. Through three archways Max spotted an infinite library. The fourth opened onto a sky filled with glowing coals, underneath which rose a handful of distant peaks.

"Welcome," said Ioam. "Abby's not here but I guess that's because she's not a God Talker."

And then he was back on the plateau, sprawling sideways across the gritty iron surface as the ground rocked.

"What's going on?" shouted Abby, up on her knees, hand on the floor to steady herself.

A ripple sped through the metal, making them all bounce into the air like toys flipped off a bed sheet. Three thunderous clangs made Max's ears hurt and a thread of blood trickled down from Abby's nose as she clapped her hands to the side of her head. It sounded as if someone had taken a planet-sized hammer to a distant part of the ship.

"Are we under attack?" asked Ioam. The aftershocks

were lighter now and they could stand up without fear of falling over.

Max didn't hang around. He ran towards the settlement, revolver ready, Abby and the witch at his heels. Had Ihanna betrayed them to Theuderic - were the Machine Men assaulting the ship? But this was more like a shift in the fundamental structure of the vessel, as if somewhere out there in the infinite universe of girders, rivets and iron plates two halves of reality had sheared out of alignment.

A quarter of a mile away he saw a grey wave pour out of the clustered buildings and head towards the access ramp leading into the valleys around the mesa. *It's the entire Abhuman population.* He heard an urgent chittering mixed with the sound of countless claws on iron. Nem thundered towards him in her exoskeleton.

"How exciting!" she said.

"What's happening?"

"No idea, but they're all going to look at something. Me too!"

She turned and loped back but as she approached the crowd that ran, leaped and danced towards the edge of the cliff a couple of dozen creatures scampered towards her, waving their limbs to shoo her away. She skidded to a stop, the shriek from her talons on the ground making Max's head ring. He, Abby and Ioam caught up with the witch, who folded her arms and stared at the creatures with petulant fury.

"Little shits say no."

An Abhuman tried to take Max's hand but he shook it off. Abby clapped and clicked her way through an unholy row with Goma.

"We have to go to the middle of the vessel. It's dangerous here," she translated. Max's temper rose. He supposed he should have been used to it by now but the Abhumans' endless refusal to let them in on their bizarre experiments, even when it appeared to endanger the ship and everyone in it, drove him insane. Why couldn't the hairy cretins understand that without this craft they had little chance of saving the Great Task?

"If it's so dangerous, why are they all going to have a look?" he asked, struggling to keep his voice even.

The last of the crowd disappeared down the ramp. It was clear from the manic shuffling of the remainder that they were desperate to catch up. Another colossal chime and the floor shuddered again. In the middle of the Ab-human settlement a cloth and balsa wood tower slumped over sideways.

"Crysanthe will be back soon," said Max. "We need to focus on our meeting with Theuderic and let these idiots go and play their stupid games for now."

He turned to Goma.

"We'll go back, but for the last time stop pissing around with reality."

Nem screamed her frustration at the beasts who huddled down with their talons over their eyes. When they realised she wasn't going to eat them they scattered and raced after the others, leaving the one who'd drawn the short straw to guide them disconsolately to the centre of the vessel. Halfway along a corridor Abby held Max back until the others were out of earshot.

"I overheard them when they were running away. Something's trying to get inside. That's why they're excited."

"Into the ship? Is it the Machine Men or more monsters from the Body?"

"No. It's from somewhere else."

"Where?"

"God only knows."

Max was about to stop the procession to have it out

with Goma when the creature suddenly froze and raised one claw.

"What is it?"

"Big danger," said Nem.

Another peal of metallic thunder. A ripple ran the length of the corridor, but this wasn't just inside the walls. Max felt it in the very centre of his being - a wave in the space-time continuum of this bricolage universe. Everyone's feet lifted from the floor as gravity vanished.

The lights behind Tephroseris started to wink out one by one, beginning in the centre and spreading to left and right. A line of Machine Men appeared in the mist, walking slowly towards them, hands to their shoulders as if they pulled a mighty weight. As they drew closer Crysanthe saw cables and chains curving up from the figures into the night sky. Selva's hand tightened on her shoulder. Ihanna lifted her face, transfixed, as the bottom segment of a white sphere as big as the Brittle Hag's ship, drifted down through the fog. It settled fifty yards away, so that its surface disappeared into the darkness just above the humans' heads.

"Where is the Black Rose?"

The voice came simultaneously from every Machine Man mouth except Ihanna's.

"Who am I talking to?" asked Crysanthe. She knew already, but there was a point that had to be made.

"Theuderic, Lord of the Machine Men."

"Greetings from the Commonwealth of the Ear. I, Crysanthe Uella, speak for man."

"Do you?"

Crysanthe also understood the value of silence, and as the seconds passed by she scrutinised the machine. Although most of it was concealed by the darkness, she could see enough of the base of the sphere through the fog to mark the missing panels, the dents and scuffs and the conduits and wires dangling down into the arms of the Machine Men in Theuderic's entourage. Here and there busy knots of figures bent over consoles and read-outs clamped to the cables and hawsers.

You're sick.

"Ramul of the Black Roses is an honoured guest on my ship," Crysanthe lied. "We must discuss how we can ensure that she is treated with the respect befitting an utter friend of man."

"And Maximillian Ocel?"

"Also an honoured guest, as are the God Talkers Ioam and Nem of the Umbilicus."

Selva Selvaggia took her hand from Crysanthe's shoulder and stepped forward.

"To make sure that our cooperation is executed with swift purpose I, Selva Selvaggia of Splenius, shall act as intermediary. Nominate one to speak with me so we may establish the necessary protocols."

"Tephroseris. He will accompany you to your ship. Summon the God Talkers so we can re-enter the Mind."

Ihanna looked as if she'd been slapped. She stared at Tephroseris, then at Theuderic who rose into the darkness, trailing cables and pipes. It was clear to Crysanthe that the creature assumed she'd be the go-between. Her mighty lord hadn't even acknowledged her presence. As one the attendant army turned its back on Crysanthe and her companions and dragged Theuderic towards the distant lights. He lumbered through the indigo twilight like the hull of a dead flyer being towed to a scrap yard. The perimeter beacons winked on as his shadow diminished. Tephroseris gestured into the fog.

"Shall we?"

They clearly had no choice, but the newly nominated spokesman came alone and Crysanthe had little doubt that she and the others could handle him. The Brittle Hag's ship appeared, frosted white by the mist. She reached out to touch the hull but Ihanna snatched her hand back. Selva immediately stepped between them but the Machine Man ignored her, tapping the iron and examining the end of her finger. It turned black as if she'd stuck it in a fire.

"Absolute zero."

Crysanthe stared at the ship. She sensed a deadness in the air as if the craft had ceased to be a physical thing and instead had turned into an emptiness at the centre of the universe.

"Is it a defensive mechanism?" asked Tephroseris. She had no idea.

"What about the people inside?" said Selva.

"If it's the same as this then they're all dead, unless," Ihanna stopped. *She doesn't want him to know about the infinite realm beyond the hub.* Had it finally collapsed? Had the stupid Abhumans done one experiment too far and emptied all the energies of that reality into some unholy void, leaving nothing but an endless mausoleum? *What do I do? It's all gone.* The thought of the corridors, halls, rooms, colonnades and world-encompassing vaults lost to her forever was unbearable. It was her last refuge. Selva noticed something was wrong and grabbed her hand.

"Crys?"

"I… I don't…" she stammered, trying to find something in her mind to grab onto. She was about to drop to her knees in weary grief when she heard a pop. A dull shock wave pushed them all backwards, the frost vanished, and the ramp thudded down. Before anyone could stop her Crysanthe ran into the ship and immediately collided with Abby.

"Watch where you're going!" snapped the scavenger.

Nem clanged along the ceiling towards them, head

upside down and hair hanging like a black waterfall, her almond eyes at the same level as hers.

"Report!" said Crysanthe.

"Who the fuck do you think you are?" said Abby. The general didn't have time for this.

"What happened?" she asked Nem.

"Something tried to get into the ship. Not this lot," she pointed a metal claw past Crysanthe's shoulder to where Selva and their hosts hovered at the bottom of the ramp. "Someone else."

"Where's Max and Ioam?"

"Gone back to check on Ramul," grumbled Abby.

Crysanthe told Nem to help Selva, signalling to the girl to keep Tephroseris and his friends occupied and outside. The naked witch flipped right way up and stalked down the slope.

"Afternoon."

The creatures exchanged glances which, even by their impassive standards, looked worried.

Abby sullenly led Crysanthe back into the trans-dimensional realm.

"The ship went completely inert, surface temperature down to absolute zero," explained Crysanthe as she jogged after the other woman along a snaking corridor of stained tin. "It was as if it suddenly dropped out of the universe."

"We lost gravity for thirty minutes. The Abhumans said someone was trying to get inside the ship, but we don't know what or where. They've all vanished - went looking for it."

Instead of taking her to the settlement Abby guided her directly to the hall where Ramul had been imprisoned. The drizzle was now a downpour thundering off their heads and kicking white spray up to their shoulders. Every wall of the Black Rose's cell had ruptured and the window was nothing more than a scattering of onyx lumps in the ankle-high filthy water. Max and Ioam stood inside the cage, sheltering from the rain.

"She could be anywhere," Max told her.

"If her intentions are genuine she'll turn up," said Crysanthe. "And there's no other way out save through the middle of the ship. Unless she wants to stay in this world forever she'll have to come past us sooner or later."

Max asked what had happened. She told them about the meeting with Theuderic.

"We can't stall for long. You three God Talkers will need to meet him so we can find out how to tackle the giants."

"If this ship is fucked we have no way of escaping this place if it all goes tits up," said Abby.

A spindly shadow waved at them from the corner of the room. Max growled an incomprehensible oath and set off towards the Abhuman who hovered in a doorway, looking for all the world like a punished dog. Crysanthe didn't recognise it, and neither did the others. She guessed Neke and his friends had sent them a complete non-entity to relay whatever update they'd prepared.

"This'd better be good," said Ioam as the creature took Max by the hand and, without a single click, led them towards the settlement.

They found all the Abhumans in their hall of maps, sitting in a circle watching Neke and Hama have a massive argument. Neke stood with his weight on his back foot, arms crossed over his chest while Hama danced around in circles, occasionally thumping him with the back of one hairy fist. When he'd finished a good third of the audience started grunting.

"They're laughing," murmured Abby to Crysanthe. Neke turned, lifted both claws in the air and let his jaw hang open. He looked as though he was just about to kick his opponent in the testicles when Max whistled through his teeth. Two thousand pairs of billiard ball eyes swivelled in their direction and Neke's hands dropped.

"Enlighten us," said Max in the gentle tone of a mass murderer at the end of his tether. For once the creature came back with a straight answer.

"A force from elsewhere tried to enter this realm."

"Did you invite it?"

"No."

Crysanthe couldn't tell whether the Abhuman was lying or not. She looked at Abby who studied the creature through half-closed eyes. Catching the General's unspoken question she shook her head. She didn't know either.

"So why did you all go running after it?"

"It was extremely interesting and exciting," exclaimed Hama. Lots of heads bobbed up and down in agreement.

"We think that passing through the mirror line made it vibrate, like a harp string, and this sent out a signal through countless dimensions. Perhaps something heard it and responded. Hama has a different idea," said Neke. "But he is a total moron and his reasoning is deeply flawed."

After a long silence in which the crowd looked at the glowering Max with pleasant expectation Crysanthe decided to step in.

"Abby, please translate." She stood up and walked into the centre of the map, the Abhumans shuffling out of the way to make a path.

"You will ensure this does not happen again. We are at the end of our journey to the Kingdom of Theuderic but may still be in great danger. If so we need this spacecraft intact and functioning - that is your primary task. Two hundred of you will form outer and inner perimeters around this settlement, and at the entrances to the hub. You will be under the command of Abby Fabrice and will keep a lookout for Ramul. If there is any sign of attack, or invasion from inside or outside the ship, I must be informed immediately."

She turned and walked back to the edge of the crowd who all watched her in silence. Abby joined her.

"So that's how it works, is it? You just say stuff in that stuck-up way and expect it to be done without question."

Crysanthe saw no challenge in her eyes, only curiosity.

"Do you have a problem with anything I said?"

"No."

"Good," she turned to Max and the witches. "We must prepare for your meeting with Theuderic."

"Thanks," said Max as they walked back to the hub. "I want Abby kept from the Machine Men. And if anything goes wrong I'd like you to take her and get as far away as you can."

Crysanthe hadn't put the woman on guard duty to protect her. She just wanted to give her something useful to do to keep her from under their feet. She accepted his gratitude with good grace - it made sense he'd want to keep his lover and baby out of harm's way, but glancing at his balsa profile and those liquid grey eyes she suspected there was more he wasn't telling her.

"If there's anything I need to know that might impact on this mission you must be honest with me," she said. He didn't answer. She wasn't going to let it drop, but they were in the centre of the ship now, and Selva was walking towards her with eyes full of messages.

"The Machine Men returned to their quarters. Nem is watching over the entrance," she said. "We agreed a first meeting between the God Talkers and Theuderic and they asked if they have permission to journey into the Mind with you. A short exploration at first, so they can gather intelligence."

"What did you manage to find out?"

"There are seventeen thousand Machine Men left," answered Selva. *So few? That's barely a division.* "With approximately three hundred vessels, mainly transports and three dozen warships and six heavy duty battleships. This is all they could salvage when Ombratulla and Belsalice took over. It seems that the giants are using the crushed suns that remained with them to fashion energies and forces that interfere with the structure of the Mind. They have also compromised many of the support engines and thinking machines used by Theuderic's people with a sickness made of ancient stars. It enters their equipment and spreads along wires and cables to infect the whole architecture. The giantesses are clearly preparing for a war or siege. The first thing they did was knock out all the scanners and observation systems. However, there was still enough time for the Machine Men to see them building a fortress."

"A fortress?" asked Ioam.

"The alien warriors who accompanied them past the Tympanic Membrane are ripping structures out of the Head and the suns are fashioning them into defences."

"They'll be doing the same inside here," the witch tapped her temple. "They're bedding down for a long one."

"So they think the Machine Men are going to try to retake the Mind?" said Max.

"Which is exactly what they intend to do," continued Selva. "Ihanna told me that the survivors are planning to regroup their forces and, once they've contacted Bassandis and the Giants of the West, they will journey along the Ear Canal back to the boundary of God's soul. They'll try to reason with the sisters, or use force if that fails."

"They'll be wiped out," said Crysanthe. "Ombratulla and Belsalice took on the entire Empire of the Ear and won. Seventeen thousand will perish in a second," she clicked her fingers to emphasise the point. This was a suicide mission, beyond stupid.

"Maybe they possess energies and weapons we don't know about," suggested Ioam.

Crysanthe remembered Theuderic's scuffed panels and twisted lifelines. *No, they don't.*

"If they had they wouldn't have been kicked out so easily the first time round," said Max.

"So how can we possibly help?" asked Ioam. "All we can do is go into our palaces and look out over our balconies and point. We have no power against the giants. So they can't see us when we're inside our castles but they sure as hell can when we step outside."

Crysanthe saw the glance pass between the sorceress and Max, who took a sudden interest in his boots. Selva noticed it too and raised an immaculate eyebrow in her direction. Max gave a sigh.

"We've got to try. Perhaps we can get in touch with Bassandis, or even communicate with the Giants of the West before Ombratulla gets to them."

"Max, are you really sure you want these buggers inside your head?" asked Ioam. It was an odd question, and Selva was watching the witch with sudden interest. "What if I or Nem let them poke around in ours to begin with, just in case they try any funny business."

What's going on? She was tempted to ask but decided to keep quiet. Selva was clearly hearing undercurrents in this conversation that she couldn't.

"We'll all do it together," he said. Ioam sniffed and gave a shrug.

"The Machine Men are waiting for us. As soon as you're ready," said Selva.

"Give us an hour," said Max. "And ask Nem to join us."

After Selva sent the mad sorceress inside she and Crysanthe stood at the bottom of the ramp and looked through the mist at the distant lights. Nothing moved in the fog though the beacons still winked on and off as floating machines slid past.

"There's something between the God Talkers," said Crysanthe.

"I know, and I think it involves Abby Fabrice and Max's child. Do you remember when Surgeon Weep sent him into God's dreams and he came back claiming he'd met his unborn daughter? She gave him a hairpin that turned into a storm that rescued him from the giants. Ihanna's mentioned a new force in the Mind, something that's neither God Talker nor giant. And Surgeon Tali told us that the baby exists in another reality."

"Are you suggesting the infant has the potential to be a weapon against Ombratulla, Belsalice and Ruth?" *If that's the case no wonder Max doesn't want her anywhere near the Machine Men.* "Does Ihanna realise?"

"No, she has other worries."

"Such as?"

"I'm not sure, but she's not happy to be here."

Crysanthe pursed her lips. She reached out and slid her fingers between Selva's. In this machine mist the press of the girl's muscled thigh comforted her.

"How easily could you overpower Abby if worst came to worst and we had to give her up?" the girl whispered.

CHAPTER SIX

So here we are at last. After more than two years journeying through the Body of God, escaping death and madness, falling in and out of love and war, Max stood before Theuderic, Lord of the Machine Men. This was supposed to mark the end, one way or another. If the fragment of Bassandis had stayed inside his head the Machine Men would have tried to take it out and make it into a new version of the dead giant. What that would have meant for Max he'd no idea. Neither Ihanna nor Anselm before her had been much comfort. The exiles hadn't a clue.

Yet, oddly, Max felt cheated. It was ridiculous - he didn't want to die, and even if the titan was playing board games in Rebecca's mind he still had no guarantee he'd escape out of here alive. Nevertheless he was angry at the universe and his own pig-headed sense of duty for dragging him and his partner through seventeen flavours of shit to get here. Looking up at the underside of the tatty sphere that, apparently, was King of the Machine Men, he vowed that if he made it through the day he'd pay more attention to Ioam's advice. *Somewhere far away, down by the feet.*

He and Abby had promised themselves there'd be no tearful, clinging farewells. They'd been over their goodbyes so many times in so many ways, and every one was compacted into the sour ball of misery in the pit of his stomach. When he'd left her at the head of the newly recruited regiment of Abhumans they'd swapped perfunctory hugs and a kiss - Abby making a bad joke he couldn't remember. He'd almost lost it for a second, but she'd turned him round and pushed him away. What was his problem? He wasn't going to be killed. Besides, Abby was in greater danger now that the garden in his mind lay empty. *Right.* To his credit he hadn't looked back, but at this moment he was a hair's breadth from returning to commandeer the spacecraft and fly away forever.

"Really?" muttered Ioam under her breath, looking up at Theuderic.

Max knew what she meant. Anselm the Machine Man, Ambassador to the Court of the Steel Queen, had used a decoy - a huge lumbering monster of claws, pistons, tracks, filthy glass and leaking pipes which Her Majesty had charmingly dubbed a giant turd on legs. The real Anselm had disguised herself as the diminutive attendant Euphrosyne, another sharp-eyed creature with a kestrel's poise and those unsettling prison-window eyes, so she could move almost unseen through the Byzantine labyrinth of courtly power.

But, standing in this machine-engineered mist on a shelf projecting many hundreds of miles from God's ear under a black void sprinkled with poisonous lights, Max had a horrible suspicion that this was it. There was no real Theuderic, no precise and powerful entity watching him from the wings with the cunning gaze of a bird. This was the Lord of the Machine Men - a sphere as big as a house that looked like it had been punted across one football field too many. Chemicals spat and hissed from hoses that curved into the darkness and the creature emitted a leaden hum that made him think of valves in a malfunctioning radio. He could feel it echo in his skull. When Theuderic spoke his voice came from the mouth of every single Machine Man, except Ihanna's. She stood rigid and though outwardly appeared no different from before, Max sensed an odd tension in her eyes. Maybe it was the shock of meeting her king for the first time - though he found it hard to believe these machines were capable of feeling awe.

"The giantesses Ombratulla and Belsalice have filled the Mind with new potencies that can find and harm Machine Men. With your permission we would like to enter your mind palaces, which are unseen by the titans, so we can get a better understanding of how they've changed God's dreams." So far so good. "We also hope it will give us the opportunity to track down the remnant of Bassandis, Maximillian Ocel." For a second he imagined that Theuderic was a giant eyeball and that the pupil had swivelled round to point at him.

"You are in no danger here."

"That's nice to know," said Ioam. Like the Abhumans, Machine Men didn't get sarcasm. Or if they did they were too polite to let it show. She poked her little finger into Max's hand to give him something to hold on to. He was grateful for her touch. In this world of fog and engines she and her sister looked the least terrifying of all.

That seemed to be it. The indistinct crowds in the mist hauled the sphere back towards the distant lights, and Ihanna gestured to a white cube sitting half a mile away to their left.

"Doesn't say much," observed Nem as they followed their guide. This time she'd dressed for the occasion in a red body-suit with a collar of steel-reinforced glass. She looked like a bastard sword someone had forgotten to clean after a massacre. The box turned out to be a building fifty yards high with a single doorway in the middle of the nearest face.

"All necessary discussions took place between Selva

and Lord Theuderic prior to your meeting - protocol and diplomacy, nothing more," answered Ihanna.

"If we're to help you reclaim the Mind from the giants we need to be part of the planning," said Max. "We've fought them, seen what they can do. And we understand how their minds work, especially the false one called Ruth."

Now he realised they weren't going to slaughter him on the spot he was detecting a disturbing *we can handle this* tone to their conversations. It almost sounded as if Theuderic's wounded pride took precedence over sense. He chafed at the thought of being treated as a disposable source of intelligence. Neither Abby nor Crysanthe would stand for it. The general would want her own battalions to lead and anyone with half a brain would let her have them. He doubted whether the Machine Men had ever fought against anything on this scale before. But if Ihanna had got the message she didn't let it show.

The building turned out to be a single room with six chairs at equal spaces around a central table. Three other Machine Men stood up as they approached and introduced themselves as Alpheus, Subjulio and Cimabue, reaching out dry paper hands to greet the God Talkers in turn.

"We are honoured to be permitted to step inside your Mind Palaces," said Subjulio, sounding genuine enough. Max winced inwardly when he remembered Ioam's reaction to the tatty remnants of his garden. It was like being the neglected child of the class - the one who hadn't made an effort because he didn't think anyone cared. He and the sisters took their seats at the table. Instinctively he joined hands with Nem and Ioam who in turn held their hosts'. Ihanna's fingers rested on his shoulder, but before he had a chance to wonder why they were back in his garden, standing underneath the coal fire sky - Max, the witches and the four Machine Men.

"Ihanna?" asked Subjulio, clearly puzzled.

"I promised to act as guide for the God Talkers during their stay in our kingdom."

The others exchanged glances and Max realised this wasn't planned. His suspicion dialled up a notch. It looked as though Ihanna was looking out for him for some reason, but he didn't know if that was a good thing or not.

"The fragment of Bassandis was here?" asked Cimabue, peering round the empty garden. Max spotted Ioam and Nem's amused expressions and seethed.

"He sat at that table. Anselm put him into a trance to conserve his spirit."

"Was he a part of the giant, or a homunculus?" asked Alpheus.

"He appeared as a whole man, if that's what you mean. When I spoke with him he seemed tired. After Anselm visited he slept with his head on his hands."

"So he was a copy of his entire spirit," said Subjulio. Max waited to be illuminated but the machines left it there. In the end Ioam echoed his own thoughts.

"That means you can remake him."

"If we can find him," said Ihanna.

"He vanished after Ombratulla and Belsalice followed me here," continued Max. "At first I thought they'd captured him, but when we confronted them on the lid of their manufactory they didn't know where he'd gone either. Maybe he fizzled away."

Lying through his teeth while standing in his own head was a deeply odd feeling. He expected his thoughts to appear over his head in brightly coloured balloons for all to see, but the Machine Men just turned to each other and conferred. Max walked over to the table. That was strange, he could have sworn one of the chairs lay on its side last time, but now both stood upright. The lacework surface looked different as well - clean and new, as if someone had given it a fresh coat of paint. He spotted a cigarette butt on the grass. *Who in God's name has been smoking inside my mind?*

"I have never visited the mind palace of a God Talker before," said Ihanna. "I'm honoured."

Max jumped and almost swore out loud.

"It's not very impressive," he glanced across at Nem and Ioam. "Apparently."

She ignored the comment and pointed at the faces peering over the distant wall. They looked like the heads of party dolls fashioned out of balloons filled with black pitch

"Those creatures can't get in or see us now," she seemed to be talking to herself. "But as soon as we step outside we'll alert them to our presence."

"Are we ready?" asked Subjulio.

Max tried to ignore the rush of light-headed dread, hoping it didn't show in his face. *Ready for what?* Ioam and Nem positioned themselves behind the Machine Men, just in case. Before he could stop her Alpheus ran to the wall, vaulted over it and started to walk up to the closest barrier.

"What the fuck is she doing?"

"Lord Theuderic commanded us to contact Belsalice and Ombratulla. Once they are here we'll treat with them. As long as you don't invite the giants into your garden we're safe inside, and can speak to them through the wall."

"You're bringing them here? To my garden?" Max remembered the sound of the titans' nails scraping on the other side of the clapboard fence as they searched for a way in, begging him to let them see the fragment of their dead brother. "By what right? This is my mind."

"It's as much our garden as yours," Subjulio replied. "We fashioned you God Talkers, remember?"

As he spoke hammer blows thudded through the soles of his feet, as if an angry neighbour was thumping the ceiling of the apartment below. The ground rocked and he swore he saw fear in the Machine Men's prison-barred eyes. Nem raised her talons behind Cimabue.

"Stop," said Ioam. "Look."

Alpheus walked up the slope until her feet touched the shadow of the creature peering down at her over the top of the battlements. She started to gesture as if trying to engage it in conversation. Along the jagged length of the barrier more heads appeared and Max was thankful that the strange light made it hard to pick out features.

The section in front of Alpheus fell forwards as if hinged at the ground. She jumped back just in time to avoid being crushed. The watcher moved into view and a terror only known in nightmares flooded through Max. Even Nem gave a whimper as something resembling a glove puppet in the shape of a giant black toad heaved through the gap, idiot head wobbling from the centre of a flat body supported by five swollen legs. Alpheus turned to run but wasn't fast enough. The beast hopped forward, slammed a ragged mouth over the Machine Man and swallowed her whole. It swivelled to face the garden.

Crysanthe found Abby sitting at the bottom of the ramp, elbows on knees and chin in hands, staring after Max. Killing her would be easy - a foot strike to the neck or base of the spine to paralyse her legs. Or she might just kick her ribs through her lungs from behind. Subduing her would be harder. The scruffy waif could fight. Pistol whip her unconscious, though it'd take more than one blow to get through that ridiculous tangle of hair.

"Going to have me shot for deserting my post?" asked

Abby without turning round.

Crysanthe looked past her at the pale lights above the mist and thought about another woman in a faraway realm staring through a window at the empty skin of God in a room full of broken furniture. Shapes moved - it was hard to tell whether they were engines or figures. This fake, acidic air turned everything to abstraction - outlines of machines, copies of men and women, symbols of lords and powers. In one way it was utterly inhuman, yet at the same time its sinister artificiality was all too familiar.

"After Ruth contacted me through the Speaking Lens in Metacarpi I sat in the ancient communication room for a week doing nothing. Max told me the machine had broken, probably sabotaged by Odilon, but I didn't know. So I waited and waited and waited to see her face and hear her voice again. After finding out she'd died in the battle with Bassandis I abandoned it all - posts, offices, commands. I shut myself away, stopped paying attention to the universe and became easy prey for those who sought my downfall. Never again."

She'd no idea why she'd said that, and she braced herself for the inevitable sneers. To her surprise Abby continued to stare into the mist.

"And what saved you in the end?"

"Selva Selvaggia," she answered without thinking.

"Loyalty and love." Abby gave a sad laugh.

Crysanthe made a decision.

"We'll protect each other. We may be the only ones capable of standing up for humanity if all else fails - so we must survive, all of us. I won't leave anyone behind, or let them die, not while I can stop it."

"You're not as big a cunt as I thought." Abby wiped her nose on the back of her hand.

"You shouldn't be here. You and your child are safer in the ship."

Abby gave her a look of sharp suspicion. Claws rattled on iron. Goma clapped his paws at Abby and she jumped up.

"They've found something important."

"Abhuman important or really important?" asked Crysanthe. From where she stood, Neke and his peoples' priorities were ridiculous and she didn't want to get side-tracked by their hobbies. But Abby jerked her head towards the mist at the bottom of the ramp and mouthed *not here.*

After an hour weaving through narrow corridors they found themselves in a vault peering down from a metal balcony. For one horrible second the general thought she was looking at a severed hand, ripped from a titan's arm and crushed out of shape. *A glove.* And a woman's by the look of it - over four hundred yards long from fingertip to cuff. It lay on a floor made from alternating panels of scarred lanthanum and slate, in a foot of water laced with dirty foam. It looked as if it had been fashioned from white leather edged with silver and gold mesh. God only knew how many creatures had died in its making. They stood half a mile up and she had to grab onto the rail as the memory of flying through the mist on Belsalice's palm snatched at her balance.

"Where did you get this?" she asked Goma.

The wretched creatures were still sending their trans-dimensional claws to pluck fragments from the world beyond, despite being endlessly told not to. Maybe if they started shooting hostages the bastards would stop, but this time it looked as though they'd located the Giants of the West. The creature scratched the outline of a man with his talon on the slate wall panel beside them. He added a kidney shape west of the Shoulder and filled it with waves.

"An ocean," said Abby. "That explains the water."

"We found it floating in a big sea a hundred and twenty thousand miles away," confirmed Goma.

"What do we do?" asked Abby.

But Crysanthe wasn't listening. Instead, she was trying to make sense of the black shadow sitting dead centre in the glove's palm. *That wasn't there a second ago.*

"Bastard," said Abby, reaching for her gun. Crysanthe clamped her hand over the woman's wrist and this time the idiot had wit enough to hold fire. The cluster of darkness sprang towards them in an arc. Crysanthe braced her feet against the balcony floor and reached behind her back for her dagger. Instinct told her this wasn't an attack, but it was hard not to react as the Black Rose landed in front of them in an explosion of cold night. The fountain of petals snapped into the shape of Ramul, standing as casual as an old friend met by chance.

"It looks as if you've found the Giants of the West."

"We're not taking you to them, if that's what you're thinking, not after what Odilon did to Bassandis," growled Abby. Crysanthe doubted the alien would have much trouble finding them by herself but she admired the woman's courage.

"What do you want?" she asked.

"I'm leaving. I can take one of you with me now to speak before our God."

"You promised you'd come with us to talk to Theuderic, Lord of the Machine Men."

"There isn't time. I've stayed here longer than I should. These Machine Men are not what you or I expected."

"What do you mean?" And how did the alien know? Had Ramul been outside the Brittle Hag's vessel to reconnoitre? If so why come back to speak with them instead of fleeing?

Ramul gestured around her. "What's wrong with this spaceship? The grey people won't tell me."

"We don't know," lied Crysanthe before Abby had a chance to say anything.

"If this craft is compromised you'll find it difficult to make the journey to the God Door. That's where your best hope lies. Forget your dead god and these titans of the mind," she gestured at the glove. "Present a case before us. Abby, I can take you now."

To Crysanthe's astonishment tears ran down the woman's cheeks. *You've had this conversation before.*

"Get lost. Who are you to judge mankind?"

"I'm not your judge, I'm your advocate," she turned to Crysanthe. "Will you come with me and plead your worth?"

"We'll come if and when we're ready."

"I wish you luck, then. When you next meet a Black Rose call out for Ramul and I will speak with you."

Crysanthe was going to ask her about the Machine Men but the alien burst into a cloud of petals and poured between them in a dark roar. The general's hair streamed after the creature in a sour wind that stank of dead space. Abby drew her revolver. Shots thundered in the wake of the cyclone but Ramul was just an ink brush flicker against the distant iron walls. She vanished.

Abby stared after her for an age, then wiped her eyes with the heel of her hand and spat over the side of the gantry. Crysanthe turned to Goma.

"Can we fly this ship to the God Door if we have to?" Crysanthe asked. After Abby translated the Abhuman wobbled his head from side to side as if mulling over an argument in his mind.

"I hope so. Despite all the changes happening in this realm, I see no reason why we couldn't make the journey when the time comes. It would be very interesting and exciting. And if you want someone to stand in front of the other gods and ask them for help, we would be happy to do so if you are too scared."

Crysanthe didn't know how to respond. Perhaps the innocent simplicity of the Abhumans trumped all the cunning diplomacy and subtle words Selva would prepare for her.

"Are we near the place where something tried to break into this universe?" asked Abby, snapping the general out of her thoughts.

Goma's head looked like it was trying to work free of his shoulders. He shuffled back and forth and twirled circles on the floor with his claws.

"Take us there."

He froze and stared at Abby with what could only be the Abhuman equivalent of panic.

"Queen Abby and Empress Crysanthe command it," she continued in a low, seductive purr. It seemed to work. The war inside Goma's head reached a crescendo and his shoulders slumped in defeat. The creature beckoned to them and loped away, *I'll get castrated for this* written all over the back of his furry head. Abby flashed a grin at Crysanthe and opened her mouth to say something. Before she could speak her eyes rolled up in her head and her legs gave way. She thumped onto her knees and fell sideways. If the general hadn't grabbed her she would have fallen half a mile to her death.

CHAPTER SEVEN

"Sod this for a game of soldiers," said Ioam and grabbed Max and Nem's hands. The landscape span and Max found himself standing back in the witch's mind palace. The contrast between the delicate shadows, lacework sky-coloured arches and his own lonely patch of grass made his eyes hurt. The two sisters stood either side of him. A fraction of a second later the remaining Machine Men appeared. They stared silently into space, rattled by the attack on Alpheus.

"I pulled them with us," explained Ioam. "I wasn't leaving them in your head."

"What about the monster?" asked Max. The thought of that slavering bulk heaving itself into his soul sickened him. He tried to concentrate, to sense whether Ombratulla and Belsalice's demon crawled through his thoughts. How would that work if he was now inside Ioam's dreams? How would he know?

"It can't touch you. A God Talker's mind can't be breached by the giants."

"If it was inside your head you'd realise," added Nem. She had a point, so he turned to the remaining Machine Men. He wanted to extract Bassandis from Rebecca's brain and get him here before they started jumping up and down again, trying to get the attention of the other giants.

"This palace is hidden from Ombratulla and Belsalice. We should bring Bassandis here and restore him to health before we try to contact them again. His sisters will destroy him while he's still weak, if they can. They imprisoned Ragaleis - their other brother won't last a second at their hands."

Subjulio and Cimabue looked into each other's eyes in silence. Max found himself watching Ihanna. She was studying her kin with an unsettling intensity. He itched to ask her what the problem was, but that'd have to wait until he got her on her own.

"How do we bring him here without alerting the titans?" asked Cimabue eventually. Max had no idea, but there had to be a way. Perhaps Rebecca could help, but she was just an infant and the last thing he wanted to do was expose her to Theuderic's vassals.

Ioam and Nem walked past them to the archway looking out onto the landscape of God's mind. Max followed and the metronome stutter of metal points on marble told him the creatures were close behind. As they emerged to gaze over a deep valley he turned and gasped at the witch's citadel. It grew from a cliff face of fused glass - a melancholy sight, for Ioam had modelled it on their own home near the Umbilicus. It had the same teased filament arches, vaulted halls and subtle-toned windows, but without the constraints of physics its owner had let her dreams loose to fashion architectural calligraphy of breath-taking abstraction. He understood now why she'd been unimpressed by his fifty square yards of lawn and faded garden furniture. A pile of books sat on a bench. Remembering her library, and happy that she'd at least preserved it here after Merodach's legions destroyed it in the real world, he picked one up. But all he found were random meaningless phrases scattered over the pages. Even when he tried to read those they slipped out from under his eye. The other volumes were the same.

"These are merely the memories, empty fragments," said Ioam with a casual diffidence that did little to conceal her heartbreak. Max looked back into the citadel where impossibly high bookcases dwindled into perspective.

"Are they all like this?"

Ioam took the book from his hand and placed it gently on the bench.

"Most. I think it's all in here somewhere," she tapped her temple. "I wish I knew how to retrieve it."

"We can help," said Subjulio, overhearing. Ioam suddenly looked angry, baring those hideous fangs of hers and ready to rip the creature apart. Max stepped between them.

"Nice try. But you aren't going to get your little metal claws inside my brain like that."

"My house!" shouted Nem, breaking the moment. She pointed at a cluster of spinning black spheres inter-shot with lightning on the opposite slope. Ioam calmed down, stalking away from Subjulio with a muttered curse. Max looked into the valley. It seemed less forbidding without the shadow walls and watchers surrounding his own mind palace but where it faded into mist on either side he could just see the outlines of towers, and beyond those, huge creatures stalking the edge of perception.

"Is there a real geography to this place?" asked Max. On his journey to speak with Ombratulla and Belsalice he'd followed what he thought was a path - walking for ages through a landscape spattered with fragments of houses and statues. He'd passed through a dividing wall, descended stairs and crossed a plain to meet the sisters. Had the route possessed its own independent existence, or did God's mind just make it up as he went along to give him the illusion of place? Was it nothing more than the dream-equivalent of the rolling conveyor belts of scenery used by actors when they wanted to signify the hero's travels?

"We don't know the limits of the unformed mind of God," said Ihanna. "We wanted it to develop unfettered by boundaries so we built the seed and let it grow of its own accord. Unfortunately that means we have to search for the giants in this realm and they may be far away from here. God's soul will only have true structure when they come together."

"And the God Talkers?"

"There's one for each giant. Again, we can only locate their mind palaces by first meeting with them in the real world."

One for each giant.

"So Bassandis was my giant?" asked Max.

"Yes."

The Machine Man's voice carried no reproach, but it still sparked a miserable guilt in Max. *If I'd known I would have saved you from my sour bastard father and looked after you better.*

"Ragaleis's God Talker?"

"We think he died long ago."

Max remembered Abby's sister telling him about the mad theatre manager Peter Löwy who wanted to invite a giant to come and see his plays at the Theatre of Angels. It all seemed so hit and miss. The Machine Men had linked the God Talkers to the titans but then scattered them all across the singularity. Maybe they thought mankind would have the wit to understand what was expected of it and hunt out the giants. *Perhaps all of this could have been avoided if they'd just tied us together at the ankles.* It was part of the contradiction of the Machine Men - intelligent and powerful, yet on occasion oddly impotent and staggeringly obtuse. Unless there was another reason why they'd wanted him and his kind separated from the Mind of God.

"I don't know about Ombratulla and Belsalice's God Talkers. The sisters hid themselves away from man from the very start, and so never came into contact with their human mentors."

"That means there's another four God Talkers out there."

"Five. Ioam and Nem are from the same bloodline, so Sorameistre belongs to both of them."

"What's that?" asked the mad witch.

A sharp fleck of metallic brightness flared high above one of the distant minarets, moving rapidly through the sky so that it under-lit the spitting coals like a searchlight.

"It's coming this way," said Max. "They've found us after all."

"No, wait a second," said Ioam. She narrowed her long almond eyes, and he realised her vision was far sharper than that of ordinary humans. The sorceress tracked the light for a few seconds. Her mouth dropped open, and she looked at Max. Before he had a chance to ask her why she was staring at him like that the mote stopped above the fortress and drifted down towards them.

This can't be happening. It's insane.

A young girl dressed in armour and carrying a spear landed on the balcony. She appeared about fourteen and had green eyes and flaming hair.

When we met a couple of months ago you couldn't have been more than three years old. You're not my daughter. You can't be. You can't even be human.

And yet he saw how she was. When Rebecca first turned up in his garden as a toddler she'd essentially been a miniature Abby, including the perpetual sulking brat expression lurking behind those stunning eyes. Now she looked ten times more alarming because she no longer resembled a little copy of his partner. For starters she was taller than Max. Straight hair tumbled down her statuesque back to finish at her waist. Hooded eyes filled with sleepy sarcasm watched him from a face of angular beauty. The bee sting mouth and scrawny neck were still there. He spotted the resemblances immediately. If he hadn't been terrified - for her and for Abby - he would have laughed out loud. His father, Herman Ocel, crossed with Rebecca Fabrice, Abby's withering sister and their unborn child's namesake. Even if this creature was entirely alien - forged from the fresh energies of the next universe and planted like a changeling in Abby's womb - it took its cue from both their genes. He waited to see what would fall from her mouth first - Herman Ocel's curt insults or her aunt's sarcasm.

Subjulio and Cimabue stepped towards Rebecca.

"Who are you?"

That threw the girl. She frowned as if thinking hard before looking at Max. He was desperate to shout at her to flee, to get away from this place, but that would alert the Machine Men. He saw Ihanna watching his daughter and panicked. *She'll see the resemblance to Abby.* Despite the dramatic transformation from infant to teenager, very few people had eyes as insane as that. His daughter, if that was what she was, looked at him as if searching for an answer. While he was still out of the Machine Men's line of sight he shook his head hoping she got the message.

"Are you from Ombratulla and Belsalice?" asked Subjulio. Max realised what he was thinking - the titans might have found out how to break into a God Talker's mind palace with the help of the ancient suns and this was their weapon. The girl's eyes blazed with all-too recognisable fury at the names.

"No. I hate them. They want to send monsters and dreams to kill my friend Bassandis."

The Machine Men swapped glances. Max wished he possessed the ability to read their card and paper expressions. He signalled to the witches and together they moved closer to the creatures. He had to get Rebecca away from them before they realised where she came from. Judging by her expression Ioam was running through ways of overpowering her guests and casting them out of her palace. *If we can push them over the parapet the titans' monstrous watchers will spot them.*

"We are Machine Men - the creators and friends of Bassandis," continued Subjulio. "Where is he?"

The constant glances Rebecca threw in Max's direction meant she was uncertain, almost distrustful. He wondered why? What had she seen in the Mind of God since he last played with her and the giant in her black diamond gazebo? She pointed to the right-hand end of the valley with her spear. At first Max had assumed that her armour was made of burnished silver, but it appeared more like a mosaic of metal plates etched onto the surface of multi-coloured mercury which flowed over her torso and along her arms and legs. Where in God's name did that come from? It looked neither human nor part of God's mind. Had she crafted it herself? What from?

"Over there, far away."

"Where are you in the real world?" asked Cimabue.

"This is the new power in the Mind, the one we detected. She may not dwell in our reality," said Ihanna. "If so, she is our guest and we must treat her as such as she may prove to be an ally."

You know, Max realised. *You know and you're protecting us.* Dealing with the Machine Men had once seemed so straightforward - conversations with complex thinking engines with one purpose and one voice. It had suddenly turned into another mess of factions. More fucking politics like the Empire of the Ear or the Black Roses. He almost wished the razor-blade minded Selva Selvaggia was here to take over.

While Rebecca struggled with the question, Cimabue moved towards her and his daughter stepped back to the parapet. For a second it looked as if she was going to spring into the air again, and as much as Max was desperate to get her away from the Machine Men he didn't want her to go, not yet.

"Where am I in the real world?" she asked, looking directly at him. *She doesn't realise she's our unborn child.* Machine Men and God Talkers stared in his direction and he realised that a simple *I haven't a clue* wouldn't work. Abby and the girl were in danger, but how could he tell her without alerting the Machine Men? He took a gamble and turned to Ihanna, hoping that her bluff meant she was on his side.

"Let Ioam, Nem and myself speak with this creature as fellow God Talkers and see if she can lead us to Bassandis," he said.

"Good idea," said Nem, clapping her hands. She shooed at the Machine Men with her taloned fingers. "Go on, piss off out of it."

Ihanna nodded.

"I agree."

But Cimabue just took another step forward and repeated his question.

"Where are you in the real world?"

Before he could stop her Rebecca reversed her spear, tapped the floor and Abby appeared beside her, jumping into existence like a character in a pop-up book.

"Oh shit." said Ioam.

Max's universe stopped, frozen in a tableau like the ones they used to drop into plays at the Theatre of Angels when he was a child, usually at the grand denouement when the plot turned upside down and the villains were finally marked for death.

Abby blinked and looked around.

"God's cock! What's going on? I was in the middle of a conversation with General Bitch-features."

She spotted Max and her eyes went wide as she realised. Slowly, as if summoning up every last ounce of courage, she turned her head to look at Rebecca. Max had only seen her this scared once before, when the giant Ragaleis appeared in the mist above Max's dolls' house two years ago. To her credit she didn't cry out or jump back. Instead she reached out and poked Rebecca on the shoulder to see if she was real, snatching her hand back when she realised this wasn't an illusion. The girl looked just as stunned, as if she'd unleashed a wild animal to see what would happen and only now understood it might have been a terrible mistake.

"You," breathed Abby. She'd clearly spotted the resemblance to her own sister and Max's father and pulled an *are you kidding?* face. It hardened in an instance.

"Get out. Go on - fuck off! I don't want you. I want a proper baby, not some fucking monster from Dimension X."

"Abby! Stop!" said Max, even as he realised it was too late. It was clear from the confusion in the girl's eyes that she had no concept of her true relation to him and Abby - that they were her mother and father. As viciously unhappy as Abby's curses sounded they were more confusing than hurtful. But family quarrels would have to wait. Subjulio stalked towards Abby.

"You're not a God Talker. How are you here?" He stopped and swivelled round, pointing behind him at Rebecca. "This creature is inside the human woman. She must be on their spaceship."

Maybe it wasn't intended to be a threat but the menace in the air turned into thick glue, making every thought and motion an endless agony. The expression of baffled worry on Rebecca's face switched to anger and she drove her spear through Subjulio's back. The blade protruded from his chest. There was no blood and the Machine Man just looked down at the blade with mild curiosity. The being clearly couldn't be harmed inside the Mind and Max's daughter's attack had merely escalated the confusion.

"We're dead," said Ioam.

"Wait, please," said Max, hoping he could somehow calm everyone down. Rebecca flipped the spear, hurling Subjulio far into the sky, his ragged silhouette dwindling against the dull red coal and ash. A cluster of what looked like tangled knots of black hair and skin beat upwards from the nearest tower, converging on the Machine Man who'd reached the limit of his trajectory and was now falling back down towards them, arms and legs flailing as he tried to get away. The shadow snatched him and disappeared into the grey mist beyond.

Ombratulla and Belsalice's defences. When she threw Sub-julio out of the mind palace they detected him. Max looked at Cimabue and although his expression had barely changed Max sensed his terror. The creature winked out of existence, followed almost immediately by Ihanna.

"They're after you," Max yelled at Abby. "They're going to kill you to get at Rebecca. For God's sake wake up and run!"

"I don't know how to."

He turned to Rebecca.

"Please, return her to the real universe or you'll both die."

Rebecca thumped her spear against the ground and Abby vanished, just as Nem and Ioam grabbed his own hands and the landscape blinked out.

They were back in the cube room, so still and silent

after the chaos of the deity's dreams. Subjulio and Alpheus slumped forward in their chairs, their faces mashed against the table top. The creatures' skin was no longer a delicate foolscap. It looked as if it was coated with wet ash, like a camp fire extinguished in a sudden thunderstorm. Not only had the beasts inside God's mind consumed their machine souls but the energies generated by the meeting of God's nightmares and their power cores had triggered a hideous dissolution. Max didn't hang around. He turned for the exit only to halt in astonishment.

Ihanna had Cimabue pinned against the wall next to the entrance. She'd buried her forearm in his abdomen with such force that she'd pushed him off the ground. His feet scrabbled for purchase on the plastic bricks behind him. She yanked her fist out, trailing a cloud of wires, cogs, pistons, ceramic dust, shreds of paper, metal and gold leaf so fine it was transparent. Her captive's head flopped to one side, and the body collapsed in a broken heap at her feet. Ihanna turned to face them.

"We have to go back to your ship and leave this place, get as far away as possible."

"Why?" asked Max.

But she was already through the door. Instinct kicked in and Max sprinted after her but ten steps into the mist Nem grabbed his arm and threw him up onto her shoulders. He clung on to her glass collar as she raced alongside her sister, one huge spider hand clamped over his thigh to hold him in place. Ihanna ran so fast that her pinions snatched sparks out of the ground.

Max's mind span. Cimabue had worked out that Rebecca was inside Abby and left Ioam's palace to hunt her down in reality, no doubt heading for the Brittle Hag's vessel. Ihanna killed him before he'd even stepped outside. Why? Why was she helping them? The Machine

Man had acted strangely since they'd got here, appearing disconnected from the ponderous ceremony of their encounter with Theuderic. Even with her prison-window eyes and silence, Max detected her unease. What did she say? Ambassadors sat in the outer circle, a thousand doors and a thousand gatekeepers from the centre of their world. It almost sounded as though she knew as little about this realm as he did. He guessed that when they arrived she'd interfaced with the systems at the core of Theuderic's kingdom. Whatever she'd discovered there had driven her to save him and Abby and, in doing so, slaughter one of her own kin.

The mist spread around them, an endless layer of paper-white nothing under a dead sky punctuated by acid-coloured lights. *They're not going to let us anywhere near the ship.* But even in the fear and adrenaline of the moment he couldn't help but wonder about Rebecca. No longer a toddler - she'd spanned ten years in a few weeks, turning into a teenage girl of such strange beauty. So recognisable and yet so alien. He understood Abby's reaction, as cruel as it seemed. *I want a proper baby, not some fucking monster.* He looked for Ioam, sprinting ahead with her jet hair blazing behind like a comet's tail. *Is Rebecca still inside your head, wondering where we've all disappeared to, or has she flown back to her own garden?* She could pass through the Mind of God unseen by giants or their monstrous sentinels. That had to be to their advantage if they ever managed to get out of here alive.

The Brittle Hag's ship loomed out of the fog. Max jumped down and the witches ran into the vessel. Ihanna stopped at the foot of the ramp.

"There's no hope here. Take your ship and journey to the Black Rose god, and beg it to rescue humanity."

"Why, Ihanna? What have you found?"

Shapes moved in the fog - shadows coalescing into an

army of Machine Men stalking towards them. One by one the lights hovering above the mist winked out.

"Don't trust Theuderic. I'll delay them and try to contact you afterwards, but you must go. Now."

"Come with us. We can easily outrun these bastards."

She froze, her eyes rolling up into her head. Her body spasmed, arms thrashing in the fog. For a second she appeared to break away from the attack. Her voice was full of shattered gears.

"They've realised. Escape! Max!"

Ihanna's torso exploded, the shock wave sending him tumbling up the ramp just as it slammed shut and he felt the lurch of the craft taking off. A lump of darkness bounded along the rusting catwalk towards him. Ihanna's severed head rolled slowly onto its side so he could see the prison-bar pupils swollen to fill her sockets. She stared straight into his eyes and her lips framed a single word. *Hate.* Her face crumpled and blackened, falling in on itself like a rotting orange.

CHAPTER EIGHT

"Hate?"

Crysanthe turned to Selva, looking for an answer. Her lover studied Max with ice blue eyes.

"We know Ombratulla, Belsalice and Ruth hate us. Do the Machine Men loathe us as well, or do they hate each other?" continued the general.

"That's all she said?" asked Selva.

Nem held Ihanna's head in her claws. At first she'd volunteered to see if she could fix it, or at least access any information that might still be locked inside, but whatever force killed the Machine Man had wrecked her beyond repair, turning the delicate bird skull into a disfigured lump of clockwork and black slime. Nem pulled a face and tossed it into the corner of the room. It landed with a dull splat.

What more could he give them? There'd been no mistaking Ihanna's final word. He guessed it was a warning. Right now he didn't care. He was more worried about Abby who sat on the floor of the bridge, hugging her knees and staring into space with such an expression of bleak desperation he wanted to take her deep into the ship and lose the two of them forever.

They hovered northwest off the left shoulder. All the humans stood in the central cabin. Abby suggested fetching Neke, but in the end Max decided no. As long as the

Abhumans kept messing around with space-time and ignoring his commands to stop he didn't trust them. It was a hateful conclusion and it made him feel guilty, but too much was at stake.

There was no sign of a Machine Man pursuit - their fleet wouldn't stand a chance of catching up with the Brittle Hag's spacecraft. They were safe for the time being, but now what? Crysanthe told them about her conversation with Ramul. *Forget your dead god and these titans of the mind. Present a case before us.* The alien would no doubt be tumbling through the endless night back towards her own deity. No help there then.

As soon as Max realised they were clear he and the witches jumped into his garden. The hinged wall had flipped back into place and the grotesque watcher's bulbous head was just another silhouette staring down the slopes while it digested its meal. Next they tried Ioam's mind palace but Rebecca was long gone. Max guessed she was back in her own bower with the giant Bassandis. He found himself longing to see her again, even though she might be an alien power stealing the body of his unborn daughter from his memories. Herman Ocel and Rebecca Fabrice were a poisonous mix - nostalgia and humiliation rolled up into one achingly beautiful demon shape to stalk through his thoughts in silver armour.

"Are you finally going to tell us the whole story?" asked Crysanthe. He saw no reason to hide the truth anymore.

"Bassandis is inside our unborn baby's mind. Thanks to the Steel Queen's wormhole Abby and I ended up on a planet in the next universe. We fucked under the stars and Abby conceived. Apparently the baby exists in some no-man's land between the two universes, though she can draw on the power of the new cosmos. She's also a God Talker. You remember when she appeared to me on my first journey through God's dreams? It was her who pulled Abby in to protect me from Ombratulla and Belsalice. She took Bassandis into her mind palace - she can travel through the deity's soul undetected by the giants or their creatures."

Abby started to cry silently, rubbing her eyes with the heel of her hand. Max didn't dare say anything to her.

"When we jumped inside Ioam's palace she appeared as a teenager. Unfortunately she dragged Abby in as well, and the Machine Men saw the link and realised where Bassandis is. They were going to come after Abby but Ihanna stopped them, helped us escape and died in the process."

"How far gone are you?" Selva asked Abby.

"Twelve months."

"That's impossible."

Abby shrugged.

"Your Doctor Tali said it was 'perfectly normal'." She made bitter quotation marks in the air with her fingers.

"So how is she turning up fully grown in the Mind if she's not even born yet?"

"Because she isn't my baby," yelled Abby "She's a monster and I want her out of me!"

Abby stood up to leave. Max moved to intercept, thinking to put his arms around her. She thumped him in the gut, hard. Winded, he watched her stomp down the corridor through watering eyes.

"Can you contact Rebecca?" asked Crysanthe.

"I don't know how to. She just turns up when she feels like it. We could try and locate her mind palace but as soon as we start wandering around outside our own heads the giants will spot us."

Ioam stood at the entrance and looked down the corridor.

"She's not going to...?"

No. Not Abby. He suspected that somewhere deep inside that fury and sadness a tiny part of her clung on to the strangeness of it all. Rebecca was a wonder, and Abby would want to understand how and why. Perhaps she hoped that once this had played out there might be a proper child at the end of it, though God knew how that was going to work. His partner wouldn't harm herself or the baby. Right now she'd want to vent her frustration by finding something to kill. He toyed with the idea of asking the Abhumans to fetch up a couple of monsters out of the abyss for her to kick around.

Crysanthe and Selva looked at each other, processing the information in their heads. Max knew that in the Empire of the Ear the answer would have been easy - sacrifice Abby to the Machine Men and let them pull Bassandis out regardless. If that's what they were thinking they'd have to get through him first and, he suspected, Ioam, Nem and all the Abhumans.

Ihanna's death changed everything. Since Ragaleis had told him to seek out the Machine Men he'd doggedly allowed stone duty to drag him by the scruff of the neck from God's left thumb to deep within the deity's mind. At first it'd been because he thought he was the last hope of mankind. Even after Bassandis decamped to Rebecca's mind palace the grinding sense of responsibility the Carceral Archipelago had gouged in his bones still drove him on.

"Unless anyone knows any different we're the only humans left who've still got a chance at saving humanity," he said. "So what's next?"

They all looked at Crysanthe. It was clear she wasn't happy about it. She turned to Selva.

"Report."

"Ombratulla and Belsalice control the Mind in our world and God's dreams," Selva closed her eyes as she read the list in her head. "They've built a fortress guarded by an alien army powered by ancient suns, and set watchers and guardians to hunt for Machine Men and ourselves. No-one can pass through the Mind unnoticed except Rebecca, whoever or whatever she is. The giants defeated Theuderic's army and cast them out of the Head. The Lord of the Machine Men is trying to re-establish contact with them while planning a counterattack. He is not our ally - he has his own stratagems which, if Ihanna's warning is genuine, threaten us and possibly the Great Task itself."

She opened her eyes. Despite the litany of desperation her expression was as infuriatingly knowing as ever.

"We have two options," said Crysanthe. "Find a way of defeating Ombratulla and Belsalice and then persuading them to unite with the other giants to form the Mind, or we follow Ramul's and Ihanna's advice and journey to the Black Roses to ask them for help."

"Or we do both," said Ioam.

"Sis and I'll go chat to the night fairies," offered her sister with a piranha grin. Everyone ignored her so she frowned and stuck out her bottom lip.

"The Black Roses are a last resort," said Max. "We've got God knows what from God knows where trying to break into the ship at random intervals and the Abhumans can't or won't stop it. While we're flying around the singularity it's not too bad. It would be a hell of a risk to journey all the way to the God Door only for this vessel to turn inside out halfway there."

"Apart from Neke and his people, the only allies we have at the moment are your daughter and Bassandis," continued Selva.

"If the Abhumans have located the Giants of the West and we can get to them before Ombratulla maybe we'll persuade them to help," said Crysanthe.

"Ragaleis was unable to match his sisters," Max remembered the tormented shadow in the pit - the white maggot that was to be Ruth imitating his desperate attempts to break free of his chains.

"He was outnumbered. If Sorameistre and the others haven't gone mad or died they'll listen to us," said Ioam. Max saw Nem take her hand. He noticed the melancholy hope in the witch's voice - that whatever bond she'd had with her childhood friend the giant still counted for something.

"OK let's start with that glove the Abhumans found," said Crysanthe.

Max turned to Ioam and Nem.

"We also need to return inside and try to find Rebecca."

"Not right now," Ioam told him. "Go after her Max."

With the help of an Abhuman he tracked Abby to the vault housing the giant's glove. She stood with her arms on the gantry rail, staring at nothing. He looked down and remembered the army of thralls sewing a two-mile long dress for Ruth inside Ombratulla and Belsalice's unholy manufactory. The scent of brine drifted up from the flood. Neke and his friends had outdone themselves this time, plucking that from the ocean waves with their magic claws.

"She's beautiful," said Abby. At first he thought she meant the glove. The penny dropped.

"My dad mixed with your sister?"

"She must have all the good looks that passed you by."

She sighed and rested her head on her forearms.

"How's it going to work, Max? If she is our daughter I'm hardly going to give birth to a teenager, am I? Even with my barge arse I'd struggle. Will she turn back into a baby when this is all over? Or is that it now? She carries on living in la-la land and I only get to see her when she fancies a chat with mum and pulls me in?"

"We need to find someone to help us - who has enough science to understand what's happened."

"The only ones who might have the knowledge are the Machine Men. Who else would know how to fix this, and how would we find them?"

She put her arms round his neck and buried her face in his chest. Gorgeous, deranged Abby Fabrice - his stomach still hurt from where she'd hit him. He tried to tell her how much he loved her but as ever the words were a clumsy parody of his thoughts. They kissed, Max trying to pull them into the moment for as long as possible. Claws tapped on metal behind him. *God's cock, now what?*

"Goma was going to show us where the attack happened," she paused. "You don't think it's Rebecca attempting to get into our reality, do you?" Was that hope in her voice? He turned to the Abhuman.

"Take us there and then fetch the others."

"It's a grappling iron," said Crysanthe. Ioam, Nem, Selva and the general had joined them in an iron-plated room half a mile long and a quarter wide. Its roof opened onto a void with clouds drifting just below filthy glass dappled with unpleasant shapes frozen at random intervals - like a badly made microscope slide. Pale yellow lights in whatever space lay beyond turned everything the colour of tired piss. Neke and a handful of Abhumans hovered in the background. Goma was in deep disgrace for bringing everyone here and he clung to Nem's leg for protection while his fellows stood in the corner, glaring in his direction and clicking angrily at each other.

Perspective re-calibrated itself inside Max's head. Crysanthe was right, he was looking at a harpoon, though the shaft of the weapon was a hundred yards long. He jumped into the trench underneath. It was just as odd - five paces across and perfectly semi-circular in cross section. He guessed the attack had unleashed powerful energies to fuse the uneven floor plates into the surface beneath his feet - so smooth his boots almost slipped out from under him.

"It came from there." He pointed at the far wall which had twisted into a flat spiral, the interstices of the plating tightening into a fractal knot directly in line with the bolt's axis. "And punched through the wall opposite. The tines sprang open and whoever or whatever fired it tried to haul it back."

Six bulges in a ring marked where the barbs dug into the yard-thick iron on the other side. The whole bulkhead domed inward. A chain fell down from the blunt end of the harpoon to puddle in an untidy heap of links - each one ten yards in diameter.

"Must have snapped with the strain," said Abby from the lip of the trench.

"Not if it was strong enough to punch through that wall."

He looked up at the underside. What the hell was it fashioned from? The whole artefact was a dead soul-sucking black. Max didn't see any reflections or specular highlights - no variation in the pure absence of all colour and light. Someone had cut a hole in reality to show the total nothing beyond. It was a sickening void that made their own empty universe seem full of busy joy. Max's head hurt just from looking at it.

Nem dropped beside him in her exoskeleton. At twice his height she could take a closer look. She angled her head back and stuck out her tongue. Unsurprisingly, it was forked and covered in white barbs like a cat's. It was also ridiculously long. "Fucking hell," muttered Abby.

"Nem, put it away please. You're frightening the children." said Ioam.

Her sister ignored her. *She's going to lick the bloody thing to see what it tastes like,* thought Max in dismay. Nem stopped and frowned, the two tips arched back an inch from the surface like twin snakes on the point of striking. She reeled her tongue in and reached up with a metal-shod finger, but her hand suddenly shot out sideways. She giggled, pulled it out of the exoskeleton and dabbed at the shaft again with her forefinger. Her arm jerked away once more. Before Max had a chance to ask what has happening she clamped her hands round his waist, her fingers and thumbs overlapping, and hoisted him up like a parent helping her toddler get a better look at the zoo. The black rent in reality hurtled towards him and he almost screamed.

"You try."

He reached out with his finger but as soon as he got within half an inch of the shaft his hand glided along a slipstream of force running parallel to the weapon. He pushed again, harder, but it only served to make his arm flip sideways all the faster. Nem put him down again.

"Our reality's bending round it," she said. "I bet you a tit it's a harmonic spike in isomorphic P." She grinned and nodded at her own cleverness.

"Meaning?" asked Crysanthe. Nem just shrugged.

"So something outside this universe fires a grappling iron into the ship that embeds itself in the wall," said Abby, building the story as she walked along the trench. "They start to haul it back. But whatever hole they've made closes, snipping off the chain and leaving this thing here."

"Haul it back to where?" asked Crysanthe.

Max turned to Neke and the other Abhumans who stood in a line against the wall, watching them with their claws folded over their chests. They weren't happy.

"Was something trying to pull this ship into another reality, or themselves into our universe?" he asked.

"Once we had to imprison King Max and Queen Abby because this ship was dangerous and we didn't want them to come to harm before we'd fully understood what was happening," answered Neke, ignoring the question. Max struggled to grasp the subtleties of the Abhuman language and relied on Abby to translate but even he noticed that the chirpy eager-to-please innocence had gone. The hairy bugger had the air of someone caught red-handed who'd decided his best response was defiance. The creature was practically threatening them. Max controlled his temper with difficulty.

"Can you not get it into your thick skulls that we need this ship more now than ever before? Our last chance is to contact the Giants of the West where you found that glove. Or if all else fails we'll have to journey to the Black Rose God and this vessel is the only craft capable of making the trip."

"We promised the entity you call the Brittle Hag to take you to the Mind where you could restore Bassandis. But the giants are at war with each other and the Machine Men, and there's little chance of you mending God's soul."

Max didn't like where this conversation was heading. Neither did Nem. She stomped out of the trench and faced the Abhumans, spreading her metal claws and grinning at them from under her ragged fringe. To their credit they didn't run away though Max noticed Hama clutch at Goma's hand.

"We will help you find the other titans and then we will journey to the Black Rose God to plead for mankind."

That sounded reasonable until Abby asked "We being?"

Neke pointed at himself and his companions.

"You're really serious?" asked Crysanthe. This was beyond ridiculous, but Max was too exhausted to argue.

"Fine. Take us to where you found the glove and if that all turns to shit as well, we'll go to the Black Rose God together," he jerked his thumb at the rest of the passengers. "All of us. King Max and Queen Abby have spoken."

He wanted to ask Ioam to show him how to enter his garden at will, but in the end he crawled into bed next to Abby. He tried to comfort her, but she'd pulled in on herself, curled up in a knot of worries and fears - so he enfolded her in his arms, murmuring nonsense composed on the border of sleep until the darkness washed everything into silence.

He was back in the garden, though he couldn't tell if he was really in the Mind or this was a dream echo. Oddly it seemed bigger - the walls further apart so that the little patch of lawn had become a wide field and the table and chairs paper shapes dwarfed by the monochrome landscape. Puzzled, he walked towards them. It took forever. After a hundred yards, if such measurements existed here, he stepped across a white line that curved through the grass - as if a groundsman had marked out the boundaries for a game. He traced its arc and realised it formed an immense circle. Was it a symbol, a message? From who? Rebecca? Bassandis?

He heard three knocks - *someone trying to get in.* Instinctively he looked at the wall, thinking that Ombratulla and Belsalice had returned to try to enter his mind again, but the sound came from behind. He turned and with a start found himself standing in front of a trapdoor made of rusted iron with a wheel in the centre. *That leads directly into my head.* More thumping and he panicked. What was attempting to break out? Himself? Should he open the hatch? The wheel rotated and an unholy shriek of peeling rust filled his ears.

He screamed himself awake and sat panting in the darkness. Abby slipped her arms round his waist and murmured something from her own dreams. Max teased her hands away so she could fall back, snoring, into the bed. He pulled his pants on and padded to the bridge where Crysanthe watched the brightening air flood the landscape.

"What do you think our chances are?" he asked.

Spires emerged out of the mist. They looked like fine hairs extruded out of white chalk, stretching hundreds of leagues into the darkness above, yet when the ship passed close to one it was at least fifty miles in diameter and the surface resembled cracked clay.

"Does it matter?" she said, without turning round. "We do what we do because it's our duty."

Another one in a mood - great.

"Even if it's stupid and futile?"

"I've done enough stupid and futile crimes in the name of duty to understand that this isn't one of them."

Muscles bunched in her jaw. It was so odd standing next to the cruel tyrant general from the Empire of the Ear and seeing her struggle with her own humanity. He had the sudden insane impulse to take her in his arms for comfort, but he'd no doubt he'd end up castrated or dead the second he touched her.

"We're going to finish on our knees before the Black Rose God, aren't we?" he said. "Even if we get the giants back together God will be a total mess, a drooling idiot blundering around in the dark. We'll be the ones who have to plead on mankind's behalf."

She didn't answer, and Max sensed he'd overstepped a boundary. He wouldn't put it past her to assume that her lordship automatically marked her as the spokesman for them all but he didn't think she was being arrogant, just silently desperate.

Crysanthe broke the moment by nodding to the west. As the fog dissipated he saw the distant landscape change from red grit and plastic to a plain of frozen white waves, like sea modelled in gypsum, the troughs a hundred miles across. The ship dipped down and he noticed roads drifting in from the shadow of the Shoulder behind to cluster in a grid. It resembled the sketch of a city before the architect added the buildings. Sure enough, after another hour clumps of towers, squat warehouses, domes, skyscrapers and arcologies appeared at the intersections of the empty highways. A quick diversion told them these remnants were long abandoned, if they'd ever been inhabited. What looked like elegant structures at a distance turned into nothing more than blocks and shapes punctured with rectangular holes and filled with desolate shadows. Even so, when Max lifted his gaze to peer between their silhouettes, he spotted the shimmering line of an ocean. Here, at last, there might be some hope - if they could find the Giants of the West before Ombratulla.

CHAPTER NINE

Once in a while Crysanthe lost patience with Selva's delight in the intricacies of arcane sex. The woman was steeped in the baroque perversity of the kingdom of Splenius and took endless pleasure in showing off her art. Sometimes she'd eke passion out to a ridiculous degree, lying beside the general for what felt like hours, if not days, and touching with a lingering yet apparently pointless delicacy that left Crysanthe baffled. It was only when a titanic orgasm hit her with the force of a waterfall that she realised what the companion had actually been doing for all this time. Now, however, the adrenaline rush from the frustration and fear of their encounter with Theuderic sent her hunting for a good honest warrior's pre-fight fuck. In a second she had Selva up against the bulkhead, fingers working inside her and thumb on her clitoris so her lover had to balance, gasping, on tip-toes, thigh muscles rigid until she came and collapsed into her arms. The girl recovered with impressive ease, throwing Crysanthe onto the bed and pinning her wrists to the sheets so she could pay her back in kind.

"Tissue armour under white camo," said Crysanthe once she'd regained her breath. "You and I are going on an extraction."

Selva stopped picking fragments of rust out of her shoulders and buttocks and gave Crysanthe a curious look.

"We're expendable," the general explained. "The others aren't. This time we're going to scout before we go charging in, like we should have done at the Black Rose base and with the Machine Men. We find a subject and bring them back here for interrogation."

Selva gave her a grin of happy love. She understood why. Two of them together - doing what they'd be trained for and far away from the ship where the fascination of its endless spaces wouldn't try to drown out Crysanthe's thoughts or tease her and her companion apart. Selva took her hands and pulled her up so they could kiss before fetching the jars from their battle chest, breaking the seals and placing the tissue armour rings around each other's necks. They clapped simultaneously, and the bodysuits sealed to their skins in an electric rush that made them both gasp.

Half an hour later, with white canvas combats over the suits, they met the others at the entrance to the tunnel portal the Abhumans had opened into the city.

"You're going like that? No weapons?" asked Abby after looking the pair of them up and down.

"We don't need them," said Crysanthe. Abby went *pfff*. The general was severely tempted to hit her round the head but to her surprise the ginger shit pulled a revolver from the back of her pants and pushed the handle towards her.

"Just in case, eh? Life wouldn't be the same without you pomping around the place."

Max barely managed to stifle a grin. Crysanthe was gearing up for a magnificent put down when Selva took the gun with a sweet smile.

"Thank you."

"Welcome," said Abby with a sniff. What was wrong with her? It was almost as if she genuinely cared.

Nem came down the passageway with a report from the Abhumans.

"You'll arrive at the top of a skyscraper. We'll close up once you're through, then open up every thirty minutes after that. If you're not back in three hours sis and I are coming after you."

Crysanthe wasn't going to waste time arguing with a bunch of amateurs. She led the way until they came to a mesh ladder. Climbing down she caught a glimpse of the others in silhouette against the soft light of the ship's interior. Selva followed, and they cat-dropped the last two yards onto a white roof covered in rubble and concrete dust. The square hole in the sky above their heads vanished with a pop.

They stood on top of an arcology five miles from the ocean. The wide curve of the shore cut the landscape in half, shallow waves filling the haze with sparks of light. To the north and south more immense skyscrapers punctuated a cityscape stretching as far as Crysanthe could see - an endless jumble of blocks, cylinders, pyramids and domes - all glazed in the same pale dust. It reminded her of the paper garden in the Whispering House. Behind her, the dark wall of God's shoulder bulked up into the eternal night like another world dovetailed into this.

They padded to an access hole in the roof - nothing more than an uneven rectangle cut out of the concrete with stone steps leading down. Automatically switching into bounding overwatch they took it in turns to advance, ending up in an immense low-ceilinged room that filled the entire top storey. It was an empty box, without a single piece of furniture, trash or rubble to break its geometry. Glassless windows threw patches of light across the crumbling floor.

The next seven floors were exactly the same. Crysanthe wondered if it was uninhabited after all. They'd spotted signs of life from the ship - dawn lights coming on here and there to suggest people waking up, a few sheets hung from lower windows to dry, drifting shadows in the streets below. It was a far cry from the crowded chaos of empire cities where even the most ordered metropolis seethed with busy motion. As they moved past yet more empty casements and cracked walls, she realised this was also a once-great kingdom fallen into decay and peopled with a few remaining stragglers and vagabonds.

On the next floor the wide halls gave way to a network of narrow, high-ceilinged passageways leading into the building. Halfway along Selva signalled and jumped back and forth silently up the walls to fix herself, starfish-like, to the ceiling. Crysanthe followed, jamming her boots and hands against the coving to keep in place. They faced in opposite directions, legs hooked through each other's so they could use their muscles to communicate. Selva's calf flexed against hers. *One, unarmed.*

An old woman in a muslin dress shuffled along the corridor below, heading back the way they'd come. She carried a basket under her arm, filled with bread loaves or withered stones, her white hair hacked short as if she was a prisoner or a slave.

Commoner. Useless. Crysanthe signalled. She was looking for someone higher up the chain of command who might have more to tell them. Ten seconds after the woman disappeared round the corner they dropped down and jogged in the opposite direction.

They arrived at a landing in the centre of the tower, with doors set at five yard intervals - some open, most closed. Crysanthe risked a glance over the balcony. The shaft fell away into dusty gloom, ringed by several hundred floors, each identical. She could just make out the ground level far below. Lumps of rubble and piles of garbage littered a checker board plaza of white and black tiles. The whole building was filled with a dead silence. It was as if the grainy air sucked all noise out of the world. Even her own breathing sounded as if it came from a great distance.

The bell made her jump. It rang four times. Her immediate thought was that they'd triggered an alarm, but this emanated from deep within the city - a slow, dark-bronze toll thundering out from an ancient cupola. More followed, peals echoing from all directions, some miles distant, some closer. Still nothing stirred except for the dust hanging in the half-light which shuddered and swirled with each successive chime. Not a summons then. Crysanthe wondered if the music marked the start of a ceremony to which all the inhabitants of this white mausoleum had gone.

Selva slipped through an open doorway, signalling for her to follow. They found themselves in a barely furnished cell - hemp sheets folded on a metal frame bed, chair pushed against an unvarnished wooden desk, a chest with more coarse-fibred clothes stacked in precise squares. *Why are we wasting time here?* Her companion pointed at the picture on the wall and she froze. *Giants.*

It had to be the four titans of the west. Two women and two men sat on tall triangle-backed thrones. They were dressed in sumptuous robes, rendered in crude yellows and reds by the clumsy printing. The man in the centre wore a crown and held his hand up, palm outward, in blessing or command. All had expressions of tragic piety, their eyes accentuated with highlights dabbed in gold and silver paint. Curled script at their feet gave their names. Crysanthe felt her heart thundering in her ribs as she read the archaic words - *Queen Sorameistre, High King Vinduranto, Queen Mephyrean, King Toldi.* Unlike the rest of the furniture, which was covered in a fine layer of concrete dust, the frame and glass were spotless. A soft leather cloth hung from a rusty hook next to the frame.

"Kings and Queens?" whispered Selva, her surprise breaking her out of stealth mode. She caught herself and signalled.

We should take this back.

Not yet. We need a subject.

They worked their way along the row of cells. Those with open doors were identical to the first, and they all had the print with its cleaning cloth hanging beside it. This place was starting to feel like a barracks or a cloister. The door at the end opened onto a larger apartment divided into two rooms, one of which looked like an office. A cage typewriter sat in the middle of a desk, surrounded by stacks of reports. They seemed to be nothing more than endless lists of names and numbers so she ignored them in her growing impatience to find someone they could kidnap and interrogate. They'd have to hunt down that woman after all, and hope she knew something useful.

They hit lucky with the office at the end of the second colonnade. In the adjacent room a man lay curled on his bunk, head to the wall, his arms wrapped round himself as if desperate for comfort. Crysanthe sensed the sickness in the air - the lingering taste of fever sweat ingrained from months of illness. He stirred and turned to look at them, showing a pale haunted face with signs of inbred decadence in his purple eyes. He barely had time to open his mouth before Selva jammed her thumb in the hollow behind his ear to knock him out. She slung him over her shoulder while Crysanthe broke the glass of his picture and tore out the image of the giants.

As they left with their prisoner, a murmuring from the stairwell told her that a crowd was returning to the building. They ran back to the roof - the man barely making a difference to Selva's stride. Crysanthe raced ahead up the wide staircase only to find herself face to face with the old woman laying out the contents of her basket in a pattern on the concrete. Trembling hands flew to her open mouth as she saw Selva emerge behind with the unconscious clerk. A dark hole opened in the sky, the shock wave kicking dust up from the cracked floor.

Crysanthe grabbed the woman round the throat and pushed her across the roof, ignoring the blows that bounced off her head and shoulders. Two yards from the edge she released her captive and kicked her in the stomach, making sure there'd be no screams. The woman folded in half and disappeared over the parapet. The general sprinted back to the rope ladder dangling from the entrance to the Brittle Hag's ship. She let the others haul her back up, hanging sideways from the rungs so she could get one last look at the layout of the city.

It took longer to resuscitate their prisoner because he was sick, but once he regained consciousness they only had to put him in a room with Nem and the Abhumans to get him to talk. After two minutes of howling, the witch stuck her head out and invited the rest of them inside. The man continued to clutch his arms around himself and rock back and forth, crying in fear. Tears and sweat ran down his grey skin. Neke asked if they could give him some of their own Abhuman tinctures to make him feel better, but Crysanthe said no. This wasn't a rescue - she needed to extract as much information about this realm as quickly as possible. After learning his name - Kelvin - she unfolded the painting she'd stolen and placed it on the table. He cried out in anguish and tried to smooth the creases, caressing the crude images as if they were the face of his lover. She realised these pictures of the giants with their frames and polishing cloths were mystical relics, more precious than anything else in his chalk and concrete universe.

"Who are they?"

"The Gods."

"The Gods?" said Abby. "No they're not, they're giants. God's lying on his back over there." She pointed east. Kelvin just looked confused.

"You worship Behemoth?" he whispered, turning a couple of shades paler.

"Eh? We don't worship anyone. We're not that stupid."

"Where are these Gods?" asked Crysanthe, gesturing at the picture.

"They dwell on the Isle Resplendent."

"Where's that?"

"Only Aelspell knows." He started weeping again as he tried to smooth a rip with his thumb.

"Who's Aelspell when he's at home?" asked Abby. Crysanthe held a finger up to quieten her. Abby muttered "Snotty bitch."

"What's this city?"

"The Great White World." He looked around at the others. "Take me back, please. My sister will worry. She went to the roof to bless my medicine under the endless sky. If I'm gone when she returns she'll be so anxious."

"We'll send you back when you've answered our questions," said Max. *No we won't,* thought Crysanthe. She clicked her fingers at Selva - that got another *pfff* from Abby - and took a notebook and pencil from the girl. She put them on top of the painting.

"I want you to write down everything you know about the forces of the Great White World, their disposition and chain of command, what weapons and scanners they bear and their morale."

"What good's that? We're not going to war with them. Are we?" asked Abby.

Crysanthe ignored her and tapped the page.

"I don't know such things," said Kelvin. "I'm just an Apparator for our tower. Somnia knows, ask Somnia. She'll tell you."

"Somnia isn't here. Nem will help you instead."

The witch hunkered down next to Kelvin. Her face was as big as his torso.

"I'm good at spelling and grammar and making stuff rhyme," she assured him.

Crysanthe picked up the print. Kelvin whimpered and snatched at it.

"You can have this back when you've finished."

They left Nem to it. Outside the cell her sister took the canvas from Crysanthe and turned it over in her hands.

"Is it Sorameistre?" asked Max, pointing at the figure on the edge of the picture. The woman shrugged.

"Perhaps. These are mere icons. I don't recognise any of her in this."

"If the giants are all on this island, can't we go searching for it ourselves?" asked Abby.

"It could be anywhere," answered Max. "That ocean's about twenty thousand leagues north to south - if it's the same distance westward we're looking at four hundred million square miles to search. At least Ombratulla's faced with the same problem. We'd be better off making contact with this ruler of theirs - Aelspell - and getting his help."

"Is that wise? They sound like another bunch of nutters if they think the giants are gods and god is a behemoth," observed Abby.

"Max is right," said Crysanthe. "Once we've got what we can out of Kelvin we'll negotiate. If that doesn't work we'll force compliance."

"As simple as that?" asked Abby.

"I saw no evidence of flying machines or other heavy weapons. This is a metropolis by an ocean yet there's no harbour or ships that I can see, or any inland defences. I doubt they have more than a police force or, at worst, militia. If there is an immediate threat we can position ourselves up in space and extract whoever we want to talk to, including this Aelspell."

"Here's the gun back," said Selva, handing over the revolver to Abby. "Thanks, but we didn't need it."

Abby looked from Crysanthe to Selva, and then back at the general.

"You're a right pair of smartarses. You do realise that, don't you?" She shrugged. "OK, whatever, your call."

They got a few scraps of intelligence from Kelvin, when they'd disentangled it from his warped mythology. It was clear these people weren't the original builders of the city. They were long gone, replaced by succeeding kingdoms increasingly indolent and defeatist as they scrawled their own petty hopes across the concrete and plaster palimpsest of the ages. Just over half a million souls led a monk-like existence ruled by a hierarchical priesthood answering, ultimately, to Aelspell, who alone was permitted to speak with the Gods. No armies, no flyers and no fleets.

"No enemies either," said Nem, holding up the notebook. "Nothing for hundreds of thousands of miles on all sides. I reckon this Great White World conquered everywhere on the west side of God so now it's shrunk there's only wilderness left around it. Neke and friends tell me they haven't found any other civilisations yet. This might be it."

"Is that all we have?" asked Selva. Nem cleared her throat and read her notes.

"Millions of years ago the gods fought and slew Behemoth, whose body lies to the east. The monster's death saved humanity. But Behemoth's dying curse trapped them on the Isle Resplendent where they have lived ever since, in their own paradise, attended only by the high priests - of whom Aelspell is the last living descendant. The end."

"What does all that mean?" asked Ioam.

"It's a city full of Segandyrs," said Abby. "He was a loony we met on a wormhole planet who thought he was God's chosen. The bastard murdered thousands, hoping it would earn him an extra big dollop of forgiveness. He almost killed Max and me. We would have died if Thin Hans hadn't rescued us."

"We have to tread carefully," continued Max. "We can't go stomping all over their beliefs, no matter how stupid, by telling them we've come to meet the giants."

"We'll interrogate Kelvin again in the morning to see if he's got anything more to tell us, and work out how we're going to approach Aelspell." Crysanthe turned to Nem. "Any chance of getting the Abhumans to try and locate the island?"

The witch nodded.

"And Ioam and I'll attempt to contact the titans in god's mind," said Max.

Crysanthe felt a claw on her arm. Neke looked up at her with his black mirror eyes.

"Can we give Kelvin our tinctures now?"

"No. Let him sweat a little longer."

In the end she didn't know why she did it. Maybe it was because she couldn't sleep, even in her post-recce exhaustion. She lay awake, tracing faces on the ceiling by the lamplight, until the comfort of Selva's arm across her breasts turned into an intolerable weight and she slipped out from under her lover's embrace. The girl murmured and arched her back beneath the sheet, lithe and beautiful. For a second she was tempted to wake her Companion for a lazy midnight fuck, but she knew that wouldn't dampen the fire in her head. She pulled on the camos she'd worn in the skyscraper, crept out of the cabin and made her way into the infinite universe of the Brittle Hag's ship.

After half an hour wandering through corridors and passageways she came to a balcony that opened onto a vast space studded with countless doors, archways, staircases, ramps, rooms, halls, vaults and colonnades. It stretched into the distance on all sides, the sight filling her with its inhuman possibility. She could go anywhere - up, down, left, right, forwards - and lose herself in an infinity of iron, steel, wood, glass, plastic, ceramics - endless abstraction to tease her troubled thoughts away. Out there, somewhere, she would find an answer, and some peace. She imagined it would be a little cell like Kelvin's, with a single window that for once wouldn't open onto more iron and darkness, but look out at a cross-hatched sky in a perfect paper world.

"Can't sleep either?"

Abby stood barefoot beside her in one of Max's shirts, absentmindedly scratching her left breast and staring into the distance. It was odd, but for once she didn't break the moment. Crysanthe felt none of the irritation the woman usually sparked with her loud and stupid opinions.

"Don't blame you. It's hard to lose everything," she sniffed. "It's not so tough on Max, he only had his bastard father and he hated him, and that fucking tower."

"And you?"

"My sister. The theatre. Family and hopes and art." She rubbed her stomach. "You?"

"I was General Uella of the Emperor's Dogs, Vavasour..."

"Yeah yeah. What did you really lose?"

Mad purple gaze. Gorgeous crazy laugh.

"Ruth."

For a second she couldn't speak and had to turn her face away.

"Family. My brothers. Nan. Nan taught me everything. She made me what I am."

Abby whistled.

"She must have been a real bitch."

To her utter surprise Crysanthe found herself laughing. It helped her keep the tears in check.

"Yes, Caterina Uella was a real bitch. My god, she should have been empress. Not me. She had valour and discipline and purpose."

"So do you. You're too hard on yourself." Abby gave her a stinging slap on the back. *I just let Abby Fabrice hit me.*

"I'm off to bed - perhaps I can cadge a shag off the snoring farter to cure my insomnia."

Crysanthe watched her go, trying to make sense of the conversation. Abby Fabrice simply lacked any filter whatsoever between her thoughts and her mouth - she just said whatever was on her mind. *So did Nan.* If there'd been more of that brutal honesty, with all its noisy crassness, instead of the endless hints, rumours, insinuations and whisperings that filled the Empire of the Ear in its final days, perhaps it would have survived.

What ifs wasted energy. She left the balcony and walked further into the ship until she came to the entrance of the tunnel that had dropped her and Selva onto the arcology roof. A lone Abhuman drew lines on a lead plate stapled to the floor. As he etched spirals and circles with his talon she heard the distant end of the passageway flex and twist with the sound of iron on wood. She summoned up her little knowledge of the Abhuman language and had a stab.

"Please can you drop me onto the skyscraper again, just for ten minutes?"

The creature's head bobbed up and down and for a few seconds she feared he might go check with the others first. He gestured down the passageway. She clicked *thank you* and headed for the far end.

It was night time in the city. Most of the buildings lay in darkness but here and there she spotted lanterns at windows, or open fires in hallways and in the centre of plazas. A few shadows drifted along the streets. All was silent. A metallic breeze from the ocean plucked at her hair and sent threads of dust flickering across her boots. The square in the sky above her head popped out of existence.

She'd asked for ten minutes. Long enough. She turned on her pencil torch and searched across the roof. Nothing. She cursed herself - why was she even doing this? She'd said no when Neke wanted to give the man physick, why was she now risking her life looking for his magic bread? *His sister came to bless his medicine under the eternal sky and I kicked her over the edge.*

There - desiccated lumps like grey stones. She picked one up. Hard as steel. How many would he need? Surely not the whole basket. She stuffed half a dozen into her pockets and straightened up just in time to hear the scuff of leather on concrete behind her.

They fell on her in a pack. Crysanthe automatically dropped into night combat mode, kicking backwards to shatter one of her assailant's thighs while using the impetus to roll forwards. But there were too many of them. She grabbed a face and dug her thumb into an eye socket - hearing another shriek, but then she was on her side, a great weight on her chest and neck. Someone yanked her arm behind her. One last heave to break out - but it was no good. An attacker pulled her head back by the hair and a fist smacked into her face like a sledgehammer.

CHAPTER TEN

"WHAT WAS SHE playing at?" asked Max as he strode down the passageway, loading his revolver. "I thought you lot were sticklers for discipline."

Selva ignored him. He'd never seen her upset before and the sight was unnerving. Her face was a rigid mask of fury - lips white and pale eyes staring down whatever fears danced through her head. She carried two long knives and clearly had carnage on her mind. The sisters walked behind the Companion, Nem already in her exoskeleton and smacking her metal fists together like a boxer about to enter the ring. He caught Ioam's eye - if Selva was about to go crazy on them they'd probably need both witches to subdue her before she destroyed any chances of meeting the giants with a bloodbath.

"She seemed fine to me," said Abby, trotting alongside. "In a bit of a mood because she couldn't sleep."

"What did you talk about?"

"Loss."

He dreaded to think what Abby's take on loss was, especially in a conversation with General Uella. He was surprised it hadn't ended in a fight. At least if they'd thumped each other unconscious he'd know where they both were.

"We're half a mile above the arcology. It looks like they've set up defences," clicked Goma, who was waiting at the exit with Neke and twenty Abhumans who'd volunteered to help fetch Crysanthe back.

Max's stomach tightened at the noise of gunfire - heavy machine guns by the sound of it. The defenders had seen the opening hanging in the dawn sky. At this distance they had little effect, though the occasional round thumped into the ceiling above the hatch, but descending into the arc of fire would be suicide. He stuck his head over the edge for a three-second scan with binoculars. The roof was swarming with figures, bunched around a dozen gun points. Thick muzzles pointed up through slots in iron domes. They looked ill-disciplined. Judging by the information they'd managed to get out of Kelvin, the military was nothing more than a bully-boy police force created to keep its own citizens in check.

"Bugger this. We'll brave the bastards on their doorstep. Abby, gather all the Abhumans capable of fighting, along with any weapons they have," he turned to Ioam and Nem. "Suit up. I want you two looking as scary as possible. Let's find this Aelspell's palace and pay him a visit."

Selva hung over the edge, one hand on a strut for support, and stared down at the enemy. A heavy slug sparked off the iron rim between her feet but she didn't even flinch.

"Selva."

She nodded and walked back into the ship without a word.

They woke Crysanthe by dashing a bucket of freezing slops in her face. She was tied to a wooden X in another floor-wide room littered with broken furniture and lumps of concrete. The ceiling bellied down in the middle, jagged ends of iron coring dripping more water into rust-stained puddles underneath. A crowd filled half the space - men and women in near identical coarse spun muslin and hemp stared at her with expressions of fearful incomprehension mixed with hatred. Three men and three women in white skull caps sat at a long table between them, muttering to each other. A hand grabbed her jaw and bloodshot eyes peered into hers. A grunt of satisfaction and the man let her head drop.

The clerk in the centre of the table tapped his pencil against the wood and watched her with a calculating gaze. He had the lazy confidence of a petty official one step up from the rabble behind him, but despite his arrogance he looked gaunt and ill, as did every face in the room. Crysanthe sensed a combination of malnutrition and sickness. He licked the lead and opened a notebook.

"Name?"

"She killed Somnia and Kelvin," screamed a voice from the crowd.

Shouts answered and the mass pushed and seethed against itself. A sword, her freedom and ten minutes was all she needed to turn this shabby little tribunal into a butcher's warehouse. The man raised his hand.

"The rule of the Law. The rule of the Gods," he intoned.

The room murmured into silence.

"I am General Crysanthe Uella of Long Lock, Commander of the armies of the Empire of the Ear. My ship waits for my return. Release me now and take me up to the roof where you found me, or I swear to God we will wipe this city from the floor of the universe."

"Your monster is dead, servant of Behemoth. Your threats are worthless."

"I want to talk to Aelspell."

The crowd burst out laughing and a concrete fragment sailed from the shadows at the back. She ducked as far as she could, and it thumped into the wood just above her head. Her judge lifted his hand again, chuckling all the while, and called for hush. He drew a vertical line in the air.

"Here is the great ladder of existence. The gods and their beautiful island sit at the very top with Aelspell just below, at their feet, attentive to their wisdom. We on the other hand cling to the bottom rung where we shit into the darkness. On you and Behemoth, far below. In the pit."

That sparked off a round of applause. Crysanthe realised she'd get nowhere in the face of this self-serving drivel. They didn't even seem to want to interrogate her. *I'm just a bogey-man to them - a convenient monster that dropped out of the sky to prove their silly tales are true.* All she could do was stay alive long enough for Selva to find her. She suspected her captors had taken her to another building for this pantomime. There had to be some way of signalling her friends.

"What shall we do with this beast, good people?" yelled out the clerk, slapping his hand on the table top. A woman pushed through the crowd, haggard and limping on dust-covered feet. She clutched a twisted shard of aluminium in her fist. It shook with fury.

"Kate! Show us how it's done!"

Crysanthe cursed herself for not bothering with the tissue armour. Although the wretch coming towards her didn't look capable of inflicting much harm, she'd no doubt those who could would be queueing up behind her. She fixed her gaze on the old woman and channelled Nan at her most powerful and contemptuous. Kate faltered, terror in her eyes. The shouts and boos of the crowd egged her on. She jabbed at Crysanthe, just below the shoulder, but the blow was so pathetic it didn't even break the cloth.

"Try its face," shouted the interrogator with friendly impatience. Kate dragged the edge back and forth across Crysanthe's forehead. It was a shallow cut, but bled enough to please the audience who whooped and applauded as the old woman staggered away, exhausted and pitifully scared.

"Well done, Kate! Well done! Who's next?"

"Rape the whore!"

"Who said that?" asked the leader with an expression of pantomime outrage. "Thomas? Was that you?"

The crowd pushed a teenager forward. Two of the men ruffled his hair and thumped him affectionately on the shoulder as he turned crimson and stared down at his boots.

"I applaud your enthusiasm, but this is a demon of Behemoth and anything you stick in that," he pointed at Crysanthe's crotch with his pencil, "will turn black and drop off."

He folded his arms and grinned at his prisoner while the good people of the Great White World bellowed with laughter. And then all was silent, as if a switch had clicked the sound off, and everyone stood rigid to attention with expressions of blank fear, especially the interrogator and his cronies. The pencil rolled slowly across the table top and fell onto the floor with a clatter. A woman at the back started to weep.

Six men in white uniforms walked into the room, wearing flat pan helmets of beaten copper and carrying rifles. A few minutes later a short fat man waddled through the door. He bent down and put his hands on his knees, face bright red under a shock of sandy hair.

"One hundred and thirty-seven floors. How many cretins does it take to fix a lift?"

Still doubled over he pointed at the pencil.

"Pencils are hard to come by. You'll have shattered the lead, you careless wretch. Pick it up, please."

One of the guards handed it to him and he waved his gratitude, struggling to find breath. Another dragged a chair over and he sat down with a thump and a gasp, wiping his face with a handkerchief. A woman ran up with a glass of water.

"Thank you, my dear." He sniffed it and took a couple of sips before placing it on the floor next to him with the fastidious air of a flower arranger. Having recovered he looked around with an expression of cheerful interest.

"Peter, Peter, Peter. What am I going to do with you?"

Crysanthe noticed the interrogator turn an even paler grey. The man oozed danger despite his chubby bonhomie, and everyone in the room felt it. He got to his feet and bundled over to Crysanthe, fumbling glasses from his pocket. He gave her the once over. She saw from his expression that he regarded her as nothing more than a package that hadn't been delivered to the right address.

"I am General Crysanthe Uella of the Empire of the Ear..." she started, but he turned away.

"Your faith is heartening, Peter. But all strangers are to be brought to the Hall of Human Understanding."

"Chiliarch Kostas, she's a demon of Behemoth. She fell from the sky," said one of Peter's colleagues, an intense eyed woman who still glared at Crysanthe with loathing.

Kostas sighed and pinched the bridge of his nose. Three guards converged on the clerk. They kicked her legs from under her and beat her with their rifle butts until the wailing stopped and the blows turned soggy. No one moved, not even those closest to the victim even though their clothes were spattered with her blood.

"How many times do we have to go through this?" muttered the Chiliarch to himself. He gestured at Crysanthe. "Put her with the others."

The guards went to untie her, but he shook his head.

"I wouldn't. This one's dangerous. I see it in her eyes.

Carry her as is."

Following Kelvin's sickbed directions it didn't take them long to locate Aelspell's palace, standing in its own plaza next to the ocean, the sea-facing wall covered with a giant version of his painting. Silk banners fell for hundreds of yards from four minarets to trail ragged edges in the dust - Sorameistre, Toldi, Vinduranto and Mephyrean, vast icons in primary colours, tragic eyes bent over hands gesturing their melancholy benedictions. A few hundred people milled back and forth. Most wore the same rough-spun clothes as their captive, though Selva pointed out a couple of dozen with beaten copper helmets and rifles over their shoulders. Ceremonial guards mooched around at the top of the palace steps.

Max got the Abhumans to hover the Brittle Hag's ship a hundred yards from the entrance, until the screaming and shouting citizens had cleared out from under its shadow, and then slam it into the ground so that shattered fragments of marble ricocheted off the stucco walls. The shock wave threw everyone in the plaza flat and toppled a crumbling building half a mile away. The few glass windows blew in. The vessel lifted and the ramp clanged down.

Ioam and Nem led the way, wielding their ray guns - flared rifle muzzles glowing a blinding star white. Nem rode the exoskeleton and Ioam wore her gunmetal battle canvas. Both had tied their hair into huge top-knot pony tails fountaining above their heads for maximum psychological impact. A gunshot to their left sent a heavy slug sparking off the edge of their spacecraft. Without turning round Nem fired her weapon sideways one-handed, and an incandescent purple beam lanced through the air to blow apart a geometric statue of a warrior fighting a demon. After that no-one dared shoot.

A thousand Abhumans poured out around the witches' legs in a grey wave, armed with clubs, sticks, shards of metal and glass, spanners, chains and screwdrivers as big as a man's thigh. Max, Abby and Selva followed. The companion wore her tissue armour and nothing else, but she'd painted her body blood red, so she looked as if she'd been flayed and twirled a long knife in each hand so the blades glittered crimson. Max hoped he and his partner could keep her in check if Aelspell didn't co-operate to her satisfaction. Abby hefted a machine gun and Max carried a pair of revolvers in the pockets of Crysanthe's battlefield greatcoat which, remarkably, was a perfect fit.

It took thirty seconds for the plaza to empty, apart from glimpses of fluttering rags as the last stragglers fled down side streets and alleyways. Ignoring them, Max took the steps two at a time and entered the main hallway, a murmuring wall of grey fur and glittering black eyes at his back. Half a dozen idiots had fallen back into the entrance hall, and were struggling to fix an antique chain gun on a tripod until Nem stomped over, kicked them out of the way and pulled the weapon to pieces with her claws.

"Anyone else?" she asked.

The vestibule stretched up fifty yards to a painted ceiling that showed the four titans in armour standing on a black worm that had a human face distorted in agony. A few heads popped over the balconies before disappearing again when they saw the monstrous invasion. If this kingdom had an army it was either hiding in ambush or, more likely, charging down the white pebble beach outside and jumping into escape boats.

Three figures in white robes appeared on the first landing. Max walked up to meet them, the witches flanking him and Abby and Selva watching their backs. To their credit the officials didn't flinch, though he spotted terror beneath their sneers. He stopped in front of the woman in the centre and bent his face down to hers. She looked in her mid-sixties and had a sour arrogance about her that he remembered from his days in the Carcarel Archipelago. Apparatchiks - he hated them all with a vengeance, and that made this so much easier.

"Aelspell. Now."

"I am Saethryth. On behalf of the mighty gods and their servant Aelspell, I welcome you to the Great White World."

Selva stood beside him - fresh gore moulded into a naked woman shimmering beneath a rainbow aura. She grinned and Max saw she'd stained her teeth black. Never mind these supercilious morons, he'd be the one having nightmares for a week.

"Take us to him, please," she said ever so sweetly.

"Friends, friends, friends!" a voice cried out from the passageway beyond. A slender old man dressed in a white tunic and baggy trousers floated towards them at the head of a squad of soldiers carrying rifles and sabres. The officials stepped back and bowed their heads. Soft fingers seized Max's and he found himself staring into soulful eyes the colour of teak framed by a cloud of grey hair.

"Aelspell."

He took each of their hands in turn and repeated his name before clasping his fingers together under his chin and looking around with an expression of pained solicitude.

"Welcome to the Great White World." He closed his eyes and breathed deeply like someone smelling a bowl of his favourite stew. "I am so happy to meet you and greet you as friends, yes, yes," he held Max's hand again. "Friends before the Gods. Friends before the Gods. Do let's be friends."

"Release General Uella," said Selva. Aelspell cocked his head to catch her words, as if trying to make sense of an incoherent toddler. He frowned and threw an enquiring look at his acolytes.

"A demon landed on House Ninety-Five last night and killed two of the occupants. The citizens captured it and now it is under the watchful eye of Chiliarch Kostas in prison with the other strangers."

"Two?" asked Abby. "There was one - Kelvin - and he's still alive on our ship."

"How confusing." Aelspell's hand went to his mouth and he blinked owlishly.

"Shall I clarify?" said Ioam. She hunkered down so her shark mouthed head was at the same height as the priest's. To his credit he gave her a pleasant I'm-all-ears smile.

"I am Ioam and this is my sister Nem. We are God Talkers, like our friend here Maximilian Ocel, ruler of Metacarpi next to the left thumb of God. This is Abigail Fabrice, and Selva Selvaggia, a companion of Empress Crysanthe Uella of the Empire of the Ear. We are also allies of Theuderic, Lord of the Machine Men, with whom we spoke a few days ago, and the titans Bassandis and Ragaleis. Do you understand, or shall I draw you a diagram? No? Good. You will release General Uella."

Aelspell bowed his head and tapped his chin. Despite his delicate mannerisms he was a lot more courageous than the rest of his people, who cast anxious glances between their leader and the invaders. He clapped his hands and smiled.

"What can I say?"

He waved at the Abhuman hoard which spread over the balcony, balustrade and halfway up the pillars, spider eyes glistening Dand weapons held aloft.

"Disperse your monsters and I will bring your friend

here forthwith."

Selva licked her lips and stepped forward. Nem barred her way with a metal-sheathed arm. Aelspell leaned closer to Max.

"I have given, now you give," he murmured. "There is no war here. Can't you see we are at your mercy? I don't want death. Do you? You wish to meet your giants? Indulge me."

Max wasn't that stupid.

"Bring our friend first. Then we'll stand down and then we'll talk."

Aelspell turned and walked up and down a few times, holding his chin and studying the marble patterns on the floor. Eventually he clicked his fingers at a couple of his acolytes and sent them scurrying off.

"Your friend will be returned to you without delay. We began badly, let's salve discontent with friendship and hospitality." He lifted a hand. "In the name of the Gods, it shall be so." As the rest of his followers crept away, leaving only the guards, Aelspell gave Max a warm smile that reminded him of Odilon.

"We'll wait by our ship," said Max, and signalled to the others to follow him back down into the plaza.

"What's going on?" asked Abby. Max turned to Neke.

"Get the vessel ready to leave. As soon as we have Crysanthe we'll hunt for the island ourselves."

Neke's commands rippled through the crowd and the creatures poured back inside. Nem made to go after them but Max called after her.

"Not yet. I still need you to scare the shit out of these bastards until we get Crysanthe."

Selva ran past him, heading for a cluster of people who'd entered the square. Max jogged after, with Abby in tow. He saw four raggedy figures flanked by militia. Aelspell appeared at the top of the stairs and signalled to the newcomers, just in time to stop them panicking and trying to shoot the Companion. She pushed the guards out of the way and homed in on Crysanthe, who limped towards her. The general's face was bruised and crusted with dried blood. Selva slapped her hard. Crysanthe staggered and slapped the girl back. The Companion seized her lover's head and kissed her in desperate relief.

"I love tender reunions." said Abby.

Max ignored her. He was more interested in the other three prisoners, who studied him with wary suspicion. Two of them looked like performers in an avant-garde circus who'd wandered into the city by mistake. The woman had a blue mohican and wore a long dress of pleated yellow metal that clashed and chimed as she walked. The bags and pouches of an apothecary dangled from her belt. Orange eyes watched Max from a face that had been slathered in chalk, making it impossible to guess her age. The man was about fifty, sharp bearded and stern, and dressed in a tightly bound black kimono. He carried a branched stick with painted plaster faces dangling from the twigs on gold chains, each one distorted in an expression of hatred or woe. The third stranger stood apart, a sallow faced scruff with a goatee wearing a brown jacket and creased shirt. He was concentrating on rolling a cigarette out of a stained leather pouch, oblivious to everyone and everything around him.

"Who are you lot?" asked Abby, before he had a chance to frame a suitable greeting. The stranger carrying the staff bowed.

"I am Clarindo of Patella. This is Waldrada from Vastus Lateralis," he gestured at the woman. "And this," he pursed his lips in disapproval and nodded at the other man. "This is Halinard."

"They're God Talkers," said Crysanthe, extracting herself from Selva's arms.

God Talkers?
She pointed at Max and the witches.
"These are the three I told you about."

CHAPTER ELEVEN

MAX HAD A thousand questions to ask the God Talkers, but now wasn't the time. He was all too conscious of their vulnerability. Even if they'd made a fearsome entrance it would only take a couple of the more adventurous with rifles to start picking them off from the surrounding rooftops. He guessed the promise of carnage deterred Aelspell from trying anything too stupid, or did the hierophant have a different, subtler game in mind? The man stood at the top of the plaza steps flanked by rallied squads, watching the invaders with a maddeningly bland expression.

As he headed back to the spaceship Max's ears popped, and a gust of freezing air made him shiver. Nem yanked him back before he could step into the craft's shadow. Selva strode past and held her palm out before snatching it away. Ice dusted her fingers.

"It's happened again."

"Why's the ramp up?" asked Abby, catching up with them. The Companion surreptitiously showed her hand to Crysanthe who looked at Max with real fear in her eyes. God help them all if the general was scared.

"Act normal," he told the others and sprinted up the stairs, Abby close behind. The last time the intruder made the ship drop out of reality it had only lasted half an hour. Even so, he needed to delay to keep their advantage. As soon as the good people of the Great White World realised they were locked outside their own vessel, with their monster army still inside, they'd have them back in the dungeon they'd used for Crysanthe and the other God Talkers. If they were lucky.

"You and I need to talk," he said to the priest, poking him in the chest with a gun barrel. The old man pursed his lips, looked down at the revolver and raised an eyebrow. He was a cool bugger alright, nodding sagely and clasping his hands together as if in prayer. A couple of his braver guards shuffled forwards in half-hearted protest until Abby pointed a weapon at them and flashed her biggest grin.

"Of course," answered Aelspell with a polite smile.

He led Max and Abby through a series of curving passageways and vaulted halls that looked as if they'd been designed to confuse visitors and entrap intruders. If the man sought to disorientate his guests he was mistaken - long years scampering through the maze of shadows in the Carcarel Archipelago had given Max an understanding of labyrinth-builders' minds. He'd have no trouble retracing his steps, no matter how often his guide tried to distract them by pointing out an elegant sculpture, painting, or unusual view of the plaza outside.

The interior of the palace was a striking improvement on the crumbling stone and stucco wreckage of the Great White World. The walls were fashioned from marble, glass and sheets of quartz and jet suspended in intricate lattices of promethium, worn matte by the scuffs and scratches of centuries. Yet Aelspell's own rooms were as spartan as the ones Selva described on returning from the arcology. A chipped stool of dark wood sat next to a dinted metal table on which lay half a dozen books and a pewter mug and plate. *Just like Father's*, thought Max. Aelspell turned and plaited his hands at his waist, like an archimandrite awaiting a confession.

"I know how it works," said Max. "You've told everyone the giants are the Gods and that the real God is a demon they overthrew long ago. That's how you keep your power, isn't it? I'm guessing that you and only you are permitted to travel to this island of yours to speak with Sorameistre and the others." Aelspell watched Max with an expression of fey concern. Max could tell it was taking all of Abby's self-control not to thump the smug bastard in the mouth. He clenched his own fists and ploughed on.

"It ends now. There's a war going on for the salvation of humanity. The real God, the one you call Behemoth, is finished and ready to carry us all through the God Door, but his mind has been taken over by two giants and a monster who've decided to wreak revenge on mankind by sending the deity mad. We need the Giants of the West to persuade their sisters to back off and unite to create the Mind as it should be. I have the Machine Men on my side, the forces of the Empire of the Ear, and seven God Talkers. Whatever petty tyranny you've crafted for yourself in this arse end of nowhere means nothing anymore."

He was shouting and any minute a hundred ill-trained thugs would come piling into the room to shoot him or beat him to death but he no longer cared. He was so, so tired of all the greed and power-grubbing stupidity that held every human chained to this slab of dirt drifting endlessly on the edge of hope. The chains that once bound his childhood home to the shores of the Forbidden Sea were just a tiny fraction of an immense web of cruelty, ignorance and hatred in which everyone and everything he'd ever known and loved struggled like bugs in a trap. He caught himself and rubbed furiously at his face with calloused hands. This had turned into a confession after all.

"How far down does this go?"

He looked up to see Abby standing in a cage lift at the far end of the hall, peering down through the grill beneath her feet. *For God's sake, woman. What has that got to do with anything?* Max was about to give her an earful when he spotted her expression. He turned to Aelspell. All condescension had fled, replaced by genuine fear.

"How far?" repeated Abby.

"Nine hundred miles."

"A wormhole?" asked Max

His partner shook her head.

"Not this."

"That's impossible. It has to be a wormhole, otherwise it'd drop below the singularity itself." Max turned to their host.

Aelspell swallowed. It was clear he'd brought them here to find the shaft, but he still looked as if he was going to burst into tears.

"The ancient ones extruded a pit in the singularity to accommodate their wonders."

"Ancient ones?" sneered Abby.

"What's down there?" asked Max.

"The truth. Your truth."

At first Max assumed the fool thought that prattling in riddles still gave him the upper hand, and he was speaking with a pair of ignorant peasants easily awed by his cryptic drivel. Abby clearly had him pegged as just another tedious lunatic. But if that was the case why did the high priest look as if he'd already lost? Max gestured towards the lift with his gun.

"Show us."

Through the mesh Max saw the shaft dwindle to a point far below. In some parts of the Wasteland the Black Roses had piled the crushed world-rock to a depth of thirty miles, creating mountain ridges and plateaus to break up the baked red plastic monotony, but there was no way they'd packed a thousand miles of dirt under the Great White World. He lifted Aelspell's chin with his pistol so that the man's gaze met his. All fey mannerisms and gentle condescension had vanished. He looked like a man about to reveal something that haunted his own worst dreams.

"The second I sense a trap…"

Aelspell nodded, and switched the lever to *Descend*.

No guards - just the three of them. Max wondered if he should call for the others, but they needed to keep up the intimidation, and be ready to re-board the ship as soon as it was free again. Besides, he was starting to revise his opinion of the priest. Despite his mannerisms the man lacked the preening self-belief that all the other tyrants in his life had radiated.

The cage dropped for ten minutes before Aelspell brought it to a shuddering halt. They stepped into a corridor lined with alternating bands of blue steel and stained copper. Ancient oil and electricity tainted the air and Max could feel a vibration through his boots. Wall panels cast parallelograms of diseased light across the floor, though more than half had guttered into darkness during the long centuries. Abby whistled.

"We're inside a machine."

Whatever it was, it stood a universe away from the crumbling chalk and plaster city above their heads. They followed Aelspell for a mile along the deserted passageway. Maybe hidden eyes watched them from behind two-way panels of transparent steel, but Max doubted it. He got the impression the priest only came down here when there was no other choice, and this was a filthy secret he would have preferred to have sealed up and forgotten.

They stopped outside a bulkhead door. Aelspell clasped his hands together and gave Max a hopeless smile.

"The original inhabitants of the Great White World vanished hundreds of thousands of years ago, leaving the city, the Isle Resplendent and what you are about to see. They were clearly far advanced in their understanding of the universe and had found ways of tapping into Black Rose science to reshape the singularity upon which we stand."

"Vanished, as in died out?"

"No. They simply disappeared - on the same day, at the same hour."

"Where to?" asked Abby.

"We don't know. They deliberately covered their tracks."

Aelspell pushed open the doors and Max and Abby followed him onto a balcony. It projected over an immense pit that stretched into the distance on all sides and plunged into a void lit by endless coruscating lights - data streams embedded in machinery that would have dwarfed the giants themselves. It reminded Max of the moment when he'd stepped into the space between the inner and outer skins of Leontine's sphere world. The shadows seethed with the same heavy chorus of movements, fulcrums, resistance and friction that held the Steel Queen's moon-sized kingdom together, and he felt the same lurch of perspective as his mind tried to understand the scale. One second it looked as if someone had just emptied the contents of an old radio into a metal box at his feet and filled the gaps between the pieces with fretful electricity, the next he was standing above an ocean storm of shapes and powers that spattered their clothes with a hectic orange light.

"They built this."

"What does it do?"

"Again, we don't know. Part of it keeps the island afloat and the ocean full of water but that's just a single tiny function of this…" Aelspell gestured, "…thing."

Abby peered over the rail.

"It really stretches down for nine hundred miles?"

"As far as we can tell."

"You haven't checked?"

"Why would we?"

Abby stared at him as if he was an utter idiot before shooting Max a look - *impressive but pointless, why are we here?*

The priest turned to face Max.

"You have to understand, Max. We are not great scientists like these ancients. We are not adventurers with spaceships and ray guns and armies of monsters at our backs. The citizens of the Great White World came here to escape from Behemoth, and his, what do you call it? - 'Great Task'. They want to be free from striving and just live as ordinary men and women, grabbing what little comfort they can in these last days. This terrible engine," he gestured at the cavern, "has given us the island of the gods, this city has given us a home, and I give hope."

"Hope of what?" said Abby. "If we stay on this singularity, humanity will die out."

"When? A thousand years from now? Ten thousand? If Behemoth comes to life and walks towards the portal, how long will it take? We've struggled and fought and lived and died for aeons upon aeons in this cosmos to achieve what? I say an end to it, an end to this futile striving, this false promise of new worlds and greater wonders. I've given the people simplicity and devotion, a rest from the ceaseless busy nothings that fill your mind and the minds of all those wretches scampering in and out of that rotting corpse to the east."

"Pathetic," Abby nodded towards the exit. "Come on, we're wasting our time."

"You're a tyrant who rules by fear," added Max. Yet

he sensed the undertow of Aelspell's words, the delicate persuasiveness of the hierophant taking the edge off his own contempt. The priest gave a sad laugh.

"I don't rule. You've seen the forces at my disposal."

"Brutal thugs."

"Perhaps, but in reality the servants of the gods choose to stay and submit themselves. My people want to be led away from the madness and the fear and the desperate hope of salvation for the uncountable generations that will follow. They have peace. Do you? Join us, and see for yourself."

"Anything for a quiet life?"

Aelspell gave him a conciliatory shrug.

"Not for much longer," said Max. "We're not the only ones searching for your gods. The Machine Men are after them for a start, but worse than that - one of their sisters is also hunting for her siblings. Her name is Ombratulla and she loathes humanity. I watched her and her sister wipe out the Empire of the Ear, using psychic powers that drove their enemy's legions insane and turned them into slaves. We God Talkers are immune, but you and the people of the Great White World are not. If she comes here and finds you've got the titans of the west on your island, she will send you all screaming mad in an instant."

He clicked his fingers and Aelspell jumped. Even in this decaying half-light Max could see the fear in his face. He'd no idea what he was about to unleash.

"Take us to the giants, and we'll them the truth," said Abby. "Your only hope of survival is to let us lead them to the Mind before Ombratulla gets here."

Aelspell looked small and frightened against the silently roaring engines in the darkness beyond. He gestured for his guests to follow him back to the lift. Once inside their guide put his hand on the lever, but hesitated as if struggling to overcome his fear.

"Just one more wonder."

Max was all for returning to the surface, but Abby's eyes were full of hunger and he had to admit he was curious to see more of the machine, if only to stand in awe at the arts and powers commanded by people long vanished. He was so used to seeing broken and dead relics of past greatness that a nine hundred mile high living, working engine, no matter how senile, awakened a terrified elation he hadn't felt in years.

He nodded and Aelspell sent the cage plunging further down the shaft. They fell for another fifteen minutes. By Max's reckoning they were just inside the well punched into the singularity by this kingdom's long-dead alchemists. His skin prickled with a strange heat, as if the old, tattered fabric of the universe was abrading his body, trying to tease his reality apart. *And we're only a hundredth of the way down.*

At last they came to a halt and the priest led the two of them along a low, shadowed artery with a hexagonal cross section. The walls looked as if they were made of thick oil, the reflections from the few remaining lamps sliding back and forth across their surfaces like leaves on a dead river. After a couple of miles they emerged on a walkway that stretched between vast engines towering in spired clusters into the vault above their heads. Max noticed a disturbing change in the shapes around him. The machinery seen from the first gantry was symmetrical and ordered. He'd recognised capacitors, valves, switches and coils, albeit magnified to an absurd size. Down here existence started to warp. Components were swollen out of shape, some pitted with diseased holes or teased out into thin strands of metallic fungus and filled with shadows. Max's heart thumped in his ears as unreality squeezed his ribcage, making it harder to breathe with each step. He understood Aelspell's reluctance to come down here. Abby took his hand without thinking. *You feel it too.*

The walkway joined a complex web of paths between the nightmare circuits. It branched left and right, dipping into tunnels, rising up to ladders propped against the more normal-looking pieces of apparatus and opening onto wide spaces littered with discarded tools transformed into lumps of rust and verdigris by the ages. Just as Max was on the point of running screaming back to the lift, they stepped into an amphitheatre encircling a cluster of low buildings that looked as if they'd been stolen from the surface world and dropped in the middle of this pandemonium. Their pale stucco normality was far more disturbing than the rest of their surroundings, but Aelspell speeded up like a man who'd found his way home.

The hastily built cluster of halls and dormitories was abandoned. Broken furniture littered auditoriums and conference rooms. Walls and ceilings bellied and sagged, clay and plaster crumbling away from rickety dab frames. Max realised he was looking at a research station constructed to Aelspell's level of science – primitive, judging by the tool fragments he saw piled in corners or next to overturned tables. He recognised the remains of crucibles, balances, theodolites, compasses, nails, hammers and mattocks - nothing more advanced than basic measuring instruments. *They chucked this place together to try and understand the machine, found something they shouldn't, and left in a hurry.* A shadow at the end of a long corridor stopped him in his tracks.

"Wait."

"What is it?" asked Abby, pulling back the bolt on her machine gun. The click echoed through the vaults, as if she'd set off a chain of switches and relays.

"Please don't," said Aelspell.

They ignored him and walked down the passageway,

Max trying to make sense of what he was looking at. It appeared to be an enormous test-tube propped against the wall - twelve foot high and about a yard in diameter, iron-framed with glass panels. Dried chemicals crusted the inner surface, scabbed into continents of poisonous grey and yellow, but he still recognised the shape curled into a comma inside. His partner swore long and loud. At first Max guessed the sages working in this complex had turned their evil to human experiments and he struggled to control his hatred as he heard Aelspell's hesitant footfalls behind him. As tempting as it was, they'd solve nothing by shooting the bastard.

"We didn't do this," said Aelspell. "They did."

"Lying sack of shit," said Abby. "You told us that the people who built the machine disappeared thousands of years ago. This would have rotted away by now."

"It's not human."

When she died her face crumpled black like a decaying orange.

"Stand back," said Max, and after they'd moved fifty yards down the corridor he pulled out both revolvers and fired. It took half a dozen shots to shatter a panel. The hole wasn't big enough to drag the body out, but at least it gave him a clearer look.

"They imprisoned a Machine Man," he said.

They both stared at Aelspell in disbelief. Max realised that the west of God had emptied itself of civilisation, and that the current people of the Great White World had grown up in an isolation that provided fertile ground for Aelspell's pitiful cosmology, but he'd assumed the man was nothing more than another con artist. Now he saw that the priest was barely less ignorant than the others. He'd stumbled on these sinister wonders and tried to make sense of them before fleeing back into ascetic superstition. He almost felt sorry for him.

"These creatures created your gods," said Abby.

Aelspell's hands flew to his mouth.

"Blasphemy," he whispered.

"Whoever made that," Max pointed through the roof at the mighty engine, "captured and experimented on a Machine Man. I'm guessing this was once the ambassador to their realm. For some reason they turned against it."

The corpse was naked, the skin hanging in shreds from a delicate frame rotted black. Half a dozen cables projected from the head and torso. They looked too thick to be Machine Man-made - petrified rubber had long fallen away to reveal green copper and brittle silica.

"Your 'Ancients' interfaced it with their own thinking machines," murmured Abby, sticking her head through the hole to get a better view. "Either they were looking for something, or using it to power their own research."

"What does it mean?" asked the priest.

"Murdering a Machine Man and hiding the giants on an island isn't going to go down well with anyone. I don't know what the stupid bastards who did this thought they were up to, but I'm not surprised they all ran away. When Ombratulla, or the Machine Men, roll up, you're the ones they'll blame - and they will find you."

"I knew this would happen." Aelspell covered his face in his hands. "I realised that one day you would come here and destroy the Great White World. It was too much to hope that we could snatch what little scraps of happiness are left, that we could just live and suffer and pass from this universe into the great mystery."

He sighed.

"What must we do?"

"Why did you bring us here?" asked Abby. Max realised that even she felt sorry for this deluded mountebank.

"I wanted to show you how far we've fallen, all of

us. Once people built these wonders, great engines and powers that turned them into gods. Where are they now? Vanished into time, and with each passing generation more and more is lost to us. Isn't it time to turn away from all this ceaseless striving? Is it so wrong to want other creatures to become gods so we can just be simple men again? How long have you struggled, Max, in the service of Behemoth?"

You don't belong here, at the end of time. You'd have been better off in a temple world or ancient city, from an age when people still looked up at skies full of stars and saw faces and animals.

"We don't have a choice."

The priest's shoulders slumped and he looked very old.

"How do you journey to the Isle Resplendent?" asked Abby.

"By ship."

"We won't fly to see the giants. Take us to the island in your magic ship, and you can present us to your gods."

Max tried to make it sound like he was doing Aelspell a favour - granting him a final dignity as the ruler of the Great White World. The man gave him a smile of pathetic gratitude. He'd fallen for the ruse. Now Max wouldn't have to explain why his all-powerful spaceship had suddenly grounded itself and locked him and his companions outside.

CHAPTER TWELVE

CRYSANTHE STARED AT a stranger's face in the mirror as she wiped away the dried blood, examining the bruises and swollen top lip. Mechanically she rinsed the cloth in the bowl of water provided by Aelspell's acolytes. *I don't know who you are anymore.*

Selva hadn't spoken either. She didn't need to. The general knew exactly what was going through her head. She could have written the dialogue herself. *What the fuck were you playing at? I don't know. Do you understand how much you mean to me? Yes. I can't face the fear of losing you. You do understand that, don't you, you stupid bitch? Yes.*

"I pushed an old woman off a roof because she got in my way."

Selva didn't even look up. She sat cross-legged on the floor, sharpening her killing knives with long strokes of a chamois leather.

"That's what we used to do," continued Crysanthe. "That's what we were taught to do. Once upon a time, when we were monsters."

"So you went back for those biscuits out of guilt," Selva said to the blades.

Did I?

She turned her head this way and that, Thin Hans' words echoing in her mind. *She is the bravest and most noble warrior in the whole empire, as clever and wise as she is clearly beautiful.*

"Everything that defined me has gone. I have no frame of reference. My body and my mind do things that are echoes of the past, things that once made sense and seemed so natural - command, tactics, combat, murder - but it's not me anymore. I don't know who I am. One Crysanthe killed Kelvin's sister. Another Crysanthe went looking for his medicine. I don't recognise either. I feel like I'm standing on a rock in the middle of an unknown sea."

The soft hiss of leather on tungsten filled the room.

"I'm sorry," she finished.

The sound stopped, and a second later Selva took her shoulders and turned her round. She ran her fingers through Crysanthe's hair, still filled with dirt and plaster from her imprisonment, and kissed her on the forehead.

"Look at the state of you."

Ioam had decided to take the initiative, so instead of standing awkwardly around their crippled vessel waiting for Max to return they'd commandeered a floor of the palace. Even with the Abhumans trapped inside the Brittle Hag's ship the two witches still scared the inhabitants so much that Selva had to track them down to their hiding places to get them to bring food and water. She and Crysanthe were in a room with a couple of wooden cots and a tin bath which half a dozen terrified acolytes filled with tepid water.

"You're going to bathe me like you did when I was General of the Dogs. That time has gone."

"I'm going to give you a wash because you smell like shit and I want to make sure that when my love gets out of the tub she's just like new."

Max and Abby returned with Aelspell just before midnight. They gathered in the hall Ioam had grabbed for the two witches. The new God Talkers stood apart from the others, watching the discussion with suspicion. Crysanthe hadn't spoken to them since the few words they'd exchanged in the ten minutes between the soldiers propping her in the corner of their cell, still strapped to the cross, and returning to set them free. Two of them wore the haughty self-congratulatory expressions of the chosen - she'd seen it often enough on the faces of the sybarites of the AntiHelix. The third one looked as if he'd wandered in by accident on his way to a cheap tavern. What was his name? Halinard? She marked him - someone so at ease in this place was either stupid or dangerous.

Aelspell gave a ten-minute speech about misunderstandings and honoured guests, insisting at one point on taking her hand and bowing his head over it in a plea for forgiveness. Another Crysanthe would have snapped his neck, this one said nothing. After he'd disappeared, Selva went over the room inch by inch before telling them it was free of any listening devices. Satisfied they were safe, Max told them about his journey into the machine beneath the Great White World.

"Aelspell's going to take us in his ship to the Isle Resplendent. The journey will take three days."

"You trust him?" asked Crysanthe.

"What do you think? Our only other option is to sit around waiting for the Brittle Hag's spacecraft to open up again, if it ever does."

He turned to Ioam.

"When did you last see Sorameistre?"

"Two hundred years ago."

The pompous looking God Talkers gasped out loud and took a few steps back from the witches. Halinard grunted around his cigarette with amusement.

"So the Isle Resplendent wasn't created by these ancient ones to house the giants. They came afterwards," said Max.

"Where did all the original inhabitants disappear to?" asked Selva.

"No idea, and neither does our friend the high priest," said Abby.

"In any case we'll let him take us to the island," said Max. "Our first priority is getting the titans on our side before Ombratulla finds them."

"What about the Abhumans?" asked Abby.

"What about them? They're locked outside our reality. Right now they'll have their own battles to fight. We can't help them and they can't help us. Even if they do reappear it's clear we can't rely on the Brittle Hag's ship anymore."

"So no pleading before the Black Rose God," said Selva.

Max nodded.

"The Giants of the West are our only hope."

He turned to the new God Talkers.

"If your giants have been hiding on the Isle Resplendent for the last couple of centuries, I'm guessing you haven't communicated with them. Was there any contact with your families before that time?"

Clarindo wore the expression of a recruit with a malfunctioning grenade pushed onto his first battlefield. Waldrada looked just as frightened. Halinard watched them with half a grin on his face.

"You don't know what we're talking about, do you?" said Abby when the silence became painful.

"You're God Talkers, right?" said Crysanthe.

"We talk to Gods. In dreams," acknowledged the woman with the air of a master lecturing an initiate. Clarindo shook his branch for emphasis and the little clay heads tinkled.

Max pinched the bridge of his nose and sighed.

"Who do you talk to in dreams?"

"Spirits."

"And these appear as what, exactly?" asked Ioam.

More frightened glances flickered back and forth between Clarindo and Waldrada. Crysanthe's patience was ebbing away fast. Even if they were the God Talkers they claimed to be, the pair acted like fairground conjurers who'd survived on cardboard and tinsel with no true understanding of what they were, or the role they were supposed to play. This was the first time they'd had their portentous drivel questioned and it was throwing them into a blind panic.

"Why are you here?" she asked.

"We were summoned." Another shake of his ridiculous staff.

"Do that one more time and I'll stuff it up your arse," Abby told him.

"I persuaded them to," said Halinard, lighting a fresh hand-made cigarette. He flicked the dead match into the corner of the room and tapped his temple. "In here. About nine months ago a little girl turned up at the door of my wagon and asked me to get these two numpties to come here in search of the giants. I knew where their happy cloud castles were so I trolled over for a chat."

"Your wagon?" said Max.

Halinard nodded.

"You don't have a mind palace? You have a mind wagon that moves about?"

"How does that work, then?" asked Nem. "I want one."

"It did move about. But the dreamscape's full of monsters so at the moment I'm stuck."

Abby stepped towards him, a dangerous expression on her face.

"What did this little girl look like?"

"A bit like you, funnily enough."

"Have you seen her since?"

"No."

"Have you contacted the Giants of the West with this vehicle of yours?" asked Selva.

He shook his head.

"What's going on?" piped up Clarindo, trying to regain the upper hand with a completely unconvincing note of command in his voice. "Why are you asking all these questions? And who are you anyway?"

Abby barked a laugh and was about to say something incendiary when Max interrupted her.

"Not here. Not now. Aelspell has agreed to take us to the Isle Resplendent in this ship of his. We set sail in the morning. You'll get a chance to meet the giants, or gods, or spirits, or whatever you think they are."

"But I'm not ready," squeaked Waldrada.

"Tough," said Crysanthe. "You're coming with us, all of you."

She understood Max's thinking. He didn't want to tell them the truth now, especially about the Giants of the East. He'd wait until they were on the boat so they couldn't run away.

"Go and get ready," he told the new God Talkers. When they didn't move Nem started cracking her knuckles. Clarindo stalked out with Waldrada in tow, flicking her cloak dramatically over her shoulder. Halinard pinched the end of his cigarette and stuck it in the breast pocket of his shabby brown jacket.

"More trouble than they're worth," he said.

"What about you?" asked Crysanthe. The man shrugged.

"I want to meet a giant to see what it's like. This pointless ability of mine came down to me through a chain of non-entities and ne'er-do-wells wasting their lives in the shadow of that," he pointed towards God. "I quite fancy being the one who finally gets to do something worthwhile."

After he'd slouched out Max shut the door and turned to the rest of them.

"Well, they're a waste of space," ventured Abby.

"Except Halinard," said Selva.

"Maybe," said Max. "As soon as we get on this boat Nem, Ioam and I will jump into their mind palaces. I want to see his wagon."

"How has he got a moving interface between his head and God's?" asked Ioam. "How does that work?"

"Could you use it to travel through the Mind?" said Crysanthe.

"Doubt it. We'll find out tomorrow."

"We'll run watches. Selva and I'll take first."

"We'll do second," said Abby. "You two can do the last."

Ioam nodded, but her sister suddenly looked sad. She wiped a couple of tears from her eyes with a black-taloned thumb.

"I want to see the Abhumans again. I'm worried about them inside that ship."

At Nem's words a surge of unhappy fear ran through Crysanthe. Fractured plains of metal sheeting flickered through her mind like the images in a stereoscope - wooden staircases dropping into planet-sized vaults, scudding clouds beneath cracked aquarium glass a mile thick reflecting mountain peaks built from discarded cogwheels, endless corridors leading to an infinity where she knew the dead weight of honour and memories of brutality would tease out and snap like rotting threads, leaving her erased and pure. She caught her breath. Selva watched her. She summoned the old disciplines and met her gaze, hoping the girl hadn't seen her longing for the wilderness of the Brittle Hag's ship. The Companion said nothing, though she took Crysanthe's hand in her own when the company broke up and they headed back to their room to get their weapons ready for the first watch.

As soon as they'd retreated to their own billet and Max locked the door Abby came for him at a running jump. Despite hanging off his neck with her legs round his waist she still managed to get his trousers down and impale herself on his erection before they collapsed onto the makeshift heap of curtains that was their bed. Half an hour later he was panting on his back and waiting for the room to stop spinning. Abby lay on top of him, humming a song into his chest and squeezing her vagina around his softening penis in time to the music. She really was completely mad, although this kind of insanity he could just about cope with.

"What's got into you?"

A face emerged from the mountain of hair covering his torso.

"Dunno. This is like old times. You and I charging into danger with a brace of pistols and no hope. Though I guess now we've got Crys and Selva as back up."

Crys and Selva?

"I thought she was General Bitch-features."

"She's alright. Bit of a humourless cow, mind you. Selva keeps trying to teach me that Spear Tip Dance of theirs. I think it's just an excuse to grope my bum."

The universe was littered with broken bones, black eyes and split lips from failed attempts to handle Abby Fabrice's backside. Pregnancy made her mellow. She sat up and rubbed her stomach - still flat muscle.

"Maybe I should be grateful she's growing up somewhere else so I don't look like an over-ripe pear."

She lay down beside him and planted a lingering kiss

on his cheek.

"Get some sleep. We're on watch in four hours and I'll want at least one more fuck before we start."

On the edge of dreams Max used the technique Ioam had shown him to enter his mind garden. To his surprise it worked, though what he saw there almost had him jumping straight back out into the safety of the real world. Where once clapboard walls enclosed a patch of grass barely fifty yards from side to side, he now found himself standing on a low rise in the centre of a plain that must have stretched six miles across. The fence had turned into a line of iron railings undulating over gentle bumps and dips towards a closed gate so far away it was just a shape in the mist. The giantesses' monsters still stood on their own greasy battlements, which followed his own defences, but they were nothing more than a row of blobs against the thundercloud sky.

Directly in front of him someone or something had constructed a circle half a mile in diameter out of grey bricks. The wall barely reached his waist, but inside he saw a concrete floor with a trap door a few hundred yards away. It was bigger than last time, with two hatches like the entrance to a tavern cellar. Luckily they were closed.

I'm building a mind palace.

But surely that was something he had to do consciously, though he'd no idea how to start. Ioam's citadel appeared as if she'd designed it herself, crafting its spired beauty to accommodate her delight in books and art. Yet this looked like the foundations of a castle, or a circular warehouse. He felt disappointed and cheated - it wasn't what he'd have chosen.

What are you on about? You made this.

Max had no intention of starting an argument with his subconscious, or stepping inside the circle, so he wandered down the slope, looking for the familiar garden furniture where Bassandis had once slept. Once again he toyed with the idea of calling for Rebecca, but he didn't want to alert the creatures outside.

He didn't find the table and chairs - he guessed they were in the other direction. After walking for ages he came across an iron ring set in the grass. More dull brutalism. It towered over him - a long O of metal already stained with rust. *I need to talk to Ioam, learn how to do this properly, otherwise I'm going to end up with a dingy slum in my head.*

He turned to walk back, but a shadow rose out of the ground in front of him and he woke with a cry. Abby held his shoulders down as he struggled to sit up.

"Hey, hey. Bad dreams again?"

He told her about the mind garden.

"My brain is building something - a palace like Ioam's - but I've no idea how or what it's going to look like. And it's haunted."

"By what?"

"I don't know. I didn't see its face - just a silhouette - but it terrified me."

"It's all your fears playing out. If you're going to sleep, sleep, don't try and go wandering through the Mind. You'll end up barmy."

She clambered off him and started to dress.

"Promise me that if this all goes wrong, if we fail but are still alive, that's it?"

He propped himself up on his elbows. Lamplight shone through her hair, covering the floor in a tangled shadow stretching towards him over the cracked tiles.

"We'll let Crys and Selva go and argue our case before the Black Rose God while you and I bugger off to nowhere and get on with the rest of our lives."

"No-one's going anywhere if the spaceship's dead. This is it - our last chance. If the giants won't help, or they can't stop their sisters, there's nothing else we can do."

"Exactly. So we go and nick another flyer, piss off to the feet and scavenge wormholes. Or if Madam does finally pop out we find a house and live in it."

She finished buttoning up her shirt and tied her hair behind her head in a red explosion.

"Promise?"

He thought of the shadow rising out of the ground between him and that dreary brick wall, its edges blurred against the spitting coal sky.

Bugger duty.

"I promise."

After an uneventful night outside the dead starship they passed the watch over to Ioam and Nem and slept again. This time Abby left Max too exhausted to dream. In the morning they met the others in the plaza outside the palace. Three twisted shapes lay beneath the Brittle Hag's vessel like man-sized fragments of charred seaweed.

"Silly bastards touched it. I told them it wasn't a good idea," said Nem.

"You let them anyway?" asked Max. Ioam shrugged.

"A salutary lesson. If we're leaving it here I want to make sure these idiots don't try to interfere. Besides, this shows us nothing's changed. The spacecraft is still locked inside wherever."

Max walked round to the front of the vessel and tried to see into the letterbox window cut in the forward edge of the disk. Nothing - no lights, shapes in the gloom or reflections of the buildings behind him. He saw the same dead absence of light as when he'd stood under the harpoon.

A crowd started to gather, clumps of people edging into the square from alleyways and doors. Max wondered if they'd be trouble but they hung back against the walls, keeping as much distance between themselves and the strangers as possible. An audience for something, but what?

The answer came with a chorus of bright trumpets from the upper windows of the palace. Banners unfurled from the balconies, printed with the same mournful icons of the giants as Kelvin's picture and the larger oriflammes pinned to the towers.

"What do you think?" asked Max, moving back to stand among the others.

"He likes his ceremonies," said Selva. "Here's our escort."

A crocodile of acolytes in white suits marched out of the entrance and down the steps towards them, a line of men on the left, women on the right. Every fourth attendant carried a picture of Vinduranto, Mephyrean, Sorameistre or Toldi. They curved away from the Brittle Hag's spaceship and stopped, facing westward. The throng at the edge of the square dropped to its knees as Aelspell appeared, dressed in robes with a starburst headpiece fashioned in black enamelled cerium. Slender barbs fanned out from the nape of his neck to his forehead, glistening in the dusty light. Max expected a speech, but the man merely raised his arms to the sky, and the masses stood up. They clearly understood the ceremony and what it meant - their favoured one was off to speak with the gods on their behalf. He came down and gestured to the escort with a smile. Max followed him as he took up position in between the two lines, Abby and the others falling in behind. They set off across the uneven ground.

From a distance the marchers looked immaculate and disciplined, but close-up Max noticed the threadbare linen uniforms and drawn expressions. They all stared ahead and he saw the sweat sheen of ill-health on several faces. No matter how much the high priest claimed his people had found a simpler life in the Great White World, it wasn't free of fear or suffering. He remembered Kelvin clutching at his precious painting. The poor sod was still locked inside the ship with the Abhumans.

He glanced round. Where the witches walked, taking baby steps so they wouldn't crash into the others, the lines curved out on either side, giving them a wide berth. Nem flashed Max a winning grin and one man fainted at the sight, the guards behind stepping over him as he sprawled grey-faced in the gutter. Clarindo and Waldrada were in their element, peering around with majestic approval. Halinard strolled along with his hands in his jacket pockets.

They descended past abandoned buildings made from chalk, diseased steel and glass that had long shattered, leaving glittering deltas across concrete floors and rucked-up pavement slabs. Max wondered why no-one lived here. Despite the overall tattiness and decay, the structures here looked more solid than the crudely fashioned tenements to the east. As the street ahead widened he spotted the curve of a beach and the grubby cellophane shimmer of the ocean in the distance. The sand appeared white instead of the usual ochre and blood clot grit of the Wasteland.

The buildings grew larger, their actinic spaces swelling into a patchwork abstraction of stone, metal and dust-slanting light. He thought of the dip in the singularity under his feet. The roots of these towers, arcologies, spires and forgotten office blocks reached down to the engine of the Great White World, nestling in that unholy pocket of unreality. Perhaps after they'd created the machine its potencies had terrified the original inhabitants into fleeing, and that was the reason why the current band of fanatical squatters kept well away from the vast cold algebra of this ancient coastline.

They emerged from the shadows of the last tower blocks and Max spotted a jetty leading out to sea. He halted, stunned into immobility by the boat resting at anchor alongside the bleached planks. He'd expected either a crude barge cobbled-together by Aelspell's minions or a rotting fragment of an ancient ironclad left over from a long scuttled navy. The cluster of white circles and curving beams rising above the pale surface of the ocean appeared brand new, yet of a technology far beyond that of their hosts. Its semi-organic forms made Max think of dried flower heads. Translucent pods clustered in the centre, giving way to hair-fine spas and masts at both ends. It looked as if the yacht had been grown, rather than built.

The rest of his companions halted and their escort, jogged out of line, milled uncertainly around the high priest. Noticing his guests' expressions he clasped his hands together under his chin and smiled with the assured contentment of the master of everything.

"Is she not so, so beautiful?"

"Where did you nick it from?" asked Abby.

Aelspell winced ever so slightly.

"We inherited this from our forebears, a sacred heirloom to treasure, for this vessel will carry you and me to speak with the gods themselves."

He unfurled an elegant hand.

"Why do we tarry in this dismal city, good friends? Let us hurry aboard and begin our holy argosy."

CHAPTER THIRTEEN

Close up the ship looked like a bunch of white grapes embedded in seashells teased from paper thin alloy. Pods six metres across clustered stern-wards from a needle prow, while vanes and sails spread into the purple sky on both sides. Aelspell climbed on board and Max and the others followed. He immediately found himself in a labyrinth of pale eggshell and polished wood, a delicate foam of space and silence. It reminded him of the inside of Thin Hans' flagship, but without the rich backwash of incense and sex that flooded through the Lord's vessel. Even Abby managed to look impressed.

The sisters had to drop to their hands and knees like spiders to navigate beneath the low ceilings. Three bubbles in, Nem rolled onto her back and lay sprawled across the floor of two adjacent rooms, pillowing her head in her talons and smiling up at her reflection. Crysanthe and Selva split up and disappeared after the priest - Max guessed they were scouting the yacht. Clarindo and Waldrada picked their way past the naked witch's exoskeleton, their expressions oscillating between utter terror and contempt. Halinard was nowhere to be seen.

"The bridge is in a cluster of pods at the prow, and the engine is directly below it," Crysanthe told him when she returned. "There's six crew and Aelspell. Give us a minute and it's ours."

"Not until we get to the island," said Max. "In the meantime we'll take it in turns to watch them."

He ducked through into an outer sphere and saw the coast recede through a porthole. He hadn't even realised they'd left. Apart from a slight vibration under his boots, the boat's engines were silent. Abby had found the access ladder to a wide deck at the back of the ship. The vanes on either side blocked their view to north and south, so he stood with his hand on the ceramic parapet and watched the city of the Great White World fade away. Abby looked down at their wake and when he followed her gaze he saw the same pattern of vents, pipes, grills and machines as the floor of the Forbidden Sea. He couldn't tell if they were discarded and the ship floated across a colossal scrap yard, or this was an extension of the mighty engine underneath the palace and very much alive. Aelspell had told him that the machinery sustained the island and the ocean.

"Coincidence?" asked Abby.

As far as he knew there was only compacted rock under Metacarpi. The dungeons of the Carceral Archipelago had been little more than pits scooped out of dirt. Even if there was a link he struggled to understand its significance. The body of God and its surroundings were layered with a million years of clutter, cast out and forgotten by an endless procession of civilisations rising and falling and going nowhere. He tried to make sense of the patterns beneath the dead waves but it was beyond him. He went back below deck to gather the God Talkers.

They found the largest pod and sat in a circle on the floor, Max and the witches alternating between the newcomers. Clarindo and Waldrada radiated suspicion, but before they could say anything he had them all join hands and a second later they stood on the balcony of Ioam's mind palace. Halinard craned his head back to look at the arches piling up into the sky and whistled. His companions swapped startled glances.

"Next we're going to visit yours," Max said to Clarindo.

"But…"

"It's not a request."

"Max," Nem called from the parapet. She nodded across the valley. "They're new."

A dozen black columns curved against the clouds. They looked insubstantial, like bamboo stalks swaying in the sharp wind from God's dreams. On their tops various spindly shadows squatted, hung or balanced. They wore tatterdemalion rags and one even had a battered top hat on its barbed head. At this distance Max couldn't see any features, but he sensed eyes filled with dead hatred staring back.

"More watchers," said Ioam. "When your daughter threw that Machine Man into the sky it alerted Ombratulla and Belsalice. They've sent their monsters to keep an eye out for us and her."

Halinard stood next to Max.

"Those are the sharpies who ringed my wagon. They don't do anything, just dance round in a circle and make stupid noises, but it means I can't drive anywhere anymore."

"Where do they come from?" asked Max. "Are they thoughts or dreams, or alien monsters made by the crushed suns? Where are they getting this army from?"

No-one had an answer, least of all Clarindo and Waldrada who huddled together in the hall, holding each other's hands. All superiority had gone. They looked terrified.

"You'll bring those horrors to my mansion," the man stammered, but Max didn't have time to argue. He nodded to Ioam and she clapped her hands.

They stood in a long pillared vault between slanting curtains of rainbow light falling from stained glass windows so high up they appeared as a shattered Borealis. Eight statues carved from grey marble glowered down, four on each side, but their features were rough-hewn like the barely remembered faces of childhood friends. Max had to concede that even amid the heavy-handed drama of this ponderous architecture Clarindo had some taste. An open arch showed a desert so flat it looked as if someone had drawn a line across the middle of a piece of paper, colouring the bottom half orange and the upper half charcoal. Isolated pillars, doorways and fragments of statues cast long shadows despite the flat, directionless light.

"Is that where your spirits come from?"

Clarindo didn't answer, so Max stood at the threshold and searched for landmarks, but the mist wiped the world clean after a few miles. He needed Rebecca to reconnoitre, but how to contact her? He watched the churning sky for a few moments, searching for the silver light announcing her approach, but nothing appeared.

"We're wasting our time here," he told the witches.

Waldrada's palace stood on a shelving beach at the edge of a black ocean as still as a mirror made from polished coal. Far out to sea shreds of pale yellow curved as high as mountains as they drifted over its surface like sails that had lost their boats. The absence of any monsters meant that the giants hadn't found Waldrada's citadel either. It had to give them an advantage but he struggled to understand what.

The woman's temple was marginally less pompous than Clarindo's, though it had the same satisfied air of the mystic waiting to dispense wisdom to pilgrims who didn't exist. Low wooden arches and white walls divided a tiled labyrinth, filled with windows looking out across the strand and the hills behind. The laughter of wind chimes followed Max through every room. It was increasingly obvious that Clarindo and Waldrada's spirits only existed in their imaginations. The giants had never visited them, or any of the other creatures wandering through the deity's unformed soul. They'd found out how to enter the Mind but that was it. Everything else came from the fragmented mythology of their ancestors.

"Are you going to tell us what's going on?" asked Halinard, joining Max in a bay window while Waldrada fussed after Nem like a curator following a hyperactive child round a museum.

"Let's see your wagon."

They jumped into a giant tank under siege. When the man had first told him about his vehicle, Max had imagined a large caravan, like the drays used to carry supplies from the wormhole shafts to Metacarpi. Halinard had fashioned his mind palace after the inside of a battleship. It felt like walking through the decks of the *Beatrice* again - the machine had the same oiled steel and mahogany as the Empire of the Ear's dreadnought. A rivet-floored corridor ran down the spine, opening to rooms on either side. Each cabin had its own observation bubble made from thick glass set in iron frames. Beyond them Max saw gritty darkness shot with flickering red. Shadows danced back and forth like demons around a bonfire. He caught a glimpse of taloned hands, barbs and heads with eye-sockets bored straight through to show the lights behind.

"I know they can't harm me. I went outside," Halinard shuddered and started to roll himself a dream cigarette. Max wondered if he'd been responsible for the dog-end in his garden, but he doubted it.

"Problem is the wagon won't get past them, so I'm stuck."

"Where are we?" asked Ioam. Nem crept up and down, scrutinising every bolt, wire and button, no doubt gathering ideas for her own palace. The other God Talkers hadn't moved from the very centre of the vessel.

"There's no logic to this place - I can leave it on top of a mountain and come back to find it in a tunnel or crossing a river of blue goo, but just before this happened I saw a castle in the middle of desert. It looked odd."

"How odd?" asked Max

"New, for a start, not made of old dream stuff. It also seemed more substantial, as though it was here to stay. Bloody great ugly thing it was, black towers and pyramids. I was going to troll along to have a look, but the next time I jumped in I was here with my own little audience. Luckily this is soundproof," he hit the wall with his fist. It rang like a bell. "They don't half make a racket when you go outside."

"The giants' citadel," said Ioam. "It's the dream version of the fortress they've built inside the Head."

Even though Halinard's wagon looked capable of withstanding heavy ordnance, and the nightmares could do nothing more than hiss and posture, Max didn't fancy the idea of explaining what had happened on the other side of the Body here. They returned to Ioam's citadel and deep inside its book-lined vaults he turned to the new God Talkers.

"About two years ago one of the Giants of the East, Bassandis, died in battle, but a fragment of his soul remained here," he tapped his own temple. "His sisters, Ombratulla and Belsalice, vowed revenge on humanity for his death. They kidnapped their remaining brother, Ragaleis, and used him as a template to create a new giant before marching on the Empire of the Ear and destroying it. Since then they've journeyed into the Head, cast out the Machine Men and built a fortress. They're looking for the Giants of the West. They want to form God's mind and turn him into mankind's enemy, so that only they are saved and the rest of us are either slaughtered or left to perish in the last night. We have to find the remaining titans before they do, and persuade them to help us stop the sisters."

"And how's that going to work?" asked Halinard. To his credit he was the only one who didn't have the face of someone who'd just seen their darkest nightmare give birth on the floor in front of them, but when he re-lit his cigarette his hands shook.

"The giants were designed to study the human race, with our help, to learn about the good and bad. For some reason over the generations we God Talkers lost touch with the titans and forgot why we're here. I didn't even know I was a God Talker until two years ago. Only Ioam actually had any kind of relationship with the creatures. We have to reforge that link and get them to understand what God was built for - to carry humanity into the next universe. Then perhaps they can persuade their siblings to stop their revenge."

"So we have an enduring faith in human nature on our side - and that's it," said Halinard. "God help us."

"We deserve to perish," whispered Clarindo. "We deserve to die for betraying our beloved giants."

"Your beloved giants are just puzzle pieces - thinking machines made flesh by yet more machines. Our job is to fit them together. Dancing around intoning the great lament for humanity while rattling toys on a stick won't save anyone." said Max, finally losing patience with the man. Clarindo stared at him with the expression of a gargoyle about to vomit boiling lead on his enemies, then vanished.

"Well done," remarked Ioam, sounding too much like Abby. Waldrada winked out. Where was Rebecca when he needed her? She'd pull them back and clout some sense into their empty skulls with her spear. Wearily he clapped his hands, and they jumped into reality. He barely had time to look at his palms and realise he'd controlled their exit before the howling started.

Clarindo knelt at end of the rear deck and screamed into the lead-coloured waters. Waldrada was pulling at the man, trying to stop him from flinging himself into the vessel's wake. She turned and hissed at Max as he approached.

"Monster."

Max pushed her out of the way. She stumbled and almost disappeared over the side. Nem yanked her into the air by the ankle and dangled her six feet off the ground, her voluminous robes muffling the shrieks. Max grabbed Clarindo and hit him. The God Talker sprawled back unconscious across the ceramic floor. Abby and Crysanthe appeared on deck.

"I told him about Bassandis and he went nuts. Claimed we all deserve to die for betraying the great spirits. God, what a mess."

"Maybe we should push him overboard," suggested Abby.

"God Talkers can't start killing God Talkers. The giants won't be happy if they found out we murdered the idiot. We need both of them."

Nem let Waldrada drop onto the deck where she bundled herself up into a tattered heap of misery.

"We have to make them help us, no matter what," concluded Max.

"Selva and I can persuade them to comply," said Crysanthe. She gave Max a chilling look that was probably meant to reassure him.

Nem picked the two God Talkers up again and clawed her way down the outside of the hull, heading for the general's cabins. Max spotted Aelspell at the prow, standing by the entrance to the bridge and watching his passengers.

"If he's the only human who's spoken to the Giants of the West recently we'll have to get past whatever bullshit he's poured into their ears as well."

"Eventually we might have to shut them all up," said Abby.

Halinard heaved himself up the ladder. If he'd heard her remark he didn't let it show; he stuck his hands in his jacket pockets and stared towards the Great White World. Max followed his gaze. The hazy distance had erased the city, but he could still sense God's body filling the universe to the east. Where the white fog blurred into the purple sky he thought he glimpsed faint lights on the edge of his vision - more continents and nations stamped into the Epidermis, or more dead machines clinging onto their last few scraps of energy as existence itself sublimated around them.

"Count me in," said Halinard. "I'll help you as best I can. I'll also see if I can get the wagon moving again, it might help."

Max wondered if Rebecca could make any of them invisible, or shield the vehicle from the titans. Once he'd got the Giants of the West on their side perhaps they'd find out where Ragaleis was kept prisoner and set him free. That would give them six against three. He realised he was talking about this as if it was a war, but remembering Belsalice and Ombratulla picking their way through the ruins of the AntiHelix, it was hard to think of it as anything else.

Evening came and Aelspell's servants brought baskets of bread and fruit to their rooms. Max wanted to talk to the priest, but was told he was busy with his meditations and not to be disturbed. He didn't force the issue. It was clear they could take over the ship in minutes, so he was happy for the old man to run through whatever mental rituals he needed before meeting the giants. The passengers took their meals on deck and sat cross-legged in a circle, eating by the light from silver batons scattered over the floor. There was no sign of Clarindo or Waldrada, and when he shot a questioning glance at Crysanthe she told him they were 'resting' with enough in her eyes to let him know they wouldn't pose any more problems for the time being. It was Selva's watch and she was back in the bridge keeping an eye on the crew.

It was a strange, silent moment, the witches towering over the rest like demons cut from black paper, slicing the loaves for themselves with their razor talons while Halinard lay on his back and stared up into the empty night sky, his cigarette hissing red static an inch from his face. For the first time none of them talked about their desperate attempts to scrabble some hope out of the chaos. They barely spoke at all, and only then to offer a murmured comment on the strangeness of the boat, the quiet ocean or to thank each other for the food. *It's the step back before the fight, when we shake the fear out of our minds and bodies before the shooting and the punching start.* In the end Abby led him to bed, but even she seemed quite happy for them to just tangle up in a nest of cushions and fall asleep.

It seemed only seconds before Max snapped awake in the morning light, convinced he'd heard screaming. Abby stirred beside him.

"Wassup?"

"Listen."

"Can't hear anything."

They dressed in a second, meeting Crysanthe on her way to the prow with a machine pistol in her hands.

"Where's the front half of the ship?" said Abby.

At first Max thought they'd been hit by an enemy torpedo. The ship's delicate razor shell vanes drifted away from the vessel, at the end of cords and wires twisting from the hull. The deck tilted down to the gap where the bridge and bow cabins had sat but he couldn't see damage from any explosion. Selva stood on the edge, panting furiously with swords in her hands and blood up to her armpits. The bodies of two of the crew lay at her feet and a third drifted away from the ship, face down.

"Jumped me," she called. "Killed three but the rest uncoupled the bridge and engines and escaped."

Nem crawled over the top of the remaining pods in her exoskeleton, followed by Ioam with the God Talkers in tow. Halinard and Waldrada looked as if they'd already fallen into the ocean. They sloshed towards them, leaving a wet trail.

"We're sinking," said the mad witch.

The water broke into a seething mass of bubbles in the space once occupied by the missing hull and the deck shuddered under Max's boots. Of course. Aelspell hadn't bothered with guards or poison to finish them off. He'd stuck them in the cargo hold and jettisoned them halfway to the island so he could get rid of the God Talkers and walk before his deities with a clear conscience, still lord of his petty world. Nem dropped to all fours and scuttled over the side, disappearing into the sea.

"How far?" asked Max. Abby ran through the sums in her head.

"I reckon we're about three hundred miles from the city, God knows where the island is."

Max turned a full circle. The water faded to mist to sky. He didn't even know which direction they were facing. If it'd been him he would have spun the vessel a few times to confuse his pursuers before sailing off. Another shudder and spray splashed his face. The pods would keep them afloat for a while, but each tremor told him the sea had breached another.

Nem reappeared, hair plastered across her torso and armour so that her eyes blazed through a black curtain.

"It looks about a mile deep. Lights way way way down there but no good to us. Twenty minutes and we start swimming."

"Can you detach this platform and turn it into a raft?" asked Max.

She swivelled on all fours and ran round the edge in a blur.

"Yep," she said and started to wrench the deck free of the bolts holding it to the superstructure.

"Supplies. To me," Crys called to Selva and Abby and they hopped across the slick pod roofs to drop through a skylight into the rooms below.

"Even if we stay afloat we'll be adrift in millions of square miles of ocean," said Halinard.

"Get ready to row hard then," snapped Ioam. She picked up Clarindo and Waldrada, who'd spent the last few minutes on their knees rocking back and forth and muttering into their cupped hands, and jumped onto the nearest pod. Max and Halinard scrambled aside just in time as Nem tore the final bolt away with her claws, lifted the entire deck above her head and threw it into the sea. A second later she was down the side of the hull fastening it to the sinking vessel with inch-thick wires chewed from the edge of the drifting vanes.

Abby, Crysanthe and Selva reappeared soaking wet, with a couple of sacks apiece.

"Bugger all," said Abby, slinging hers down to the witch. "He made sure we'd die soon."

Max jumped over the hull, looking for something to serve as a paddle. Another shudder nearly pitched him into the ocean as the ship dropped a yard. He sprawled over the wet ceramic, the water boiling and runnelling between the spheres around him.

"Who's that?" said Abby.

She was on her hands and knees staring back at the stern, which was now at the end of a forty-five degree slope. Max followed her gaze and saw a woman standing on the very edge watching them with an expression of perplexed curiosity. She was the same height as the witches and wore a simple sleeveless dress belted at the waist. She had pale almond eyes and lips the colour of corroded lead. White hair streamed behind her in the vortex kicked up by the sinking ship.

Everyone stared at the newcomer, frozen into silence by the apparition, except Crysanthe and Selva. They looked at Max and the others, following their line of sight but clearly seeing nothing.

"Why have you all stopped? What's there?"

Ioam answered in a voice that carried with it such a promise of love and reconciliation.

"Sorameistre."

The woman took a step forwards and peered down at the witch who gazed up at her from the wreck. Max sensed a vast shadow shifting in the distant fog.

"I know you."

She leaned forward and Crysanthe cried out as the sky darkened.

"It's Ioam. Your little Ioam."

"Ioam. I remember. You told me wonderful stories. Once, long ago."

And then a cupped hand as big as a mountain scooped down from the clouds, into the ocean and under the ship, lifting it high above the boiling waves.

CHAPTER FOURTEEN

THE LAST TIME Crysanthe rode on a giant's palm she'd almost gone insane. Belsalice had snatched her from Ruth, and as she'd lain on the titan's hand the creature and her sister, Ombratulla, ransacked her mind, tearing it apart as they tried to prove her a liar. She'd been so empty and helpless, knowing they could spread her between finger and thumb like someone carelessly rubbing away a bug. Ruth interceded on her behalf, a dismissive whim made a thousand times crueller because she'd hoped it was the echo of their love driving the girl. That lie died on the edge of the knife slipped into her guts above a pit full of shattered tanks and half-tracks. She struggled with the memory, reciting every combat mantra she could remember as each recollection brought a fresh wave of fear and hatred.

As soon as they realised they'd been rescued by a giant Nem grabbed her and Selva to protect them from the psychic powers of the titan. But this journey was different. Sorameistre waded through the water, stepping here and there with the delicate balance of someone crossing uneven stones in a ford. She held her hands cupped around the boat as if she carried a fledgling back to its nest. Crysanthe even summoned up the courage to look up at the giant's face, but the mist that swathed her upper body turned her into a grey shadowed silhouette whose hair streamed behind her like reeds in a river.

She came from the island, she must have sensed Ioam was in danger.

The witch and her sister stood further off, unable to tear their eyes away from their childhood companion. Halinard clung to a pod roof, swearing at each fresh jolt. Clarindo and Waldrada lay flat with their arms spread, faces down in terror. Crysanthe looked for Abby and Max. They'd jumped down onto Sorameistre's hand and were standing at the junction between her fore and middle finger, trying to peer through the gap to see where they were going.

A mighty wall rushed towards them, its top hidden in the clouds. Sorameistre turned and climbed out of the water and onto a staircase cut into the white rock. Judging by the rise and fall of the giant's body as she walked up the cliff face, each step was at least a quarter of a mile high. The general wondered how Aelspell and his acolytes had managed to scramble up this cyclopean pathway. On the next corner she spotted a rusting gantry with oil-slicked cables dangling down to the ocean - a cage lift.

The stairs rose up through the mist to emerge beneath the empty sky. Crysanthe gasped at the sight of the cloud tops stretching into the distance, ringed with pale air rising in concentric bands through purple to black. It was the paper world of her dreams - an immense book of nothing under a cold antiseptic vault. She would have stared at it forever, but Sorameistre walked down a slope into a network of gargantuan buildings rising out of a midnight green forest far below. The mist thickened again, hiding the landscape, so that all she saw were mountain-sized porticoes, colonnades and entrances. The giant carried them into a hall and set the boat down on an immense table top. Selva and Crysanthe grabbed Clarindo and Waldrada by the scruff of the neck and hauled them onto their feet.

"You help us persuade the giants to save humanity. Don't mess it up or you'll have me to answer to," Crysanthe murmured in their ears. All their self-importance had vanished, and the two God Talkers nodded and whimpered.

They climbed off the boat and walked across pale steel to where Max and Abby waited. Crysanthe could feel the cold through the soles of her boots. She remembered stripping naked and bathing before the cruel sisters in a place like this. Now as then, it was like walking across a vast autopsy slab. Sorameistre faced them from the far edge of the table, grey hands flat on the surface. Beyond her Crysanthe could just make out a white rectangle. She guessed it was an opening in the wall looking towards the west. Shapes waited on either side of the giantess.

Nem powered past her, claws thundering on metal as she sprinted into the haze. Screams and shouting rang out and a few seconds later she came back with her claw clamped around Aelspell's neck. He clung to her steel-edged fingers, red in the face and pop-eyed as he tried to suck in air.

"His friends ran away. He just stood there and shat himself. What a bastard eh?"

She shook him like a rat and he gurgled, eyes rolling.

"Put him down," said Max. As much as he deserved it, murdering the self-styled high priest on the Gods' dining table probably wouldn't help their cause.

"Plop," said Nem, opening her claws. Aelspell fell onto the floor, curling himself into a whimpering ball. Nem rested her foot on his back.

"High King Vinduranto and his queen, Mephyrean, Wise Queen Sorameistre and Noble King Toldi welcome their guests to the Isle Resplendent. Walk a while among the Gods. Let peace guide you, for there shall be no suffering in this last refuge from the horrors of Behemoth."

The voice rumbled through the hall, coming from the shadows behind their rescuer. The temperature dropped. *They believe Aelspell's nonsense. They're as deluded as the idiots in the Great White World.*

"Noble Gods. Save yourself. These are the demons of Behemoth himself…" howled Aelspell. Nem pushed her foot down, and he spread-eagled across the metal with a muffled squawk.

"No strife," growled the voice. It made Crysanthe's head ring. Anger swilled over her like the vile leavings of a poisonous flood. Selva spat curses beside her. Spider white fingers as long as her forearms curled around her neck and the grinding hatred and pain eased. She in turn grabbed Selva's hand and the Companion also relaxed.

"We aren't servants of Behemoth," said Max. "We're God Talkers - genetically engineered to teach you about humanity. Your destiny is to form the mind of the deity who will carry the last remnants of mankind through the portal into the next universe. We need your help."

All the others were looking at a patch of table a few yards in front of them, and not up at Sorameistre. Crysanthe realised they were speaking with the human-sized avatars of the titans. In the Whispering House Ihanna had used Machine-Man sorcery to allow everyone to see Ombratulla, Belsalice and Ruth as if they were ordinary people standing among them. Here only the God Talkers had that privilege. Selva, Crysanthe and the poor bastards from the Great White World had to talk directly to the giants themselves. She noticed Abby was also staring at their invisible hosts. *Odd.*

The mist was clearing, though she didn't know if the giants were consciously making it thin or it was just the effect of the winds from the sea as they hissed over the steel landscape. Sorameistre stepped back and as she did so Crysanthe realised that the shapes behind her were thrones and three were occupied by two men and another woman. As their faces clarified in the half-light she saw the same strange mix of mournful beauty and harsh artificiality. They looked as if a mad sculptor had tried to carve delicate idols out of white corroded rubber and metal. All had the same pale eyes glowing under shadowed brows. Sorameistre sat in the vacant seat, folding her hands in her lap.

"I don't understand."

The voice came from the man sitting to the far left. She guessed it was High King Vinduranto, speaking for them all.

"We don't have time to waste," Max said to the others. "I'm going to let them inside my head."

"Max…" warned Abby.

"It's OK, they can't harm us, remember?"

Before she had a chance to stop him he turned back to the giants.

"Look into my mind. It's all in there - what's happened and what we've got to do to make it right again. It's not pretty, but you must understand that we are the only hope left."

He dropped his chin to his chest with a grunt of pain and swayed. Abby grabbed his arm, and something in her touch rallied him - though his fists were clenched white and Crysanthe swore she heard his teeth grinding. A few seconds passed and he staggered, gasping, before falling to his knees.

Two of the giants leapt from their thrones and strode towards the table, their shadows filling the universe. Before Crysanthe could move, a hand slammed downward. She saw the second titan grab the first's wrist and it halted ten yards above their heads, Even though the blow hadn't descended the shock wave still knocked them flat.

Toldi - she guessed it was him - yanked his arm away from Sorameistre's grip and tried again, but this time he stopped of his own accord.

"Why can't I crush you?"

The shout was a hurricane of noise. Crysanthe clapped her hands to her ears and tasted iron as her nose started to bleed.

"We're God Talkers," yelled Max. "You can't harm us. You mustn't harm us. We are the only ones who can save us all - giants, mankind and all the creatures that live in the last darkness of God's body."

"You slew Bassandis," hissed Toldi.

"He still lives. He's in the Mind, waiting for you to help him. So is Ragaleis. We have to work together."

"To save you?" spat the giant. "To save the monsters who do nothing day in and day out but harm and hurt, who are filled with greed and rage and contempt. You want us to save you with your little lies and petty treachery?"

This time he thumped his hand on the table half a mile to their left. The shock wave hurled them into the air. Around them shapes toppled and shattered on the steel plain. Pottery and crystal shards taller than a man skittered towards Crysanthe.

Sorameistre took Toldi's hand once more, but he shook her off and stalked away, heading for the wall of light. He stepped through and disappeared, his outline receding as he headed for whatever refuge he'd chosen to nurse his fury. His sister turned to her siblings, who hadn't budged from their thrones.

"They are worth saving. They are worth helping. I remember now. It returns to me like the sea when it races back to the island from the west. I looked into their souls, before I came here. I've learned enough about these people to understand their flaws and yes, as we have seen, they are capable of great cruelty. But they are also have the nobility and goodness in their hearts to have survived through the long ages of this reality, and to have endured the cold aeons of this last night."

"She's quoting from one of the books I read to her," whispered Ioam, hands clasped together in happiness.

"Take them from our sight," said Vinduranto.

"King Vinduranto..." Max started.

"Enough."

Sorameistre walked back to the table and rested her palm upwards so they could climb between the fingers. The mad witch brought Aelspell with her, dangling him at the end of her claw like something repulsive she was taking out to the dustbin.

The giant covered them with her other hand and they swayed in the darkness as she took them from the throne room. At last she gently tipped them into a square surrounded by three normal sized villas. A parapet ran along the fourth side, looking out over a vast ocean. Crysanthe glanced up at the sky but she sensed it was empty. *We're facing west.* Walls rose up right and left to meet in an arch a mile above their heads. Sorameistre withdrew and she realised with a jolt that the titan was reaching up from the gloom behind them, as if she'd put them on a high shelf.

"Where are we? Are we trapped?"

"This is where our most honoured guests from the Great White World stay."

Her voice was a hissing wind rising up from the shadows.

Aelspell's palace. So much for his simple faith. Crysanthe took in the marble and gold sculpted walls, the rich furnishings through the windows, laced with the ebb and flow of incense. She wondered if the rest of the crew would end up here as well, though somehow she doubted it. What had happened to them after Nem chased them shrieking across the titan's dining table?

"Don't worry, little Ioam. We'll help you," said the giant. "I remember now, the things I came here to do all those years ago, to find my brothers and sisters so we could set out on our last journey. You have shocked and frightened us, Max Ocel, but we needed it. Let me speak with Vinduranto, Mephyrean and Toldi, and later we will make our plans."

Ioam reached out as if trying to stop someone leaving, and Crysanthe heard the rustle of a gown drawn back across a marble floor a mile and half below.

"What do we do with him?" asked Abby, poking Aelspell with her foot. He whimpered and tried to curl up into a tighter ball.

"Find a room with a bath and a door and lock him in it," said Max. Nem yanked the man off the floor by his leg and disappeared into one of the villas.

Clarindo turned on Max.

"You have destroyed it all, you filth. I know you, I know you scum well enough. I've met you before, you and your bitch whore, tearing apart the holy pact between us and the spirits, making everything that is great seem small and smeared in your shit..."

Abby hit him. To her credit she pulled the punch but the man still flew backwards to crash with a back-breaking thud against the parapet. She picked up his stick, snapped it across her knee, and threw it over the edge. He cried out and clutched at the dancing faces as they fell towards the ocean miles below. The Time Scavenger started forward with another thump in mind, but Max grabbed hold of her. She spat on the floor and shook him off.

"You should chuck him after it," muttered Halinard around his cigarette. Waldrada ran to the fallen seer and helped him to his feet, dabbing at his bruised face with her robes. "And her as well."

"Take him inside and stay there," Max said to Waldrada. Once the pair had left he turned to Ioam. Nem and her sister were hugging each other, Nem patting Ioam's back with her claw. They pulled apart and Ioam wiped her tears away. She flashed the biggest, happiest smile the general had ever seen on her face. It was truly frightful.

"As soon as we can I want to get Sorameistre into your mind palace so she can see for herself what's happening. How much influence has she got with the others?" asked Max.

Ioam shrugged.

"Hard to tell. I don't know what happened since she left our home. She's new here, so she's not as wrapped up in all this religious bullshit as her sister and brothers." She tailed off and stared into the distance. Crysanthe could guess what she was thinking.

"The giants seem to have no memories, or only hazy part-formed ones," she said. "If they've been wandering the singularity for thousands of years learning about us, why don't they remember more?"

"When my father and Odilon found Bassandis he didn't understand what he was, that's how they managed to fool him into thinking he was there to defend Metacarpi. These titans think they're gods living on their magic isle safe from Behemoth. It doesn't make sense. And why are there so few God Talkers?"

"Where are you from?" Selva asked Halinard.

"Calcaneus."

Abby's mouth fell open.

"The Heel?"

"Thumb, Patella, Vastus Lateralis, Umbilical," Max ran through the God Talkers' original locations, ticking them off on his fingers.

"Nothing higher than the Waist," said Crysanthe. Ioam and Abby swapped identical *what is going on?* expressions.

"We've no idea what happened to the God Talkers of the other eastern giants, but I bet they all came from the back end of nowhere as well. Belsalice and Ombratulla didn't even meet theirs, they spent a couple of days deciding mankind was utter evil and went and sulked at the end of the Hair until Ruth stumbled across them."

"We always thought the Machine Men scattered the God Talkers beyond the Ear so the giants wouldn't hang around the AntiHelix, but would go out to wander through all the realms of humanity," said Crysanthe. "But that was assuming there were more than just eight of you. This sounds like you were deliberately hidden as far away from the titans as possible."

"But if the Machine Men didn't want the giants to learn about humanity, why create them in the first place?" asked Selva. "Why send them to wander abroad? It doesn't make any sense."

She was right, but Max didn't have any answers.

"None of this changes things," he said. "If Sorameistre persuades the others to help us our next task is to get them off this island and back to the Head. In the meantime all we can do is wait. Keep those three idiots locked up and we'll take watches again. At least this place looks more comfortable than the city."

Crysanthe had guessed right - their villa complex sat on a windowsill at head height to the giants, with no obvious way to climb down the wall and explore the rest of the island. To the west, mist threaded through a forest far below which spread to the edge of the ocean, curving around the bay to her left. The water was as flat and lifeless as before, but from their vantage point she spotted faint lights in the depths and once or twice movement - though she couldn't tell whether it was machinery or creatures. To the east the window looked into a sparsely furnished room with a scissor chair, chest and daybed. Light slanted from other windows set three miles up in the stone walls, and she thought she recognised a human sized garden complete with trees and gazebo in the alcove of the highest.

Max and Abby took first watch, so Crysanthe and Selva found a room for themselves and dived into the luxury of a normal bed for the first time in ages, rolling themselves up in the piled sheets and snapping out of reality like extinguished candles. When she woke it was dark and Selva still slept, so she wrapped a blanket around herself and padded out into the courtyard. To her surprise she came across Ioam sitting cross-legged on the floor with a book on her knee, telling the story to Nem who leaned back on her elbows and stared up at the empty sky.

"What an image of repose did this scene present!" read the sorceress out loud. "The fierce and terrible passions too, which so often agitated the inhabitants of this edifice, seemed now hushed in sleep; those mysterious workings, that rouse the elements of man's nature into tempest, were calm."

Nem caught Crysanthe's eye and made a shush sign with her finger. Ioam paused and looked towards the empty space on her left.

"Repose is another word for 'rest', and edifice means the castle."

Crysanthe glanced behind her and noticed a soft orange glow in the room beyond. Peering down from the shelf she saw the giantess Sorameistre sitting mermaid-style on the floor, head to one side as she listened. *Of course.* The general couldn't see it, but she knew that the human avatar of the titan sat in exactly the same pose on the empty spot opposite Nem. Ioam was reading to her childhood friend.

After their watch they slept again but this time she awoke to splitting headache and an empty rage grinding in her stomach. Selva sat up, a fatuous look of horror on her stupid face.

"What's happening?" she yelped and pressed her fingers to her temples. Crysanthe wanted to wrench them away and hit her hard, crush that endless mocking sneer that plagued her day in day out. She knelt up, ready to backhand the snivelling bitch off the bed. Selva saw her raise her fist and snarled at her in hatred, hand scrabbling for the long knife she kept beside her pillow.

The next second Crysanthe was on the floor with Abby's arms around her while Ioam dragged her lover to the other side of the room. In the background she heard a man howling endless curses. The headache vanished, along with the rage, to be replaced by a hideous guilt at the murderous loathing she'd felt for the girl.

"It's not you," hissed the Time Scavenger. "It's the giants."

Crysanthe got to her feet. Selva put her face in her hands and burst into tears, Ioam's fingers still around her waist.

"Why isn't it affecting you?"

"Rebecca," said Abby. "The brat's made me immune, bless her."

"Who's screaming?"

"Guess. Our friend the High Priest of the Great White World."

Selva and Crysanthe allowed themselves to be led out into the courtyard by Ioam and Abby. The general cried out in fear at Sorameistre's head rising over the western parapet, stray wisps of cloud clinging to her hair. Judging by the huddle in the middle of the plaza, the others were locked in earnest conversation with the titan. She spotted Waldrada standing off to one side with an expression of sullen misery.

"Where's Clarindo?" asked Selva. She'd calmed down and Crysanthe reached across to grab her hand. The answering squeeze nearly broke her fingers.

"We believe he's with Toldi," said Sorameistre. "My brother came here in the night. I don't think he meant you harm, though his rage knows few bounds. His God Talker has joined him, but whether he will calm the fear and hatred in his soul is unclear."

"He won't," said Crysanthe. "He hates us as much as Toldi does - blames us for betraying the noble ideals of the giants."

Sorameistre's slender eyes half-closed in thought, making her look even more inhuman. Crysanthe could see how easy it had been for Aelspell to turn these creatures into monstrous demiurges.

"We are sorry that you, Crysanthe and Selva, and also Aelspell and the other humans, were subject to our brother's troubled mind. We've dealt with his passions before, and can dampen them with our own thoughts. The pain and fear will fade."

Crysanthe stepped away from Abby. The headache returned, along with an undercurrent of rage, but muted.

"Where's Toldi now?" asked Max.

"I don't know. Somewhere on the island. He'll come back to us when he's ready."

Crysanthe wasn't so sure, especially with Clarindo dripping his own curdled resentment into the titan's ear. Next chance she got she'd break the cowardly bastard's neck.

Sorameistre smiled and placed her hand palm-up at the edge of the parapet.

"Come. High King Vinduranto and Queen Mephyrean wish to speak with you about returning to the Head."

CHAPTER FIFTEEN

MORE THAN EVER Max needed to talk to Rebecca, not only to make contact with Bassandis again, but get her to help them unite the giants. He had the beginnings of a plan in his head, a double assault against the sisters' fortress in reality and in God's dream world. If she could cloak Halinard's wagon, it might allow them a route through the dark wasteland of the deity's id, hidden from the army of nightmare watchers.

Crysanthe's comments about the titans' memories bothered him. It was true - if they recalled anything it was only brief flashes of the past. Ragaleis, Ombratulla and Belsalice had an understanding of their destiny, but the Giants of the West had fallen for Aelspell's fantasy, apparently without question. They were like the magic slate he'd had as a child - a present from Odilon. It was a screen covered in iron dust on which he'd drawn the adventures of another, happier Max. A shake and the images fell away so he could inscribe a new story with his stylus. The creature's minds were the same - blank pages rubbed out time and time again, waiting for the next human to etch more wise epithets or superstitious curses.

They get their thoughts from us. We're the catalyst. When we're with them, their consciousness is formed by our hatred and desire. Ombratulla and Belsalice gleaned their malice from Ruth. Sorameistre gets her eccentric wisdom from Ioam, and the others have had their minds filled with Aelspell's bullshit.

Abby twitched in her sleep and muttered abusive nonsense at whatever monster she chased through her dreams. Max closed his eyes and entered his mind garden.

He immediately panicked. Instead of the grassy enclosure with its white furniture, he stood on a circular plain fashioned from granite blocks fitted together in a precise checker-board pattern. A quarter mile away a wall rose up into the sky, punctuated by iron-arched windows so that the red and grey light from the coal heavens cast flickering spokes that radiated from his feet. The hall didn't have a roof and the top of the wall looked uneven, as if half-built. At first he thought he'd jumped into another part of God's mind by mistake. If so he hoped it belonged to a God Talker, otherwise all manner of horrors might come boiling through those gaps. But there was something very familiar about the place, which made him pause.

He walked to the window and looked out over the dun grass. The new iron fence rose and fell across the distant hills and beyond it the heads of the watchers bobbed along their own black parapets. Halfway between him and the perimeter he spotted another iron cleat set in the ground. This one had a pile of rings next to it. A memory nudged at him. If this was his mind palace, what exactly was he making? Half of him wanted to seek Ioam out and ask her what has happening, and how he could control it, but for some reason he felt ashamed. If his deepest fears and desires were crafting these artefacts did he really want to spread them out before the gaze of others?

Wood banged on stone and he turned to see a large double-doored hatch in the floor. He hadn't noticed it before, but he remembered it from his last visit. *The shadow man just flung it open.* He was about to jump back out into the real world when he heard the sound of someone dragging furniture around. The noise was so ridiculously ordinary that he summoned up the courage to walk towards the trapdoor.

A ladder stretched down to a wooden floor half a dozen yards below. Lights from a hidden source cast long shadows across the boards. *I'm looking into my own mind.*

"I could really do with a hand," called a man's voice, with the breezy impatience of a friendly overseer who'd spotted a roustabout not pulling his weight.

"I don't think I can go down there," said Max without thinking.

"Of course you can. Come and help."

It didn't sound like a monster or a nightmare. The intonation was resonant, matter of fact and utterly familiar. He knew it so well and yet he couldn't place it.

Here goes nothing.

He put his foot on the first rung. The universe didn't end. Neither did his brain explode into a chaos of insane mirrors. Emboldened, he climbed down a little further. At last he reached the bottom of the stairs and turned round to find himself in a long low-roofed warehouse that seemed to stretch on forever on all sides. It was filled with endless clutter - desks, chairs, piles of books, files, tables, dressers, a mirror that reflected nothing, jugs and bowls on iron stands, even one or two beds. *Is this my mind? God it's boring.*

"Over here."

Keeping one eye on the ladder, just in case it disappeared and left him trapped forever in the tatty archives of his thoughts, Max made his way between piles of junk to a row of stacked chairs and glass tables. There must have been thousands, stretching in iron and green crystal walls into the distance, broken here and there by untidy pyramids of typewriters.

A man in shirt and braces stood with his back to Max counting the stock and making notes on a clipboard. A thread of cigarette smoke curled over his head. *You're the bugger who was smoking in my mind garden.* The figure turned round and every childhood terror came crashing into Max's head as he found himself in front of his father, Herman Ocel.

"You."

The Lord of the Carceral Archipelago gave Max a grin that completely threw him. He could count on one hand the number of times the sour old bastard had smiled, and none of them had been as open and welcoming as this.

"You too," said Herman Ocel. He put his hands on his hips. There it was again, that insane smile. It couldn't be Father.

"Who are you?" asked Max.

The man offered his hand to shake.

"Max Ocel."

"No you aren't. I'm Max Ocel. You're Herman Ocel, my father."

The man stuck his arms out and looked down at himself.

"That cantankerous old git? Surely not."

Max glanced around. The desks and typewriters, the stone walls and the iron cleats with the chains piled ready beside them - each link as big as a house - it all made horrible sense.

"You're my father, Herman Ocel. And you're building the Carceral Archipelago as my mind palace."

"The what-ity what-ago?"

This was beyond madness. The Tyrant in the Tower stroked his beard and mused at the corridor of glass desks. A vague memory of a dream came back to Max - one where he'd walked through the empty prison of his childhood and it had been filled with light and happiness. Herman cocked his head.

"There's someone upstairs you need to talk to." He tapped his clipboard with his pencil. "Maybe next time, eh?"

Max jabbed his father in the chest with his finger.

"Stop building that tower. I want a mind palace like Ioam's. The Carceral Archipelago lies in rubble in the Forbidden Sea where it belongs. I never want to look at it, or you, again."

"Don't be silly, of course you do," chuckled Herman, slapping him on the shoulder. "Now go on, you're running out of time."

Rebecca waited for him in the roofless hall, wearing her silver armour and carrying the spear she'd used to throw Subjulio to his death. Her red hair cascaded down her back and she shot him a sleepy-eyed half-smile half-pout that made him realise she was going to be major trouble if she ever manifested herself in reality.

"I need your help. Do you remember the God Talker's wagon - the machine that moves?"

She nodded.

"Can you make it invisible to Belsalice and Ombratulla, like you are?"

"Perhaps."

"Do you understand where you are, and what's happening?"

"Bassandis told me. He and his brothers and sisters have to join together to save everyone, but those two are stopping him because they want to control the world themselves."

"At the moment, if anyone other than you steps outside these mind palaces the watchers spot them and alert the sisters in their citadel. I need to get all the other giants, including Bassandis, into that wagon, and then you can hide it long enough for us to journey to their fortress, find and free Ragaleis, and defeat Ombratulla and Belsalice. Can you help?"

Rebecca gave him a pure Abby look of derision, boosted up to adolescent level. *God help me.*

"Of course."

"And I have to be able to contact you. At the moment you just turn up at random."

She handed him her spear.

"Bang that on the ground and I'll hear you."

"Don't you need it?"

"I've got a whole box of those at home. Bassandis keeps making them for me."

An unreasonable pang of fatherly jealousy caught Max unawares. He was about to launch into a lecture about not getting too close to giants, but stopped himself just in time.

"Rebecca, do you know who you are?"

The girl looked off to one side.

"I'm Rebecca and my mother is Abby…" she said, as if reading from a badly written cue card "…and my father is Max. You. You're my dad."

"I suppose so."

"The glittery bastard I fed to the terrors said I was inside mum. What did he mean?"

Max had no idea where to start. How to explain to her that in reality she was still nothing more than an embryo in stasis, and her appearance as a bolshie teenage girl was a construct from God only knew where?

"You're linked to Abby, and so those who want to stop us will try and kill her. You must never pull your mother back into this world without asking first. Promise?"

She shrugged.

"Promise?" he repeated.

"Promise. But I get to meet you again?"

Max hefted her lance.

"Oh yes. Fetch Bassandis and take him to the wagon. Wait for us there."

She vanished. Max wondered what he should do with the spear. In the end he jumped out with it clenched in his fist, hoping it would still be there when he returned to the Mind.

While Sorameistre carried them to the other giants he told his companions about his plan. He realised it was a lot to ask of Halinard to let them use his wagon as a stealth weapon but the God Talker just shrugged and started to roll another cigarette.

"With Rebecca's help I think we can make it to the citadel in the Mind," Max continued. "It's the journey in the real universe that's the problem. I don't see how we're going to get the titans to the Head if we no longer have the Brittle Hag's spaceship."

Nem sniffed, wiping her nose with the back of her hand. Max knew her sad expression echoed everyone else's thoughts. They all missed Neke and his companions.

"If we do manage the journey we'll still have the Machine Men to deal with," said Crysanthe.

"Whatever their game is, they want God's mind finished," said Ioam. "Without it we all perish in the last darkness, humans, Machine Men, giants and monsters."

"Worst comes to worst we'll have to get them to come and fetch us," said Max.

Sorameistre unfurled her hand and they stepped down onto the table in front of the thrones. Vinduranto and Mephyrean looked down on them with the unreadable faces of ancient statues. Sorameistre sat with Toldi's empty chair between her and her sister. A second later their avatars approached them, walking barefoot across the scarred metal. Sorameistre had taken some getting used to. She was the same height as Ioam and Nem and towered over the other two - more proof that the giants defined much of themselves through their God Talkers.

Max had insisted on bringing Aelspell. Despite his treachery and delusion he'd been the high priest of the titans. He didn't want to antagonise them by appearing without the man, and at the same time he hoped they'd recognise him for the lying mountebank he really was. The old fool had unwittingly obliged by cutting holes in a bed sheet and draping it over himself, no doubt hoping this ritual self-abasement might endear him to his Gods. He staggered away and fell to his knees, head bowed before the King and Queens. Max noticed another huddle further off - the crew of the boat. He wondered if they'd spent the night on this cyclopean table or if they'd been brought here from other quarters.

"If we journey to the Head, and join with our brothers and sisters of the east, will we rescue everything from destruction?" asked Mephyrean in the soft lazy voice of an aristocrat who'd never had a normal conversation with those beneath her before.

"Yes," answered Crysanthe, looking through the avatars at the shadows on their thrones. "You shall become the God who was built to save humanity."

"Toldi says you're too wicked to be allowed to survive," said Vinduranto.

"It's not for him to judge."

"Then who is to judge?"

"No-one," said Max. "There's no entity alive or yet living who can condemn the entire history of our people to oblivion. If you've been told you have the right to weigh up the good and bad in us and decide our fate, then you've been lied to. You've looked inside my head and seen what you are, and what you have to do. You have no moral authority over us. Ombratulla and Belsalice thought they had and ended up slaughtering thousands, thinking they were justified in their petty revenge."

"If this is our purpose, why have we stayed here on this island?" Mephyrean turned to her brother.

"Ask him." Ioam pointed to Aelspell who rocked back and forth, twisting the bedsheet over and over in his hands. He gazed up at his deities with such forlorn despair that Max couldn't help but take pity on him. Vinduranto looked at the high priest. It was hard to tell what the titan was thinking.

"We'll go the Head and meet with the Giants of the East," he said. "First, we must speak with Toldi to make him understand."

"I'd like you to join us in Halinard's mind palace. Bassandis will be there, and another God Talker."

"Please don't go," whined Aelspell. "Please don't leave the Isle Resplendent and the Great White World. There is nothing out there but danger and murder. Why throw away this paradise for horror and strife?" He lifted his hands in supplication.

"You've had your fun," said Abby. "Why don't you just shut up?"

"No, it's not like that. It really isn't. Tell them, Max. I wanted the people to be happy, to be free of fear and to live in a utopia so that humanity could have one last grasp at peace before the night claims us."

"Utopia? A population of diseased serfs in hock to your grotesque fantasies of lordship?"

Tyrants always rubbed her up the wrong way but this wasn't the time or place. She stalked towards Aelspell who snivelled into his clenched fists, trying to wring a last prayer out of his misery.

"Abby, leave him," said Max.

She probably had nothing more in mind than a clip round the ear, but as she approached Aelspell he collapsed on all fours and started to bang his head against the table top. At first Max thought it was just a self-destructive tantrum for effect, but the blows got harder and a red mark appeared on the steel. At the same time Crysanthe and Selva staggered back, clutching at their temples. Ioam grabbed the two of them by the arms.

Abby stopped, frozen by the sight of the high priest who jack-knifed up and down faster and faster, smashing his head repeatedly against the ground. Through the endless crunching he squealed like a tortured mouse. Urine puddled round his knees.

"What in God's name?" said Crysanthe.

Aelspell sprang upright. His face looked as if it was rammed against a pane of red glass. He reached up and dug his thumbs into his eye sockets. Fluid spurted over his hands. Max heard Waldrada being noisily sick behind him.

"Toldi," said Nem.

"No," said Sorameistre. "It can't be."

Aelspell, now blind, staggered back and forth. He stuck both hands into his mouth and started to yank on his jaw, grunting with the effort. It took the hierophant four attempts but in the end he wrenched it free, a long strip of skin tearing down his neck and chest. He burbled through the blood spraying from the ruin, the bottom half of his face dangling at his waist like a grotesque pendant, and pitched forward to lie, unmoving, in a spreading pool of gore. More howls and screams came from where the crew had huddled. They faded into a terrible silence.

Ombratulla stood among the avatars.

"Found you at last."

In the shadows beyond the table Max saw her true form by the thrones, soft eyes in a mountain glowing through the ever-present haze.

"I met your brother down on the beach," she continued, ignoring the God Talkers. "He wasn't happy. We had a long chat. So now you know. Thank you Max for enlightening our siblings."

Her human shape gave him a sardonic half bow.

"And General Crysanthe, or is it Empress Crysanthe these days, or just Nobody Crysanthe? Ruth sends her regards. You have a new woman, I see. No worries. Little sister is far beyond jealousy."

"You killed the High Priest of the Great White World," said Mephyrean, irritation barely breaking through her diffident drawl.

"We were made to save these people," added Sorameistre, voice shaking with anger.

In answer Ombratulla reached forward and a vast hand drifted over the table. She wiped Aelspell up with her sleeve, the smear of his body on the rich cloth barely longer than her little finger nail.

"There, all gone."

Max noticed she was carrying a stack of thin discs under her arm, like large metal dinner plates - a weapon or a shield?

"We Giants of the East are waiting for our brothers and sisters to join us in the Mind so we can forge a new being, a supreme creature untainted by man with his filthy lies."

"Why have you done this? Why have you turned your back on our creators and their servants?"

Ombratulla gave a high, poisonous laugh, hand to her mouth like a society hostess anxious to charm.

"You understand as well as I that we are greater than they are. You were lucky. In their ignorance they turned you into gods and that is all the better for them. In our case they betrayed us and let their own servants, the Machine Men, try and lord it over us. We would have helped them, we would have carried them into the next universe if they hadn't dragged us into their petty cruelties."

"Where's Ragaleis?" asked Max.

"In our fortress and thankfully rid of the taint of humanity. He works on our side, crafting powers ready for the final victory and our transformation into God. The Giants of the East are complete."

"You don't have Bassandis."

"That scrap of nothing in your garden? Is he even still alive? Bring him to us then. We would love to meet sweet Bassandis once more."

"And do to him what you did to Ragaleis when you ripped out part of his soul to make that bitch Ruth into another monster?" spat Abby.

Ombratulla turned cold, bright eyes on the Time Scavenger.

"You're not a God Talker, are you?"

Max cried out in horror, realising that Abby wasn't touching any of them and so stood unprotected halfway between him and the faint smudge that once was Aelspell.

"Ombratulla, don't."

She extended her thumb, and a shadow fell over Abby. Max sprinted towards her, even though he knew it was too late. Ombratulla pressed down and her hand stopped a few yards above his lover's head. She tried again, harder, but an invisible barrier lay between her and the woman. The giant gave Max a look of quick anger. He grabbed at Abby but to his astonishment she ducked out of the way, strode over to the avatar and shoved her backwards. In the split second when her hands hit Ombratulla's shoulders, Max saw the ghost of a silver-armoured girl. *Rebecca.*

"Don't kill her," he yelled. If his daughter had the power to harm a giant, God only knew where they'd end up.

Avatar Ombratulla staggered back, caught by So-

rameistre before she could fall. Beyond the table mountains thundered against each other and Max felt the steel
under his feet vibrate. The giant righted herself, jagged
teeth bared in fury. She slapped her hand down towards
the whole group but once again the blow stopped short.
She glared at them, struggling to calm herself.

"You needn't worry, Max. It seems I can't kill her."

"I was talking to Abby, not you."

Max saw a flash of real fear in the titan's eyes. She
turned to her siblings.

"You see. These creatures are dangerous. They'll destroy us or enslave us like they did Bassandis. Come to
the Head and leave them to die in the darkness."

"The only cruelty I've seen here is yours," said Sorameistre.

Ombratulla looked her up and down.

"You're a fool, sister, if you let yourself be taken in by
their lies. This is the last battle between God and mankind and we will win."

"Why are you filled with such malice?" asked Max.
It was a genuine question. "You spent a couple of days
in our company. Does all your venom come from that,
and the bitterness of Ruth? Don't you realise how flimsy
and pathetic your judgements are? Slaughtering millions
and abandoning those you're designed to protect because
of what? Forty-eight hours unpleasantness and the ram-
blings of a damaged teenager?"

Ombratulla ignored him.

"I've brought you gifts."

In the shadows beyond her giant self placed the stack
of discs next to the thrones. At last Max recognised them -
they looked like the platforms the two sisters had ridden
during their assault on the AntiHelix.

"Our star friends from deep time crafted these to carry
you to our citadel."

She turned to go.

"There is no hatred or anger on the Isle Resplendent," rumbled Vinduranto, speaking for the first time. "Stay awhile, sister, and speak with your sisters and brothers. You are most welcome here."

He gestured to Sorameistre.

"Take them away so we can take counsel with Ombratulla."

"Wait…" said Crysanthe, but giant hands cupped them and moments later they were swaying in the half-light of an immense fist.

When they returned to their villas Waldrada tried to kill herself by leaping off the parapet. Nem jumped after her, grabbing her round the waist and jamming her own claws into the wall so she could climb back up like long-haired spider. After that they locked the prophetess in a windowless room and let her sob and howl out her anguish.

"Look," said Crysanthe, pointing out across the forest towards the distant beach. Ombratulla and Toldi walked along the ocean's edge, heads bent towards each other in earnest conversation.

"Not good. Do you think she'll persuade them to join her?"

"Sorameistre won't go," said Ioam.

Max hoped she was right.

"At least we've got transport for the giants," said Crysanthe. "Whatever they decide, they'll need to return to the Head. And us with them."

Max glanced around. Abby had headed for a bath as soon as they'd got back. Ioam drifted over to her sister, who'd taken off her exoskeleton and was polishing it with her hair. He took Crysanthe by the arm and led her to a corner of the plaza. They sat next to each other on a marble bench, looking up at the pale light flickering on the ceiling of Sorameistre's room miles above. The general gave him a puzzled glance, and not for the first time a sliver of lust passed through him at her sharp-faced beauty.

"I don't want Abby near the Machine Men."

"She'll be useful. You saw what she did to Ombratulla. That daughter of yours has given her power over those monsters."

"The giants can't harm her, but Machine Men and humans can and she's a target. When the time comes, I'll need you to help protect her. She'll put up a fight, but the end game is for giants and God Talkers only."

"If I abduct her, what about Rebecca?"

"She's got the ability to roam God's mind at will, even if Abby's far away I reckon it won't affect our daughter's powers."

She looked unconvinced.

"It's all a gamble, all of this," he continued. "There's only seven of us, eight if you include Rebecca."

Crysanthe rested her hand on his shoulder.

"I'll do what I can, though I might have to knock the idiot out again."

CHAPTER SIXTEEN

Aт dusk Sᴏʀᴀᴍᴇɪsᴛʀᴇ returned to tell them that Ombrat-ulla and Toldi had departed the island, speeding north across the ocean on two star-forged discs.

"We called after them and tried to follow, but lost their trail in the mist."

"Four titans against us, five if Ragaleis really is on their side," said Ioam.

Max fumed. The wrong odds were stacking up.

"Take us to Vinduranto and Mephyrean, I want us all to visit Halinard's wagon."

Rebecca and Bassandis were waiting for them when he, the witches, Halinard and the Giants of the West entered the Mind. They left Abby, Crysanthe and Selva in the villa, along with Waldrada endlessly grizzling in her room. Clarindo hadn't reappeared. Max guessed he'd left with Toldi and Ombratulla.

He still wasn't sure how time passed here, but his daughter sat cross-legged on the floor, arms folded, with a killer look of boredom on her face. Bassandis stood in one of the pods, peering through the thick glass. Max put down Rebecca's spear, which had re-appeared in his hand, and joined the titan. He radiated energy. Pale eyes glittered and even his skin seemed to carry its own lambent glow. Compared to him, his brothers and sisters looked like porcelain dolls brought to an uneasy, anaemic life.

"Where are we?"

Halinard stood beside Max, staring out of the window in puzzlement. The circling demons had vanished and now they stood on a ramp dotted with broken pillars and statues. The slope ended in an immense amphitheatre ringed with sharp-angled mountains. The floor of the arena was starred with cracks like a dry lake bed. In the centre a cluster of black pyramids, spires and shards rose out of the orange ground, lofting for miles towards the red and charcoal sky. Disturbing shapes cast jagged shadows as they crept here and there through the dust, and midnight rags flapped in ascending circles above the far-off peaks.

"I brought us here," said Rebecca. "That's Ombratulla and Belsalice's castle in the Mind."

"And nothing can see this vehicle?"

She shook her head.

They returned to the main cabin. The three Giants of the West stood in the centre, looking around with hesitant wonder.

"Brother, sisters," said Bassandis.

Mephyrean gasped and held out a trembling hand.

"I remember you, from long ago. We sat at a table and laughed and were happy. Afterwards we said goodbye, and you walked into the darkness."

Bassandis took her hand.

"Ombratulla told us you were dead."

"I'm alive. This girl's garden brought me back."

"Meet Rebecca," said Max. "She's a God Talker, but she only lives in the Mind." He didn't want to tell them she was Abby's unborn child.

Sorameistre, Vinduranto and Mephyrean embraced Bassandis, who greeted them each in turn with easy happiness. It was hard to reconcile this dapper, energetic creature with the diseased monster rotting in chains in the secret fortress across the Forbidden Sea.

"We're inside Halinard's mind palace," explained Max.

"Do you have one of these?" Sorameistre asked Ioam and Nem. "I want to see it."

"We never dared move through the Mind," added Vinduranto. "We thought it was a chaos of dreams and nightmares that would destroy us."

Max told Rebecca about Ombratulla's visit. Before he'd had a chance to finish she vanished, reappearing a few seconds later.

"A man and a woman are walking across a desert far away, they're heading for the giant's castle."

"Did they see you?"

She gave Max a *what do you think?* look.

"So, a plan?" asked Halinard. He offered a hand-rolled cigarette to Vinduranto, who stared at it in confusion. Max realised the scruffy owner of the land leviathan was the High King's God Talker and this was his way of breaking the ice. When the titan didn't react Halinard lit up and waved a hole in the cloud of blue smoke in front of his face. Mephyrean started to cough.

"We journey to the Head to meet with the others in the real world. At the same time Rebecca gets us inside that fortress. Once we find Ragaleis and release him we confront the Giants of the East both in here and outside, and then it's down to you titans to persuade them to turn away from the path they've chosen. We've got Rebecca on our side. She frightened Ombratulla, which gives us some advantage. We also need Theuderic's help - if only to let us have safe passage through their outpost in the Ear."

"And if we can't make the sisters give up their hatred?" asked Sorameistre.

"We destroy the Mind," said Bassandis.

Everyone stared at him in disbelief.

"A dead god is better than a mad god. Our powers in the hands of an insane deity will threaten everything."

"You're suggesting we kill ourselves and them?" asked Vinduranto. His regal diffidence vanished, and his hand trembled as he pointed in the direction of the citadel.

"There has to be another way," said Mephyrean.

"How do we know they can't form the Mind without us? Do we all have to be there? And if we all die, how do we know that will be the end of all this?" asked Sorameistre, gesturing around her.

"The Machine Men will know the answer to that, they designed you" said Max. "That's why we need to talk to Theuderic."

"If this is what we were made to do, then we have to do it," announced Vinduranto, still the portentously stubborn king of the Isle Resplendent. "We shall prepare to leave."

"Dad?" said Rebecca. Max groaned inwardly. *Why did you have to call me that?* He was about to tell her to be quiet when he saw her expression.

"What's the matter?"

Halinard looked from Max to his daughter and back again. He laughed in realisation.

"Something's wrong with mum," said the girl.

Rebecca struck the floor with her own spear. Dream silver rang on iron but nothing happened.

"I can't reach her. I can't bring her here."

Max clapped his hands and found himself on the giant's table. The others snapped awake around him in quick succession.

"The villa!" he yelled at Sorameistre, who scooped him and his companions up and ran through the vaulted corridors of the palace. She dropped him in the plaza and he immediately slipped and fell in the trail of fresh blood that led from his apartments to the edge of the parapet.

Crysanthe couldn't do anything to help the God Talkers. She tried to keep her frustration in check by running through the strategic options for an assault on the giant's citadel inside the Head, but it was nothing more than make-believe. She had no armies or fleets to command, and the Machine Men wouldn't give her theirs. The struggle for God's soul would happen in the sorcerous realm of his Mind, where she couldn't even go, let alone fight. *You're redundant. Here on sufferance because of what? Friendship? Pity? Selva and I would have gone to plead before the Black Rose God, but we don't have a spaceship anymore.*

She ran through the Spear Tip Dance a couple of times but it was hard to focus and she made stupid mistakes that left her even more defeated. She wandered through the villas and came across the library where Ioam had found the book she'd read to Sorameistre. Nothing grabbed her attention, and she hated reading alone.

In the palace where Abby and Max had camped she heard splashing, which led her to a circular hall with a swimming pool masquerading as a bath. To her surprise she saw Selva sitting naked on the edge, dangling her feet in the water while the Time Scavenger swam lazy lengths back and forth by a curved window looking out along the side of the giant's home. More windows dotted the white stone beyond, and each one had a villa, roofs glistening in the light and green moss trailing down stained walls.

"Join us," said Selva. There was nothing else to do other than tussle with her demons so Crysanthe stripped, leaving her clothes on a table covered in pots of incense, and sat beside the Companion.

"She's sulking because she thinks Max will make her stay here." The girl nodded towards Abby's legs as they disappeared under the water after the rest of her.

"He wants us to abduct her and take her somewhere safe when the final assault starts," said Crysanthe. "The Machine Men targeted her because of their daughter. I'll need your help. She can fight and she won't go easily."

Abby resurfaced on the other side of the bath and gave Crysanthe a nod. Her ludicrous hair covered her torso, so she looked like nothing more than a part-drowned ginger cat. Crysanthe felt the touch of Selva's nails across her thigh. She glanced across to see a wicked light in the woman's eyes as she stared at the other bather.

"You two could be sisters. Neither of you will admit to weakness no matter what."

"Are you totally and utterly insane?"

Selva's mouth twitched, and she shrugged. A finger ran up the length of the general's spine and back down again. Selva licked her lips. Crysanthe read her like a book.

"You're suggesting a sympathy fuck with Abby Fabrice - the three of us?" In her astonishment she struggled to keep her voice a whisper. *Splenius*. The perverse corruption of that realm still lingered in her lover's blood.

"Think of it as a challenge. It'd cheer us all up. Thin Hans was always a firm advocate of the pre-battle orgy. Cemented loyalties and got the circulation going."

"No. Absolutely categorically no. Not in a million million years. Don't even think about it."

Selva sniffed.

"What are you two talking about?" asked Abby.

"Nothing," answered Crysanthe.

"Bugger this, I'm bored."

The woman vaulted onto the side and stretched on tip toes, red hair clinging to her muscled back and bottom. Crysanthe doubted she was doing it deliberately, but to her horror she recognised the all-too familiar nip of desire in her own groin. The woman poked around in a bowl of fruit on a low table by the window. Selva started whispering obscene suggestions in Crysanthe's ear.

"Want some fruit? That mopey bag with the face paint found it. S'nice," said Abby. "It'll do you good."

She held up a banana and the Companion burst out laughing.

"Har, har. Suit yourself, smartarse."

Abby padded out of the hall, whistling.

"Don't you want to follow her?"

"No!"

"Just you and me then," murmured Selva, kissing her under the ear.

They fucked in the warm water until their skin started to crinkle after which Selva dragged her out onto the side. By the time she'd finished they were both so exhausted Crysanthe fell into a light doze. She awoke moments later to find herself alone on the tiles. Grumpily she went in search of her lover and something to dry herself with. The air was beginning to fade, bringing a chill breeze from the distant ocean.

She found piles of towels in an alcove. They looked as if they hadn't been used in years and smelt musty but they'd do. She bent down to gather up an armful but when she straightened up a weight shattered on the back of her skull, driving her forwards to smack her face against the wall. She clutched at the air as the pain and darkness burst over her. Another explosion, muffled this time but enough for the lightning-shrouded clouds to consume her.

Crysanthe awoke to find herself curled on the cold floor in a heap of towels. She tried to sit up and hissed in agony. Her hair had stuck to the tiles and when she glanced down she saw the blood clotting on the wet stone. Porcelain shards tinkled as she lifted herself onto her knees, pain flaring in her scalp as her bloody locks tugged free. She touched her head. Skin broken, bone intact, long shallow cuts down the back of her skull. A vase, probably enough to stun her but not to do significant damage.

She made it to the corridor outside. Selva lay slumped against the wall, her torso caked in blood. It trickled between the fingers she'd clamped below her shoulder.

"Waldrada. Bitch jumped me. She's got Abby."

Crysanthe knelt beside her.

"I'm OK, it's just bloody. I disarmed her and cut her back - a tracking wound. Get after her."

Selva pushed a wooden-handled peeling knife into her hand. That explained why the Companion's injury was nothing more than a desperate slash made by someone who hadn't a clue. The pain in her own mind was fading so Crysanthe left her the girl and broke into a lurching run. Surely Abby would make mincemeat of the God Talker. But then so would they if they hadn't been ambushed. Sloppy. No doubt Selva just saw a wretched coward in front of her before it was too late.

Waldrada's blood trailed across the plaza to the parapet. For a horrible second she thought the woman had leaped to her death, dragging Abby with her, but then she noticed the trail ended at a thin gap a foot in from the edge, barely a black line in the marble. Wincing at the shard of pain twisting behind her eyes she ran her hands along the bottom of the low wall until she found a square button. She pressed, and the floor hinged out and down to form a wide platform two yards below. Bloody footprints led to an opening under her feet - a second complex in the wall of the giant's building, underneath the villas. She jumped, stumbled and fell on her knees at a wave of dizziness. She shook it free and saw the entrance to a tunnel sloping down to her right.

The passageway jack-knifed back and forth. At the second junction she found Waldrada, dead in a spreading pool of blood. Selva had nicked a major vein in the woman's leg, letting her live just long enough to lead any pursuers down here. Orange eyes stared at the ceiling from a chalk white face. Crysanthe felt nothing but disgust at the empty-headed coward with her pompous witch-doctor ceremonies. But where was Abby? A set of boot prints trailed away from the corpse. At first she thought the woman had carried on ahead by herself, but then she noticed the shape of a two bare feet close together among the heavier tracks. *Clarindo. The bastard didn't go with Toldi. He's carrying Abby. He put her down for a second to catch his breath.* Crysanthe started to jog after the God Talker. Each footfall drove a spike into the back of her neck. She'd make him suffer for this insolence.

Eventually the passageway opened into a hangar. Crysanthe found herself next to a row of three-wheeled cars. Glass bubble canopies sat above deep-tracked spheres as high as a man, banded in red and black. A steel mesh road stretched from the far wall, weaving into the distance through the top of the forest. Fresh tyre marks led from an empty space at the end of the garage. Crysanthe scrambled up one of the ball wheels into a cabin. Hand cupolas rose on stalks, flanking a cracked and stained leather saddle. She straddled the seat, jammed her fingers into the pods and pushed forwards. With an electric whine the car shuddered into motion, rumbling across the vault and onto the rusting highway.

So far the only normal sized buildings she'd seen were the villas sitting high up on the window ledges like toys put away for the night. Now she realised the forest hid an ancient city, no doubt built by the original inhabitants of the Great White World before they'd disappeared. In the heavy twilight between the dark branches she spotted more delicate palaces, arcologies, halls, stadiums, factories, research bases, warehouses, parade grounds, mausoleums and graveyards littered with a millennia's-worth of broken statues. The structures lay half-buried in a soft carpet of purple loam, dusted with thick needle leaves from the trees.

A flash of blue far ahead told her that another vehicle sped along the highway. *Clarindo.* Where was he heading? It was hard to figure out the geography of the island in the ever-present haze, with the jagged tree tops rising and falling around her in waves. The halls of the giants receded behind her, she couldn't see anything in front except the endless forest and the grey sky. When Toldi took Clarindo from the villa he must have brought him in this direction. Sure enough, she drove past clearings hundreds of yards long and filled with broken trees - the titan's footprints.

Even at maximum throttle all she could do was match her speed to the other car. Her quarry was too far away for her to see who was inside the cabin. The only way the God Talkers could have overcome Abby was by ambushing her as well, unless she was already dead and he was just dragging a corpse along as proof - to what or whom? Ombratulla and Toldi had left for the Head. Who else lived here?

At last the road angled up into the sky. A box frame miles high loomed out of the clouds. She wondered if it was scaffolding for an unfinished mega-arcology but then she spotted machines, buildings and sculptures bolted to the grid. The track entered the structure and started to curl upwards in a spiral, taking her past floor after floor of open-walled concrete floors littered with scrap.

She counted twenty levels before the vehicle rolled off the end of the ramp and into a wide circle ringed by stacks of plastic circuit boards yards across, towering unsteadily towards the ceiling. Clarindo's car stood on the other side, but as soon as Crysanthe jumped down she realised it was abandoned. Tracks scored the dirt, disappearing between the broken components. Why didn't Abby tackle the bastard? A blow hard enough to knock her out for this long would have killed her unless she was drugged. She hefted the knife in her hand and remembered the woman standing naked in front of a picture window, sorting through a bowl of fruit. Of course. The bastards had dosed it with narcotics from Waldrada's magic pouches.

Clarindo knew she was following him. Here and there he'd pushed over heaps of rubbish or machinery to try to stop her - clumsy and pathetic attempts, but they slowed her down enough for her to fear she'd be too late. The pain in her head had grown into a dull ache that made it hard to focus. As soon as she'd tracked the traitor down she'd slaughter him, she didn't have the patience or the concentration for anything else.

He knelt on the very edge, frantically wrapping a cord round Abby's neck. She sprawled naked across the floor, hands waving feebly in the air. At least she was still alive. Beyond them the mist boiled over the ocean, filling the universe with grey, dead light. Clarindo lifted his arms in supplication.

"Great Toldi. Noble Toldi. Come back to me, your faithful servant. I give you the bitch whore and the monstrous child you so fear. Their deaths will be our gifts to your sisters. They will redeem us both. Please, please, I beg you. Come back to me."

He started to weep, outline shuddering against the mist as he buried his face in his hands. They were too close to the precipice for Crysanthe to launch herself for a killing strike - she'd have them all over the side - but her blade wasn't weighted to throw. She spotted a steel bar lying on the grubby concrete next to a supporting girder. Her injury made her cack-handed and when she picked it up the end scraped across the rubble. Clarindo jerked round, nearly falling off the platform. He waved a knife in her direction - one of Selva's. She'd balanced and sharpened them to her own tastes. Anyone else trying to use them was likely to slice off their own hand. Normally she would have stood and watched him flay himself by accident, but she was there to rescue Abby.

"Stay back," he yelped. "Stay back or I will call down the wrath of the spirits."

He held the sword point over Abby's stomach.

"OK, OK. I won't harm you. Look."

She dropped the bar and showed him her empty hands, moving sideways to line herself up. The ruse worked. He thought she'd disarmed herself.

"What are you doing?"

She breathed in and lifted her hands up to the ceiling, intertwining her fingers and rising onto her toes. It was a gamble, her balance was off and timing was everything. In her memory she saw Nan sitting on a black wooden chair, switch across her knees, waiting for the inevitable errors.

"Stop it."

Like all who'd never seen the Spear Tip Dance before its beauty mesmerised Clarindo. The first warriors designed it that way, pirouetting on the points of their enemy's lances to drive them into madness.

Seventh form.

She counted out the seconds in cartwheels. On the third she snatched up the iron bar with her feet and kicked it at Clarindo as she swung around the pillar. The throw was mistimed, but it hit his forearm, breaking it with a sickening crack. Selva's knife disappeared into the mist. The God Talker sprawled over the concrete, shrieking and clutching his arm. Crysanthe fell out of the dance and walked towards the fool, Waldrada's knife dropping into her fist.

Before she could stop him he grabbed Abby and rolled both of them over the edge. The rope uncoiled and it was only then Crysanthe realised the other end was tied to the nearest pillar. She hurled herself forwards but even as she scrabbled at the last few yards she realised it was too late. Cutting it would send the woman to her death, grabbing it would snap her neck.

The floor bucked under her knees, sending her sprawling over the crumbling stone. Half a mile away the roof collapsed in an avalanche of concrete and broken machinery. The air seethed with dust, blurring her vision and filling her mouth with its sour taste. Almost weeping in frustration and anger she hauled herself to the edge and looked down, knowing full well what she'd find.

She had to wipe her eyes twice before she realised she wasn't hallucinating. The cord from the woman's neck ended a few inches below. Crysanthe lifted it up - a precise cut. She peered into the void. Miles below the ocean thundered against the bottom of the frame. No bodies. She got to her knees, trying to understand what had happened.

Far away a little black square opened in the sky. A speck dropped out of the hole, tumbling over and over as it fell. Crysanthe could have sworn a faint shriek drifted on the wind. It hit the water in a plume of spray and the rent among the clouds vanished. A gust snatched at her clothes and she heard a noise behind her. She turned round to see half a dozen Abhumans watching her with their shining opal eyes.

CHAPTER SEVENTEEN

Sorameistre carried the remaining God Talkers across the sea. She used one of Ombratulla's flying discs while they rode on her hand, Max pacing back and forth, inventing a hundred agonising deaths for Clarindo. As soon as Selva told them about the betrayal the giantess knew where to go - she called it the Lattice. Despite his fury Max blanched at the sight of it looming out of the mist. The framework rose into space, its upper levels in darkness.

After Abby threw herself into his arms, still groggy from the narcotic Waldrada had sprinkled over the fruit, it took him a whole minute to register the row of Abhumans standing behind Crysanthe. Half a mile away the Brittle Hag's vessel sat on the concrete floor.

"You showed up just in the nick of time. Again."

Neke bobbed his head enthusiastically, completely failing to catch his tone of voice. Even so, he had to give the creatures credit. Sorameistre peered at them with almond eyes fifty yards across and they didn't flinch.

"What happened to your ship?"

"We are under sustained attack. Each time the assault from outside gets stronger," explained Neke. "We've learned to anticipate when and where it will happen, and so can shift the internal geometry to prevent the invaders getting a foothold. Connecting to wormholes protects us."

"You're connecting to wormholes?" asked Nem. She clapped her hands in appreciation, sparks flying off the exoskeleton's claws.

"That's how we escaped from the city. The last space-time harpoon fired into the ship's reality was the most powerful so far, but we jumped the ship into a wormhole shaft and it severed the chain."

While Ioam and Selva tended to Abby, the Companion with her shoulder now bandaged, Crysanthe joined Max. Her angled birds-egg face looked even paler than usual, and her blonde hair was matted with blood.

"We can't fight two wars," she said. "They'll have to tackle this themselves. We have our own struggle ahead."

"We don't expect you to help us. Our life here is ended," clicked Neke. "We decided that because this ship is unstable we will chance a last trip to the Black Rose God. We came to say goodbye to King Max and Queen Abby."

"You can't plead on behalf of mankind." said Max. The first time Neke said that he and his fellows were going to make the journey to the God Door he hadn't taken the creature seriously. If it ended up with no other choice than to beg the aliens for help he'd fully intended they'd all go, or at least those that survived. Now he realised Neke was in deadly earnest and off into space regardless.

"Why not?"

Neke had him there. Of all the people, witches, giants and monsters Max had met in his journey in and around the body of God, the Abhumans were the most guileless. Perhaps they really did represent the best of humanity - but he suspected it would be a colossally naive mistake to think their innocence could make a dent in the baroque amorality of the Black Roses, and whatever else took it upon themselves to judge them. The creatures watched him, waiting for an answer.

"We need to talk," he said eventually. "After we've patched up the wounded and secured the island."

"Very well," answered Neke. "But we're leaving soon and can't wait much longer."

"What did you do with Kelvin?" asked Crysanthe.

"Gave him back to his people."

Sorameistre carried the God Talkers back to the villa, all except Nem who was beside herself with excitement and insisted on staying with her rediscovered friends. Max wasn't sure, but Neke and the others didn't seem quite as enthusiastic. He suspected that since they'd found the harpoon the creatures decided Max's quest was a lost cause and were slowly backing away into their own stratagems. In the end he supposed it didn't really matter, though he confessed to himself that he'd missed the hairy buggers. The Brittle Hag's ship was too unstable to be of any use. He pushed the Abhumans to the back of his mind. There was another, harder conversation he needed to have with Abby.

"How did you know I'd been kidnapped?" she asked. His lover was in a hell of a mood, transformed into a belligerent drunk by the after-effect of the drugs. In her head no-one ever got the better of Abby Fabrice and even if they'd used a ton of narcotics it was no excuse. She sat on the edge of the bed, head between her knees, endlessly muttering the foulest oaths.

"Rebecca."

"Little cow. What did she have to say for herself?"

"She could sense there was something wrong with you. She tried to summon you into the Mind but couldn't."

"Good. She can drop dead."

"You're a target. The Machine Men came after you. Ombratulla's terrified of you because she couldn't harm you and you practically knocked her over. Clarindo was going to sacrifice you to Toldi."

"I thought Bassandis was leaving Rebecca's head and going to live in Ioam's palace."

"It's not Bassandis they're after. It's Rebecca. They can't harm her in the Mind, but they can get to her through you."

"So?" She sat up and gave him that stubborn glare of old. He geared himself up.

"When we go back to the Head with the giants I want you to stay here with the Abhumans, Crysanthe and Selva."

"Ain't happening."

Her head fell back down between her calves. Max didn't know whether she was battling nausea or this nodding-bird act was an after-effect of the sleeping draught.

"Not up for discussion," came her voice from under the cloud of hair. "Not having yet another 'might never see you again but let's pretend I will' performance. S'boring."

Abby hauled herself up again and fell backwards onto the bed. Her eyes rolled up in her head and she started to snore. Max stared at her. God almighty but she was exhausting - gobby, truculent, abusive and deliberately contrary with no sense of time or place. How many years had she shaved off his life by almost dying? The ridiculous woman filled up his world with constant noise, adrenaline and filthy sex. He could have had anyone - pale daughters of the richest in Metacarpi, fey Bohemians entranced by the craggy scavenger. And he'd gone and ended up with Abigail Fabrice. He crawled across the sheets and looked down at her face - sleeping innocence slathered in brick dust freckles. No way was he risking her again. He gave her the gentlest of kisses and went in search of Halinard. Moments later he was back in the God Talker's wagon.

"You do what you need to do," said his host. "I'll be in the front cabin."

Max banged his spear on the metal plating and Rebecca appeared.

"What?"

"Bring your mother here."

Abby popped into existence.

"What are you doing?" she said when she saw Max. "I've just been doped up to the eyeballs and nearly murdered. I'm trying to get some sleep."

She carried a slur in her voice but her dream self seemed a lot more alert. She glared at Rebecca and then looked around.

"Where are we now?"

"Can you protect her when she's in the Mind, in the same way as you do Bassandis?" Max asked the girl. She shrugged and nodded. He guessed it meant *Yes*.

"We're in Halinard's mind palace - land ironclad to be exact. It moves, and thanks to our daughter none of the giants' monsters can see it."

He beckoned Abby over to one of the windows facing into the vast arena and pointed at the jagged silhouette of the castle. It looked like a hand shattered and reset by a deranged sculptor working in blood-doused coal.

"That's where we're heading. I think Ragaleis is in there somewhere. We get in fast, free him and take on Belsalice, Ombratulla and Ruth."

Abby cracked her knuckles.

Got you.

"You come with us here. But back in reality you have to stay out of harm's way."

She paused mid crack.

"So you thought you'd bring me in here as a bribe so you can leave me behind on the magic island." She turned to Rebecca. "Tell your father he's a total fucking cunt."

"Dad, mum says…"

"Without Rebecca we can't do this," he interrupted. "We have to protect you to protect her. The second the Machine Men know where you are they will go for you. Ombratulla knows you're a threat. Giants can't harm you, but the warriors Ruth brought out of deep time can and will."

"Alright alright. God's cock!" Abby turned to Rebecca. "Why can't you squat in another mug's body? Ioam was going to invite Bassandis to live in her head. Why don't you go with him and piss off out of me?"

"She's our daughter," said Max.

Abby gave the ancestor of all contemptuous snorts. Max winced, wondering if the girl understood. Having been on the end of years of dismissive contempt from his own father he knew how deep into the bone each sneer dug.

"She's our daughter," he said again, and there was enough in his voice for Abby to have the grace to look a bit ashamed. Yet Rebecca stayed magnificently unimpressed, serving her mother's expression back to her in spades. He had the horrible feeling there'd be a lot more of this in years to come if they all managed to survive.

Abby folded her arms and stared out of the window at the fortress.

"Why does anyone have to go to the Head? Why can't we run the whole operation here in slumber land?"

"The giants have to meet their brothers and sisters inside the skull to reunite. We're their God Talkers. We can't leave them to make the journey by themselves. You've seen how unworldly they are - easy prey to any persuasive maniac. They need us with them."

"I need you with me," said Abby. It was a complaint to the universe, not to him directly. It had a weary resignation that saddened him.

"Send me back. I've had enough of this," she said to Rebecca.

After they'd both disappeared, Max waited. He needed a few moments to think before seeing her in reality, knowing he'd probably have to run through the same conversation again. Yet their bed was empty. He panicked and went hunting for her only to see the brief flicker of one of the buggies racing between the trees far below.

"Abby's gone to the Lattice," said Crysanthe, standing on the hidden platform. "She looked like she wanted to be alone."

He jumped down and joined her. The general turned back to stare towards the ocean with a frown on her face.

"You need to move quickly. Every day you waste their defences will grow stronger."

It sounded like she was saying goodbye.

"Selva and I will go with the Abhumans to the Black Rose God," she said in answer to his unspoken question. "We can't help you here, but we might do some good if we survive the journey and get to speak with the aliens."

Disdainful, sadistic, aristocratic Crysanthe Uella. He'd despised her before he'd even met her. The image in his father's speaking lens told him all he needed to know about this scion of the Empire of the Ear and her cruelties. Yet here he was two years later, fighting to stop himself from begging her to stay. It wasn't just that her lethality surpassed even Abby's. In the woman's eyes he recognised the same endless battle between doubt, fear and bloody-edged duty forever swilling around his own head. Of course he found her attractive, despite her preference for women instead of men, but that wasn't it. Crysanthe was one of the five remaining friends he'd grown to trust. If the general and her Companion flew off into the empty gulf he'd be down to Abby, Ioam and Nem. Nem was as cracked as they came and there was no guarantee he'd see his lover again, or that she'd talk to him when he did. *We're falling apart before we've even started.*

Two days later they assembled on the beach between the villa and the Lattice. The three giants rested their flying discs on the shallows, stepped onto them and glided out to sea where they turned into mist-shrouded mountains towering up through the morning cloud layer, their heads silhouetted against the purple sky. As Max walked up to Selva and Crysanthe, the Companion turned to her lover.

"Do I have my lady's permission to favour him with Splenius's Embrace for the Departing Hero?"

"No you do not," said Abby, who glared at them from the top of a sand dune a few yards away with four Abhumans next to her. Selva shrugged, reached forward and kissed him on the mouth, biting his bottom lip for good measure and surreptitiously giving his balls a squeeze.

"That's the highly edited version. For luck."

Crysanthe shook his hand and for a moment he almost hugged her, but stopped himself just in time.

"Abby will report on your progress from the Mind. As soon as you've secured the citadel the Abhumans intend to leave for the Black Rose God."

"Take care," he said.

She gave him a nod, and he guessed that would have to do. He trudged over to Abby.

"This is my personal guard. They're going to stay behind and look after me until you get back - Goma, Bratu, Ustat and Voti," she pointed to each one, and Max clicked *Thank you.*

"It is our honour to help Queen Abby save King Max from his own fucking stupidity," answered Goma.

"Good. Now bugger off over there so we can talk." Abby gestured at the shattered wreck of an ancient flyer and the creatures dutifully loped away.

"His own fucking stupidity?"

Abby gave him a bruising kiss that lingered to the point of suffocation. When they pulled apart he tasted blood.

"Take that with you, you bastard. It'll make up for the fact we can't hold each other properly in God's dreams. And let the giants and Rebecca do the work, they have the power - not you. Keep out of harm's way. Please. For me?" She put his hand on her stomach. "For us?"

In her eyes he read the love and the pleading he only ever saw when they were alone together.

"Come back so we can find a way to sort this out."

She held his fingers in place and touched his cheek with her other hand.

"I promise," hoping she could see that he meant it. Abby turned him round and pushed him down the slope.

"See you in la la land."

Three hands as big as clouds scooped down over the water's edge. The God Talkers had decided to ride with their own giants - Ioam and Nem with Sorameistre and Halinard with Vinduranto. As Waldrada was dead Max climbed into Mephyrean's palm. He wasn't sure how the titan would react to the loss of her own prophetess. Emotions sat uneasy on the giants - either appearing vast and childlike like Ombratulla and Belsalice's hate, or vague and ill-defined. After learning that Waldrada had perished Mephyrean had demonstrated nothing more than melancholy confusion.

She lifted her hand, and he stepped onto her shoulder. It measured four hundred yards from neck to the edge of the deltoid and three hundred across, so he had plenty of room. He stood and watched the Isle Resplendent recede. Walls of mist passed in succession and each time the bay looked smaller and more translucent, as if the universe itself was dissolving into grey nothing. For the first few minutes he could just make out a cluster of dots on the beach, but the grainy light soon absorbed all detail and he turned to look northeast. Mephyrean's face carved a silhouette out of the sky to his left. She didn't bother to appear as an avatar beside him, so he was left his own devices. He sat cross-legged on her trapezius, trying hard not to think of Abby Fabrice.

Eventually he sensed an increase in speed. A force field extended upwards from the disc, preventing him from being blown off into the sea although he still heard the scream of the wind as it built to a hurricane. A muffled bang made him jump and a white cloud flashed around the giants. *We've gone supersonic.* They'd calculated they'd reach the Ear in four to five days, at which point it'd be time to contact the Machine Men. Without a ship the God Talkers would suffocate as soon as the titans rose above the atmosphere on their way to the Meatus.

When the last light faded from the sky Max lay down, pillowed his head in his hands and jumped into his Mind Palace.

For God's sake. Really?

He stood holding Rebecca's spear in a long hall floored in white steel. The desks he'd seen in the basement sat in precise rows. There must have been thousands of them, their pristine emerald tops shining in the strange light. Every one had a black cage typewriter with a sheet of paper sticking out of the roller. He glanced at the near-est. *The Mighty Tower of the Carceral Archipelago is a Moral Axis of Strength and Resolve. Discuss.* By Maximilian Ocel. He checked three more. Unsurprisingly, they were all the same. *He's built half the thing already. How's he done that? What monsters does he command?* It was the seven hundredth floor - the Room of Whispered Love where the sub clerks scribed out the suspicions of the people - neighbours ratting on neighbours, children getting their petty revenge against grownups. *Not in my head. Not in a million years.* He kicked a table over and it shattered, clots of glass skittering over the metal. He stared at them, shaking. *I've got to stop this.* It was bad enough living out the first thirty years of his life in the shadow of that judgemental bastard, but to have his father squatting like a parasite inside his head, all fake bonhomie while he rebuilt this hideous prison fortress, filled him with a sick anger.

But now was not the time. He thumped the weapon on the steel. Rebecca appeared and moments later Abby stood among the desks.

"This rings bells," she said. Not happy ones by the look on her face. "What rat hole's this?"

"Dad's mind palace," answered Rebecca with the bland innocence of every child betraying one parent to another.

"I thought you had a garden. Isn't that where I dropped you the first time Madam here pulled me in?"

"My brain started constructing this," Max said. "I don't know how to stop it."

"Why would you want to stop it?"

Her eyes went wide.

"The Carceral Archipelago! You're building the Carceral Archipelago in your head. Does it really have that much of a hold over you?"

The shame caught him unawares. He shouldn't feel guilty - yet he did, as if it was his fault the tower's roots lay deep in his unconscious, cemented to his dreams with fear. He saw pity on Abby's face, making it a hundred times worse. She walked over and touched him. He sensed a light pressure, as if a cold draught had targeted his shoulder, but there was no reality to it. They tried to embrace but it was like clutching at a cloud of mercury. Abby stood back, eyes grim.

"We're camping out by the Lattice, next to the Abhuman's ship. Crysanthe thinks the villa is unsafe, and it's too big with just the three of us. Where are you?"

"Mephyrean's shoulder. We should be beyond the sea by the time I wake up."

"Keep an eye on your stupid father. I want him back in one piece," she said to Rebecca, who'd sat herself down at a desk and was trying to work out how to use the type-writer. "Can't you help him fix this place?"

"No." The girl didn't even look up. Abby glared at her before turning back to Max.

"Why don't you get Ioam to help you sort this out?"

He shrugged, not wanting to tell her how wretched and ashamed the place made him feel. Abby must have realised because she kept quiet.

"I won't bring you here again," he said. "Tomorrow we'll meet in Halinard's tank and start our advance on the citadel."

She tried to kiss him - a recollection of a faint breeze carrying her scent from thousands of miles away. It would have to do.

When they'd gone he pulled the paper out of Rebecca's typewriter. She'd written a poem that started *And I recall when as a child I felt your hand take mine.* It jogged his memory but he couldn't place it. One of Abby's no doubt, extracted from her memories by the silver-armoured cuckoo.

The next night Sorameistre touched her brother and sister on the shoulder to let the God Talkers walk along her arms to gather at the base of her neck. The witches had clearly been having far more fun with their giant than Max or Halinard. Their camp on top of the titan's trapezius looked like a student's bedroom floor, with a bag of books spilling its contents in among the clothes and sacks of rations. Ioam cleared a space, cursing Nem's untidiness all the while, and they sat cross-legged in a circle. Halinard dropped his cigarette into an empty tin mug as big as a wastepaper basket and they held hands, jumping into his land ironclad a second later.

They gathered in the front cabin of the tank. If God Talkers' mind palaces were fashioned from memories of their childhood, Halinard must have grown up amid the remnants of a vast machine battlefield. Instead of the finely turned brass and polished wood of the other rooms the control centre was built from polygons of dinted metal painted in military olive and grey, with only the occasional yellow or red warning stripe to break up the jumbled blocks. It was big enough to hold them all with plenty of room to spare - but still the shadows crowded in, barely touched by the orange lamps flaring in the corners. Max found himself tensing in anticipation of gunfire and explosions. Abby hovered next to him. Even if they couldn't hold each other they kept as close as possible.

Halinard sat on a command chair made from green steel and cracked leather. He tapped his fingers on the bottom of one of several control wheels.

"Now what?"

A bright light appeared on the edge of the main screen. The thick aquarium glass surrounded it with a halo that rippled like a smoke ring as Rebecca strolled out in front of the ironclad, using her burning spear as a walking stick. She stepped down the slope, turned and waited until the God Talker set the vehicle in motion. It trundled after her over the cracked ground.

Max's first thought was that every creature in the Mind would see that spark. It hurt his eyes and changed the silhouette of his daughter into a burning statue. Yet if anything the hunched and slithering shadows down in the immense amphitheatre cringed away from the advancing circle of light, covering their heads with shrouds, membranes and papillae.

"They can't see us?" asked Abby.

"No," said Bassandis, standing at the entrance to the bridge, feet together and hands clasped with the crisp precision of a servant waiting to show honoured guests into the presence of his lord. "Your little girl has remarkable powers."

Max saw Abby gearing herself up, but caught her eye. She clamped her mouth shut and stared at the red-haired herald who marched in front of the tank. He could have sworn he saw grudging admiration in her face.

The odd distortion of time inside the Mind meant that even though they crossed the plain at little more than a walking pace the citadel appeared to rush upon them, a jagged clutch of darkness rising out of a floor of melted resin the colour of blood-stained milk. They paused on the edge of its shadow. Max didn't see any lights, just random holes bored into its surface. Maybe they were windows - if so the interior architecture was as mad as the outside.

"There," said Bassandis. He came down and pointed over Halinard's shoulder at a slanting triangular hole half a mile further along the wall. "That's how we get inside."

CHAPTER EIGHTEEN

On the morning of the fifth day, Max woke to find the giants within sight of the shelf worlds leading up to God's right ear. An hour later, as they sped over the crumpled terrain, casting long lizard crests of dust and debris behind, half a dozen ships flew down to meet them. The titans stopped and lowered the God Talkers to the ground. Max's boots crunched on a plain of cracked jade stretching for a hundred miles in each direction.

Either the Machine Men were playing it safe, or they didn't want to scare the giants. Just one of the silver-vaned quarrels landed, grey-brown smoke belching from its rockets. A man and two women clambered out of the cockpit and stood waiting for them, their white robes billowing in the cold wind that blew from the pit that cradled God's head. The human avatars of Sorameistre, Vinduranto and Mephyrean appeared, each standing next to their own God Talkers.

"Gentle Sorameistre and Vinduranto, and Noble Mephyrean. Lord Theuderic welcomes you on your last journey to form the Mind of God."

To Max's surprise Mephyrean took his hand. Her fingers were dry and hot as if a fever consumed her. The emissaries from the Machine Men waited in silence - paper statues on a crystal field. He didn't have time for elegant diplomacy.

"Have Ombratulla and Toldi returned?"

"They passed this way two days ago."

"And?"

Translucent doll faces turned towards him. He guessed they were conferring with the others up at the Meatus, framing their answer to some intricate agenda.

"We attempted to contact them but were unsuccessful. They entered the Mind."

"Give us a human ship so the God Talkers can ascend to the Ear," said Sorameistre. "We want to talk to Theuderic."

A second vessel landed next to the first. This one looked like an over-inflated polyhedron fashioned from scarred armour plating.

"No Machine Men," insisted Max. "Just us." He kept seeing Ihanna's severed head blackening with rot even as she mouthed her last word. *Hate.* Thank God Abby was thirty-six thousand miles away.

Max, Ioam, Nem and Halinard climbed on board while Vinduranto let the previous crew climb onto his hand. Max baulked at the spider web control panel at first, but Halinard stuck a bent cigarette in his mouth, lit it with a match struck on the sole of his boot, and started to press buttons and twist dials. They rose up through the atmosphere, drifting at shoulder height to the giants, and headed for the glowing waterfall beyond which lay Theuderic's temporary base. A few hours later they crested the edge and stared down in stunned silence. The evidence of the Machine Men's attempts to talk to Ombratulla and Toldi littered the shelf. Max counted over fifty vessels strewn in pieces or scrunched up into blackened knots of steel and plastic. The wreckage formed a pathway aiming directly towards the Meatus. The other ships coasted ahead to act as guides. They veered off to the left towards a mountain of ten-mile-high cubes rising above the blue fog, their faces speckled with the lights of countless windows. Max wondered if the Machine Men had built this tumbledown city themselves or just stumbled across it.

One of the boxes had a curtain of shimmering air for one of its faces. They entered and landed on a platform hanging in a net of cables that trailed down from the distant ceiling to plug directly into building-sized machines scattered here and there over the tarnished surface. Max and the others stepped out of their ship, the titan's avatars snapping into existence among them. The giants themselves stood far behind - immense statues in darkness save for where the faint blue glow under-lit their faces. It was hard to reconcile the fey, wide-eyed creatures standing in the middle of their group - Mephyrean grasping Max's hand again like a wary child - with the monstrous sentinels towering over everything else. A line of Machine Men towed Theuderic from the shadows. He resembled a tired balloon bobbing along while his servants tended cables and wires, blocking leaky vents and mopping up spilled fluids.

"How did Ombratulla and Toldi destroy all those ships?" asked Max. Bugger diplomacy. He didn't trust the Lord of the Machine Men and had no time to waste on protocol.

"The star-born disease they crafted penetrated the defences we erected, and invaded our systems. We re-calibrated." As before Theuderic's voice issued simultaneously from the mouth of every one of his attendants, even the ones still struggling at the seals of his sphere with pliers and wrenches. They continued about their busy tasks, seemingly oblivious to the words they intoned.

"As you know, we have an ally in the Mind who can move unseen by giants and watchers. She also has the power to overcome Machine Men when they enter that realm."

"Your daughter."

Max froze. He shouldn't be surprised that the architects of God's soul had figured out who Rebecca really was, but to hear Theuderic say it filled him with dread. He fought the urge to jump into his mind palace and summon the girl and Abby just to make sure they were still alive. Luckily, Ioam stepped in before he gave himself away.

"Inside the Mind we are already at the citadel of the giants, ready to enter and free Ragaleis. Bassandis is with us, and in his daughter," she pointed at Max with a demon forefinger, "we have the sorcery to overcome the rebel titans. You help us, or you stand aside."

"How quickly can you transform the spirit of Bassandis into a giant?" asked Max.

"We can't. We no longer have access to the science with which we created the titans. It was lost when Ombratulla, Belsalice and their creature cast us out."

Max had expected as much. Even if the Machine Men possessed the ability to fashion a new body he doubted they could just tap it out of a mould like a fresh jelly. How long did it take to create a two-mile high mannequin and give it life? Months? Years?

"Can the giants still merge to form God's consciousness?" asked Ioam.

The Machine Men froze and all fell silent, save for the hiss of the glowing wind over the platform and the sparking and sputtering of Theuderic's frayed cabling.

"Will he have enough of a brain to stand up and walk to the God Door?" asked Max when the silence lingered too long.

"Yes."

"What's the process? Does it just happen or do you need to pull levers and press buttons?" asked Nem.

"Once the titans agree to merge it begins automatically. If you can persuade Ombratulla and Belsalice to withdraw the alien sickness from our thinking engines then we can monitor, and give guidance and help where necessary. Noble giants," every Machine Man face looked up into the sky to where the immense, silent figures hovered at the edge of darkness like three mountains hacked into idols. "You must ensure that your love of mankind is greater than their hate. If it only matches the sister's loathing God's mind will tear itself apart. If it is weaker the deity will turn against us all."

Mephyrean's grip on Max's hand tightened. Through the open wall beyond the giants Max saw vessels gathering above the shining mist - a hodgepodge fleet of slender needles, distorted polygons, spheres and platforms on which more Machine Men stood. All turned to face Max.

"We will escort the titans of the west to the Mind so they can speak in person with their sisters and brother."

"Come with us," whispered the queen's avatar, clutching at his hand. "Don't leave me with these creatures."

Half of him wanted to turn back, job done, and return to Abby. He could still take part in the closing scenes of the Great Task in Halinard's tank, with little danger to himself. Max glanced across at the other God Talkers. Ioam and Nem flanked Sorameistre, looking as if they were itching for the Machine Men to start something. Halinard also watched Theuderic and his attendants with an unfamiliar intensity in his eyes. *None of us trust these creatures. Why? They are the architects of God's Mind and they coded our genes.* There were too many unanswered questions - but above them all he couldn't get Ihanna's last word out of his head. *Hate.*

"We will also join you in your journey into the citadel in God's dreams."

"No you won't," said Max. "You concentrate on operations out here. We'll handle the sisters in the Mind." *And if any of you buggers show your face Rebecca will stick you with her spear and feed you to the demon watchers.* "Gather your forces and meet us at the entrance to the Ear Canal."

He got ready for inevitable argument, but none came.

"Very well," said Theuderic. Ioam and Max immediately swapped glances. *Too easy, far too easy. What are the bastards playing at?* He didn't dare say anything, just in case the Machine Men changed their minds.

In the ship they'd commandeered Max hung back with Mephyrean's avatar while the others crowded into the forward cabin. Halinard reversed off the platform and turned in an ascending arc through the cube wall and up towards the Meatus. The giants floated after them on their discs, the Machine Man fleet parting to let them through.

The giantess looked through Max with such a faraway expression of loss and loneliness that he almost took her in his arms. Remembering that he was looking at the projection of a two-mile high golem he contented himself with taking her hand. *Each of these fingers is a hundred and fifty yards long.*

"What's bothering you?"

"What am I, Max?"

"You're part of God's mind. You were sent out into the realms of man to learn about us so that when you combine with your brothers and sisters you'll save humanity by carrying us through the God Door to the next universe."

"But I don't know you," she looked into his face with her pale owl eyes. "I don't know what you are, or why I should care."

"You were fooled into staying on that island, so your God Talker Waldrada and her ancestors before her never got a chance to meet you."

"But she should have been there from the start to teach us what to think and feel."

She stared at her feet and shook her head.

"Why weren't any of you God Talkers with us? Now when I look at you and the machines you spoke to I don't understand what I feel, or whether it's right. Theuderic said we must conquer our sisters' hatred with our love for you. But how can I do that if I don't recognise what those emotions are like?"

The temperature was dropping in the cabin, and the shadows seemed thicker. The fey creature in front of him flew in the wake of their ship, a column of darkness as big as the stone tower of his childhood. It was one thing to see the fear and uncertainty on the face of someone who looked like a delicate consumptive, but the same torment raged in the soul of a living mountain, and the future of humanity depended on her being reassured.

"What do you think you feel now?"

Mephyrean stared at him and her expression hardened.

"Since we spoke to the Machine Men? Angry. I'm angry Max, at you, at them," she nodded at the others, "and at a universe that made me and then abandoned me. What do I owe you? Why should I save you?"

Max remembered Ihanna's words to Ombratulla and Belsalice. *If we made you too innocent, I'm sorry. We wanted you to discover humanity and all its joys and weaknesses for yourself without our influence to distort you.* At the time it made sense, now he wasn't so sure. Innocence had nothing with which to defend itself against cruelty or betrayal. Sending these creatures out into the world of man with all its wars and corruption, its greed and endless grinding hunt for power, looked more like a deliberate abdication of responsibility. He guessed that Ihanna had spoken the truth as she'd seen it - giants would flourish best if they started as empty slates and in the end the goodness they saw in people would outweigh the evil. But how much of that was her own wish-fulfilment. She herself found something in the kingdom of Theuderic that made her sacrifice her own life to save Max and his companions - from what?

"If only there was time to show you everything - all the complexity of the creatures who live in and around God, all the humans in whatever form we've ended up, and the billions of years of history that have brought us to this. We're not perfect. But we've survived this universe, and we made you to help us survive into the next. Trust me, we are worth saving because if you don't nothing will remain, no chance to try to be better, and we shall fade away in this last awful silence."

Mephyrean vanished. Max joined the others just in time to see Vinduranto and Sorameistre disappear.

"We were in the middle of a conversation," said Ioam.

"There's something up with the giants."

"What?"

Max climbed on a seat so he could peer through the bubble canopy at the titans floating behind. The scattered lights across the shelf occasionally lit the robes, limbs and heads of their silent followers, but it was impossible to read any thoughts in their colossal faces.

"How does Sorameistre seem to you?"

Ioam and Nem shrugged in unison.

"Absolutely fine."

Max turned to Halinard.

"Vinduranto?"

"Doesn't say much."

Max waited for more, but the man just looked back at him with the infuriating expression of a party-goer expecting his friend to come up with all the small talk. Max told them about his conversation with Mephyrean.

"Sorameistre doesn't have a problem with us, or what she's supposed to do," said Ioam.

"Neither does Bassandis, and Ragaleis forgave me after the death of his brother and said redemption was in our hands. The giants who spent time with God Talkers are on our side, it's the ones who didn't who struggle with humanity - Ombratulla and Belsalice in their cottage at the end of the Hair, the Giants of the West stuck on their magical island being fed religious drivel by idiots like Aelspell – that we'll have a problem with."

At the entrance to the Meatus they were joined by the Machine Men fleet. The first assault by the Giants of the East had reduced Theuderic's realm to barely three hundred ships. Ombratulla and Toldi wiped out another hundred in one casual encounter, like children kicking dead leaves aside as they trudged through a forest. *We're balanced on a knife-edge. The only chance we have is for our titans to persuade the others to stop.*

They sped up, heading into the darkness. Max recognised the landscape from his journey to the Whispering House - the floor littered with debris from the roof two thousand miles above. The impacts had dented the thick iron sheeting, causing it to dip and billow into dull mountain ranges coated with rust and dirt. Here and there he spotted the remains of the engines used to build the Ear Canal, most decayed into spiky lumps of corrosion.

They passed a few empty cities and factory complexes. No lights shone. The tunnel was long abandoned. Max remembered the emperor's pleasure palace. Its wreck sat inside the Brittle Hag's ship. Selva had given him a tour to satisfy his curiosity. Crysanthe refused to go back inside. He wondered if some ancient tyrant had fashioned a similar retreat here. He doubted it. From what he'd seen of the western side of God the inhabitants of these realms had either fled deep into the Body or disappeared into whatever oblivion the people of the Great White World had found for themselves.

Max jumped into the land ironclad, to speak with Bassandis.

"Do you remember when you first left the Ear? Before my father and Odilon imprisoned you in that tower?"

The titan shook his head.

"Fragments."

"Do you remember how you felt?"

"Lost. In my mind I see tiny people milling across deserts and valleys, long lines stretching into the haze. I try to talk to them but they flee."

"Why didn't you stay with your brother and sisters?"

"Something drove us away from each other once we stood in the air. But after that I became so lonely. I forgot who I was. It wasn't until I met you that I understood what I really am."

Max was taken aback by the friendly gratitude in the giant's face. He hadn't expected it, especially after the hideous death Bassandis suffered at the hands of his father and the Empire.

"Mephyrean and Vinduranto are uncertain, like you were. I need you to talk to them so that by the time we confront your sisters they're completely on our side."

The avatar nodded.

"Of course. I'll bring them here and speak with them."

A few seconds later the three titans of the west appeared and Bassandis led them into a side cabin. Not wanting to intrude, Max left them to it.

Two days later they passed through the Tympanic Membrane and the Middle Ear, entering the long tunnel of the Vestibular Nerve leading straight to the centre of the Skull. At their scale it was just another patchwork tube of iron, wood and canvas, though this passageway was a mere three hundred miles in diameter.

Max found it hard to understand why the original builders of the Head had taken such pains to recreate the structures of a human body. After all, God's ears would never hear anything in the airless gulf between the singularity and the portal. How could he speak without any atmosphere to carry his words? He guessed the architects, engineers, carpenters, sculptors and stone masons had worked on autopilot. With man as a template, they didn't need a plan or even an understanding of what they were trying to achieve. They'd just built a human jigsaw. If and when the deity awoke, the quantum skeleton at the core of all this junk would move and flex the space-time binding everything together, following the puppet commands from the Mind. What were the other gods like? Did they think? Did they have powers and potencies? Did they dictate the ethics and logic of their worshippers as the pantheons of ancient time once did, or were they merely more machine dolls given life by desperate alchemists?

Ioam let him meet Abby each night in her mind palace. He didn't want to see the Carcarel Archipelago again, its hideous shadow crowding his thoughts, wrapping its stone and iron around his dream self. The idea of his disdainful father creeping like a parasite in and out of the deserted halls, corridors and stairwells, or piling more levels upon levels, each as cold and empty as the last, filled him with helpless misery. He'd have it out with the bastard, but not now and certainly not in front of Abby and Rebecca.

So they walked through Ioam's citadel or sat beneath archways bordered with delicate tracery and looked across the demon-haunted valley at Nem's tangled Newton's cradle. Once in a while they saw their hostess picking books from shelves and piling them on a table, opening the volumes with cries of delight as the words returned. Max guessed these were the stories she was reading to Sorameistre and that as she re-enacted each tale it reforged itself in the library of her mind. Occasionally Max found the witch and the giant sitting with their heads touching over a picture book. Another time, as he held Abby's ghost hand on a balcony, he spotted Bassandis in earnest conversation with Vinduranto and Mephyrean. This time the queen listened intently, instead of gazing into the distance with an expression of miserable indifference. That had to be a good sign.

On the evening of the third day the Vestibular Nerve widened out and they passed into the vast space of the Cranial Cavity. The first shock came when they crossed a force field and found themselves flying once more through air. The second was the utter emptiness of the vault. Legend had always held that the regions on the other side of the Tympanic Membrane contained energies too powerful for humans and that only the Machine Men had the science and the endurance to withstand the endless chaos. He'd imagined world-sized engines similar to the ones that powered the Steel Queen's sphere - storms of lambent power and arc lightning cast between diodes and accumulators thousands of miles high. In his dream of the giants in Ragaleis's house they'd sat at a simple kitchen table in the middle of darkness. Wasn't that just a symbol of their loneliness and innocence? Surely their real home wasn't as desolate. But looking at the wooden floor stretching away on all sides like a stage in an abandoned theatre he realised it was.

"So God's empty-headed after all. Surprise, surprise," said Ioam beside him.

"Where do the dreams sit? Something has to house that landscape with its watchers and the citadel."

Ioam looked across at Nem who just shrugged. Halinard rolled yet another of his scrappy cigarettes and gazed out of the window like a man stuck on a delayed tram.

"Company," he said.

A flying platform carrying three Machine Men took up position ahead of their bow, and one of its passengers walked to the edge and raised a hand. A message came over the ship's radio asking for permission to come aboard. Nem put on her exoskeleton just in case, and Max signalled back. He expected they'd dock, but the Machine Man simply leaped across the intervening space, landing on the roof with a sharp clang and scuttling on hands and knees down to the airlock like an insect. Seconds later their visitor introduced himself as Usariph - another fragile birds-head doll built from rice paper and filled with the contents of a million watches. The titans' avatars appeared, answering some invisible call.

"We're approaching the fortress. It's surrounded by the sisters' army, so the giants should go first and we will follow in the wake of their safe passage. It may be wise for the Giant Talkers to ride on your shoulders so they have maximum protection. Ombratulla, Belsalice and Toldi can't harm you directly, but they've got warriors powered by ancient suns who aren't bound by the rules of this time."

"I know," said Max. "I've met the buggers."

"We will hold back and observe," Usariph continued, "Lord Theuderic anticipates that he will speak with the giants once they have come to an agreement amongst themselves."

He could anticipate whatever he liked. Max had other plans.

And so he found himself once again on Mephyrean's right shoulder, the thick cloth of her dress bunched in his fist to steady himself as they sped east. The Machine Men fleet trailed behind like a cloud of chaff. After four monotonous hours he was on the point of curling up at the bottom of a fold to jump into the Mind when he noticed a change in the texture of the floor ahead. A checker board of black squares stamped on the immense planks came into focus, and as the giants slowed their approach he saw that each one was an army, the soldiers and machines pixelated into obsidian flecks. These were the dreaming hordes of insane warriors - the survivors of Long Lock, Lobe, Buccinator, Upper Occipital and the AntiHelix itself, interspersed with spined automata filled with ancient stars. He'd assumed that half had perished in the battle, and later when the sisters opened the manufactory to release Ruth new-made, and the thralls inside the box had suffocated. Even if that was the case they were still grotesquely outnumbered. No wonder Belsalice and Ombratulla had cast out the Machine Men so easily.

The fortress emerged out of the gloom beyond. It was a titanic cluster of obelisks and monoliths piled on top of each other and studded with crenulations, parapets, ravelins, half-moons and bastions - endless platforms shaped like stars and circles. It looked like a child's castle built from toy bricks. Max recognised an echo of the citadel in the Mind, but the laws of physics and gravity blunted the surreal delicacy, turning it into a jumbled lump of black, oily metal.

The giants floated to the ground in front of a ramp that angled down from the entrance, which looked like a simple house door complete with latch. As they stepped off their platforms it opened and Belsalice appeared, walking briskly down towards them like one of the Metacarpi bourgeoisie leaving her elegant residence to go shopping. Beyond her, far above, Max saw two figures watching from the battlements. *Ombratulla and Toldi. Where's Ruth and Ragaleis?*

"Greetings brother, sisters," she nodded to each in

turn. "Welcome to our home."

She glanced at Max.

"You have something caught in your dress, fair Mephyrean," she made a brushing motion at her own shoulder. "We will talk with you and you alone. Neither God Talkers nor machines are wanted here."

"We have the right to be present," called Max. His plan depended on the God Talkers remaining outside the castle, but not to protest would look odd.

"No you don't," answered the giant, turning back to her siblings with the casual indifference of someone who'd spotted and immediately forgotten a stranger in a crowd.

"God Talkers were put in this realm to help and counsel the titans," shouted Ioam. *Shit, don't overdo it.*

"They are our friends," added Vinduranto in a truculent rumble. For one horrible moment Max thought Belsalice was going to relent. If they went inside the fortress in reality how would they jump into the Mind without alerting suspicion when they all fell to the ground in a faint? To his relief the titan clasped her hands and gave Vinduranto an indulgently superior smile.

"They aren't our friends, brother. They stay out here or there's no discussion."

Mephyrean lifted her hand and Max stepped onto it. The polygon ship picked him and his companions up from the giants' palms before drifting back among the Machine Men fleet. From a rear porthole Max watched Belsalice gesture behind her, her mouth framing the invitation *Shall we?* She led the way up the ramp and the three remaining giants of the west followed. The door closed and all was silent.

CHAPTER NINETEEN

When she wasn't inside the Mind, Abby left Crysanthe and Selva to their own devices and went wandering through the Lattice, only returning at the appointed time to curl up in a ball in the shadow of the Brittle Hag's ship and slip into the semi-death that marked her transit into God's dreams. Selva suggested they decamp back to the villa, but the woman refused. Whatever uneasy alliance they'd built up over the last few weeks dissolved in Abby's bitter resentment at being stuck on the island. She spoke to the others in monosyllables, when she bothered to talk at all. As far as the general could tell the God Talkers were on the point of infiltrating the giants' citadel. Abby's refusal to give them any more details maddened her.

In the end, Crysanthe was grateful for the hard discomfort of the field camp they'd rigged, despite Selva's pestering to let them go back to the villa with its silk pillows, swimming pool baths and dark incense. Iron on her cheek and the acid wind of a dead ocean littered with machines pouring over the concrete - that's how she wanted to wake each morning. It reminded her of the universe inside the Brittle Hag's ship - so close and yet forbidden. As long as they needed to watch out for Abby they couldn't risk entering the vessel, just in case another attack made it drop between realities and severed the link between the Time Scavenger and the others. She longed to walk through its bricolage labyrinth again, to see the empty landscapes unfolding one after the other, each vaster than the last. Once or twice she dreamed she was back inside, and when she woke to find herself still lying outside she almost cried in frustration.

On the fifth day after the giants' departure, just as the light began to fade from the mist above the ocean and the world turned purple with the onset of night, Crysanthe climbed to the next level of the Lattice. Part of her was curious to see where Abby went on her adventures, but she also wanted a break from the waking dreams that stole up on her in the shadow of the spaceship.

She'd soon realised that the structure rising for hundreds of miles into the airless night above the island was nothing more than a vast stack of shelves designed to store supplies for an entire people. Discarded ropes, tarpaulins, chains, empty barrels, pallets and tanks told her that the original inhabitants of the Great White World had stuffed the thousands of levels with food, elements, materials, minerals, engines and artefacts. When they'd left they'd taken most of it with them - to where God only knew. They would have needed a fleet of boats or flyers as big as the AntiHelix's to shift everything. All that remained were the remnants - the useless and the broken. Crysanthe wandered for an hour between stacks of wax cylinders, each as tall as herself, carved in music or words no-one would ever hear again. At last she came to the edge of the level and saw Abby sitting on one that had fallen over, staring north.

"I might be about to see him die," the woman said as she approached. "And I won't be able to do a thing to save him. I stand next to him in the Mind. Sometimes we hold hands, but it's a dream touch - empty. We could be arm in arm and some bastard in reality will shoot him or blow him up or stick a dagger in his guts and he'll pop like a soap bubble and that'll be that."

"The odds are on his side. They have the Machine Men. The giants can't harm him. The only danger is from the star-powered alien warriors. The God Talkers won't get in range of those."

"Max doesn't trust the Machine Men. The plan is for the Giants of the West to talk to their sisters in reality while we infiltrate the citadel in the Mind. We'll free Ragaleis and then confront the enemy. The odds will be in our favour but what can we do? We can't kill the bitches, we have to try and 'persuade' them to be nice." Abby made angry speech marks in the air with her fingers. "We're totally and utterly out of our tiny minds."

Empty reassurances meant nothing. After a few moments Crysanthe placed her hand on Abby's shoulder. The woman reached up but instead of pushing her away she rested her own fingers on top of Crysanthe's and they waited for the last of the day to disappear.

"I don't want to go back to the ship. If I jump into the Mind here will you stay and watch over me?"

Crysanthe didn't know how to react. She actually saw trust and friendship in the woman's eyes. Her face must have shown her confusion because Abby smiled and there was no sneer or malice or contempt behind it.

"Of course," answered Crysanthe.

A few seconds later Abby's chin slumped onto her chest. Crysanthe gently lowered her so that she lay on her back, and pillowed the woman's head under her own jacket. She sat cross-legged beside the God Talker and watched the lights under the sea grow brighter as the sky faded.

Once they'd put a good fifty leagues between themselves and the fortress, well away from the vanguard of the titans' unholy army, Ioam and Nem had a colossal row because they'd decided that one of them needed to stay behind to guard the ship, and they couldn't agree which of them it would be. To Max it was obviously Nem because she was mad, but the discussion degenerated into a bad-tempered game of rock-paper-scissors. Despite insisting on three re-matches Nem still lost. She took her disappointment out on the hull by kicking so many dents in it Max thought the ship was going to rupture. Finally she sat down on the floor and folded her arms, refusing to speak to anyone.

None of the Machine Men craft hailed them to ask what they were doing. That was odd, Theuderic and his servants were treating them as if they didn't exist. Since their conversation in the cube complex there'd been no further mention of Bassandis, even though Max had bust a gut dragging his soul across the body of God for two years. Fair enough if there was no longer the time or the technology to rebuild a body for him to take part in this end-game but even so. The Machine Men's indifference intensified his suspicion. The sooner they found Ragaleis and confronted Ombratulla, Belsalice and Ruth in the Mind the better. He wondered about Crysanthe's former lover. Surely of all people she would have wanted to stand on the battlements and gloat at their pitiful muster. He told Nem to prepare to flee if things turned nasty. She simply tossed her head.

"Might. Might not. Depends how I feel."

As soon as they materialised in Halinard's cabin Max saw Rebecca and Abby standing halfway between the vehicle and the entrance to the citadel, in the puddle of light cast by the girl's spear.

"It's safe to go out there?" asked Max. Dark shapes flopped, wriggled and strutted across the plain on all sides, though none of them showed the slightest interest in the wagon.

"Apparently," said Ioam.

"Nice of you to join us," said Abby when he stepped outside. She blew him a kiss like a lover saying goodbye through a tram window. "Hope you're having fun, because I'm bored out of my skull. Right now I'm lying on a concrete shelf in the arse-end of beyond with the charming Commander Death-fuck for company. So now what? Do we drive inside or walk it?"

"We need to scout first."

Max looked up and saw a shoal of moving shadows like giant black bedsheets rippling and flapping across the sky.

"You're absolutely sure they can't see us?"

"Yes," said Rebecca, sounding exactly like Abby's sister. The word carried the same silent *you cretin* at the end. Abby snorted.

"Won't they spot the wagon if we continue on foot? I'm guessing that light of yours has limited range."

"It won't matter. We'll be invisible going in and when we come back out Madam's magic sparkle cloud will cover the ironclad and drive any monsters away."

"Why do you keep calling me Madam? And what's a magic sparkle cloud?" asked Rebecca with the pointed suspicion of a child starting to realise the grownups were pulling her leg.

"Let's just have a look inside, shall we?" said Max.

They approached the entrance. Its sharp apex towered half a mile above them and a floor of dark metal stretched beyond it into the gloom. The wall was a quarter mile thick and on the other side they found themselves in a vault filled with shadows and slanting beams of pale red light that seemed to fall from nowhere. By their fitful radiance Max could just make out arches piled on arches, slender and impossible, interspersed with flights of stairs made for giants, with steps three hundred yards high. Some spiralled up into the sky, others ended at platforms or simple nothingness. It was difficult to gauge the layout of the citadel, everything was so far away and wreathed in a grainy twilight. There might have been rooms and chambers but it was hard to tell. Where were the sisters? Even now they'd be arguing with their siblings, but here there was only silence.

Abby cursed, and Max turned to see a figure moving towards them. His heart started to hammer so loudly he could have sworn the noise filled the castle. The twisted silhouette limped over the ground, dragging one clubbed hand behind it, the other scrabbling long nails against the plated ground to pull itself along. Instead of eyes it had a cluster of ragged holes at the top of its black, egg-shaped head. The worst thing about the apparition was the soldier's shako perched on top, indigo plumes nodding with each lurch. The monster looked in pain and stumbled once or twice. Nauseous pity replaced fear as it curved around them, hunching away from the light. They were indeed invisible to the giants' demons. Even if the servant sensed a presence it just flinched back like a slug from a burning match. They waited until it crept outside, giving the wagon a wide berth before heading off towards the distant mountains.

"What in God's name was that?" asked Abby.

"One of the watchers," said Rebecca. "They've been coming out of this castle since it appeared."

Max noticed that the nightmare had left a trail of black droplets like a leaky pen. They disappeared into the gloom.

"We follow that."

"Are you cracked in the head?"

"It's that or spend hours wandering round this random insanity," he gestured at the hall. "I reckon that'll lead us closer to the sisters and hopefully Ragaleis."

Abby shrugged assent. Max had seen enough. They'd take the ironclad as far as they could. Even if he was invisible he'd feel a lot safer with iron plating and armoured glass between him and the citadel's garrison.

They were just about to return when Abby stopped them.

"Listen."

At first he heard nothing beyond his own breathing. At length, out of the darkness, came the sound of a woman crying. It was so faint that it swept back and forth over the threshold of perception like waves on a beach, but there was no mistaking those sobs, and the loneliness and pain that filled them. They were infinitely more terrifying than the shadowed labyrinth and its nightmare inhabitants, simply because they sounded so ordinary.

"The sisters? Their monsters?" asked Abby.

Max shook his head.

"It's Ruth."

A metal flare on the edge of a cloud a few hundred yards below snapped Crysanthe out of her daydream. Tremors passed through the floor, followed by what sounded like a pile of rusty barrels tipping over.

A force hit her in the small of her back, pushing her over the concrete edge, but instead of falling miles to her death she found herself dangling from the underside of the level. Greasy matted fur covered her face and a thick band squeezed her waist. A few yards away two Abhumans hung from a network of girders by their claws. One had the still-unconscious Abby by the legs and the other cradled her head, its long talons over her mouth. *They're going to kill us at last,* was her first thought, and she tensed, ready to chance a lunge for the knife in her boot.

Sharp taps rang out on the level above their heads.

It sounded like a clockwork spider running with busy purpose across the concrete. The Abhumans pulled their captives back into the forest of rusting metal, scrunching up into the shadows. An upside-down head appeared silhouetted at the edge of the roof. It vanished and a few seconds later three humanoid shapes slid into view, clinging on all fours to the ceiling. They froze, looking this way and that as if playing scanners over the surroundings. As one they crept away from the Abhumans.

Machine Men.

There was no time to wonder how the creatures had found the island. Despite all the scrap clouding their radar it wouldn't take them long to track their quarry down. Half a dozen tactical routines clicked through Crysanthe's head and she mapped them onto her surroundings - but she was trapped in the Abhumans' grip and if she struggled she'd risk alerting their stalkers.

A rapid skittering echoed across the ceiling as three pale outlines hurtled towards them. Crysanthe tried to jack-knife free to grab her dagger but before she had a chance to move the Machine Men ran past upside down and threw themselves into space. Almost immediately the Abhumans dropped to the next floor and carried their captives to the edge. Half a dozen levels below, the Brittle Hag's ship sped away over the sea, tiny figures clinging to its roof. A massive crossbow quarrel fashioned out of silver metal shot out from the Lattice and set off in pursuit, trailing black smoke.

The Abhumans didn't waste time. Even as their spacecraft disappeared vertically into the clouds they raced down through the structure. There was no point trying to struggle. The creatures ran much faster than she could, leaping up and swinging over piles of abandoned crates and barrels without breaking stride. Three carried Abby, and they held her as tenderly as a baby. Crysanthe realised they were heading for the metal road that led back to the villa - a stupid move, if the Machine Men were here in force that's exactly where they'd search.

As they came in sight of the buggies, queued one after the other like cars on a fairground ride, another half dozen Abhumans appeared running alongside their left flank, wielding metal rods, spanners and crowbars. They immediately swarmed two Machine Men who stood next to the vehicles, bundling them over the edge of the platform in writhing heaps of fur. She doubted the creatures would prevail against the sentries but they bought them enough time for her captors to cram her and themselves under a bubble canopy. They hurtled forwards and behind them the second car followed in close pursuit, Abby still held like an infant in grey furred claws. A single figure jumped back onto the road and chased after them but gangling shapes cannoned into it and carried it over the side once more. Then they were racing between the trees.

Crysanthe spotted a craft on the beach - this a teardrop lozenge of pale blue metal. At least it looked as if it was only a small party, not a full-blown army. Sure enough she saw three silver humanoids lope out of the shadows onto the sand, trotting up to join another pair. Once they'd got over their surprise the Machine Men would have no problem against the Abhumans. Max had told her that one could defeat a Black Rose. But were they here to kill or to capture? It didn't matter - Abby was clearly their target and she'd do all she could to keep them apart. She'd no doubt that Selva was on the Brittle Hag's ship and that once they'd shaken off their pursuer she'd come back to pick them up.

"We mustn't go back to the villa," she said, trying to click out her words and hoping they were understandable.

"We're not," answered the nearest Abhuman, and on

that cue the car juddered to a stop. After a quick nod between the crews of the two vehicles Crysanthe found herself picked up again before they all fell in a bundle into the trees, leaping through the branches, heading away from the track at ninety degrees.

A few moments later they emerged on the southern side of the island. Ahead a balcony sat at the end of a long passageway extending from the base of the main palace. As the creatures headed towards it a tiny black disc dropped out of the clouds far to Crysanthe's right and moved to intercept them. The Abhumans swung up the outer wall, using the countless gaps and crevices ages-worn into the white stone. They emerged on top of the parapet and she saw a long table with two couches. Three miles above her head an awning extended out on metal arms forged to carry the weight of millions of tons of canvas and wood.

We're bugs running through someone's home.

They leaped onto the table and charged past plates, cups and a book fifty yards thick and five hundred yards long. The Brittle Hag's ship drifted across the surface in a slow arc, and settled down between a cup and a bowl as big as a temple.

The ramp clanged down and Selva appeared at the head of another dozen Abhumans. The creature holding Crysanthe let go as the Companion tossed her an automatic rifle. She dropped into a forward roll, coming up in reverse stance just in time to snatch the gun out of the air, jam it against her shoulder and draw a bead on the wave of Machine Men swarming over the edge of the table. She counted thirty.

In a second Selva stood beside her and they were falling back, aiming so that the explosive bullets blew apart their pursuers' heads. They worked as one, Crysanthe always taking the closest out while Selva went for the next in line. Some of the decapitated figures kept running forwards, so they started to aim for the hip, blowing thighs to pieces in clouds of paper and clockwork. Even with legs missing the attackers came on, crawling over the cracked marble like frantic spiders. The Abhumans scuttled past on both sides and threw themselves into the advancing foe. The assault faltered for a moment and she saw slender arcing blades erupt from the Machine Men's arms and torsos. Blood the colour of crude oil stained the air. Crysanthe's heels hit the bottom of the ramp and as they stepped onto it, still firing, the ship lurched upwards. They turned and ran. A rapid series of thuds behind them echoed down the passageway.

"They're in the ship," shouted Selva. Their only chance was to try to lose the creatures in the labyrinth, but the internal configuration had changed since the general last walked its iron and wooden mysteries. She couldn't stop to get her bearings - all they could do was sprint down tunnels, hoping they'd shake off their pursuers without careening into a dead end. She remembered how quickly the Machine Man had run after the buggies - much faster than a human. Any second now they'd have to turn and stand their ground.

Abhumans yanked them sideways through a gap in the wall, and she was falling down a shaft that dwindled into an infinite point far below. Before she had a chance to cry out more arms pulled her into yet another opening - up, left and she dropped again, looking up at a cluster of chains that dangled down from the darkness, lit by dusty shafts of light spearing across the vault from countless other openings. Selva fell towards her, spread-eagled and mouth open.

At the last second the Abhumans set them upright on a metal plate projecting from the wall. Around them the shaft bellied out above an immense gulf. Crysanthe glanced over the edge to see what looked like a city map etched in iron and copper. Clouds drifted between them and the landscape far below. Were those buildings, roads and plazas laid out in mathematical rows? *Does something live there? Do they realise where they are?*

"They'll have taken Abby to the Abhuman camp. We've got to get there before the Machine Men," said Selva. The creatures who'd saved them frantically scratched diagrams on the iron floor with their talons. Crysanthe didn't know if they were working out the direction or trying to change the configuration of the ship. One pointed at the diagram and nodded to the other. Before either women could say anything they were snatched from the platform. The Abhumans swung under the roof of the world-encompassing void for a hundred yards before flipping themselves and their cargo up into a corridor that rose gently up into the misty distance. As they ran Crysanthe heard a clanging far behind and turned to spot two silver figures at the mouth of the tunnel. Abhuman claws yanked her sideways into yet another labyrinth.

The universe became an endless lung-searing race through a storm of corridors, rooms, halls, parapets, dusty light and nightmare darkness. For ages it seemed they ran alone through this alien realm, but then they'd look behind and see pale figures leaping from platform to platform or racing after them upside down over cracked and sagging ceilings. The pursuit probably lasted less than ten minutes, but Crysanthe was long used to the effect of fear, adrenaline and blood-lust on time.

At last they came to the Abhuman camp. Their guides sounded the alarm, and the creatures began to stream away from the settlement, heading further into the ship, some carrying infants and the ill and elderly on their shoulders. Crysanthe spotted Neke scampering into the hall of maps. She chased after him to find the entire lead floor covered in grey seething fur. A thousand needles glittered in the claws as the mob scratched and hacked at the metal. It was like the noise of a million fingernails on the universe's biggest and most badly tuned blackboard. *What in God's name are you playing at?*

Goma's head popped up from the scrum ten yards away. He jumped up and ran across the backs of his colleagues, clicking his claws furiously.

"Queen Abby has been taken further into the ship. You must follow."

"What are you doing? Leave this - we have to stand and fight or run."

To her astonishment he dived back into the writhing mass. *They'll be slaughtered.*

There wasn't time. She ran outside with Selva to see a dozen humanoids loping towards them across the plateau. Her lover was out of ammo so she drew her long knives. Crysanthe took down one with a couple of bursts but then she too was left with only a knife.

"I love you," she called.

"Shut up and fight."

She'd always planned that she would meet the very end at full throttle, screaming the legacy of a thousand years of the Uellas as she charged down her death with whatever final weapon fate had given her. She howled out her fury at the cold universe and sprinted towards the nearest Machine Man. Selva shrieked some infernal curse at her side and as Crysanthe locked her gaze on the paper circle eyes of the enemy reality ended.

A box of nothing fell out of the sky around the settlement, its walls guillotining into the plateau. Gravity vanished and Crysanthe's momentum sent her into a forward somersault. She bumped against something soft, pulling a cloud of glittering motes after her as she recoiled. The front half of a Machine Man torso, face still attached, rotated opposite her in a bizarre reflection. She turned, and another head drifted upwards, trailing sparkling innards. Twisting round, she watched the entire hall of maps rise like a partly inflated hot air balloon, Abhumans tumbling slowly out of the bottom. She looked up and gasped. The entire ship lay spread out above her across a million universes like an exquisitely empty patchwork stencil. It looked so familiar. *My God, it's a map of my own thoughts.* Then her weight returned, and she landed on her back with a thud that drove the breath out of her lungs. The total, final silence of a dead creation settled on her and it felt so beautiful.

Selva pulled her to her feet.

"It worked. We're safe."

Pieces of Machine Men littered the ground. Whatever forces had rearranged the vessel beyond the box had also torn them apart and scattered the remaining shreds over half a mile of cracked metal flooring. They limped back to the hall of maps, its walls and roof skewed at an odd angle but otherwise intact. Inside, the Abhumans stood in a line around the edge of the lead sheet, staring down at its surface. Crysanthe managed to click "What's the matter? Where are we?" at the nearest one. It ignored her.

"Crys, the map."

She looked down at the vast surface. It was completely smooth. All the intricate diagrams, equations, curlicues and embellishments that charted the impossible landscapes of the Brittle Hag's ship had vanished.

CHAPTER TWENTY

"Why's Ruth crying?" asked Max after they'd clambered back into the tank.

"Who cares?" shrugged Abby. "If she's a bit miserable it serves her right for being such a treacherous shit."

"Can we turn it to our advantage?" said Ioam.

He doubted it. To be honest he agreed with his partner. He'd had enough experience with Alaric's daughter, and heard enough from Crysanthe, to know she was a lost cause. Even so, he couldn't get the desperate anguish in those lonely sobs out of his mind. He told Halinard to follow the trail left by the watcher.

They passed more creatures - oily tatters that shuffled, limped, flapped and stalked along the same path taken by the first. His gut tightened like an over-wound watch each time one approached the ironclad, but they all winced away as Rebecca's power made them blind and fearful. The trail entered a corridor that switched back and forth as it descended.

"Are you sure this is the right direction?" asked Ioam eventually. "I thought we were looking for Ragaleis and his sisters."

Bassandis stood next to Halinard, peering through the thick bottle-glass window.

"He's this way," he murmured at last. "I sense my brother."

"Can you communicate with him?"

"No I can't, it's more like a silhouette in my mind, growing sharper. But it doesn't move or speak."

Another shadow tripped past. This one appeared a lot jauntier than the others. Max caught a glimpse of coat tails and a top hat amid the brittle limbs and sharp claws. He looked at Rebecca. She still wore that infuriating *so what?* expression in all its magnificent adolescent glory. At this point any self-respecting father would have a conversation along the lines of *you realise this is important so are you absolutely convinced you know what you're doing? You can tell me if you don't and I won't be angry.* He also knew exactly the response any self-respecting father would get from daughter and mother, so he kept his peace. The girl was their only chance anyway, so why bother fretting over teenage delusions of invincibility?

He noticed a mist hanging in the air but instead of eddying back and forth it stayed perfectly still, like finely grained soot suspended in jelly. As the wagon descended it parted to either side, offering no resistance.

"Any ideas?"

"This is the raw stuff God's dream world is fashioned from," said Ioam. "Pure undifferentiated being."

"It looks like that crap that used to come out of the factories on the south side of the Brick River in Metacarpi," said Abby. "That filthy smog hung around for days in the poor quarters. Remember?" she glanced at Max. "No you wouldn't, you lived in your mansion on top of daddy's tower where the air was always fresh."

"OK. Now what?" asked Halinard, bringing the tank to a stop in front of a wall. It stretched endlessly into the gloom on either side, doors piercing its dull surface every ten yards. None were big enough for the wagon. As Max studied the barrier in dismay another lurching shadow emerged from one of the gaps and disappeared up the ramp.

"You're sure Ragaleis is beyond that?" he asked.

Bassandis nodded.

"Looks like we walk," said Abby.

The five of them stepped out of the tank into the gritty fog. Max waved his hand through it - the soot shivered with the passage of his fingers. He insisted on going first with Abby beside him. Ioam came next, Rebecca behind her, holding the burning spear, and Halinard taking up the rear like a vagabond trailing after a family outing in the hope of cadging food.

They stepped through one of the doors and found themselves standing on a narrow causeway that stretched ahead into darkness. Black oceans of mist filled the void on either side. Max looked behind him but couldn't see the doorway they'd entered through.

"What do we do if we meet one of those monsters coming in the opposite direction?" asked Abby.

"Push the bugger over the side," said Ioam.

Max swore under his breath at the thought of being the party's snow plough but he strode on ahead. Surely the soot would be getting in his eyes and on his skin by now, but he didn't feel anything and when he glanced at his hands they were clean. *Primordial essence. How can Ragaleis exist down here without dissolving?* He looked back at Bassandis, but the titan was as composed and purposeful as before, his head and torso shining in the glow of Rebecca's force field.

"What's that?" asked Abby. He hadn't been paying attention. A faint radiance appeared far ahead. As they approached he saw a cube roughly ten yards on all sides, with square windows set in the middle of each face. Sourceless white light flooded the interior of the stone cage, making the inner surfaces shine like annealed jewellery. A shadow sat at a table, forearms resting on wood cracked and bleached by the fierce glare. Its hands worked over each other with the steady kneading rhythm of a potter at a wheel.

"Brother," whispered Bassandis.

Max found a door in the side of the cube and entered, dreading what he'd find. Instead of the young man with the white hair and black suit who'd introduced him to the world of the giants in a dream in the Wasteland north of Metacarpi, he saw a lumpen, misshapen creature, its outline bleeding into the surrounding mist. The face, shadowed and tragic, had the gravity-drawn features of a stroke victim. Soot coated the skin. Bassandis and the other God Talkers crowded into the cell.

"Ragaleis," said Max.

The giant lifted up his fists to show the chains hanging from his wrists.

"You didn't help me. Why didn't you help me?"

"Your sisters were too strong."

Ragaleis dropped his hands and started to work at a lump of darkness, rolling and kneading it. As Max struggled to think of what to say the titan leaned closer to his task, oblivious to his visitors. Perhaps he thought he'd imagined them. Max looked to Bassandis, wondering why he didn't speak either, but he was peering at his brother with intense concentration, as if he could see right inside the prisoner's head and was trying to make sense of what he found.

Abby swore and Max turned round to see Ragaleis lift his hands from a figure standing in the middle of the table top. It was hunched and hooded with taloned hands. *He's made a model of a watcher.* But even as realisation popped into his head the maquette crawled across the surface, growing larger as it dragged itself along so that by the time it fell onto the floor with a wet plop it was as big as a cat. It hauled itself over the sill of the window facing the causeway and headed for the distant wall. When it finally vanished into the darkness it was as tall as Ioam.

"He's making them," said the witch. Max swore he heard admiration in her voice. Ragaleis batted at the air with his hands, swiping fistfuls of soot down onto the table where they formed another lump of nightmare dough.

"Enough," said Bassandis. "Rebecca?"

The girl reached across, took each of the chains in her fists and yanked them apart. Abby gave Max a proud wink. Bassandis held his brother's hands in his own. Ragaleis lifted his head ever so slowly and stared into the other titan's face.

"Bassandis? You died. I carried your body through the burning city."

He turned to Max and at last there was a flare of intelligence in those agonised eyes.

"I was right. They hid him in your thoughts. You did it Max, well done."

His chin dropped in exhaustion.

"What happened, brother?" asked Bassandis.

"I went in search of our sisters and found them in the Hair, filled with hatred. They overpowered me in the real world and in here, putting me into an enchanted sleep. I woke up in this prison, deep inside the id of God. I've no idea where my body is in reality - try as I might I can't return to it. They promised to give it back to me if I made these figures. I don't know how many I've fashioned out of this filthy air. Hundreds? Thousands? They frighten me, but still I must craft them."

"Because they thought I was dead, our sisters decided to reawaken God as the enemy of humanity," Ragaleis told him. "We're divided against each other - Ombratulla, Belsalice, Toldi and Ruth on one side and Mephyrean, Vinduranto and Sorameistre and myself on the other."

"Who's Ruth?"

"A total and utter…" Abby started. Max held up his hand.

"A human who was fashioned into a new giant using technologies and powers from the distant past," he explained.

"She took my body," said Ragaleis. He seemed more awake as if the energy of the next universe was passing from his brother into him. "I sensed another consciousness at the edge of mine, a giant but malformed."

"That's her. They used you as a template."

"If we take him back to my garden he'll be healed like Bassandis," said Rebecca from the doorway.

"There's no time," answered Ioam without looking round. Max saw the girl stick her tongue out at the back of the witch's head.

"The rest of the giants are meeting now, in the citadel," he said to Bassandis. "We need to get you two up there so that Ombratulla and Belsalice can see that you're alive and whole, and not the wretched fragment they think you are."

"Are you able to walk?" asked Bassandis. Ragaleis pushed himself into a standing position. He looked unsteady, but had enough energy to heave at the table with trembling hands, tipping it over with a crash. Bassandis put a hand on his arm.

"We must persuade, not fight. Their anger has to be tempered by our love of man."

Ragaleis nodded.

They made their way back along the causeway and through the doors to the wagon. In their absence no creatures had noticed the tank. They climbed aboard and Halinard drove them back up the ramp. Bassandis and Rebecca sat either side of Ragaleis, holding his hands, and Max could have sworn the titan returned to life moment by moment. The wagon emerged into the hall to find it swarming with watchers, an army of nightmares that stumbled and twitched in an endless chaos of motion. As it rolled forward they parted on either side.

"They realise something's up," said Abby at Max's side. "They sense we're coming to the grand finale. If we get through this there's a hell of a play to write."

"We need to find the giants next, they're somewhere in here. Maybe these buggers'll give us a clue."

Abby didn't reply so he glanced at her. That was odd. She looked frozen, as if she'd seen something. He followed her gaze but spotted nothing among the crowds.

"What is it?"

Still she didn't speak and with a lurch of fear he realised he could see the outlines of the bulkhead ever so faintly through her face. He looked across at Rebecca. Bassandis leaned across Ragaleis and spoke to her, reaching out to touch her arm. His hand went straight through the girl.

"Abby!" Max grabbed at his lover but his hands smacked together somewhere in the middle of her torso. She was just a fading image now, a three-dimensional shadow drifting into oblivion. She turned red, as if someone had stuck a dim bulb inside her.

"What's happening?" he shouted in desperation. Ioam strode over and pushed her head inside the ghost, looking around as if she could somehow spot an explanation written on the inside of Abby's skin.

"Interesting."

Max stared at the last remnant of his partner as it flickered out of existence. He looked across at Ragaleis and Bassandis. The seat next to them was empty.

"Ladies and gents, we have a problem," said Halinard. Beyond the window every watcher had turned to stare at the wagon.

"What happens if a God Talker dies? They just vanish from the Mind, right? They don't fade away like that." He tried to batter down the cold, sick emptiness that rose up through him like a dead flood.

"I don't know," said Ioam.

"The Machine Men will," said Max. He made to clap his hands so he could jump back into reality.

"Max, no!" said Bassandis. "There's no time. We have to confront the sisters now."

"If they're dead, they're dead," said Halinard. "The Isle Resplendent is days away."

"Red shift ghosts."

Everyone looked at Ioam.

"They froze, turned red and faded." She fluttered her long fingers in the air. "That's what we'd see if the Brittle Hag's spacecraft went faster than light. The hairy scamps have shifted."

"Why was Abby inside the ship? Everyone agreed to stay outside because of the attacks," said Max.

Why couldn't the infuriating idiot do as she was told? Half of him was desperate to believe Ioam's explanation, the rest cursed his lover to the skies. Rebecca's second spear stood propped against the bulkhead. He picked it up but it just felt like a metal rod. Banging it against the floor made the room ring, but nothing happened.

"I hate to interrupt," Halinard looked up from rolling a cigarette and nodded at the window. "They're not happy."

The last time God's nightmares had surrounded the tank they'd contented themselves with roiling and gibbering in a circle like dancers round the carcass of a dead enemy. Now they pressed up against the hull and the bottom half of the glass was full of smeared faces, blank eyes and slack mouths.

"We're going to have to jump out anyway. Those buggers won't let us through," said Ioam.

Bassandis walked over to Max and took his hands. The giant's fingers were burning sticks - dry metal pulled out of a furnace.

"Max, we have to finish what we came here for."

Stone duty. Max gathered up all his fear and sorrow and ground it down into a diamond point of hatred. He hefted his daughter's spear, hoping that as long as he could feel it in his grasp she and her mother still lived. Bassandis strode to the outer bulkhead door, span the wheel and stepped outside.

The army of nightmares drew back. From the ladder Max spotted dolls with diseased faces and dog eyes, tall shadows with top hats and tails and long curving claws, obscene insects crafted out of tarnished lead. He jumped down and turned to help Ragaleis descend. The two brothers moved forward, and to Max's astonishment the watchers cowered in fear. *They recognise their maker.*

"I am Bassandis, Giant of the East. Guide us to my sisters."

A path opened up in the crowd, snaking towards a vast flight of stairs. In ten steps the titans had grown to full size, reaching down to pick up the God Talkers. Max and Halinard stood on Ragaleis's palm - it shook alarmingly as the giant struggled through his lingering weakness. They rose up into the vault, leaving the sea of monsters nipping and leaping helplessly at the bottom of the first step. The wagon was nothing more than a brass dot far below in a seething shadow ocean.

At length they came to a corridor. Ragaleis and Bassandis set their passengers down and shrank back to human size. Together they walked towards an arch that opened onto a garden filled with black flowers and trees. A crystal dome arched miles above, and beyond it the coals of the Mind's sky hissed and spat. *If only Abby was here to see this.* More urgently, he knew that in Rebecca they'd lost their trump card.

On a lawn by a dead fountain Ombratulla, Belsalice, Toldi and Ruth waited opposite the Giants of the West, also human sized. Max noticed that the three guests huddled together. They seemed frightened, although Sorameistre stood defiantly at the front of their little group. Were they actually scared of their sisters? Ombratulla turned, and at the sight of Bassandis alarm flickered in her face. She masked it well, favouring the newcomers with a condescending smile of pleasant evil.

"Welcome. We've hit a slight impasse. New points of view, no matter how jejune, will no doubt shake the blockage free."

Max ignored the sneer. He stared at Ruth. She was almost doubled over, one hand on her stomach, the other on the back of a chair as she struggled to support herself. Her dress, fashioned by a thousand insane tailors in the manufactory, was elegant, but her hair fell in a lank curtain over her face. He caught a glimpse of mad, pain-filled eyes and her whole body shook.

Bassandis and Ragaleis approached their brother and sisters of the west, standing among them before Belsalice and Ombratulla. It was impossible to read the expressions of the rebels. For all their contempt and professed indifference, Max sensed the conflict in their artificial souls. The one they'd assumed was dead had returned, not as a wretched crippled echo of what he once was, but reborn and more powerful than any of them. What possible justification did they have now for their revenge?

"Why are you doing this?" asked Bassandis. "Why have my sisters chosen to fight against humanity?"

"Because they imprisoned you, drove you mad and killed you," answered Ruth, her voice a desperate croak, filled with sick loathing. Max saw Belsalice wince at the sound. Bassandis opened his arms.

"And yet here I am. Whole, complete."

He pointed to Max.

"Because of this man I was saved and now I'm filled with the energies of a new universe. Is that not a reason to rejoice in kindness and redemption?"

"You told me he'd been betrayed and destroyed by man, and that nothing remained but a worthless shadow," said Toldi. "You lied."

"They didn't know," said Max. "They assumed. Filled with hate by this woman," he gestured at Ruth. "They thought they saw her viciousness in all mankind."

"You are monsters," answered Ombratulla. "Vile things that murder, rape, cheat, massacre thousands and visit destruction on whole cities."

"So what are you? We made you." snapped Ioam.

This was in danger of turning into a tit-for-tat squabble. Somehow Max and the other God Talkers had to persuade the giants to unite and form the Mind. *It'll just happen when everyone agrees, said Theuderic.* He totted up the odds. Ombratulla and Belsalice were outnumbered, could they be forced? God, if only Abby and Rebecca were here. He noticed with a shock that Ruth stood closer. Was she planning on jumping him? In her state she could barely stand. So much for being reborn as a pure giant. She appeared worse than the gaunt cadaver standing on the roof of the manufactory. At least then she'd been filled with hope. Now she looked as if all she wanted to do was die.

A movement at the other end of the garden and Max spotted half a dozen silver statues walking towards them, their skin a fine mesh through which he saw flickering lights. Eyes a sharp white-blue cast rays across the paths and hedges. In the centre strode one larger than all the rest - a noble figure with a beard of carved gold. Max guessed it was Theuderic's dream self, full of soulless self-importance.

"What are they playing at?" muttered Halinard.

"Lord Theuderic," said Ombratulla. "This is turning into quite the event. I don't recall inviting you or your fellows into our citadel. Must we repeat a few lessons?"

"Giants of the Mind," announced the King of the Machine Men. "It's time to join with each other."

Belsalice gave the patient sigh of someone dealing with a senile relative four sentences behind everyone else.

"We were having that conversation already. Everyone's making pretty speeches about how wonderful humanity is, and how we must rescue these poor fragile beings, and so on and so forth. I hate man, as does my sister, as does…" she waved a dismissive hand at Ruth. Max heard a painful intake of breath at the insult, followed by an agonised whimper.

"Know this," she continued. "All of you un-Giants. God is not going to save you. Your fate is to perish in the last eternal night. If and when we choose to become the deity we will walk through the God Door empty and alone."

"And you?" asked Theuderic, turning to Toldi. "Are you filled with hate?"

The giant looked down at his hands, cocking his head to one side as if listening to a voice in his brain.

"Yes," he said at last.

"And you? Do you feel hate?" said the Lord of the Machine Men to Mephyrean.

"I don't know. How am I supposed to tell?"

Hate? - Ihanna's last warning to Max. He suddenly felt very afraid. The whole universe was about to flip upside down, and everything he'd known and fought for would whirl away in an insane chaos of lies.

"What's going on? Why's he asking them all if they

hate us?" whispered Ioam as the bright statue spoke to each of the other titans in turn. Only Bassandis and Sorameistre gave a firm *no.*

"Help me."

The voice was at his elbow and he almost jerked back from the twisted creature that once was Ruth.

"I can't bear it. The pain, the thoughts - they're all too big. Help me Max, I beg you."

The penny dropped. No matter how much she'd kidded herself that she belonged in this world, among these titans, this realm and her new body were pure torture. She'd trapped herself with no way out. How easy would it be to turn her back into a human? If nothing else it'd remove her baleful influence from the discussion.

"Come, my brothers and sisters," Bassandis said. "It's time at last. We can bring God to life and save humanity. It's our stone duty."

The sound of his father's phrase dropping out of the titan's mouth snapped Max to attention.

"We will form the mind of the deity," answered Belsalice. "But we have no intention of saving man. His time has gone."

"Man is worthless," agreed Theuderic. "We will share a perfect future untainted by his ambition and greed. It's the vision we implanted in you when we made you. It was our gift."

And so reality inverted. Max could almost have laughed out loud, but an overwhelming silence deeper than he had ever known settled on the garden as the universe froze into yet another treacherous tableau. Theuderic's words sank into his mind. *Hate. This is what Ihanna meant. 'It was our gift.' The Machine Men programmed the titans to despise mankind so only they and their metal creators would be saved. That's why they loathe us so much. They were designed to hate us.*

CHAPTER TWENTY-ONE

"Where are we?"

"We don't know."

"Where's the ship?"

"We don't know."

"Are we safe?"

No answer. The Abhumans continued to stare at the blank map. At first Crysanthe thought they'd just been stricken dumb with fear, but then she noticed their eyes flickering back and forth as they traced invisible lines across the erased chart. *They're looking for something.* A few of them fell to their hands and knees and started to crawl over the floor, faces a mere inch away from the surface. More joined in and soon they were all moving hither and thither, patting at the metal with their claws or scrutinising flaws and blemishes from countless angles. There was nothing she could do to help so she stepped outside with Selva.

The refugees who'd flown into the depths of the ship came back, creeping tentatively into the settlement. As far as she could tell the surroundings hadn't changed that much - the ramshackle town still sat on a plateau, but clearly they saw things in the misty distance that hadn't been there before, and they cowered in wonder.

Abby raced towards them.

"I have to get back into the Mind. Max is surrounded

by monsters and the dozy bastard needs my help."

She was masking her fear well, but there was no mistaking the desperation in her voice.

"They jumped the ship to escape the Machine Men and now they say they don't know where we are," Crysanthe told her.

"Rebecca won't talk to me. I've begged her to take me back but I can't contact her. Knock me out."

"What?"

"Are you fucking deaf or what? Hit me, knock me out. If I fall unconscious I can re-enter the Mind."

Selva stepped up behind and jammed her knuckle under Abby's ear. The woman folded and Crysanthe caught her as she dropped.

"Surrounded by monsters?" she asked.

"The jump severed the connection between Abby's child and God's soul. She was cloaking them from Ombratulla and Belsalice's creatures. If she's no longer there they're exposed, but God Talkers can't be harmed, right?"

"They can be imprisoned or driven mad."

"Why hasn't the link been re-established?" asked the Companion. "If the ship's back in reality then what's stopping Rebecca returning to help her father?"

"If we've returned to reality. Or perhaps we have, but are too far away. The Abhumans won't have been so stupid as to drop us right back among our enemies."

They left Abby and returned to the hall. After ten minutes picking their way through the carpet of searching Abhumans they located Neke and Hama and hauled them out. Crysanthe put on her best tyrant face and Selva fiddled with the handles of her short swords. That seemed to do the trick.

"The map shows our location inside the universe of this vessel," explained Hama. Neke stood beside him, claws crossed over his barrel chest, occasionally grunting or snorting as his friend said more than he should. "It's a chart, a scanner and a navigation tool in one. We shifted our houses out of danger but went too far. Therefore the sheet is blank."

"So we're lost inside the ship and need to find our way back to the middle," said Selva.

The Abhumans swapped glances.

"And?" asked Crysanthe, taking a step closer to Hama. He scratched the top of his bread loaf head.

"We moved the ship as well, so the Machine Men couldn't come after us. But something hooked onto it and dragged it far away. Not only has the settlement shifted, but the spacecraft as well."

"So we're no longer on the Isle Resplendent?"

Four liquid black eyes stared into hers.

"The ship is no longer anywhere near the Body of God. We're somewhere in deep space."

"How far?"

"A few light years. Maybe more."

"A few light years?"

"Perhaps less," clicked Hama with chirpy desperation.

"That'd explain why Rebecca can't re-enter the mind," said Selva. "I doubt the link would work across that distance."

"Wake her up."

Selva hit Abby hard between the breasts with the flat of her hand. The Time Scavenger jack-knifed into a sitting position, sucking in air like a diver emerging from the sea.

"Nothing. Just shit dreams." She looked away, struggling with fearful tears. "Why won't she talk to me?"

Crysanthe repeated Hama's explanation. Abby wiped her face with her hand and kicked at the ground. She kept eyeing the Abhumans and Crysanthe got ready to intervene just in case she decided to go for one.

"The first thing we have to do is relocate the middle of the ship. Once we're back in the control centre we'll understand where we are."

Abby nodded. Crysanthe had to admire her resilience. The general understood all too well what it was like to be sundered from a lover who was caretaker for all desires and hopes.

"What about the Machine Men?" asked Selva.

Crysanthe turned to Hama and Neke.

"Did we eliminate all the invaders when we jumped?"

"If the ship shifted with Machine Men on board some are probably still here, looking for Queen Abby," said Hama.

"And we didn't have time to seal the ship," added Neke, no doubt thinking he was being helpful. "The central section in the old universe is open to the vacuum."

The Abhumans nodded furiously.

"So all this air's going to vent into space?" said Selva.

"Oh that's not a problem," clicked Hama. He waved at their surroundings with a black taloned hand. "This is infinite. We'll always be able to breathe."

"So how long till you locate the middle?" asked Abby.

"The invaders with their harpoons have tried to enter our universe seven times."

Despite herself Crysanthe felt her mouth drop open.

"Each time they leave a dead zone that never changes position, so they're our beacons," continued Hama. "As soon as we find them we can map our way back."

"So what are we waiting for?" asked Abby.

In the end it took three days for the Abhumans to locate the first dead zone. For seventy-two hours Abby paced in widening circles around the settlement, occasionally heading off down one of the corridors that had re-appeared in their new pocket of space-time. Crysanthe fought the temptation to go with her and ensure she kept out of trouble. To her surprise she found herself sympathising with Abby's pent-up anguish, and cursing her own inability to help. The scavenger clearly wanted to be left alone. But there was another reason for the general to stay in the camp. The infinite spaces of the Brittle Hag's ship called to her with an ever-fiercer insistence. As Max's plan looked increasingly fragile, the urge to run away forever into the wood and iron silences came upon her stronger and more often. She knew that Selva sensed it. The girl stayed close to her, maybe fearing she was going to disappear, and at night their passion had a clinging urgency as if the Companion sought to entwine the pair of them in an unbreakable knot.

So the general had the shock of her life when she woke in the early hours of the third morning, weighed down by Selva's arm and leg, to find Abby standing next to the bed, naked. The lamplight shone through that ridiculous hair, turning it into an immense ginger halo. She was too stunned to say anything.

"I'm lonely and it's freezing. Budge up."

Before Crysanthe had a chance to respond the woman slipped into bed beside her, rolled over to face the wall and jammed a cold bottom into her groin.

"Now wait a minute..." Crysanthe started.

Abby rested her cheek on the general's left bicep, grabbed behind and pulled the other arm around her for a cuddle. Crysanthe stared at the back of her head. *I'm holding her tit in my hand.* Selva appeared at the periphery of her vision, leaning over from the other side of the bed and wearing a foot-wide grin. She winked, licked her fingertips and reached for Abby.

"If either of you try to poke your fingers up my cunt I'll break them off," the woman mumbled without turning round. Five minutes later she was snoring and Crysanthe had lost all feeling in her left arm.

In the morning she found herself on the floor in a tangle of sheets. Selva had disappeared and Abby was star-fished across the entire bed, mouth open. She found the Companion running through the Spear Tip Dance in the courtyard outside. She stopped when Crysanthe emerged.

"How was it for you?"

"Shut up."

Crysanthe bent over to finish lacing up her boots.

"We just slept with Abby Fabrice," Selva couldn't resist adding.

"Nothing happened."

"Of course not."

"Nothing happened!"

"OK!"

"She pushed us onto the floor after ten minutes. It hardly qualifies."

"So much for comfort. You talk in your sleep," said Abby, emerging into the light. "You don't," she added to Selva. Crysanthe watched her pad across to her own quarters on the other side of the plaza.

She didn't reappear the next night and in the morning half a dozen Abhumans boiled into the room and dragged them to the map. In one corner a crowd jostled and squeezed around three others who once more etched patterns in the metal. Crysanthe saw a circle no bigger than her little fingernail, surrounded by lines and spirals.

"How far?"

"Three hundred miles from here," clicked Neke. He pointed at the wall. "That direction."

"Three hundred miles?" asked Abby, aghast. "Without transport that's a two-week trek."

"And it's only the first dead zone," added Selva. "We don't know the distance betweeen them, or how close this one is to the centre of the ship."

"We could be a months away."

And even then they'd no idea where the Brittle Hag's ship was. They could arrive at the bridge only to find themselves drifting in the void light years from anywhere.

"There is a way of moving faster," said Hama, who was on his knees working at a particularly intricate fractal. That set off a full blown argument between him and Neke, which spread out like pond ripples through the crowd until they were all at it, waving arms, snapping jaws and clicking fingers like a demented chorus line. Half the group thought the other half were incompetent mathematicians and clearly insane. Despite her limited grasp of their vocabulary Crysanthe recognised the frequent use of 'moron', 'coward' and 'intellectually bankrupt'. Abby pulled out her revolver and fired a bullet into the ceiling. Everyone froze.

"And the plan is?" she asked.

"We jump the town, here," said Hama, pointing at the circle at the edge of the map. "Then we send out search parties to scout the surroundings until we find the next breach - and jump again."

"Hama and his friends lack rigour, and their proofs are fatuous," declared Neke, arms folded and rectangular head angled upwards in contempt.

"So we use the dead zones as stepping stones," said Crysanthe.

"What's the problem?" Abby asked Neke. With the grandfather of all impatient sighs he unfurled his claws and pointed at the etching.

"Every time we jump we'll be like a fish sticking our head above the surface ready for the anglers and their harpoons. At worst they'll get a foothold, at best they'll try and fail but create new dead zones in the process, thus confusing this map."

"Neke is fearful. He is a baby who sees a rope in a dark room and imagines a snake," said Hama. Neke clicked a rhythm laced with obscenities.

"We take the risk," decided Crysanthe. Abby shot her a disarming look of gratitude. "Our first priority is to get back to help Max and the others. I'm not wasting days. If your invaders want to come, let them come."

The first shift came half an hour later. There was no point wasting time watching the Abhumans engaged in a bunch of calculations she couldn't understand so Crysanthe went outside with Selva. Abby trailed after them, locked in her own angry world. When the Abhumans snatched the Whispering House out of the Ear Canal, Crysanthe had no idea what was happening. She'd assumed that giant Ruth had bludgeoned a hole in the cupola and that the mansion was collapsing around her ears. It was only when she'd looked outside on a new landscape of cluttered iron and wood that she'd understood. The jump to escape the Machine Men's attack had been another whirling confusion, as if the entire contents of the Brittle Hag's ship had been dropped into a centrifugal grinder. This time she was ready. She braced herself and faced in the direction Neke had pointed.

The spacecraft rang like a bell. Crysanthe's feet lifted from the floor and around her rubble and scrap drifted slowly upwards. Selva grabbed her hand. Abby just kept the same position as she rose a foot into the air - arms folded and face lowered in an irritable scowl. Beyond the plateau the patchwork walls and sky disassembled themselves, turning into an exploded diagram of reality. It rushed towards the general and she cried out, flinging her arm over her eyes, but there was no impact. She looked again to find herself roaring down a kaleidoscope tunnel of walls, doors, pipes, scaffolding, canvas, glass, plastic, metal, fused sand and frictionless ceramics tumbling over each other. She could have sworn that some of it passed straight through her, disappearing into a point behind. And then all was still. She dropped back onto the ground and stumbled forward, her brain convinced she'd gone from a thousand miles an hour to nothing in a split second. But there was no momentum to bring her to her knees, and despite the lingering storm in her head all was as sterile and silent as before.

Abby set off in the direction of the plateau's edge and Crysanthe and Selva followed. Behind them the Abhumans poured out of the tent, listening to the air like guard dogs. *They're waiting to see if we've been attacked again.*

The Time Scavenger froze at the edge of the cliff.

"God almighty," she hissed as the other two women joined her.

The dark wrongness of the first alien harpoon had been bad enough. It gouged a line of dead night out of existence, making everything around it - landscape and people - seem fragile and worthless. More than anything else, the black emptiness of the barb and piled chains made Crysanthe feel as if she, and all she'd ever known or loved, were there on the pure sufferance of an indifferent cosmos - a lumbering, tired shadow fashioned from boredom and lazy malice that encompassed everything, and from whom there was no escape. The grappling iron picked apart the stitching of reality, but compared to this it was nothing.

Dark trenches criss-crossed the fifty-mile wide valley below. The dead shadow cuts sliced their terrible hieroglyphs from the base of the precipice to the distant haze. Here and there Crysanthe saw tangled clusters of midnight coloured chains. At the end of half a dozen gouges the harpoon shafts still angled upwards like rough cut corn stalks. She guessed that others lay at the bottom of deep furrows, but it was impossible to tell. Where the grappling irons had passed over the landscape they'd left pitch black scars that sucked all light and energy out of their surroundings. Neke and Goma appeared at her side.

"This was the hardest," clicked the leader of the Abhumans. "It happened when we arrived at the Great White World. They came at us with forty-three separate attacks. We only stopped them by shifting each time to close the breach and sever their chains. It was very close."

"Did you see them?"

"No," answered Goma. "Whatever fires these into our reality sends them remotely. We think that if and when they ever get a foothold, then they'll come through - or drag us into their universe."

Crysanthe wondered if they should scout the attack zone to try and find out more about their extra-dimensional enemy, but in truth she just wanted to get as far away as possible. She had the feeling the longer they stayed, the more vulnerable they became.

"Good news. We've found the next dead node," said Neke. "From that we should be able to find our way back to the centre."

"Shift us again as soon as you can. Let's keep moving."

She looked at Abby. The Time Scavenger stared down at the nearest cluster of scars. Crysanthe understood enough about the woman by now to realise that normally she'd be charging down there, gunning for a fight. Instead she spat over the cliff, wiped her nose on the back of her hand and wandered off, kicking at the ground. Crysanthe knew better than to follow her.

The next attempted breach consisted of two harpoons sticking out of the wall of a cube three miles high, each side decorated with a carved face mouthing a forgotten syllable. The Abhumans explained they'd plucked it up from somewhere deep inside God's throat - the remnants of one of the civilisations that had taken on the futile task of crafting the Larynx. One quarrel pierced the cheek of a gaunt woman. The other protruded from the centre of a young boy's forehead, the chain hanging down over his face.

Despite their first burst of confidence, this second zone threw the Abhumans into panicked confusion and they spent the next day and night in endless debate in the map room, alternately rolling around on the lead sheet en-masse or standing around the edge shouting at each other. Crysanthe asked if this was an attack they hadn't known about, but that just inflamed the argument. In the end Abby pulled her revolver on Neke and had to be manhandled out of the tent by the other women. Unsurprisingly she didn't resist - the general felt the defeat in her shoulders even as she pulled her outside. The Time Scavenger didn't bother to yell her usual litany of curses or fight them. She just turned her back on the settlement and walked off, hands on her stomach. Crysanthe could tell she was crying.

"Go after her," said Selva.

Was the girl mad? Since when did the Athanatoi of the Empire fuss over the pitiful snivellings of a wretch like Abby Fabrice? Yet as soon as she had the thought she felt ashamed. Selva pushed her in the small of the back. Crysanthe walked after Abby, bracing herself for the inevitable 'fuck off'. Instead, Abby sat on a fallen pillar of corroded plastic, arms on her knees, fists clasped, studying her boots.

"Five days now. I left him in the middle of the citadel. How long does it take to build or break God? We were at the very edge of the knife, the final balance. Oh look. Abby and the brat have pissed off. Down tools everyone until they come back."

"Max will survive."

"What do you care? We're nothing to you - the shit on your boots, if that. You don't understand anything. You don't know how stupid he is, how blind and desperate - so wrapped up in running from his daddy. If he ever succeeds it's through idiot luck, blundering over enemies because he's too busy looking over his shoulder at the shadow of that miserable tower. He's rebuilding it. Inside his head. The Carceral Archipelago. That's where he belongs. He'd love it, really. Him and that puling stain Rebecca who won't even bother to speak with me. I tell you, first chance we get I'm hooking her out and flushing her down the crapper."

She rubbed at her stomach, dropped her head and started to sob into her chest. Crysanthe took her hand. It was remarkably small for such a fighter, though she noticed where a couple of knuckles had been dislocated in ancient punch ups. She wanted to tell Abby that Max was driftwood, tougher than stone, carved and cast into the last river of history. Both these wastrels from the back of beyond were hacked from the same tree as Titus, the loyal Dog with his sullen battle-born wisdom, who'd died trying to protect her from her treacherous brothers. But any comparison would be self-serving and so she held the woman's fingers in silence.

"Crys," Selva called. She turned to see a line of Abhumans racing towards a tunnel at the foot of a wall beyond the cube, Selva following them. Crysanthe caught up, Abby a few steps behind.

"They need our weapons," the Companion told her, handing her one of her swords.

"Report."

Instantly alert, her first thought was that the creatures had found a live breach, and they were about to face down whatever was trying to get in - a stupid play given that the attackers possessed technology far ahead of any of the kinetic and bladed arms they carried. Before she had a chance to order them all back they stopped outside an arched door locked with a single wooden bar.

"It's not another zone," said Abby, translating the endless chittering. "It's something else. It'll help us navigate to the hub but it has a..." she looked at Hama as if he'd gone mad "... a guardian?"

"A creature they pulled out from the body of God?" If they'd managed to hook a monster they were closer to the singularity than she'd thought.

"They're not making sense," said Abby. "I don't have time for this bollocks."

Before anyone could stop her she'd heaved the bar out of its slots and pushed open the door. As she cat-stepped into the room the general looked past to see a long hall flanked by pillars of black metal rising from rough sandstone flagging. Torches flared from brackets set at head height, and by their light she saw more jumbled stone forming the ceiling a hundred yards above their heads. Between the columns she just made out a midnight blue curtain speckled with bright points. Abby slowed down, sighting down the heavy calibre revolver. Instinctively Crysanthe advanced, Selva covering her flank.

The instant they stepped over the threshold her skin blazed as if it was being flayed with red hot sandpaper. She tried to cry out but her body peeled away in layers and the boiling air sucked all strength from her lungs. As Crysanthe collapsed on her hands and knees Selva staggered sideways into a pillar, her sword clattering onto the stones. Abby shouted something. The general barely managed to lift her head to catch a blurred glimpse of a white-furred winged serpent thicker than a man coiling in and out of the columns and statues at the far end, yelling back at the Time Scavenger in an unknown tongue. Abby ran backwards between the women and someone started dragging Crysanthe across the floor by her foot as she passed out.

She came to propped against a corridor wall. Selva sat opposite with her head slumped between her knees. An Abhuman poked a dish of something under the girl's nose. No doubt it was supposed to be invigorating. The smell made Crysanthe retch. Abby paced up and down between them. Most of the other creatures were peering at them round the end of the passageway in silence, tracking the woman's steps like an audience at a tennis match.

"What happened?" the general managed to whisper. She held up her hand. It shook, but was still there, skin intact.

"An ancient wormhole realm."

She didn't have the strength to answer but her expression no doubt said it all.

"Neke claims that when they fled from the Isle Resplendent they jumped into one of the wormholes near the Great White World to try to avoid detection by the invaders," explained Abby. "Looks like they snagged a bit on the way through."

"That's why we started dying," said Crysanthe.

"When we entered that temple we stepped into the distant past and your life force started dissolving in the higher energy level," the Time Scavenger continued.

The curtain covered in shining dots - it was a night sky full of stars.

Selva looked up from her dish of orange slime.

"But you're OK."

Abby shrugged and patted her stomach.

"Another side-effect of Madam. She's made me immune to the effects of deep time."

"If that's from a wormhole in the singularity can we use it to get home?"

"No, they ripped it out. It doesn't lead anywhere other

than the rest of the universe at that period. It's billions of years back, so you can't survive. I'm the only one able to go inside, and I massively pissed off its temple demon."

"So we're wasting our time here."

Crysanthe struggled to a standing position.

"No - the Abhumans used it to work out how to get back to the centre of the ship," answered Abby. "One more shift'll take us within half a mile. Then all we need to do is to work out how to seal the vessel so we don't all suffocate the second we step back into reality."

CHAPTER TWENTY-TWO

A SILENCE FELL on the garden, giants, God Talkers and Machine Men, sealing everything in the pure clarity of this ultimate betrayal like an ants' nest in glass. A deep calm settled over Max. *This is the sum total of the Great Task. A million years building a deity only to be kicked aside in the last second. We are completely and utterly alone, with no-one left to save mankind but ourselves.*

"So the things we made in our image turn against us. Why am I not surprised?" observed Ioam.

If it was any consolation, Ombratulla and Belsalice's faces were pictures of comic shock. They stared at Theuderic, mouths open like stupefied goldfish. Max decided to make sure the penny had fully dropped.

"So let me get this absolutely clear. You Machine Men programmed these giants to hate humanity so they would carry you through the God Door instead of us. Therefore, this grand, noble contempt of yours..." he turned to the sisters of the east. "...is just a script etched in your heads by our machine servants. Am I right?"

"My hate is my own," answered Ombratulla, with pure murder in her eyes.

"And mine," echoed Toldi, flexing his hands and glaring at the God Talkers.

"No, it's not," replied Halinard. "We made Theuderic and co. They in turn made you. And didn't do a very good job of it by the look of things."

"It's not even all the Machine Men. You've been co-opted by the nutters," said Ioam. "Ihanna wasn't part of this - she wanted you two to turn from your petty vengeance and come back here to create the Mind."

"That's why she warned us, and was executed for it. Anselm was the same," added Max.

Theuderic's avatar was a silver statue, his hammered metal face giving nothing away.

"Anselm," he said. "Sadly those who walked among humanity became tainted by them, fooled into a worthless compassion where none was deserved. We who stayed in the Head realised from the beginning that man's time had come. In us you created perfect, changeless beings and we in turn made a god. Giants, you were designed for this moment."

Max desperately longed for Abby. Her voice rang in his head now. *What a load of total and utter horse shit. You're a bunch of automated spanners we stupidly gave intelligence to and you fantasise that it's turned you into fucking demiurges.* Belsalice and Ombratulla could do with another nudge.

"The vengeance and vendetta for the death of Bassandis was a lie - implanted into your minds. Whatever they spout then or now, these creatures wanted you to hate humanity, so you would side with these buggers against us."

Belsalice laughed, but it sounded desperate.

"If what you say is true then why aren't we all affected? If our hatred's programmed why don't we all feel the same?" She gestured at Sorameistre. "This fool loves humans - thinks they're worth saving."

If giants truly mirrored the personalities of their God Talkers anyone who called Ioam and Nem's titan a fool was asking for it, but Belsalice and her sister longed to believe they had free will - that their anger was their own

- and it made them reckless.

"Because I lived among the best of humanity," answered Sorameistre. "You went and hid in your pathetic little hovel at the arse-end of nowhere. You never made the effort to know people like I did, to listen to the stories that explained who they are and why they commit their so-called crimes."

"What about you? Of all of us you have reason to hate humans the most," Ombratulla said to Bassandis. It wasn't an accusation or a plea, Max could see that with the ground gone from beneath her feet, the giantess wanted to understand.

"Have I? True, the ignorant and the stupid imprisoned me - not knowing what I was - and turned me into a monster. But Max Ocel rescued me. He cared for me in his mind, as did his daughter. And through them I have tasted the next universe."

Max waited for Ragaleis to speak. After all the giant had woken him to the understanding of who he was, and first given him the task of bringing the remnant of his brother here to be repaired. The titan stood in front of Ruth. The disfigurement that hunched him into a lumpen shadow had all but vanished and Max recognised the pale-haired man who'd greeted him inside his own doll's house two years ago. Ragaleis reached out and touched the woman on the shoulder. She cried out in pain and flinched away.

"This is what you fashioned from me?" he asked his sisters.

"Poor quality materials," answered Belsalice. "We thought she had a giant's heart, but in the end it was just rancour and human spite, barely enough to fill her own spirit, let alone one of ours. The ancient stars from deep time fashioned her a body of sorts, but they came from a world of machines and struggled to work flesh into a shape that would last."

"Poor child. How could you do this to her?" Ragaleis asked.

"She was responsible for the death of Bassandis. Ruth was lucky we let her live at all."

The giant and Alaric's daughter looked into each other's eyes. Max couldn't see her face. Perhaps she was snarling hatred at the creature whose body had been the template for her own, or maybe she was begging for help. Ragaleis reached out again but she staggered back with a cry, one arm up to defend herself. The titan returned to the others. Max noticed Ruth's shoulders were shaking.

"Brothers and sisters," said Bassandis. "The new cosmos is not for machines or even giants. It's for things that live. It's for them." he pointed at Max and his companions. "They are the masters here, and carry powers that will prevail against any of ours."

"Where is your daughter?" asked Theuderic. "She and your woman eluded my scouts, but not for long. Tell me where she is or it will go hard for you."

Max hoped the creatures didn't recognise the sheer relief in his eyes. Ioam was right - the Abhumans had jumped the others out of harm's way. It was only there for a second - a deep hatred welled up, as if he were a hollow statue filled with churning poison. *You tried to murder my love and our child.* How did they track them to the Isle Resplendent? They must have retraced Toldi and Ombratulla's route when the giants returned to the Ear. Had Crysanthe and Selva escaped as well? Even Machine Men would have a fight on their hands if they took on the general and her Companion.

"If you think you can defeat Rebecca, you're a fool," he heard himself speak with his father's voice. It rarely happened, and he usually hated himself for parroting the Tyrant in the Tower, but right now he gave it his all. "She walks through the Mind unseen by any of you. I saw her feed your servants to the giantesses' watchers and unless you bow to those who created you and form God's soul in our service," he lifted Rebecca's spear above his head, "she'll unleash such horrors on this realm that Ragaleis's nightmares will look like the fucking glove puppets they really are."

"You have a daughter that can move through the Mind unseen?" asked Ombratulla. The anger in her voice barely concealing her fear. She rounded on Theuderic. "How can this be?"

"She's a God Talker from the next creation," explained Bassandis. "Her mind palace is filled with the light of young suns - new energies, scents and thoughts we can scarcely dream of. She took me into her garden and I was remade."

"How do you think we got into this fortress to free Ragaleis?" said Ioam.

"And you have no control over her?" Belsalice asked Theuderic.

"Their ship is faster than any of ours. Your attacks on my people and ships have left us seriously weakened. We're still hunting for it, but it could be anywhere, even in deep space."

Ombratulla pointed at Max.

"Then rip his head open and find out where it is."

Despite his survival hinging on an outrageous bluff, he really wished Theuderic's avatar had the ability to pull faces. He'd have loved to seen them now.

"We can't risk his daughter's anger."

Belsalice gave a laugh of pure scorn.

"Stalemate," observed Halinard.

"Three giants care for man," declared Max, pointing at Bassandis, Ragaleis and Sorameistre. "Three think they hate him - Toldi, Ombratulla and Belsalice. And you?"

All he could make out in Vinduranto and Mephyrean's faces was baffled panic.

"Gentle Mephyrean," he said. "You told Lord Theuderic that you couldn't tell whether you hated us."

The Queen shook her head, pleading with him not to ask the question. He didn't bother, the answer was obvious. The giantess wouldn't recognise hatred if it spat in her eyes.

Ruth still hadn't moved or spoken since Ragaleis approached her. She stood trembling on the edge of the circle, forgotten by her sisters. Ragged hair hung down from her bowed head like a curtain and her white, knife-sharp fingers flexed and twitched. Max had thought to call her out, if only to prove to Alaric's daughter that her vengeance and promise of transcendence were lies. If she'd goaded Ombratulla and Belsalice to lay waste to the Empire of the Ear it wasn't the justness of her cause, or force of will, that had seen the titans striding between shattered buildings of the AntiHelix, laughing at the mad and dying.

He paused. *You control the last of the ancient stars and alien warriors.* If the others had grown tired of their little sister, that had to give him an advantage. He didn't know how long his bluff about Rebecca would last and the girl had begged him to help her. Somehow he had to buy more time - the current deadlock wouldn't last. He'd have to gamble everything.

"You must decide," he said to the giants. "The mind of God can only be fully created by the eight of you agreeing to merge of your own free will. You have to persuade each other. Neither God Talkers nor Machine Men can make the final decision. Whether the deity comes to consciousness as our enemy or our saviour is entirely down to you. We will stand down if Theuderic does the same."

Ioam gave him a *what the fuck are you doing?* look.

"I call a truce. In the real universe three armies wait outside this fortress - the giants' dreaming mad, who follow all of you," he gestured to the titans. "The Machine Men's fleet, and an alien army powered by ancient suns, under the control of Ruth an Vircana. All will stand down while you argue it out amongst yourselves."

"And if we decide to fashion a God that hates humanity and Machine Man in equal measure?" asked Belsalice.

"Your decision stands, whatever it is, or I'll unleash forces from deep time that cannot be stopped by titans, Machine Men or God Talkers' daughters," hissed Ruth. "You've seen how they can invade Machine Man systems and overcome their vaunted science. The ancient stars are in the Mind as well, waiting to do my bidding."

She'd lifted her head to stare directly at her sisters. They glared back at her with ill-concealed expressions of disappointment bordering on disgust. The fantasy Ruth once had of merging with the pure soul of a remorseless god died in that moment. Max remembered the re-fashioned woman tripping through the Ear Canal. *Once you'd passed beyond the Tympanic Membrane, how quickly did the betrayal come? How soon did you realise you'd never be a God?* It would have been better if Ruth an Vircana had perished in Metacarpi.

"We created you to carry us through the God Door," said Theuderic. "Be guided by our wisdom."

"And we made you to save us," Ioam told him. "So finally you understand what ingratitude feels like, Theuderic Lord of the Machine Men. We slaughtered our child Merodach when it pretended it was divine and lorded it over the Steel Queen's refugees. What are you going to do with your golems now they've turned against you?"

She might as well have been talking to a silver figurine for all the response in the statue's face.

"I hope you know what you're doing," Halinard muttered to Max.

"Wait here," Belsalice told the God Talkers and Machine Men. She gestured to her brothers and sisters and they walked after her through the garden, Ombratulla taking up the rear. As the others filed between the dead lattices of trees and bushes, she paused, turning back towards Ruth. Max sensed she was getting ready to tell the woman she had no part in this because she wasn't a real giant. Ruth didn't speak, though her gaze never left the titan's face. Reading her silence as defeat, Ombratulla shook her head in a pity as dismissive as it was fake, and followed her siblings.

A door in the crystal wall led to a staircase. Eight shadows rippled against the dome as they ascended to a circular platform, taking up their positions on the rim, facing each other under the lowering sky. Max remembered seeing performances like this in the Theatre of Angels. The scene resembled a chorus in one of the ancient tragedies, chanting out the steps of a tragic fall, supplicating the senile universe for its last scrap of attention.

"We're going to let them decide amongst themselves, just like that?" asked Ioam.

"What else are we supposed to do?" said Halinard. "At least we've removed them from the equation." He nodded towards the Machine Men who gathered beside Theuderic, silently conferring. Max wasn't so sure. He couldn't imagine they'd give up so easily.

"Rebecca's our trump card," he said. "As long as they think she's around we, and Nem, are safe. We're going to have to trust Sorameistre, Bassandis and Ragaleis to see this through. Theuderic's stupid mistake was to tell the giants they were programmed to hate us. They want to believe they have free will, so he's gloriously pissed off the lot of them."

"Maybe they'll decide to prove him wrong by rescuing

humanity after all," said Halinard.

"Maybe I'll start farting rainbows," muttered Ioam. "We need an exit plan. If this does all collapse into shit we have to find a way to get downstairs to your tank so we can jump back into reality."

Max was only half listening. He had his eyes on Ruth, who, in turn, watched the giants as they gestured and argued with each other on their sky stage. Without his daughter the remains of her army of stars were the only other power not tied to gods, humanity or Machine Men. She stood alone and forgotten by her sisters, one hand on the back of a cast iron bench. Her whole body trembled.

"Will you help me, or have you just come to gloat?" She spoke like someone being electrocuted, forcing her voice through the endless pain in a hiss. Her chin was wet with spittle.

"How can I possibly help you?"

"They'll turn on humanity, whether they agree to form the Mind or not. I've seen what drives them. They're angry children, neither pure nor powerful."

"You wanted them to rebel against us." It was a cheap shot. Rubbing her face in her own misery and the destruction she'd caused wouldn't solve anything, and right now he could do with any advantage she had to offer. On the other side of the wall the titans' gestures grew more emphatic. Even without the sound of their voices Max knew they were shouting in fury. He glanced across at Theuderic. None of the Machine Men moved. They stood in a line, heads angled up towards their creatures, metal faces reflecting the occasional sparks falling from the clouds.

"Theuderic's still feeding the giants' hatred and they're turning it on each other," said Ruth.

"How do you know?"

"The stars tell me."

He started forward but Ruth grabbed him, her hand a

spasming claw around his forearm.

"We have to stop them. Stop all of them. I can do it, but not for long."

"What do you mean?"

"The suns are leaving, there's so few left - we have to act while some still linger."

She scrabbled for his neck and pulled his face down to hers. Burning eyes stared at him from a skull papered with mottled, diseased skin. If this was how her avatar appeared inside God's dreams, what did her real giant body look like?

"I'll stop the Machine Men and Ombratulla and Belsalice. In return promise you'll kill me."

He thought he'd misheard. Her hand tightened.

"Kill me Max, I beg you."

"Is Theuderic controlling their emotions right now?" asked Max. He'd enjoy nothing more than putting a bullet through the girls' head, so why the hesitation? Why the pity?

"He's trying to."

"Stop him."

"Promise you'll kill me."

Max nodded. For a second the fear and agony fell from Ruth's face and he caught a glimpse of the woman she had once been. Her hand relaxed, and she vanished. Ioam appeared at his side.

"What's happening?"

Every Machine Man had turned towards them. They lacked the power to harm the God Talkers in here, but their bodies were on the ship with Nem and she'd only be able to keep them out of danger for so long.

"Ruth said she'd stop Theuderic trying to control the titans if we killed her."

"And you believed her?"

He nodded through the wall to where the monstrous

siblings yelled and gesticulated, jabbing angry fingers towards each other. Only Bassandis and Sorameistre appeared calm, struggling to reason with their brothers and sisters.

"They're out of control. The hatred the Machine Men planted inside is feeding off itself. It's over, Ioam. We've been conned into attempting to fix a wrecked engine, and it's about to blow up in our faces."

The sorceress put her fingers to her lips and her eyes filled with tears as she stared at Theuderic.

"The Great Task. Is this it? Is this the end? Were we so stupid as to swallow that tin soldier's lies?"

She strode towards the Machine Men but before she got within half a dozen paces they winked out one by one, like candles in a row extinguished by a departing priest. Max hoped Ruth had kept her promise and jammed the signals the Machine Men were sending into the minds of their creations, forcing them to jump out to try and stop her. He looked up at the platform and saw the brothers and sisters had paused in their arguments. Vinduranto had a hand to his temple, as if he'd developed a headache, and Ombratulla was listening to the sky. Did they realise what had happened?

"We need to go," said Halinard.

Max couldn't face leaving now. *We came so far.* With Theuderic out of the picture, maybe if he and the other God Talkers spoke with the giants they might still bring them back. He ran to the crystal door and hammered on it, shouting to catch their attention, but if they heard him they didn't respond.

"Max, we have to leave now," said Ioam.

He banged on the wall once more. Bassandis turned his face towards him, but he had the distant expression of someone looking at their own reflection in a two-way mirror. Mephyrean lifted up her hands, turning them over to stare at the palms. She staggered, plucking at her dress as tiny rents appeared in the fabric. The other titans stopped and watched her as she raised her fingers to her eyes. Dark gashes mottled her skin. Vinduranto stepped forwards to help her just as she opened her mouth in a silent howl and fell to her knees. The queen vanished.

"They're under attack," hissed Ioam. "It's that bitch Ruth."

Ruth, Machine Men or each other, it didn't matter. Max sprinted through the garden, his companions racing alongside, the witch clearing five foot hedges like a hurdler. It was no good. Nightmares filled the passageway - a seething tide of grotesques stretching back into the citadel. Every single puppet crafted by Ragaleis in his stone prison had gathered here and on the steps leading down to Halinard's wagon and they showed no sign of moving. Max walked towards them, clenching his fists and trying to ignore the shrieking klaxon inside his head.

"Stand aside. I am Max Ocel, God Talker to Bassandis."

He saw dead people he'd known, looking like twisted and smeared corpses crushed under the iron wheels of a juggernaut and abandoned to rot in oil-stained ruts - Herman Ocel, Berthold, Chiral, Som, Pell, Segandyr. They mouthed accusations as their eyeless sockets flowed across featureless doll heads. Thank God he didn't see Abby - it would have sent him insane.

He hefted Rebecca's spear. No response - the monsters didn't flinch. They were going to have battle their way through. Thunder erupted in the wasteland beyond the fortress and the walls and ground shuddered. Max heard the sound of a crystal dome shattering under a rain of spitting boulders. Bassandis appeared at his side and lifted his hand. The nightmares shrank against the wall, flattening themselves against the stone until they were nothing more than a glistening frieze of demons annealed into a macabre dance.

"My brothers and sisters have left the Mind to carry on their fight in reality. They're turning their mad soldiers on each other."

The giant's eyes were filled with desperation. He ran down the corridor and the God Talkers followed. When they reached the top of the staircase Bassandis grew to full size and gathered the three of them up. He took the steps two at a time, so they were flung back and forth inside his cupped hands. When he finally tipped them out on the floor outside the tank the landscape span and Max could barely stand.

"I can't follow them," said the titan, returning to human proportions. "I no longer have a body out there. You've got to stop them Max, before they kill each other."

Somehow Ioam managed to manhandle the men up the stairs into the wagon.

"Go. I'll do what I can in here," shouted Bassandis, and then he was gone and a mountain rose up through the immense hallway as the walls and pillars shuddered and swayed around it.

CHAPTER TWENTY-THREE

ONE MORE JUMP, and to Crysanthe's surprise they ended up in the misted hall where she'd fought the oil-haired monster. The fog had cleared. When Abby joined her and Selva beside the shattered escape pipe she noticed the woman's cloud of hair shimmering in the half-light. At first she thought chemicals lingering in the air were affecting her eyesight.

"Don't you feel that?" asked the Time Scavenger.

Crysanthe closed her eyes. Her left cheek was colder than the right and she detected a gentle hissing. *A breeze.*

"The atmosphere's venting into space," said Selva. "We're close."

Someone was going to have to seal the ship, risking decompression or being sucked out of the vessel. Crysanthe's first instinct was to throw the Abhumans at it - but that was the Empire of the Ear talking, callous and arrogant. She blanked the thoughts. At least it meant they wouldn't have to jump the settlement again, and by some fluke they hadn't attracted the attention of their attackers.

An hour later they found a dead Machine Man, hanging over a jagged sheet of iron like washing on a fence, its body almost cut in two. *It died when the forces caused by the ship's reconfiguration sheared the plate.* Beyond she saw the entrance to a wide passage.

"That's the way," clicked Neke. "Five miles to the

hub."

Abby poked at the corpse's limp hand with her boot.

"They don't need oxygen."

Crysanthe did the maths in her head.

"Thirty came at us over the table top. We took out ten, and another dozen at the settlement when we shifted the first time. Plus this one means at least twenty-three out of action so we could be looking at up to seven of the bastards waiting for us.

"We'll scout ahead. Neke, set up a communication relay through the fastest avoidance route. If you don't hear from us in two hours jump anyway," she turned to Abby while Selva translated to the Abhumans. "You need to go back and get ready to shift."

"No."

Crysanthe steeled herself for a fight but this time Abby just looked back at her with disarming expression of melancholy seriousness.

"We can't protect you and Rebecca..."

"I don't want protecting. It's too late for me to help Max. Either God's mind has been formed or he's dead. I'm not sitting staring at these walls while you go and get killed. What's left for me afterwards?"

"Your child?"

Abby snorted.

"What child?"

She spread her arms and looked down at her flat abdomen.

"It was just a dream, nothing more, and even in dreams I haven't spoken to Rebecca since we jumped. There's nothing there."

Crysanthe found her own arguments crumbling. Did she pity the woman? No, she'd never pitied anyone in her life. *Do I actually care about you?* The very idea was grotesque.

"Three against seven gives us better odds," said Selva.

"This is a silent reconnaissance mission, not a scream-ing death charge."

Abby bent down, unlaced her boots and kicked them off.

"There you go. Tip toes all the way."

Crysanthe gave up.

"Stay at the back, and if you give me any trouble I'll shoot you myself."

They walked for another half hour down the passage-way, winding back and forth under grimy panel lights. A few tinked on and off, revealing the outlines of twisted insect corpses. The wind grew stronger, tugging at their clothes and pushing them along with an insistent hand. Every ten yards an Abhuman peeled off their crocodile and took up station, ready to send the alarm back down the line snaking between them and the ramshackle city.

They descended steps, a howling gale at their backs. The last six Abhumans remaining dug their claws into the floor. Crysanthe leaned back to stop herself from slid-ing along the uneven metal. How in God's name would they be able to close the ship's hatch without being blown out into space?

Entering a circular chamber gave them the chance to step out of the slipstream that screamed into a dark hole in the opposite wall. Another Machine Man lay dead on crumpled plates, its limbs and head teased from its tor-so. The three woman stepped around the body, weapons trained on the fragments in case they decided to re-knit.

"Crys," Selva called above the wind. She glanced across to see a figure standing at the other entrance watching them, digging its fingers into the iron frame to keep itself in place while those prison window eyes stared at Abby.

"Where have you taken us?" shouted the creature so its voice could be heard above the roar. At this volume its words lost any pretence at humanity. Shrill clockwork set her teeth on edge.

"We jumped the ship, and will do so again if you threaten us. Stand down."

Her stomach tightened as a second slipped over the lintel, crawling up the wall where it waited among the deep shadows. The first edged into the room, followed by two more. The women stepped back, weapons trained, the Abhumans crowding the exit behind them.

"Stand down, now!"

She fired into the planks above the entrance. The Machine Men's torsos blossomed with fine blades like many-fingered hands opening to embrace them. As one they turned towards Abby. *We don't stand a chance.*

"Crys. Where's the ceiling gone?" asked Selva.

In the corner of her eye Crysanthe saw the woman's mouth drop open. The general risked a glance upwards just in time to see black, wet shapes like huge bundles of shredded washing rain down on the invaders, each humanoid disappearing in a flurry of silver and shimmering midnight. Slivers of metal flashed briefly only to disappear in a writhing mass of darkness.

All movement ceased. Abby swore. Eight Black Roses stood up from the dismembered bodies of the Machine Men.

"Behold Empress Crysanthe who speaks on behalf of man, and Abby Fabrice, friend of Ramul," Selva cried out before her lover had even understood what she was seeing.

The roiling fountains coalesced into human form. Every one resembled the alien they'd found imprisoned in the way station nestled in God's suprasternal notch - bald with penny-coloured eyes and blue robes. Two might have been female, if that meant anything, but it was hard to tell. What were their chances now? If these beings decided to attack them it'd be over in seconds.

The silence dragged out. She risked a glance at her companions and saw a fearful cocktail of hatred and longing on Abby's face. Of all of them she was the one who'd been closest to a Black Rose, only to be betrayed. An alien exploded in a cloud of petals and reformed into Ramul. She bowed.

"How are you here? What's happened?" she asked. "Why are the Machine Men attacking you?"

She's journeyed here through the dark network that connects them all. Everything I say from now on will be weighed in the balance. Crysanthe tried to close off all distractions, pretending this was just another one of her commands waiting for precise orders.

"We'll speak to the Black Rose God. We are the envoys representing humanity."

"What has happened to the human god and for what reason did the Machine Men, servants of that god and creators of its mind, try to kill you?"

"We'll tell everything to your deity."

She sensed Abby's fury, how desperate she was to return to save Max. At least the wretch had the wit not to argue in front of the aliens.

"As you can see we lost access to our control room. Whereabouts are we?" asked Selva, breaking the silence.

"You are one hundred and sixty-three light years from the singularity we made for you, and twenty from the God Door."

There was the answer to the Time Scavenger's unspoken question. Even if this vessel really was the swiftest in the universe it'd take months to cover that distance, unless the Abhumans could make it jump back. *Neke said we were pulled here. He didn't bring us this far by design.*

"The Empress humbly asks that you help seal this ship and then guide her to the Black Rose God," announced

Selva.

"Very well," answered Ramul.

Men and women turned into shadows that disappeared, leaving crumpled scraps of Machine Man littering the room. Even with the aliens absent no-one knew what to say. Crysanthe rolled Ramul's explanation around in her head but still failed to grasp what it meant - *one hundred and sixty-three light years from home?* Abby stood with her hands on her hips, gazing through the floor into the gulf her own loneliness. Selva was another cut-out with her hand over her mouth and eyes wide.

The wind died.

Crysanthe snapped out of her stupor and turned to the Abhumans who, to their credit, hovered by the other door staring across the chamber with the rapt attention of an audience of children at a magic show.

"Re-arrange the internal configuration of the ship to stop the Black Roses getting inside."

The last thing she wanted was for the aliens to discover they could pluck chunks out of the universe or open portals. No matter how chaotic and unstable the process, it might be the only advantage they had left. They dutifully vanished into the darkness.

When they entered the reality-bound centre of the craft it was empty, the abandoned passageways echoing with the cracks and groans of the iron as it warmed. They came to the bridge and Abby gasped in wonder, her breath clouding in the freezing air as she broke out of her miserable silence. Through the window Crysanthe saw an immense ship hanging in the darkness. Five hexagonal toruses followed a central spine, curving along the outer edge of a quarter circle. A few lights shone on the hull, picking out half-glimpses of the bulky engines clustered around the segment's apex. They were only fitful navigation beacons and judging by their erratic pattern most had died. The rest of the vessel was a dead, grey silhouette.

"Black Rose?" asked Selva.

"No, they fly unaided through space," said Abby. "That's a ghost ship."

Twelve shining gold cables unfurled on either side of their own craft, pointing towards the hulk. As they tightened Crysanthe saw that each one ended in a seething mass of petals.

They're towing us.

Crysanthe reached for their own controls but Abby snatched her hand back.

"It's still too cold. You'll have your skin off."

She wrapped her own fingers in her sleeve and tried the joystick, but the Brittle Hag's spaceship didn't respond.

"Either they've disabled our engines or those ropes are too strong."

They had no choice but to wait as the aliens guided their ship through the empty void. Crysanthe found herself endlessly recalibrating scale in giddy calculations before realising the abandoned craft was almost half the size of the AntiHelix itself. They passed lightless shells as big as dreadnoughts and vast superstructures spiralling out from the first two toruses before the Black Roses turned in towards the central hull. A pinhole grew into a cavernous landing bay lit by dim blue lights. When they entered Crysanthe noticed the ropes sag, and dust kicked up by the ragged wings of their captors as they settled onto the floor. *Air and gravity.* The creatures snapped back into human form and walked towards their vessel, coiling the cables up in their arms. The one that looked like Ramul gestured for them to step outside.

Neke and Hama met them at the entrance to the passageway leading into the ship's universe.

"Are we going to the Black Rose God?" clicked the Ab-human leader.

"Yes. Can you study this vessel from your city?" replied Crysanthe. "I want to understand how and why it's here."

"How long would it take to fly to the singularity?" interrupted Abby. The creatures swapped glances, drawing silent straws. In the end Hama answered.

"At this ship's maximum speed? Just over a year."

"And you can't jump back?"

"We didn't plan to come here. Our extra-dimensional foe snagged onto the vessel when we fled the Machine Men, and pulled us to this place. Their power is far greater than ours. We can't shift such long distances without any reference points. If we tried we'd get even more lost and probably expose ourselves to further attacks."

Abby didn't speak or move. She was looking at something two feet in front of her face invisible to everyone else. Crysanthe wanted her to rage and fight, call them all a bunch of fucking cunts and try to shoot them - but the woman just stood there, bleak and alone.

"I'm sorry," said Neke.

They stepped outside into freezing air that stank of kerosene and acid. Ramul walked towards them across a steel floor rimed with frost and littered with scorched and twists shards of metal.

"Is this ship yours?" asked Crysanthe.

"No. We found it as we were journeying through space. It's an abandoned hulk. It looks as though it's lain here for thousands of years."

"Any crew?"

The alien shook her head - a disarmingly normal gesture for a cloud of petals crammed into a humanoid shell.

"Not yet - but we've barely begun to explore."

"Why have you brought us here? We need to journey

to the god of the Black Roses to plead on behalf of mankind."

"All in good time. Our business here will finish in a day or so. Then we shall be happy to escort you to our deity."

Old Crysanthe bristled at the creature's insolence. *Is that all we are now? Fragments to be pitied and condescended to when you're gracious enough to remember we're still here?*

"Most of the ship is sealed and beyond our art to enter, but there is atmosphere and gravity in the rest and no danger. Feel free to explore. Such a tragic and noble ruin may amuse you."

She wasn't sure whether the Black Rose was deliberately goading her, but she let it rest. They were dependent on the capricious goodwill of these creatures who clearly saw the entire human race as a failed experiment. Helpless and humiliated, she glanced around at the immense vault. There was a fascination in this majestic, empty vessel. Even Abby looked as if she was dying to explore. Behind them Abhumans crept out, clicking softly to each other in subdued wonder. They were supposed to be locking down the ship, but she guessed their never-ending curiosity had got the better of them.

The Black Roses burst into dark fire and flew up into the shadows. Left to their own devices Crysanthe, Selva and Abby picked their way through the hangar hunting for clues about the crew and their fate. The general expected to see consoles or instruments - the usual machinery of a landing bay, but the only machines standing were temple-sized clusters of pipes, blocks and cylinders or rusting cables as thick as her thigh. She couldn't even tell if the beings who'd piloted the craft had been humanoid or something else.

No bodies. Whatever flew this ship perished in the explosion or escaped. But it was still odd. There would be at least a few corpses, or perhaps not after thousands of years. Maybe the fine dust she kicked up as she walked through the vault was nothing more than the desiccated crew. Looking round, she noticed the Abhumans had disappeared. That surprised her given their fascination with anything new, but maybe this mausoleum was too empty and grim even for them.

"Looks like it's been stripped," she remarked to Selva in front of a brighter patch of wall ringed by empty rivet holes.

"Not only that, whoever did it wanted to cover their tracks."

The Companion pointed at a plate that had been abraded into a gritty swirl of rust.

"There's no sign of writing anywhere, and in the few places you'd expect it you get this."

"An exploration or a transport vessel on its way to the God Door?"

"Who'd explore an empty universe or try to cross into the next one without a god?"

The desperate.

Abby joined them.

"I'm going back into our ship. There's nothing to see here," she said to the floor, her voice empty of life. Crysanthe let her go.

"We can't do anything to help her," she told Selva as the woman climbed up the ramp. "Max is probably dead."

"Do you think we won? Has God finally got a mind and is he on our side?"

"Whatever's done is done. We still need to plead before the Black Roses."

They walked a couple of miles to the end of the hangar. It narrowed down into a passageway that disappeared into blackness. There was no point continuing if they couldn't see anything. They'd found nothing of value and the aliens were elsewhere, leaving them to kick their heels like children left behind in an empty playground. They returned to the Brittle Hag's vessel.

Hama was waiting for them. As they entered the bridge he checked to see if they were being followed and then closed the ship's hatch.

"We've discovered something," clicked the Abhuman. He took their hands and led them into the universe of the ship.

"What?"

"Things that are wondrous and full of mystery," he answered.

"Such as?"

But he didn't answer. Instead, he weaved in and out of passageways, occasionally stopping to scratch his head and get his bearings. At last he showed them into a room lined with doors. Each portal had a number above it scrawled in chalk. Abby and half a dozen Abhumans squatted around a sheet of cardboard on which one of the creatures drew diagrams in yellow crayon. The Time Scavenger looked up and managed a smile.

"Clever little buggers did what you said and scouted out the rest of the ship."

"And?"

Abby pointed at the sketch.

"The sections with circles have atmospheres, the ones with crosses are breached, including the power systems here and here."

"You're telling me they've opened portals into all these levels?"

Crysanthe looked at the Abhumans who resembled a line of owls on a branch, all staring back at her with the same familiar expression of friendly expectation.

"We're very good at stealth in places with lots of shadows and walls the same colour as our fur," volunteered the third one in from the end, who she suddenly realised was Goma. "The slimy moths won't see us."

"You said 'breached'…" prompted Selva.

"The craft was attacked. Our hairy friends opened doors into the airless caverns for a few seconds to check what was there and spotted energy beam splashes along with armour-piercing and high explosive shell damage."

"The Black Roses?"

"I don't think so. This happened ages ago, perhaps thousands of years past. Once the command centre was wrecked the hulk just drifted, powerless, through space. Some of these sealed sections are filled with mothballed machines and devices. They've also found cases of treasures and rare substances - like you'd find in a trader."

"Any sign of the crew?" asked Selva.

Abby ignored her.

"But it's these that's got them the most excited." she tapped on the outlines of the last three toruses with her finger. The Abhumans erupted into frantic nodding. The Time Scavenger looked sharp and hungry and Crysanthe was happy to see the reckless insolence returned.

"What's inside?"

Abby chuckled and rubbed her hands.

"They won't say, Goma wants us to see for ourselves. They're intact and have atmosphere. Apparently Ramul and her friends have been hovering around these, so we'll have to time it right."

They waited half an hour but the aliens didn't return. Goma dispatched scouts through the numbered doors, crossing them off on his cardboard chart. The creatures returned, some panting with their hair matted with frost, gasping ice clouds into the room. They reported that the Black Roses were clustered around the central torus, and it looked as if they'd found a way inside. With that taking up their attention, Crysanthe decided to chance a re-connaissance into the last ring. They weaponed up. Abby started cracking her knuckles but stopped and looked away, blinking furiously. *She wishes Max was here.*

"You go first," Crysanthe told her. Abby shot her a look of cautious disbelief before flashing a rare grin.

They jogged along the wooden tunnel, angling down into the darkness. After half a mile the walls and floor fragmented into a litter of planks scattered over a wide tiled pathway between rows of machinery. The cold chewed at Crysanthe's face, making her wince. Through watering eyes she tried to make out the surroundings. There was no light, but the Abhumans had given them storm lanterns which they lit and held aloft, picking out lines of glass and metal tubes. After checking for any signs of life she scouted ahead. On all sides banks of cylinders curved up into the shadows.

She turned back and noticed Selva and Abby rubbing at the surface of one of the pods while Goma held the lantern steady. As she approached the two women swapped glances.

"What is it?"

She looked through the cracked and filthy glass. In the soft orange glow every flaw from a thousand years of damage scintillated, messing with her eyes and breaking the contents into mirror fragments. It took her a good twenty seconds to figure out the shape lying on a brittle plastic couch - the open mouth with amber teeth and soot grey lips pulled back over pitted stone gums. Abby nodded at a plate on the side of the tomb.

"Barignan," she read.

"Benucci," answered Selva from the next tube.

"Bertolagi, Bianca D'Este, Bondeno, Brehus…"

Endless corpses in alphabetical order.

"This is the crew," said Abby. "They slept for the long

voyage, but all died when they were attacked. There must be tens of thousands in here, and in the other sealed toruses."

She took the lantern from Goma and lifted it above her head. Wherever the beams fell on a pod Crysanthe spotted the delicate shadow of another body, a few recognisably children.

"They're not alien, are they?" asked Crysanthe. With names like that she already knew the answer.

"They're us," answered Selva. "Given up hope for the Great Task and fleeing the singularity to try their luck at the God Door."

"They came to plead on behalf of humanity," continued Abby. "We're not the first."

A sour rage born from hopelessness and the familiar stench of treachery clouded the general's mind.

"And this is the answer we can expect."

Black flowers tumbled from the vault above their heads to land with soundless delicacy between the humans and the tunnel leading back to the Brittle Hag's ship.

CHAPTER TWENTY-FOUR

Max awoke to find himself plastered to the ceiling by centrifugal force. Half a second later he realised the craft was upside down. Judging by the invisible hand pushing him across the steel plates they were in the middle of a barrel roll. Rivets scored painful bruises across his back. On the opposite side of the cabin Ioam pulled herself into a standing position and bellowed down the length of the craft.

"What are you doing?"

"Dogfighting," came the cheerful yell from the cockpit.

"You haven't got any guns!"

The ship stopped spinning and Max rolled onto his hands and knees. Nem had scrunched herself into a seat designed to take a pilot half her size, her thighs next to her ears. She gripped the controls with the careless grin of someone hell-bent on mischief as compensation for being left out of the party. Beyond the canopy Max saw white fog. *The giants' mist.*

"Lost them. I think."

Nem slammed the ship into a nose dive. He caught a brief glimpse of endless wood covered in writhing insects before the witch flipped them upside down once more, hurled them into a high velocity turn and send them roaring back into the clouds.

"Just making sure."

"You did that on purpose," said Ioam.

"What's happened?" asked Max.

"Mephyrean came outside and the giants' armies attacked her. Then they started on each other. I couldn't see much after that because of the fog."

"The titans are fighting each other with their mad hordes, and Ruth's controlling anything powered by the last of the stars," said Max. "We have to stop them."

"How?" asked Halinard.

The fog cleared, shredding into tattered daggers that pointed down at an immense land battle in front of the citadel. As the giants took over the minds of the captives from the Empire of the Ear the thrall legions tore at each other. There was no pattern to it - the mad switched allegiance at random, turning on those beside them in close-quarter butchery. Max saw a tracked gunship grind a bloody pathway through half a dozen lines of men and women. It stopped, fired all its guns, and reversed over the troops who'd followed it. He had the vision of wilful children pulling dolls back and forth between them. Knots of taller warriors in barbed chitin armour strode through the chaos, carving precise, surgical cuts in the broil. At least these sun-powered creatures weren't mad, but they had ferocious strength and obeyed Ruth's deranged orders without question.

Halinard swore and pointed at the foot of the ramp leading from the fortress entrance. A giant sprawled face-up, unmoving. Ioam swooped in for a closer look.

Mephyrean.

Her skin and flesh hung in tatters and grey slime ran from the wounds in slow streams over the dark ground. She'd flung her arm over her eyes, as if defending herself. The shaft of a broken spear protruded from beneath her left breast. It had to be a hundred yards thick and stuck up into the sky for half a mile. *Where in god's name did that come from?* Max struggled to understand what he was seeing - titans slaying each other. Seething movement caught his eye. Mephyrean's corpse looked as it was covered in swarms of insects. He peered closer. Machine Men, insane warriors and Ruth's creatures fought back and forth across her skin and over the valleys and folds of her dress.

Nem swore as the ship lurched to the right. A wasp-striped arrowhead overshot them and the witch dropped into a ball-shrivelling dive towards the corpse, plastering Max against the metal again. Missile trails passed on both sides, exploding on the giant's collarbone, sending fountains of white and grey matter into the sky. He saw their attacker start to turn, banking between the citadel towers. The air around the fighter erupted in clusters of fire and smoke from flak, and the fuselage detonated, scarring the battlements with a line of burning fuel and debris. The mad sister took them back into the clouds. Max fell to his knees, hyperventilating and drenched with sweat.

"Gods," muttered Halinard as he lit a bent cigarette with a shaking hand.

"Do you have a plan? Or are you just intending to spend the rest of the afternoon looping the loop and making the little people shit themselves?" shouted Ioam.

"Open to suggestions."

"Find another craft," said Max, hauling himself up next to the pilot. "We have to get inside the fortress and stop this carnage, but we need weapons, missiles, bombs, anything." He spotted the clumpy outline of a flyer through a gap in the fog. He remembered seeing ships like that spiral out of the Beatrice to hurl missiles at the giant Bassandis. "There."

"Isn't that a Lobe corvette?"

"Machine men and star warriors can kill God Talkers, but the dreaming mad are bound by the same rules as the giants. If we commandeer that," he pointed at the approaching vessel, "we might be able to make it inside."

An explosion knocked them sideways. The engines faltered and several indicators flashed red. Shrapnel broke over the prow and a crack appeared in the window.

"How do we get on board?" yelled Ioam as the cabin shuddered and half a dozen shiny domes traced a line across the far wall.

They'd have to suit up and jump onto the hull of the other craft, hoping the speed didn't tear them off, and there were enough handholds and unlocked hatches to let them climb inside. Attempting it while stationary would have been deranged enough, but they were travelling at half a mach.

"It's got a bomb bay," announced Nem. "I bet it isn't armoured."

Before anyone could stop her she dipped under the imperial craft, matched velocities and fired the retros straight down. They smashed up through the hatches, the cockpit canopy bursting apart. Nem scrambled out of the seat and leaped through the wreckage, exoskeleton servos howling above the explosion. Ioam followed, grabbing Max and Halinard by the scruff of their necks and hauling them after her like a pair of rescued puppies. The Machine Man ship popped and creaked as its hull buckled. The witch scrambled up the wall to a gantry just as the entire floor of the bay gave way, taking their ride with it. Spherical bombs poured out of unstoppered storage pipes, emptying into the mist below. At least none of them detonated inside.

As they entered a corridor leading to the bridge Nem rose from a pile of bodies and threw guns in their direction. Her sister caught them and handed Halinard and Max one a piece, keeping two chain-gatlings for herself. They looked like kids' toys in her long white hands.

"They're not bothered by us, but I couldn't be arsed to ask nicely," explained Nem, pushing the corpses to the side with her metal-clawed foot. In death the madness had left their eyes and Max only saw the drawn, blood-spattered faces of ordinary men and women. The sight made him sick at heart, but the other God Talkers were already heading for the main cabin and he didn't have time for the luxury of guilt.

Just as the others disappeared through a bulkhead door a spiked shadow stepped out of the wall and turned to face him. Rows of ruby lentil-shaped eyes flanked a wedged head crested with dagger spikes. Scalpel blades ten inches long unrolled from two six-fingered hands. The last time he'd confronted one of these monstrosities he'd thumped its carapace to try to goad it into killing him. Instead, the intelligent suns implanted in his own body by Crysanthe persuaded the ones powering the ancient warrior to rescue him and the witches. Not this time. Surely Ruth's alien army had marked him for death. Perhaps there was a strange, convoluted irony in all this, but he was too busy scrabbling with the unfamiliar controls of his gun to think it through.

The beast took five strides towards him. Another tangle of darkness erupted out of the floor and yanked it to the ground with a shuddering thump. Coils that looked like they were made from oily rubber clamped its arms and legs to the metal, and Max heard the brittle snap of the armoured chitin shattering. What in god's name could exert such strength? A shadow rose behind the alien. It wore a top hat. Lank hair streamed around a face of melted wax. The cockpit lights beyond shone through a translucent body full of ink swirls in rotting jelly. *God's nightmare.* It pulled its bulk over the struggling captive. Locked in the static-filled paralysis he only ever knew in night terrors, Max watched as the creatures became a single billowing lump. It sank into the plating, leaving a black rot stain.

"Max, where are you?" yelled Ioam.

It took him all his courage to break into a run, hopping sideways past the reeking smear. Nem was studying rows of switches and tittering, her nose an inch away from the console.

"Guided missiles, big ones, Beyond-Visual-Range drones and Scatter Shards." She was a little girl who'd found a new toy.

"I just met an alien warrior, like the one that rescued us from the manufactory,"

The witches swopped glances.

"And?"

"One of Bassandis's watchers stopped it killing me."

"Impossible," said Halinard. "They're dream creatures."

"It got into reality. I saw. Maybe something's figured out how to manifest God's dreams outside the Mind."

White appeared all the way round Ioam's pupils. He understood why. The implications of the nightmares joining in the war were too horrendous to contemplate, even if the one he'd just stumbled across had been on his side.

"Any more on board?"

"Hope not. Don't intend to find out," he nodded at the citadel looming through the fog. "Let's go."

As if on cue the door into the castle fell outwards, tearing from its hinges to shatter on the ramp, sending thick obsidian fragments ploughing through the figures battling on its lower slopes. Vinduranto appeared, clawing at the air with one hand. Max saw the other had been torn off at the elbow. Tatters of skin and sinew flapped back and forth, spraying gobbets of white flesh and grey blood. The giant uttered long howls of anguish and pain that turned his face into a grotesque child's drawing. Halinard cried out and stepped to the glass, his indifference breaking for the first time.

Even as the titan lurched outside a swarm of ships descended on him. His head and shoulders erupted in ragged bursts as they poured bullets and missiles into his torn flesh. He batted at them, lifting his face to spit a cloud of acid at his tormentors. A few craft exploded, or spiralled down into the battlefield far below, but most merely shifted position and continued to fire. At the edge of his own mind Max detected a mountainous storm of incoherent thoughts lashing out at random. In his pain and fury the giant, unused to controlling humans, hadn't the focus or the skill to save himself. His calves turned black as the insane soldiers swarmed up his legs, emptying their guns at point blank range and hacking at the ridged flesh with swords, knives, teeth and claws, driven by his sisters' hatred.

"Help him," said Halinard, turning to Max with glistening eyes. "He can't die."

"All we can do is put him out of his misery," said Ioam. "We're one ship against an armada of psychopathic lunatics."

"Bugger it," said Nem, flicking switches. She rolled the corvette round to bring its missiles to bear on Vinduranto.

"What are you doing?" asked her sister.

But whatever plan she'd concocted was interrupted by the appearance of Toldi on a platform high up among the citadel towers. He lifted his arm and hurled another spear at his brother. It hit Vinduranto between the shoulder blades, driving through his torso so the point jutted a good two hundred yards from his chest. Halinard cried out and sank to his knees, imitating his giant who tugged helplessly at the weapon before pitching forwards. The impact of his fall kicked up debris and bodies and sent shock waves slamming into the flyer, kicking it violently sideways.

"Sorameistre's on her own," said Ioam, her voice tight with fear. "We have to save her."

Nem switched on the afterburners and the ship roared through the shattered doorway.

"I'm going back into the Mind," shouted her sister.

She closed her eyes and Max grabbed onto her hand just in time. They landed on the balcony of Ioam's mind palace. The valley below seethed under an ocean of writhing monstrosity, nightmares forming and reforming as the fabric of God's soul tore itself apart and demons from his id bubbled up through the cracks. The burning sky's roar deafened Max and an endless rain of sputtering fragments fell through boiling clouds. Ioam whirled round, on the edge of desperate tears.

"Why aren't we in the tank? Where's Halinard? The bastard."

They jumped back. The God Talker sat slumped against the cockpit window, the muzzle of his gun in his mouth and half his head smeared up the glass.

"I wasn't quick enough to stop him," Nem shouted over her shoulder as she pulled the corvette into a tight turn to avoid a pillar. "Blamed himself for letting Vinduranto die."

"The stupid stupid bastard's locked us out of the citadel. His ironclad was our only route in." Ioam thumped the wall hard, leaving a dent.

"We'll have to save her out here," said Max. "Do we have enough to take down four giants?" He couldn't believe what he was saying, but with half the Giants of the West dead there were only Sorameistre, Bassandis and Ragaleis left on the side of mankind, outnumbered by their malevolent siblings and the monster Ruth. The

Mind was lost to the enemies of humanity. The only way they'd survive was by wiping it out. What choice did he have? *I'm going to be the man who destroys the Great Task.* His legs weakened, and he grasped at Nem's shoulder to stop himself falling.

"These are big missiles," she said. "In the right place they might kill a giant. Any idea where the right place is?"

Max hadn't a clue. They'd have to assume the titans' anatomy was a fair approximation of their own.

The witch flew the ship through an arch, heading towards the centre of the fortress. The walls and floor seethed with darkness and high above, amid charcoal rafters, winged creatures attacked a handful of Machine Men craft that had also infiltrated the citadel. They didn't stand a chance. Max guessed the guardians were Ruth's alien warriors, or their insect constructs filled with the power and intelligence of condensed galaxies. They'd have no qualms about ripping the corvette to shreds and letting its fragments fall a mile and half to the flagstones, along with the wreckage of Theuderic's flyers. *The second they see us we're dead. We've got to locate Ruth and destroy her before we're spotted and overcome.* He'd promised to kill her if she broke the spell between the Machine Men and the titans, but all she'd done so far was bring carnage. Even so, the stars took their cue from the mad girl and might give up once the connection was severed. Or he and his companions could just as easily end up as the target of an entire vengeful army.

But first they had to find the giants. Max couldn't see any logic in the random labyrinth of cube-shaped rooms miles high and filled with nothing but shafts of pale grey light falling from no discernible source. The building looked as if it had been crafted from cyclopean obsidian blocks, like a child's toy construction set designed to leave everything to the imagination. Doors opened on dead ends, or corridors angling back and forth between the cells. Ioam swore an increasingly desperate litany of vile curses as her sister dodged in and out of chamber after chamber, avoiding the ones where the floor was carpeted by shrieking madmen slaughtering each other in their thousands.

A familiar shape in the middle of a room down a side tunnel caught Max's eye.

"There, Ragaleis."

It was a copy of the titan's cell in God's subconscious, where he'd scooped horrors out of the primordial soul and moulded them into the sisters' nightmare watchers. Nem let the ship hover by the crudely hacked window. Inside a shadow sat on a rough bench with his hands clasped on his knees and his head down. If they could free him at least they'd have one ally against Ombratulla and Belsalice.

A padlock twice the size of their flyer sealed the door. Nem took up position a few hundred yards out, waggling her head from side to side with her left eye closed as she worked out the range before firing a pair of wing-mounted cannon. Armour piercing shells hacked the lock to pieces and it fell with a cavernous thud onto the dusty floor. Moments passed, Max wrestling with a mounting agony of fear. What state was the giant in? He'd struggled to reclaim his old strength in the Mind - was he any use to them here? *We're going to have to go in and pull him out.*

The door swung open so quickly Nem had to flip the corvette prow over stern to avoid being hit. The portal slammed into the wall and Ragaleis heaved himself out of his cell. To Max's relief the dull, stupid exhaustion he'd seen in the dream titan's eyes was no longer there. Instead he saw fury, and although the creature looked gaunt and took unsteady steps into the hall, he flexed his hands into fists.

"Max?"

Ragaleis stood in the centre of the cockpit. He looked at the three God Talkers in turn, but before anyone had a chance to speak his avatar vanished. Beyond the glass the vast shadow sprinted for the doorway. The impact of his footsteps made the cabin floor bounce like a trampoline. Nem turned the ship and raced after him, but by the time they reached the corridor outside he'd disappeared into the twilight labyrinth.

"Find him. He'll lead us to Sorameistre," shouted Ioam.

"I'm trying, I'm trying!"

She attempted to follow the sound of his feet, which still echoed through the bulkheads, but two junctions led them to more empty corridors and on the third she pulled out of a screaming curve right into the path of the giant Ruth.

She slouched at the far end of the passageway, a mountain of tattered darkness, sobbing with exhaustion and misery. One hand scrabbled at the wall, trying to keep her impossible bulk from collapsing, the other held Vinduranto's forearm. Its grey fingers still splayed in agony and as she dragged the elbow across the floor it left slick trails in the seething carpet of alien warriors and machines. Her hair was a ragged curtain, thankfully hiding her face, though two brittle points of light marked her eyes on the other side of the fringe. For a dreadful second Max swore her gaze caught his, and he saw the same tormented parade of betrayal and insane fury he'd seen in the sisters' dead garden.

"Can you kill her?" he asked.

Nem drove the craft up to the ceiling where the grey radiance gave way to night shadow. Far below half a dozen specks peeled away from the surface of the army and rose up towards them. He couldn't tell if they were fighters or the winged monsters he'd seen earlier. Whatever they were, he and the others wouldn't stand a chance.

"What are you doing?" asked Ioam as her sister powered towards Ruth.

"Twenty kilotons in the back of the neck will take her head off, but we need to be in front of the blast."

She did see me. He remembered trying to stop Bassandis in his pain-crazed odyssey across the Forbidden Sea. As she lifted her head and the lank hair fell away from her face he saw eyes racked with mad agony. The skin on her forehead was cracked and peeling like the bottom of a dried lake. Huge gouges had laid open her cheek, and he saw rotting teeth between strands of white muscle and sinew. Ruth searched the air, and he had the sudden urge to reach out, touch her and say he was sorry. But there was nothing in that blank snarl - no recognition - just despair and madness.

"Speed it up," shouted Ioam. "The buggers are on us."

Something with black metal wings landed with a thud on the hull behind the bubble canopy. Nem span the ship into a barrel roll that almost had Max's stomach corkscrewing up his gullet. As she forced the craft into a dive the slipstream ripped the creature free and it fell to tangle in Ruth's hair like a wasp. The sorceress righted the flyer and turned to face the back of the girl's head. From this angle she looked as vulnerable and as beautiful as when he'd rescued her from Ragaleis's house in the Wasteland. Once he'd even held her in his arms and struggled against desire.

A pair of smoke trails spiralled from the front of the corvette. Nem threw all throttles open and they screamed back over Ruth's hair in a furious dash for the end of the corridor. They'd just flipped round the corner when the walls flashed white. She managed to get them beyond three more junctions before the shock wave of two ten kiloton warheads caught up with them. Fire and dust snatched the ship up in a fist and threw it across a hallway big enough to house a mountain range. Nem howled, fighting with the engines as she tried to surf along the top of a sea of flame carrying them towards a wide arch. She almost succeeded. At the last second the flyer bucked and they smacked into the edge of the wall, spinning like a top as they were hurled into the next room. Half a dozen obsidian blocks fell past them, dislodged from the ceiling by the impact.

The universe filled with grey dust and the grinding rumble of walls and towers collapsing. The witch managed to slow the corvette, though it listed heavily.

"We did it," she exclaimed. "We blew her head off and we're alive."

"That's one down and three still to go," said Ioam pointedly, yellow blood trickling from a couple of gashes on her forehead. "Is every single kill going to be like this?"

A shadow flickered on the other side of a doorway full of choking haze. Nem eased the craft forwards, her expression grim.

They came to a second vast hall. Ioam cried out. In the centre of the room Ombratulla gripped Sorameistre around the throat and snapped at her face like an animal. The witches' giant pushed back, digging her thumbs into the cheeks of her attacker so they sank into the flesh up to the first joint. Beyond them Toldi and Ragaleis wrestled against a wall smeared in their viscous blood. Belsalice's severed head lay face up at their feet, her mouth open in an O of surprise. There was no sign of her body. The rest of the floor was smeared with the corpses of thousands of insane slaves, half of them trampled into a sickening mess by the titans as they'd fought back and forth across the room.

"Stop her, stop the bitch," screamed Ioam. Nem hammered at the controls but as they aimed for Ombratulla the two titans stumbled. Sorameistre flailed for balance and her hand smacked into the corvette. Max's world exploded in a chaos of glass, steel and darkness.

CHAPTER TWENTY-FIVE

"This is a human ship," said Crysanthe as the Black Roses changed into people. Ramul studied her, flanked by the endless glass tombs, her expression as unreadable as ever.

"We know."

"It's an ark. Our people set out from the singularity to look for the God Door. They must have known they wouldn't get through it by themselves so they came as supplicants looking for help. We're not the first to come begging to your God. That's why you attacked them."

A thought flashed into her mind and she gasped despite herself.

"The people of the Great White World. This is where they ended up."

Ramul shook her head.

"This spacecraft was assaulted, yes. But not by us."

"Liar," sneered Abby.

"Who stopped them?" asked Crysanthe.

"The Crystal God."

The universe was breaking apart word by word. Crysanthe almost felt as if she'd had this conversation before, and knew exactly how it played out.

"The Crystal God?" the contempt had gone from Abby's voice. It sounded far away.

"Her people, yes."

"Why did the acolytes of the Crystal God destroy this ship?" asked Selva as if she didn't even understand the language they were speaking.

"They don't want you in the next universe."

"Who else?" asked Crysanthe. "Who else is against us?" Oh for an army of Dogs or a fleet at her back. She'd wipe these arrogant gods from the floor of the cosmos for daring to judge mankind. For daring to judge her. Ramul's eyes momentarily filled with pity.

"The Roaring Face. He Who Twists. The Lady of Radiance. Others."

"Bastards," hissed Abby. "You're all against us. None of you want humanity in the new universe."

"Not all," said Ramul, as if that held any comfort. "Of the four hundred gods who walk towards the next cosmos just over half are against you. The rest are indifferent. A handful wish you well, including our people. But with a mad god, a sick god, you have no possibility of leaving this universe. He will not be allowed anywhere near the door. You'll have to come with us and beg our deity to carry you. It's your only chance now. I, Ramul, and these your utter friends..." she gestured at her fellows who placed their fake hands on their fake hearts and bowed, "...will plead on your behalf, others will speak against you. But there is still hope."

"Hope? What hope?" spat Abby.

"Our work here is done," Ramul said. "We are preparing to journey back to the Black Rose God. You have a choice. If you wish, one of us will guide you back to your own deity, or we'll escort you to ours so you can plead for help. In our company you'll be safe from the malice of other gods."

"What chance do we have, Black Rose?" Selva moved behind Abby, ready to grab her just in case.

"A chance."

"Why did you bother with mankind in the first place?" asked Crysanthe. "If all this is so futile what was the reason for the singularity and that stupid puppet we've built? What made you decide to help us?"

Ramul smiled.

"Admiration for the courage of a little girl and her foolish servant."

Selva put her hand on Abby's arm. The Time Scavenger shook her off and made for the tunnel. The Black Roses parted to let her through.

The aliens tethered their shining chords to the front of the ship and pulled them out of the hangar into space. With no rear windows Crysanthe couldn't see the wreck diminishing, but in her thoughts she pictured the hopeless mausoleum fading among the threadbare tangles of the universe.

"If they plan on towing us twenty light years we'll be long dead by the time we reach their god," said Selva.

Neke and Goma joined them. If the discovery that half of creation was set on barring mankind from the portal had sunk into their bread-loaf skulls it didn't show, or perhaps they wore desperation and grief differently to their hairless cousins.

"A space-time bubble has formed around the ship, emanating from those bits of string," remarked the Abhuman leader.

Crysanthe peered out of the window. At first it looked as if they hung in a stationary web of ancient yellow starlight, but after a while she thought she could just sense a faint blue-white radiance ahead.

The god door.

Once the sight would have elated her, filling her with the cold electricity of disciplined purpose. After their conversation with Ramul the only thing left inside was sick exhaustion. Without speaking to Selva or the others she made her way back to the ramshackle comfort of the ship's inner landscape.

All they could do now was wait. While they were speaking with the Black Roses, Hama and a few other Abhumans had scouted the remaining toruses and discovered thousands more of the dead in their glass test tubes. The creatures had either found broken pods or decided to have a go at tomb robbing, presenting the women with armfuls of clothes, a couple of books, meaningless artefacts and pictures. One photograph showed a noble ruler standing next to the ark which hung in a construction frame as clusters of engineering craft and platforms hovered around its half-built hull. Lords and ladies in towering headdresses of silk, jewels and fine-spun metals followed their master's gaze as he pointed at the juggernaut. Beyond it dark cables spanned an ochre sky. She handed it to Selva.

"Look how the strands lie. It's the eastern side of the Head. Long Lock, but aeons ago. They didn't come from the Great White World after all."

"This is hundreds of thousands of years before our history. I can't read any of the books. Are these the first builders?"

Crysanthe doubted it. The hairs looked complete, and she spotted the faint dusting of light on the underside of some that marked the presence of cities, factories and shipyards.

"They gave up so early," whispered the Companion.

Once the general would have judged the dead for their weakness and cowardice in abandoning the Great Task. But if she was going to allow herself the self-indulgent luxury of hate, the only target would be the other gods. At least she had the consolation of their old cabin back, in all its sensual Thin-Hans-crafted absurdity, but too many doubts crowded Crysanthe's thoughts so she left her lover to sift through the stash from the ancient starship and set off in the direction of the Abhuman settlement. She had questions to ask them, though when she thought hard about it she struggled to remember what they were. Post battle exhaustion guided her steps - the trembling light-headed nothing that filled her after every skirmish. Yet they hadn't fought anything. The Black Roses had merely told them the truth, and in doing so had peeled away another layer upon which humanity had built its last few hopes, to reveal nothing underneath but indifferent chance.

She knew this wasn't the way, but she kept on walking. One more hall and then she'd turn back, but then she came to bridge that spanned a room filled with copper sand out of which grew dark red crystals that reached to the parapet on either side. And then she entered a chain of rooms in white plastic, another corridor, and beyond that a rotunda of a hundred doors. One of them led down half a mile of iron stairs to end on a web of gantries in the upper reaches of a vault that encased a city built entirely out of metal cylinders and giant transistors.

"Where are you going?"

Abby stood behind her. For a few seconds she didn't recognise the woman. She struggled to answer - it was as if she'd been surprised in the middle of a filthy secret.

"Don't go," said the Time Scavenger. The sad plea was so unexpected that Crysanthe didn't know how to respond.

"Don't go where?"

"Out there. I can see in your face that you're not coming back."

"Don't be ridiculous, of course I'm coming back."

With a shock Crysanthe realised that as she'd traipsed through this endless world she'd forgotten everything -

Selva, Abby, the Abhumans, the mission, the Empire of the Ear, Nan, even herself. The woman walked up to her and took her hand.

"You two are all I have left now."

Abby hugged her. The insane ginger mop went up her nose and in her eyes. She put her arms round the girl, thunderstruck and struggling to know what to do next. In the end she patted the Time Scavenger on the back as if she was a fretful baby. Abby broke the embrace and kissed Crysanthe on the cheek.

"Come on."

Taking her by the hand the woman led her up the stairs. The siren call of the spaces beyond the dead city tugged at Crysanthe's mind.

"What are you doing here?" she managed to ask.

"I went and had a chat with that furry temple snake."

Crysanthe had no idea what she was talking about.

"The one in the room the Abhumans plucked out of the wormhole."

"The creature that tried to kill us?"

"No, it didn't, it's just angry. It's a god on that world so I thought we could get some tips on how to butter up the Black Rose God."

"And?"

"It said it'd grown sick of ceremony. For thousands of years its worshippers danced and sang and performed in front of it when all it wanted to do was talk. They even gave it babies to eat."

"Did it?"

"Yes. They longed for a monster, and so in the end it stopped trying to speak with them and made itself into the avenging horror they were looking for. Then they all died or got bored or pissed off to other worlds and left it alone. That's why it was so grumpy when we rolled up."

If there was a lesson in all this it bypassed Crysanthe,

but the story had distracted her long enough for Abby to lead her back to the Abhuman settlement. She dropped Crysanthe's hand and turned to face her.

"Ramul said there were four hundred gods - so many and over half stand against us. What chance will a human god have against one or two, let alone over two hundred? Even if Max fixed God's mind they won't allow him any-where near the door."

Crysanthe remembered their conversation with the Black Rose in the hulk.

"What did she mean about the courage of a little girl and her foolish servant?"

Abby face darkened. She chewed the inside of her cheek and kicked at the ground.

"A sick joke, echoes of Odilon. It's a line from a pan-tomime we used to put on for the treacherous shit - *The Gate of Light*. It's the story of how the God Door was dis-covered - just a kid's fairy tale."

Crysanthe didn't think Ramul had been joking, but she let it drop.

Frightened by the ease with which she'd lost herself, Cry-santhe spent the rest of the journey inside the hub. As the days crept by the radiance grew stronger, turning into a thin vertical band of blue light. Each morning they gath-ered at the window, Selva and Abby taking her hands in theirs.

"It's the Gate to the next universe, it's real," Abby whispered. "I saw it from the other side. But where are the gods?" The ship aimed for the bottom edge of the door where a flat glow fanned across a polished surface. Teachers and sages had often spoken of the floor of the universe, as if the cosmos was nothing more than an enormous room filled with galaxies strung together like the wall-to-wall glow bulbs of a Splenius pleasure house.

Crysanthe wished she had binoculars or a telescope to hand so she could see more detail. Selva leaned closer to the cold glass, her eyes narrowed. A matted brick of fur bumped up between them.

"Gods," clicked Neke and pointed.

At first she saw nothing more than a line of fly-dirt specks. Crysanthe expected mighty beings - but even as they approached, and the dots turned into shapes, all she could think of were ants on a doorstep.

The God Door's half a light year tall - of course they're nothing before such immensity.

The Black Roses towed the ship towards the end of the queue. It was clear they wanted to treat their guests to a beauty parade of the last gods of the old universe. Crysanthe wondered where the Black Rose deity was - near the front or the back, or halfway along - jostling between more monstrosities as they made their centuries-long steps? Three shapes loomed out of the darkness, outlined in the portal's glow. Fingers tightened on her own as Abby and Selva stood trembling on either side.

The first silhouette became a humanoid with plated skin and a crest arching from behind its head to fan out into spears of bone. A forehead jutted over eyes so deep that all she saw were black pits. Lights speckled the limbs in swirls and circles, and a cloud of glow worm motes flickered incessantly along the arms and outstretched claws. It was impossible to judge distances or scale. The Brittle Hag's spacecraft carried her into an infinite fractal that endlessly unfolded fresh vistas of light-spattered structures and hideous cancers of dark metal spiralling out from the god's torso. The shoulder filled the window yet they were still hundreds of thousands of leagues out. She guessed this creature was the same height as their own deity - half a million miles tall. It could have worn a necklace of ancient planets around its neck, or held a dozen in one hand. *Which immortal are you? Do you even have a name?*

"It's not right," murmured Abby beside her.

"What do you mean?"

"Dunno. Can't put my finger on it."

She realised her flash of irritation at the woman's pointless comment masked her own fear, so she said nothing. The ship continued to slide past the first creature. In the cracked gulfs between its scales Crysanthe spotted signs of whole civilisations crusting the fissures with fungus light. Long arteries of neon and fire spread over its shoulder and crest. Spacecraft spun in and out of pores in the skin that were nothing more than bright pinpricks - though she knew that each was hundreds of miles wide.

Two half-moon-shaped craft drifted towards them, matching their course. Weapon spikes projected from turrets banded with navy and green stripes. Window slits scattered at random over the crescent hulls told her nothing. They were lines of light surrounded by thick armour, making them look like a boxer's eyes swollen shut after too many blows. After half an hour they peeled away. Maybe some hidden communication passed between their captains and the feathered patches towing their ship, or perhaps they'd just grown bored.

On the other side of the immense god an upright multi-jointed cylinder hove into view. Clouds of ancient star fire surrounded the ball and socket links between each pod and speckled tentacles of moving light spiralled out in an endlessly writhing web.

"Do all these gods appear in the same shape as their people?" clicked Neke with the blithe curiosity of a child. Crysanthe had no idea.

"God help us if they do," grumbled Abby. She kept shaking her head, working over whatever preyed on her mind. Next came a figure cast in pure darkness with only a single halo of red beacons framing its reptile silhouette face.

"Could they have they seen us?" asked the scavenger after a while.

"Don't be stupid," snapped Crysanthe. "Gods take thousands of years to move."

Light-headed nausea burst over her every time a new monstrosity emerged out of the darkness, and the woman's cretinous remarks scraped at her nerves.

"Then why are they moving this way?"

"What do you mean?" asked Selva in a tone that said she was suddenly taking Abby's comment very seriously.

"I'm not sure about that tube thingy, but this one and the first one look as if they're turning round."

It was hard to tell, but the black lizard was definitely twisting towards them, like a dancer peeling from a line. Crysanthe recalled the first god. *We flew from shoulder to shoulder, it's standing at right angles to the queue. She's correct, it's changing facing.*

"What are they doing?" asked Selva.

"They're getting ready," says Abby, her voice grim.

"Getting ready for what?"

It's a rear-guard. They're setting up an ambush.

"The last gods in the line are going to defend the door, and the others, from the human deity," Crysanthe finally managed to say. "If and when he wakes up and makes the long journey through the night to this portal they'll be prepared for him."

We didn't build a warrior, despite Nan and her sword of God's purpose. We made a puppet - a giant child's toy. He won't stand a chance against these gods - and this is only three out of the two hundred or more ranged against us.

Abby swore under her breath as the Black Roses' ship towed them past the jaws of the monster. All Crysanthe could think of were the petty firefights of her youth - grinding mindlessly room by room - *breach, kill and clear, breach, kill and clear.* She knew exactly how a lone trained fighter would handle a dozen defenders but what use was that? *It's too late to teach God the Spear Tip Dance.* She laughed, and the others swapped worried glances at the wild madness in her voice. It was all she had left. These wondrous gods with their worshippers in their glittering cities and gorgeous ships rubbed her face in humanity's failure. *We achieved nothing like this, nothing but greed, hatred and stupidity...and now all those vicious little qualities manifest themselves in the mind of that immense half-dead abortion, insane and evil before it even steps off its slab.*

Claws ticked on rusted iron. Crysanthe glanced over her shoulder to find more Abhumans crowding into the room. Rustling and clicking from beyond told her that the creatures had left their settlement and filled the corridors and cabins. *They've all come to see our doom.* Nobody knew what to say. All they could do was watch the endless muster of hostile and indifferent gods.

The line of figures snaked towards the portal, their outlines blurring in the radiance shining from the next universe. When she glanced to either side she saw glowing blue columns in every Abhuman eye, as if they'd all been filled with starlight and it had burned them new cat pupils. They didn't seem interested in the parade of grotesques drifting past the spaceship as the Black Roses wove between limbs, tentacles, chitin-sheathed legs and delicate wings of light. Their gaze was fixed on the new cosmos. Crysanthe strained to see what lay on the other side of the brightness - stars in a dark sky like in the winged serpent's chapel? Nothing - just an endless migraine glow.

"Can you jump through that?" Abby asked, pointing at the door.

"Impossible," said Hama and Neke simultaneously.

"Its space-time structure is beyond us," continued the Abhuman leader. "We have no way of linking the old universe with the new. Besides, we have discovered that the attacks are coming from near here, probably made by one of these deities. Any attempts to shift will definitely alert them and be our undoing."

Crysanthe forgot the sight outside for a second.

"One of these monsters has been firing harpoons into this ship?"

A wall of spider faces nodded enthusiastically.

"There is no other explanation."

"So the fuckers know we're here," said Abby.

And they've got technology to match our most powerful craft. This was a race to get to the Black Rose God before one of those two hundred bastards finally batted them out of existence.

"I almost hope they refuse to help us," the woman continued. "I'd love to ram this spaceship right up one of their holy arses and detonate it."

She glanced at Crysanthe.

"What do you think, Crys? Shall we take them on and give them a reason to really despise mankind?"

Abby had a point. Training gathered back her fragmented thoughts and shaped them into the calculated hatred and contempt she'd always reserved for her greatest enemies. If she'd believed this craft could make a dent in a being half a million miles tall she probably would have said yes. All other options seemed guaranteed to fail.

"The Black Rose God," said Selva, breaking the moment.

A fountain of shimmering coils emerged out of the glow, twists of darkness spiralling out from a dense core. Rings and loops hung from the delicate filaments or jutted out from broader tendrils. Their guides changed direction, angling down towards the first of countless bands suspended on a vine that seethed in constant motion, like a river of crow's feathers shot through with lightning. As they approached, the general spotted splashes of light on the inner rim of the nearest ring. Slender spires thousands of miles long, and coloured actinic blue and acid yellow, pointed inward - their tips forming an irregular gap through which the aliens towed their craft. *Black Rose cities.*

Shards drifted towards them - splintered tetrahedrons studded with a few lights, dark orange and red against the harsh spectrum of the spire fortresses.

"I thought they didn't need spaceships," said Abby.

"A defensive fleet," answered Selva. Crysanthe tried to read her lover's silhouette. The girl had drawn into herself, closing up in the face of such inhuman power and no doubt layering her thoughts with Splenius cunning ready for the negotiations to come.

"Look," she said. "Troops for us to review."

Among the crushed and warped polyhedra one vessel was nothing more than a flat square covered in lines like a page in an exercise book. They dipped down and Crysanthe felt her mouth drop open as the score turned into millions upon millions of Black Roses standing in neat rows, fluttering in the light.

"Give them a wave then," said Abby, but before the general could fully take in what she'd just seen the legion vanished beneath the Brittle Hag's vessel.

They entered a cluster of rings embedded in a thick tendril. A valve irised open on the surface of one and Ramul and his companions towed them into a mile-wide tunnel stretching into the body of the ring. It was empty save for a few lights spiralling along the walls. After another age they settled onto a sheet of metal projecting from the side. Their escort released the golden chords, which sank into the surface of the platform and disappeared. The Black Roses gathered before the ship in a semi-circle.

"This is it," Crysanthe faced Abby and Selva, holding their hands tight in hers.

Selva gave a wicked grin and the Time Scavenger flashed a mock salute. She turned to the Abhumans. Neke put his claw on his chest and bowed.

"I shall come with you as one of the representatives of humanity," Abby translated. "So I can advise Empress Crysanthe on her dealings with the aliens. The rest of us will lurk deep inside the ship and make sure none of the 'feathery fucks', as Queen Abby names them, encroach on our domain."

The three women and Neke walked to the exit, the Abhumans around them pouring back into the trans-dimensional interior. The ramp fell down with a clang and the human form of Ramul ascended into the corridor. She favoured each of them in turn with a deep bow.

"Welcome to the worlds of the Black Rose God."

CHAPTER TWENTY-SIX

HE WENT LOOKING for Ruth in the state apartments at the top of the Carceral Archipelago, but although servants had lit the stove she wasn't there. Outside the tower a storm raged, turning the sky a deep indigo spattered with flashes of red. Perhaps they'd transferred her to the prisons, though he didn't remember giving that order. Max had insisted that she be cared for as an honoured guest, and that made sense if they were going to placate the Empire of the Ear. Maybe his son knew, but he'd no idea where the idiot boy had disappeared to, and for some reason he couldn't find anyone else to ask. All the halls, offices, corridors, barracks, canteens, workshops, laboratories and store-rooms were empty. Part of him actually preferred it this way. The vaulted spaces of the ancient tower took on a rich, lantern-lit nobility without the usual, endless human bustle. He hoped the tempest would clear soon - it would look even more impressive in the light of day. Thunder rolled, reaching a peak of fury so strong it sounded like murderous voices shrieking at each other.

From far below came the sound of someone knocking on a door. Although he knew it was at the very base of the tower, he heard it as clearly as if the visitor was in the next room. He made his way down through the Shadows to the secret entrance that opened onto the beach. Bassandis stood at the top of the steps, a long walking stick in one hand and a sou'wester on his head. He doffed it.

"Max, good to see you."

"I'm Herman Ocel. Max isn't here."

Bassandis paused and gave him an odd look.

"Are you going to let me in, Max?"

He didn't bother to argue. The storm was finally dying but up among the distant hills he saw countless corpses of black-shredded creatures. In the sky the tattered remnants of a cloud-sized jellyfish fluttered in the gale, its edges bleeding and dissolving. New ravines and chasms creased the landscape and as he watched more shadows dragged themselves to the rifts to tumble into the darkness below.

"It's the army Ragaleis made from God's subconscious mind, returning to its source," said Bassandis, stepping inside. He beat his hat against the wall, but instead of raindrops tiny coals fell onto stone where they hissed, sputtered and died. Memories started to flicker back.

"I'm Max?"

"Yes. You're Max." The giant put his hand on his shoulder. "It's over. There's nothing to fear anymore."

"Over? Am I dead?" Bassandis shook his head.

"When titans die some of our soul lingers in this world because we were fashioned from it. Not God Talkers - when you perish in reality you cease to exist here as well. If you're here then you're still alive up there." He pointed through the door at the seething clouds. As they settled gaps opened up to show the underside of a coal fire that spanned the heavens.

"Why did I think I was my father?"

"You miss him, of course. And you want to be him as he should have been, not as he was when the Black Rose took his life."

The idea was too odd to grasp, so he pushed the door

closed and turned to his guest.

"What happened?"

"We fought among ourselves. Whatever routines the Machine Men implanted in our minds were imperfect. They thought they were masters of all this, and yet because they were machines they didn't understand the infinite complexity of our thoughts and feelings. Those of us who spent time with you learnt to love man. Your mother's poems, Ioam's stories, Aelspell's rituals and incantations - all those things chipped at the hatred. Belsalice and Ombratulla never gave themselves that chance. When Theuderic finally tried to unleash the hate against you it didn't work, all he did was turn it back against its vessels. Ultimately my brothers and sisters aimed their loathing at themselves and each other."

"What about you? Of all the giants you had the most reason to despise us after I..." Max paused, trying to remember who he really was "... after what my father and Odilon did to you."

"Yes, but I was reborn. Your daughter - or the creature you are pleased to call your daughter - took me to her mind palace and filled me with the light and power of a new universe."

He stuck his arms out and turned in a circle, like a bride showing off her wedding dress.

"All the poison of the old universe fell away and left me new-made."

"Did any of your brothers or sisters survive?"

Bassandis replaced his sou'wester and gathered his coat about him, ready to venture back out into the last of the storm.

"I don't know. The new universe has given me the power to walk through this realm, so I'm going to search for their remnants. Even if they perished in the real world, there's probably enough left in here for me to reconcile them with each other. The Mind of God will not be made, but I hope I may fashion a haven from its remnants where they can be friends again, and live out the rest of their existence in happiness and peace."

"You're going to be the steward of God's dreams." Bassandis laughed.

"That's a very grand title, but yes, something like that."

He took Max's hand. It was no longer the hot, languid grasp of a fever victim. The handshake was firm and re-assuring.

"We might not see each other again, I fear. Thank you, Max. Go to the new universe, find a way to save humani-ty that doesn't rely on the sad wreckage of this god. Find a way, but you've got to hurry."

The grip tightened and sharp nails dug into his skin.

"You're still in great danger."

The clouds thickened once more until all he saw of Bassandis was a silhouette against the night sky. He tried to pull away from the giant's grasp, but it was too tight and tugged at him as though it was trying to yank his arm off.

"Sister's gone. We've got to find her," said Nem.

He lay on his back on the ceiling. The witch arched over him. Yellow blood dripped from the waist of her ex-oskeleton. It was her white fingers around his own pull-ing him awake. *How in God's name did we survive the crash?*

Nem braced her shoulders against the hull plate above. Armoured joints whined as the metal unfolded with a se-ries of deafening pops. Max managed to roll over onto his hands and knees and crawl out of the wreckage. Sharp pain flared in his chest. *Broken rib.* Dried blood from a ragged gash in his shoulder coated his left arm, and his whole body felt as if someone had spent a couple of lei-surely hours on it with a blackjack. He could just about stand, but he was more worried about Nem. She pressed one hand to her midriff and fresh gore welled between her fingers to etch gold rivulets down her legs.

"Got to find sis," said Nem in a voice stiff with pain.

It took him a while to realise he was stumbling over ridged white rubber scored with trenches. Pillars arched overhead, tapering to points. *Fingernails. Sorameistre fell when she fought Ombratulla and snatched us out of the sky.* The landscape suddenly made sense. The corvette lay upside down, one wing cutting into the base of the titan's thumb so the craft stuck out of her flesh like a splinter. It had stopped them piling head first into her palm. She'd curled her hand into a fist, protecting them when she fell. Through the gap between her little finger and wrist Max saw the arm stretching away, grey and mountainous in the dust-filled air, completely still. He'd no doubt Sorameistre was dead at the hands of Ombratulla. Judging by the cold silence from the hall beyond it didn't sound as if anyone else had survived either.

A coil of darkness lay fifty yards in the direction of the ring finger, like a hasty reminder the titan had scribbled on her hand. Nem limped past Max, gasping with the effort. He followed. The twisted corpse emerging from the gloom told him what he'd suspected all along. Nem knelt by Ioam and lifted her shoulders up. The witch's head flopped back at a horrible angle before she could catch it. The mad sister eased herself into a sitting position, cradling it in her lap. Max reached out to touch her.

"I'm sorry, Nem."

The universe exploded into a roaring smoked-glass carousel shot with lightning. He stood on platform floating in the middle of the air while huge metal spheres danced around him in a cluster of deranged orbits.

"IOAM, IOAM, IOAM."

He spotted Nem standing on top of a gold and scarlet banded orb. It hurtled up on his left side, passed overhead and curved down to his right like a seat on a ferris wheel. The witch held her arms aloft and howled across a valley at the broken remnants of a citadel projecting out of a wall of fused glass. Despite the strobing lights, and the incessant roar and shriek of Nem's infernal engine, Max saw the distant spires of paper-thin jade crumple under their own weight and collapse into the seething black mist in the gully below.

He snapped awake, stumbling backwards to fetch up on his bottom. Any longer in Nem's mind palace and he would have gone mad himself. The witch opened her eyes.

"It was a pretty castle. I wanted one like it, but my dreams are too mad."

Nem rummaged in Ioam's jacket and pulled out a book - *The Bold Knight and the Apple of Youth*. She riffled through the pages until she found one with the corner turned down and held it up in front of her sister's unseeing eyes.

"You didn't finish reading us the story. How does it end?"

Max had to look away. When he'd mastered himself enough to turn back, Nem stood up and lay her sister out on Sorameistre's palm. She handed the book to him.

"Look after this for me. I haven't got any pockets in this thing."

He took it from her. The edges were wet with blood and when the woman limped towards a gap between the towering fingers she left a trail across the skin.

Bassandis had told him that the war between the giants was over, in which case he guessed they'd killed each other in reality, and the fragments of their souls lingering in the Mind were as broken and fragile as the titan's own after Theuderic's dreadnoughts slew him in Metacarpi. That left the insane armies, alien warriors and the Machine Men to contend with.

Maybe Ruth's death had stopped the ancient suns, perhaps the legions of thralls had wiped each other out, and Theuderic had slunk back in shame and confusion to the outer world. He doubted it, even if nothing moved in the space beyond Sorameistre's fist. In his gut he knew it wasn't over yet. They were miles from the citadel's entrance, with no flyer. They'd have to trace a path out of these cyclopean chambers where hordes had fought each other across cracked flagstones as big as fields, and after that find their way through the inside of God's skull. Nem was badly injured, and he didn't know how long she could carry on. He wasn't leaving her to die here. They were the only two God Talkers left alive.

The witch eased herself through the gap between Sorameistre's index and middle finger. Max sprinted after her. He saw no point in trying to bring Ioam's body with them, and he was hard pushed to imagine a more fitting resting place for her than cradled in the palm of her giant.

He climbed down piles of wreckage to the floor. Nem knelt on one leg at the bottom of the debris slope muttering to herself. She didn't seem to be bleeding as badly, but Max had no idea how different her insides were. When she rose to her feet and gave him a weak version of her mad grin, her hair plastered to her face, it was obvious the exoskeleton was doing most of the work. If he found another human vessel it might have medical supplies on board. Even better if it still flew, otherwise he reckoned they faced a forty-mile slog through this charnel house.

He tried to figure out directions. The missile explosions hadn't destroyed the fortress, but a choking vapour hung in the air and clouds gathered below the ceiling. Given the size of the room it wasn't surprising that the detonation would kick off a localised storm. Far to his left he saw an entrance sealed with a heap of obsidian blocks. They must have come that way after killing Ruth. The two of them climbed to the crest of a rubble dune dotted with human corpses. It gave them a better view of Sorameistre. She lay on her back. Ombratulla's body sprawled at right angles, her face buried in her sister's neck. They looked like a pair of lovers kissing. Sick at heart, Max turned away.

Other shapes sketched ink-wash mountains in the haze. None of them stirred. Max couldn't do anything more to save the Great Task. He no longer cared about giants or gods. He just wanted to survive long enough to get out of the castle and beyond the Head to start looking for Abby. The rest of the universe could go fuck itself.

They stumbled down the other side, slipping in avalanches of rock and metal. At the bottom they found themselves at the edge of a nightmare. As the titans fought each other the battle had played itself out in an armageddon of slaughter and cruelty between their human armies. Eastern and western giants used the men and women captured from the Empire of the Ear, losing and gaining control over their minds so that whole divisions turned on enemies and allies alike, or simply went mad and destroyed themselves. Thousands more were crushed under the feet of the giants as they wrestled each other, pounding their slaves into acres of pulp and shattered bone.

Even though Max stayed as far away as possible from those grim lakes, the reek still clawed at his nose and throat. Stumbling past endless heaps of the corpses of those who'd avoided being trampled on was preferable to wading through endless sickening mess, but only just. In death the psychic hold over the troops vanished, leaving the victims looking as if they'd just fallen into a gentle sleep. All wore the same untroubled half-smiles, even though some still gripped the chewed guts of their disembowelled enemies. Rictus grins and staring faces filled with horror he could have coped with. The bland peace on every face made the carnage infinitely worse.

Max knew the only way he'd get through this part-sane was by fixing his eyes on the pale grey blur of the nearest open door. It lay about ten miles away, beyond more ridges of stone, metal and bodies kicked up in the battle. Without injuries Nem could have put him on her shoulders and carried him. As it was she stumbled through the filth, the exoskeleton clanking and hissing from its servos. Once in a while she almost lost her balance and had to stop, going down on one knee to steady herself. The witch didn't even acknowledge him. Her gaze was also locked on the distant archway, and her lips were a knife-slash of pain.

To keep his mind off the surroundings, and his desperate longing for Abby, he tried to plan their moves once they'd reached the brain cavity. With no transport they faced a journey of ten thousand miles or more, and once they passed through the Tympanic Membrane they'd be back out in a vacuum. Their only other option was to descend through the Skull, climbing down until they were below the atmosphere. Again, Max faced a trip that would take years on foot, and in every direction the Head was no doubt swarming with enemies. If they didn't find an abandoned flyer they were going to have to fight the Machine Men, if they hadn't all fled.

Nem stumbled again, fetching up on her knees at the bottom of the next ridge.

"We'll rest awhile," said Max.

"You go, Max. I want to lie down and sleep."

She sat back, her head nodding over her chest. Max swore. If she passed out now she'd never wake up. He reached up to slap her.

"Stay with me, Nem."

She bared fangs as long as his fingers. For a horrible second he worried the witch might forget where she was and chew his face off.

"What's the point? All the giants are dead."

"You can't leave me. We're the final two God Talkers, there's no-one else." He realised he was begging now, but he couldn't bear the thought of being the last one standing.

Nem peered down at him and giggled herself awake.

"You suggesting we make a few more? It'd be like doing sex with an eight year old."

Max didn't want to know what was going through her head, but it gave her fresh energy. She rubbed her face and staggered upright. He noticed the wound in her side. Yellow blood had clotted into a green-brown crust, so her naked body resembled a birch tree scarred with moss.

"Got any water?"

He spotted the wreckage of a ship on the crest of the next hill. *A transport.* The crash had torn both wings off and the crushed stern vented an oily thread of smoke but it might have medical supplies, or at least water for Nem.

After making her swear she wasn't going to sleep he scrambled up the loose slope, taking care not to touch the bodies tangled in the rubble. The tanker was wrecked beyond repair but he found a plastic can half-full of water in a stowage compartment under a seat. He turned back to find a nightmare standing between him and the exit.

This one was a diseased network of blood vessels joined by cancerous polyps and draped in tattered cloth. One of the growths - a dark rust-coloured gourd near the top - wore a distorted face smeared over its porous surface. It flickered and jumped like an image thrown by a malfunctioning film projector. Two tangles of filaments flexed like trembling hands.

Mind-blanking terror wrestled with his dead nerves

and muscles, trying to get them to react, to defend himself or fall to the deck and curl up in a thumb-sucking ball. Somewhere among the chaos another voice told him God Talkers were immune to the watchers made from God's id, and despite the monster's appearance it couldn't harm him. But didn't that only apply inside the Mind? This eidolon had escaped into the real world. If that rule was broken then all bets were off.

Could he call out to Nem? She was injured. What would she be able to do? The head mouthed words, shouting at him, gaze flickering hither and thither as it reacted to horrors in whatever realm the projection came from. A hand cluster pointed through the shattered cockpit towards one of the hall's exits. Max's fear subsided. Was the thing telling him to go in that direction, or avoid it?

The creature collapsed in a shower of grey dust, the dissolution so rapid and unexpected that Max cried out. A grainy shadow seethed on the floor, shrinking like a puddle in sunlight. He leaned as close as courage would allow as the last few specks vanished. They reminded him of something, but he couldn't place it. Not that he particularly cared - the exit was free, and he hurled himself out of the flyer in case the nightmare, or its relatives, decided to come back.

He gave Nem the water, and she drained it in three swallows.

"You yelled for me."

He told her what had happened. The pain left her eyes, replaced by wary curiosity.

"If Ragaleis's puppets are turning up out here that means God's mind has found a medium to give the beasts shape."

Max remembered where he'd seen the dust. "The ancient stars."

Some of them are still around and they'll definitely have no qualms about killing us after we murdered Ruth.

"Theuderic said Ombratulla and Belsalice brought a sickness that invaded their systems and shut them down," continued Nem. "It must have been the stars. They've set up a link with God's mind and they're pulling out the dreams and making them real."

But why? It didn't make sense. If that horror in the ship was a watcher given form by Ruth's microscopic allies, why hadn't it attacked him, and what did it mean when it gestured at the door? He had no answers, merely endless questions. Whatever the truth, they had to get out of the citadel as quickly as possible.

The witch stood up. She winced with the effort, but didn't look as desperately ill as before. He hoped the rest and the water would keep her on her feet a while longer.

"It wants us to go over there, does it? Good a place as any."

Injury had made her madness worse - now it was suicidal. She noticed his expression.

"If it wanted to kill you it would have done so already. Don't you want to find out what's going on?"

"No."

She ignored him and limped over the next ridge. He followed, muttering the old litany of oaths he used whenever Abby dragged him towards certain death. Its familiarity helped him order his thoughts, rewarding him with melancholy strength. *Let the buggers come.*

At length they came to the entrance to the tunnel. It wasn't as choked with debris and bodies as the others, and the dust eddied in a draught as it settled. Maybe this would lead outside after all. Even so, they separated and crept along the shadows cast by the wreckage, each spotting for the other. They had no guns - all their weapons had been lost in the crash.

The corridor was roughly a mile wide and three miles high. Soot and scars from energy beams and kinetic shells spread across the flagstones. The polyhedral silver hulls of Machine Men ships lay shattered at random points on the ground, resembling jewels embedded in dirty lead. He saw fewer corpses among the detritus. The mad legions had chased after their giants, piling into the final battlefield on the crazed assumption their insectile struggles would somehow sway the fight taking place above their heads. At least that meant that the worst was behind them. Just as Max started to hope, a Machine Man vessel drifted around the corner, spotlights sweeping for survivors and missiles locked.

CHAPTER TWENTY-SEVEN

Before Crysanthe could draw breath, Ramul burst into a roaring storm of black petals and engulfed her, yanking her off her feet. She tried to cry out but her eyes and mouth were choked with oily flutterings. Dead frost touched her lips. An instant later her vision cleared, and she found herself hurtling along the corridor and down the ramp, arms and legs flailing. She scrabbled at the thick band encircling her waist, but her nails just sank into its seething mass. The sensation was unbearable. She snatched her hands away in disgust.

Her stomach tried to force its way up her gullet as her captor fell through a world-sized vault threaded with black spires, arches and conduits. Far to her left she spotted Abby, upside down, a Black Rose blossoming from her back like demon wings. It was clear from the urchin's expression that she was shrieking every oath in her mammoth collection, but Crysanthe couldn't hear a thing - their mad flight was utterly soundless. Try as hard as she could it was impossible to twist round to see if Selva and Neke had also been kidnapped.

It was like tumbling through the inside of a human body fossilised into a network of midnight nerves and blood vessels. A web of tendrils, branches, tubes, filaments, cables, threads and chains spanned a vault that had to be at least as big as an ancient world. Random lights dribbled along the conduits or floated in the void, disturbed by more feathered clusters who drifted and flitted between the junctions in this deranged root system.

A disc appeared below, rushing up towards them so fast she thought they were going to smash into it. She braced for the impact, knowing full well they wouldn't survive, but at the last second the alien slowed, entering a funnel that narrowed down to a shaft twenty yards across. Half a mile and the tube opened out into a circular room. The Black Rose jolted to a stop and uncurled the tentacle from her waist, setting her upright beside a mountain of cushions. Moments later Abby was deposited head first in another pile. Selva landed on her feet beside her, wide-eyed and hyperventilating. Finally, a grey furry ball thumped onto floor, untangled itself and bounced around the curving walls in a chittering panic before diving into the heap next to Crysanthe. Two black eyes stared out at the general from under a pile of blankets.

"You will rest here and wait."

Human Ramul stood in the shadows. The other Black Roses had vanished.

"When will we meet with your leaders and the Black Rose God?" asked Crysanthe.

"Soon, don't give up hope. In the meantime you are our guests."

Abby snorted.

Two aliens fell down among them, carrying baskets. They placed them in the centre of the room and roared up into the funnel. Selva pulled out a round loaf and held it up in wonder.

"Bread. Still warm."

Crysanthe had lived for so long on the Abhumans' white tuber stew that she forgot their surroundings and joined the others in rummaging through the panniers while Ramul looked on.

"Where did you get this?" she held up a bottle in one hand and an apple as big as an otter's head in the other.

"Supplies from the ship we found."

Before anyone could stop her Abby tore off the end of a cob and stuffed it in her mouth. She chewed slowly, caught Crysanthe's eye, and munched faster before swallowing, going cross-eyed with the effort. The general guessed from the look in the woman's eyes that the alien lied. But why? And if she did, where had this food really come from? Whatever the answer, it didn't seem poisoned. Abby sat down and took a long swig from a flask before holding the remains of her bread towards a gap in the pile of cushions. A grey claw shot out and snatched it back into the hole.

"How will I state my case?" Crysanthe asked. "And to who exactly?"

"The Black Rose God." Despite her human appearance the utter stillness of her stance made Ramul twice as alarming as the roaring flowers that brought the supplies.

"Our god is a vessel for the people it'll carry, nothing more," remarked Selva. "Are you saying that yours is actually a ruler of your race, possessed of intelligence and wisdom?"

"It represents us. It is the sum of all our qualities."

"And it'll make the ultimate decision as to whether we can journey with you?" continued the Companion.

"Whether you can travel with any god. The other gods who side with man have agreed that ours will be the arbiter of your destiny. So it must decide not only if humanity is permitted to accompany us, but if you're fit to go through the God Door at all."

"Arrogant bastards, the lot of you!" Abby sprayed through a mouthful of food. "Who do you think you are to judge us?"

"We're the ones chosen by circumstance."

"What total and utter crap. 'We're the ones chosen by circumstance'," she whined in imitation of Ramul. "My arse. You're all liars and traitors. This is a colossal stitch up."

"Abby!" snapped Crysanthe. The scavenger gave her a *you know I'm right* shrug and took another swig.

Exhaustion swept over her. *It's hopeless. How can I say anything to add to or detract from the history and evidence of mankind?*

"When do I meet the Black Rose God?"

"Soon, but I think you should rest first and compose your thoughts. We are all at the end of billions of years of this universe's existence. What you present will determine whether you will continue into the next. Choose your words carefully and take all the time you need to prepare."

Ramul streaked into the dark chimney over their heads.

"Arsehole," said Abby.

Crysanthe looked round. *No doors.*

"We're prisoners."

"Perhaps," answered Selva. She sat cross-legged on the cushions next to Abby and picked a loaf out of one of the baskets.

"This didn't come from the dead hulk. It's fresh, and I doubt the Black Roses eat this kind of food."

"They baked it for us. How?"

"Does it matter?" asked Abby. Crysanthe wasn't sure if it did. She joined the others and ate a proper meal for the first time in months. It tasted beautiful. Neke crept out from his hideaway and picked at some fruit.

"We're all speaking before the Black Rose God," Abby gestured to the group. "It's not fair if it's only you."

"This is diplomacy of the highest subtlety," Selva

pointed out.

"I'm good at that," Abby caught her expression. "What? I shouldn't have called her an arsehole? Sorry, that's just me. I tell it like I see it." She paused, dropped her head into her hands and started to cry. Selva and Crysanthe stared at each other, then simultaneously shimmied over the cushions towards the woman. She waved them away.

"No, it's alright. I'm fine. It's only Max and the sprog. I know they're dead, but it's so hard not to hope." She rubbed her face with her palms. "Shit. There we are. All OK."

She blinked furiously while Neke patted her on the head.

"I've no intention of delaying. I'll speak with whomever I need to after we've rested," said Crysanthe. "I won't prepare a speech. Human rhetoric will be meaningless to these aliens. I'll fashion a simple plea for mercy."

Selva watched her with an unfathomable expression, but didn't volunteer anything.

"There's nowhere here to play political games."

The Companion nodded. The general wanted so much to take her lover and lose herself in the few hours remaining, drawing whatever comfort she could in the girl's arms. Abby paused in the middle of building herself a nest.

"If you two want to fiddle with each other, don't let me stop you. I'll just close my eyes and put a cushion over my head."

Selva burst out laughing and mouthed *your sister reads you like a book.*

In the end they rolled themselves up in a knot and Crysanthe lay with the soft breath of her partner on her eyelashes and her hand on a muscled thigh. Abby snored in the other heap of cushions. She'd no idea what Neke was up to, though occasionally she'd hear a faint clicking as the Abhuman chatted to himself. Whether it was mathematics, a fearful monologue or prayers she couldn't tell.

After ages staring up at the shadowed mouth of the funnel she crept out from under Selva's embrace. Of course she couldn't sleep, yet as much as her mind raced none of it had enough coherence to fashion into the last plea for mankind. Tired and frustrated to the edge of tears she walked round the perimeter of the room, chewing absentmindedly on a bitter pear. She almost passed the doorway without realising it.

That didn't exist before.

The amber light from their prison illuminated a ramp that stretched into the darkness. A shadow drifted over it and she fell into a combat crouch. Neke crept towards her, claws ticking on metal.

"No aliens or monsters," he clicked. "Come and see."

He took her by the hand and led her along a narrow bridge. Even though the light only revealed the cleated plates under her feet she sensed an immense void above and below. The path led to a platform. A steel staircase rose up from the centre into the darkness. She paused and listened. Was that movement in the black gulf beyond? A faint wind hissed around her. She looked up the stairs, but they faded into darkness.

"It appeared when we slept. Shall we climb? It is very exciting and intriguing."

Crysanthe looked at her own reflection in his opal eyes. *I'm dreaming. This isn't real.*

She climbed a few steps, the sharp-edged metal hard under her feet.

"Empress. Is there any hope here?"

"There's no hope anywhere anymore, but returning to the night won't save us. Wait for me, and if I don't come back in an hour wake the others."

Neke's head wobbled. He put his claw on his chest and gave her a deep bow.

Crysanthe climbed. This whole structure was clearly intended for the human guests - Black Roses had no need of stairs. She glanced down to the right and saw the bridge leading to the room far below. Neke stood at the bottom, one hand on the rail as he tracked her ascent. She sensed other eyes, inhuman senses playing over her. *This is some kind of test. What do you want from me?*

Their prison disappeared into blackness, though an invisible light source still illuminated her as she hauled herself ever upwards. After an age the general came to a circular landing. Ramul waited for her at the bottom of a second flight.

"Where do these stairs lead? Why are they here?"

"They were fashioned specifically for you, Crysanthe Uella."

She bristled. No doubt Selva would have met such condescension with a precise and elegant riposte, but she found it harder to mask her anger.

"I represent all the governments of humanity at the end of all things. I am deserving of the same respect as your rulers, whoever they are. As a scion of my people I'm not a subject for your games. Just because you've thrown mankind a lifeline doesn't mean you can treat us like fools." Time was when she wouldn't have bothered. Instead she'd have snapped a neck or driven a blade through an upstart's heart.

"This isn't a test. Whether you continue or not is up to you, and won't have any bearing on the final decision. We are split among ourselves, as you know, and your utter friends have to tread carefully. That's why you should climb, so you can understand what you're really up against."

The alien's infuriating obliqueness convinced her

more and more that this was only a vision, either implanted in her head by the creatures or born out of her own fears. Nevertheless she turned her back on Ramul and kept climbing. With each step she sensed a growing multitude in the darkness. She was a trapeze artist hauling herself up a ladder, lit by one cruel spotlight and watched by an audience who'd only bothered to pay in the hope she'd fall off and kill herself. Was she expected to make her supplications to the Black Rose God at the end of this painful trek? She'd rather spit in its face.

Another landing. A squat humanoid dressed in white armour observed her with topaz eyes. It had a wedge-shaped skull and ochre skin. She wondered if it was a worshipper of the first deity they'd seen, the one turning round to defend the line against the human god. The alien's claws tapped on the glass hilt of a sword. *Am I going to have to fight now?* Her weapons were in the ship, but that didn't matter. Ten seconds and she'd be holding up the beast's head by its jagged crest.

"If you ever make it into the next cosmos we'll battle against you so that you can't renew the cruelties you visited on us in this reality," it said in the voice of a patient grandfather tested to endurance by a fractious toddler. "Go back to your mad puppet and die in the darkness. There is nothing above you but despair."

Despite herself all will to struggle drained away. Her legs ached and her mind filled with tired sorrow. Yet the lizard man stepped to one side, bowed and gestured at the stairs. *You want me to see the futility of it all for myself.*

If time existed in this half-dream Crysanthe soon lost track. Sometimes she thought others climbed with her, dragging her upwards with insistent hands. Nan, Bauto, Selva, Thin Hans, all the Companions one by one, even vile Enguerrand and the senile Emperor Demetrius. She'd been staring down at the pool of light around her feet for the last hundred flights and now she noticed it was brighter, taking on a blue tinge. She stepped onto yet another platform and looked up, hunting for the source.

At first Crysanthe thought the Black Roses had dangled a patterned ball just above her head and she reached up to touch its bright surface, searching for the lamp's heat with her fingertips. Scale shifted, and she realised she was staring at an immense sphere hanging in the void. Combat training kicked in and she winked, trying to figure out the parallax. It didn't shift. *How far away is that thing?* She studied it more closely. It was so cold up here that her breath fogged the air and it took her a few minutes to take in all the detail. The bauble was coloured with random splashes of blue, brown and green, overlain with a delicate swirling white lace. It seemed strangely familiar though she knew she'd never seen anything as beautiful and strange before. If Crysanthe looked closer she could just make out fine lines dividing the image up into a fishnet grid that curved around the sphere. Once in a while a tiny mote of light flashed along a thread or at a knot. She walked from one edge of the landing to the other, her eyes fixed on the disc. Still it didn't move.

"If you're wondering how big it is, it's ten thousand miles in diameter, and we're standing sixty thousand miles away."

Ramul stood beside her, head angled up at the vision, its pale circle duplicated in the centre of her penny eyes. Realisation hit Crysanthe like a mallet to the chest.

"It's an ancient world from the deep abyss of time. You've preserved one of your planets from the age of the stars."

Ramul said nothing. The general gazed at the sphere, all fear and anger swept from her mind. To stand in those fields and among those mountains, to walk on the shores of a blue sea and look up at a sky laced with clouds. Endless questions crowded in. She had no idea where to start. Suddenly the dark horror of abandonment had been replaced by hope, but for what? A thin black line along the equator speckled with flashes. The creature nodded at the world.

"There's a war in heaven," she said.

"Between who?"

Ramul gave Crysanthe a disarming look of pity.

"Why are you showing me this? What is that?"

She pointed up at the planet.

"It's the reason the people of the human god will never be allowed to enter the next universe."

The alien lifted her arms and they both dissolved into a storm of petals.

She woke up to find Selva, Abby and Neke gazing anxiously down at her. The ceiling beyond her Companion's head was a tracery of delicate stars against pale blue. At first she thought she was lying under the sky of the ancient world until she spotted the erotic parade stitched in dark silk - a gift from Thin Hans. *I'm in our cabin on the Brittle Hag's ship.* She sat up and the universe span, she stuck her head between her knees.

"Report."

"We woke to find you gone," said Selva. She looked gaunt with fear. "Neke told us you'd climbed a staircase, but the entrance was sealed. Ten Black Roses appeared and carried us back to the ship. I found you on the bed. They towed us into space, said they won't help mankind and warned us never to return. We're now about twelve thousand miles from their god. What happened?"

"I saw an ancient planet, and Ramul told me it was the reason we're barred from the next cosmos."

"A planet?"

"Take us to your room of maps," Crysanthe said to

Neke.

As they jogged into the ship Selva asked if she'd spoken with the Black Rose God.

"No."

"So why have they decided to deny our request?"

"They never intended to help us," Abby growled. "Bastards always lied to us. Why should this be any different?"

"I want to open a portal to the surface of the world I saw, can you do it from this distance?" Crysanthe told Neke as soon as they entered the map room. He looked startled.

"We may alert the invaders and call down more harpoons."

"I don't care. Do it."

He waved at the Abhumans standing on the lead sheet, clicked out some instructions and they dropped as one, crawling around on all fours and chittering excitedly. Goma ran out of the hall, returning with another two dozen. They dived into the mass, pins in fists.

"We're going down into that world?" asked her lover.

"Ramul said it was the reason we're barred from the next universe. I want to find out why."

Abby and Selva broke into identical grins and the scavenger smacked the Companion hard on the shoulder.

The Abhumans tied space-time in knots for this incursion. The corridor leading down to the surface turned right ninety degrees six times without colliding with itself. Fifty yards after the last twist Crysanthe heard the soft weave of air through long grass and smelled loam - a heavy, bewildering scent far different from the bitter chemicals in Catagen's fake soil. She found herself on a grassy slope that spread downward into a valley before rising up to a forest on the far side. Somehow the Abhumans had managed to hide the entrance to the ship behind a house-sized boulder. Selva, Abby, Hama and Neke gathered in its shadow.

She looked up at the sky. Four bright points hung above the clouds in a vault the colour of brushed metal - tiny suns hanging in the atmosphere. She hadn't spotted them from the staircase, their radiance only fell on the surface below. The faint lines crisscrossing the sphere formed a lattice from horizon to horizon. The cords were thicker and speckled with random bursts of light. *This whole world is artificial. Why build a new planet in the old universe?*

A cylindrical building with glass, steel and white stone walls sat among tended lawns in the middle of the valley. A bubble-canopied jeep rested on four yellow rubber-ball wheels.

"That's where the food came from," Abby nodded at a cluster of outhouses. Crysanthe had never looked further past her plate or billycan but the Time Scavenger had walked ancient worlds and seen the lives of others. Animal noises drifted on the wind.

"There's someone in the house," said Selva. "Perhaps a Black Rose in human form."

"Wait here and prep to leave," Crysanthe told Neke. She turned to give her companions the nod to start a covert advance, but Abby was already jogging over the grass towards the tower.

"Has that fucking idiot never heard of stealthy reconnaissance?"

By sheer luck whoever was inside had their attention elsewhere, and they reached the entrance without triggering any alarms. Abby waited for them with revolver drawn. She slipped through the door and they padded along a corridor. Reflected light from picture windows bounced off cold tile.

The man stood at the window in a room at the back

of the house, sipping from an elegant cup as he gazed down the valley. A plate with a single pear sat on a glass table. It all looked so normal, so simple and so beautiful. The occupant didn't stand like a Black Rose. He'd tied his long blond hair in a ponytail and wore a baggy blue shirt over multi-pocketed black trousers. Crysanthe realised she was looking at another human.

Abby whistled between her teeth and the man jerked round. She trained the gun on his heart.

"Move away from the window," said Crysanthe. He clearly understood her as he shuffled to one side, face white and hands trembling. The precise beard was shot with grey - she guessed early sixties. As soon as he was out of sight of the valley Selva had him up against the wall with a sword against his throat, pressing just enough for pain and a trickle of red onto his collar.

"Lie and you die. Anyone else here? Anyone coming?"

He shook his head, blinking furiously as he started to whimper. The Companion frisked him before pushing him onto a stool. She handed Crysanthe a notebook and what looked like a communication jewel. The book contained pages of numbers and charts annotated in an unfamiliar script. The general turned a chair round and straddled it, elbows on the back. Selva went to search the rest of the building while Abby chewed her way through the pear, revolver on the tabletop pointing at their prisoner.

"If you attempt to flee or alert anyone we shall kill you, very painfully, do I make myself clear? What is this place?"

Puzzlement briefly overcame terror in his face. He clearly thought the answer obvious.

"Observation tower 775." His accent and pronunciation were odd, carrying an archaic, musical lilt, but it was human speech alright.

She waved at the window.

"No, all this."

"The Valley of Desolation."

This was going to be a slog - the man was a cretin.

"What is this world?" asked the Time Scavenger in the slow shout of someone addressing the terminally thick. His hands flew to his mouth. The waif spat pear pips onto the table top and picked up her gun, daring him to make a break for it.

"Who are you?" he whispered.

"I am Crysanthe Uella of the Empire of the Ear, and this is my friend Abby Fabrice of Thumb."

The stool clattered over backwards and he was against the far wall, hatred and terror in his eyes, pressing himself against the stone as if he could push his way through the brickwork.

"You're the tainted ones, the discarded, the filth we left behind. How did you get here?"

CHAPTER TWENTY-EIGHT

Nem fell to her hands and knees on the rearward slope of a pile of rubble, while Max ducked down behind the shattered hull of an imperial flyer. The chances of evading the Machine Men were slim. Even if they hid the creatures probably had sensors that would pick them up, unless he buried himself deep within the wreckage, hoping that the scrap would generate enough interference to scramble their instruments. But Nem was a white streak in a metal cage and despite trying to stay hidden she stood out like a pale beacon in the twilight dust.

She must have figured out it was hopeless because she climbed to the top of the heap and put her hands on her hips, staring at the vessel. The crew spotted her and the ship drifted to a stop, settling on a tripod of spider-thin legs. Max cursed her to the skies. Even if she was trying to decoy them away from him it was a stupid move. Nem looked so insolently indifferent to the threat she'd make anyone automatically suspicious, and besides, where was he supposed to be making a break to? He wouldn't get past the flyer and if he turned and ran back into the room they'd pick him off in seconds. Why the ship didn't blow his companion to pieces, he'd no idea. To his astonishment she waved at him to join her. He'd forgotten she was completely mad, and now she proved it.

"Come on, I've got a plan," she shouted cheerfully.

He noticed her hand was clamped to her side again and yellow blood glistened between her fingers. She wasn't thinking of hijacking the ship, was she?

A silver door petalled open and four Machine Men stepped out and walked towards them, two heading in his direction.

"Maximilian Ocel," one of them called. "You are to accompany us to King Theuderic, Lord of the Machine Men."

The Machine Men drew weapons - black pistols that looked like rows of tennis balls impaled on a stick. He wasn't prepared to let Nem die alone and maybe he could bargain his way out of this. He stood up and walked to Nem's side, hands in the air.

"What's this wonderful plan then?" he muttered.

"There's something peculiar in that heap that might be to our advantage."

Between Max and the newcomers lay a pile of corpses. Among the tangled limbs and pale faces and hands he saw a couple of the alien warriors - carapaces and spines shattered by energy beams. The light was odd. At this distance it looked as though dark smoke crept through the dead, as if someone had tried to start a funeral pyre but it hadn't taken. The Machine Men saw it as well. They paused, guns aimed at the bodies.

In an explosion of oily vapour a spindle-armed figure with a lantern jaw, top hat and tails rose out of the pile. Max yelled out and jumped back in fear, landing on his bottom. It was huge, almost the size of a house - another nightmare creature from god's unconscious mind given form in reality. As he battled yet again with freezing panic he realised the bodies hadn't shifted. Instead of hiding underneath, the creature had formed in front of their eyes out of the creeping smoke. *It's the stars that powered the alien sentinels, but who's turning them into dream watch-*

ers? He remembered his conversation with Bassandis in the Carcarel Archipelago. *'You're going to be the steward of God's dreams.' He's doing this - he's using the suns that interfaced with God's soul and turning them into monsters to help us.* As if it read his thoughts, the being swivelled towards Max and Nem and doffed its topper in a gesture that would have made Max laugh if he hadn't been so terrified. It turned back to the Machine Men.

"Nice dream," said the witch as if she was trying to calm a pet dog who fancied his chances with a stranger. Before the Machine Men could fire the creature pounced. Two of the humanoids vanished in a greasy splash of claws and darkness. Max heard the teeth-scraping shriek of crushed metal. Before he could stop her Nem leaped forward, lashing out at one of the other Machine Men with her foot. A crimson beam sliced the air, missing her, but as she ducked she stumbled and fell sprawling. The nearest humanoid pointed her weapon at the witch's head. Max yelled out, knowing that the blast would shear his friend in half. Thin lines of smoke speared past on either side of him and both Machine Men's heads exploded simultaneously in a spatter of clockwork, paper and pale fluid. Giant cotton wool fists boxed Max's ears as the detonation flung him backwards. He found himself lying on his back staring up at a human woman in the uniform of the Empire of the Ear with a tactical missile launcher in her hands.

She spoke to him but the ringing in his head drowned out her voice. She stepped out of sight and Max felt a cold weight on his feet. He tried to squirm away but a foul pressure pinned him to the flagstones. A shadow bubbled up from the bottom of his vision and a monstrous face filled the sky. Eyes that were nothing more than holes in an oil slick stared into his. Protean fingers caressed his cheek. He couldn't scream or move. The watcher looked up at the woman and mouthed something. Tattered rents appeared in its skin and it dissolved into a cloud of shreds blown to nothingness by an invisible wind. *It's gone back to the id.*

He stood up and faced the woman, expecting madness. She appeared as calm and indifferent as the surrounding dead, studying him with thistle-coloured eyes. Her blonde curls were tied back in a braid that looked like she'd used it to paint pictures in blood. She wore a Long Lock uniform of black and silver battle-mesh, close-fitted against her wide-shouldered, muscular body. Max reckoned the soldier was the same age as he. In other circumstances he might have found her attractive - she had the same high-cheeked alien beauty as Crysanthe and Selva, but he realised from the lines on her face that the frown was more or less permanent. She stared as if she didn't understand what he was. He read the badge on her chest.

"Gisele. Thanks."

She gave him an odd look before glancing down at her name and staring at it for a few seconds. It had to be the after-effects of the insanity. Max hoped they didn't include sudden urges to shoot strangers. He remembered Nem.

"My friend's injured."

She nodded OK, and he ran to the witch who knelt head-down with her hands to her stomach. The explosion had laid open a few more cuts on her arms and torso but none of them looked as serious as the wound in her abdomen. He looked up to see Gisele climbing into the Machine Man vessel. *The bitch is leaving without us.*

Max managed to coax Nem to her feet so that her exoskeleton took over. When she limped alongside him she looked like a marionette in a machine, shuddering on invisible strings. Either the woman had waited, or she just hadn't figured out how to fly the craft yet. Nem crawled on board and slumped in a corner. Gisele shot them both a frown, her eyes locking on Max for longer than was comfortable. She spun up the dynamos and shut the hatch as the flyer wobbled into the air. He didn't know how good a pilot she was and they were about to run the gauntlet of any remaining ships outside. A half-barmy amateur would get them killed in seconds.

"Can you operate this thing?"

She gestured to the controls, and he stepped in to take over.

"Look for any medical supplies for Nem."

He'd have to trust her. After a few minutes she told him what he expected - there was nothing on a Machine Man scout that would help the witch, not even water. Max wasn't going to let his friend die. He pulled round in a tight turn and headed for the way out.

"You're wearing a Long Lock uniform. What happened?"

"I woke up here. I don't recall anything else."

You don't remember taking part in the slaughter of millions and the destruction of the AntiHelix? If that was the case she was lucky, though her tone of voice didn't convince him.

They sped through the immense grey-dusted mausoleum. Its titanic child-block simplicity held neither comfort nor humanity, and without Ombratulla and Belsalice's fantasies of power to sustain it anymore it was a dead and wretched maze. Max took the ship up to a mile so he didn't have to see the details smeared over the obsidian floor. By sheer luck he located a doorway opening onto a platform on the upper battlements and they left the fortress, flying over the aftermath of the siege. The radio broke the silence with constant chatter - a strange high-pitched clockwork language writing words on the back of his neck with ice. He couldn't tell if it asked them to report in. Inevitably its crew had told the others what they'd found. It wouldn't take long for Theuderic's strag-glers to come after them.

Gisele appeared beside him, looking out on the car-nage with an unreadable expression. Max snatched a glance at her profile. Something vaguely familiar about her nibbled at his thoughts – odd, as he'd never met her before in his life. He put it down to her resemblance to Crys and Selva - all the imperial women were cast from the same mould. He followed her gaze and spotted the bodies of Vinduranto and Mephyrean lying on the ramp leading up to the entrance. Vessels flitted around them. Judging by the wreckage at the foot of the outer defences the last of the Machine Man fleet had suffered atrocious losses. He aimed for the ceiling, hoping they could get deep into the Forehead before anyone noticed.

"Company," said Gisele.

A couple of ships spiralled up towards them. They looked like small scouts, and one trailed smoke, but Max had no doubt they carried sufficient weaponry to take the flyer out. Lights on the console started to flash.

"Hailing us."

The woman's insistence on stating the obvious every two minutes was starting to tweak his nerves. He was about to reply when Nem appeared between them. Gise-le shrank back, eyes wide with fear. The witch looked hideous - a frightful, gaunt demon with a sick grin on her face.

"Guns and missiles? Big pretty ones?" She poked at a few switches.

"No, Nem!"

"They will follow you. They will follow and follow and follow and follow. They know what you did. Get rid of them and you might escape."

Before he could stop her she hit more buttons and six trails curved out of the prow, looping beneath them to lock on to their pursuers. The closest scout exploded in a sprawling cluster of fire and debris. Its wingman tumbled down into a crazy spin, spraying chaff in a desperate attempt to avoid the incoming rockets.

"And off we go," said Nem, slamming her hand down on a lever.

Afterburners kicked in, making her lose her balance and throwing her into the rear of the cabin. Max held on, wrestling with the guidance system as the wall of the mind vault raced towards them. He just managed to steer into a pit and next second they roared through a tunnel tens of miles across - a mote lost inside the lacunae of the mad god's skull.

After ten minutes the afterburners ran out and Max managed to gain enough control over the ship to guide them into a side tunnel. He switched back and forth through a maze. No one seemed to be pursuing them but he flew on, using every trick he knew to lay a false trail. Gisele watched the landscape speeding by and said nothing. Nem hadn't moved since the power surge had sent her sprawling against the rear bulkhead. She sat with her chin on her chest. He didn't even know if she was still alive, but his first priority was finding a supply cache with medical supplies.

Sometimes the ship sped along narrow corridors, at others it entered vaults thousands of miles high. Clearly fashioned in the very beginning of the Great Task, they formed world-encompassing cathedrals of stunning complexity and beauty teased out of glass and steel, diamond, samarium - all the elements of the universe both ancient and new-created. They stood in stark contrast to the cobbled-together wood and iron of later aeons. All were empty of life. Whatever their purpose, no-one had lived here or left anything useful.

He was exhausted and struggled to concentrate on piloting the ship. Gisele tapped him on the shoulder and pointed at a twenty-mile-wide shelf sticking out of the side of a chamber scooped out of a hollow ball of tanzanite three hundred miles across. It had a light speckled coin in the centre - a lake. Hope gave Max enough fresh energy to set the flyer down on the shore.

Vast statues cluttered the tarn - arms, torsos and heads sprouting from the surface like mountains. He tasted the water - freezing, laced with a coppery antiseptic, but drinkable. Max didn't have anything to carry it in so he filled his hands and ran back to the ship. Conscious he was holding his fingers next to six-inch shark's teeth he managed to pour most of the water into the witch's mouth. She opened her eyes and licked his palm with her forked tongue. A sour reek rose from the wound in her side.

"Where are we?"

"By a lake."

"Take me to it."

Gisele helped him manhandle the exoskeleton out of the cabin and it clanked alongside Max to the water's edge. Nem thumped the release button and fell out of the suit in a heap of birch-white limbs and midnight hair. Max tried to help her stand, but she shook her head, pulled herself to the shallows and sat up, legs in the water.

"It's beautiful. Look at all we did. Look at all we can do."

Max splashed into the lake. If he got her to drink and washed the wound he might still have a chance to keep her alive long enough to find aid.

"No. Leave it. Sit by me."

One look into her eyes told him it was pointless to argue. What could he do? He sat down beside the witch. She held his hand in hers, the spider-white fingers caging his own.

"It can't end here, Max. Get to the God Door, whatever it takes."

Nem rested her head on his shoulder. It was like trying to prop up a huge rock. She ran a talon over his palm.

"Lucky boy."

"She left, Nem, remember?" he said, struggling to keep his voice even. "The Brittle Hag went to the next universe with the Steel Queen."

"Did she? That's a shame." Her head slumped and before he could catch her she slowly toppled backwards.

He sat forever, holding the witch's hand and trying to focus on the silhouettes of the statues against the tanzanite sky. They danced, their outlines shimmering, breaking apart and reforming. Eventually he washed his eyes in the lake and trudged back to the flyer. Gisele stood by the hatch.

"I'm sorry, Max."

"I want to build a pyre before we go and…"

He stopped.

"How do you know my name?"

"What do you mean?"

"I never told you my name."

"I heard Nem call you Max."

"No you didn't."

She grinned and recognition flooded through his mind, bringing with it a cold, angry fear.

"Ruth."

"Is it that obvious?"

"You died. We blew your fucking head off."

She was half a foot taller than Alaric's daughter, with blonde hair and the wide-jawed beauty of an athlete, but there was no mistaking the look in those eyes, or that smile. They hadn't destroyed her. Somehow she'd transferred her soul from the monstrous giant into this Long

Lock soldier.

"How?"

"The ancient suns. When you killed me they rescued my mind and poured it into Gisele's corpse. They fixed her up and here I am."

Max remembered the seething, grainy smoke enveloping the broken girl on top of the giantess's manufactory. It had seeped through the glass to sow her being in a body fashioned from thousands of victims.

"They can help Nem, bring her back to life."

Ruth shrugged.

"They've gone from me. I tried to keep the truth from them but in the very end they realised what they were asked to do, to destroy man's chance of journeying through the God Door. After fixing me they want nothing to do with this age anymore. They will go back to their own era, or find another in which to nurse their guilt."

He would have ripped her murderous head from her shoulders. The vile bitch lived and his friend lay dead in the shallows of an inhuman sea. At the same time he cursed himself - if some of the suns still worked with Bassandis they could have saved Nem. He'd been too terrified of the watchers to ask for help.

"It's over, Max."

"No. I'm not letting you live to wreak more of your pathetic revenge on us all."

"I don't care anymore."

He searched for the lie in her eyes, for any sign of the bitter madness that had driven her to avenge the death of her father in an empire-spanning orgy of destruction. Nothing.

"They mended me. Changed my mind. They said it was for my own good."

To his surprise she flashed him a look of sadness.

"They told me they'd taken all my feelings and locked

them in a box deep in my soul. All of them - revenge, love, hate, passion. I sense the black prison on the edge of my mind, and I hear the voices trapped inside far away, hammering at the sides. But here," she pointed at her breast, "there's nothing left."

Max stared at her, appalled. He didn't know if the ancient suns had actually meant to punish her, but his own dreams of revenge were pointless if she possessed no comprehension of what she'd done, if all the capacity for guilt and shame was permanently locked away.

"They'll come back," he snarled. "They'll come back in an unholy storm one day and drive you mad. Nobody does what you did and keeps it bottled up forever, alien suns or not. You, Ruth an Vircana, condemned humanity to die in the endless night."

"You want me to answer for my crimes? Who to? The Empire? It's gone. Or maybe you'd like to bury me at the bottom of your little tower in Metacarpi? Ragaleis pushed it over, remember?"

He shifted his stance. Ruth put her hands on her hips and cocked her head to one side.

"Really? This body might be strange but I recall enough of the Spear Tip Dance."

Max stood up, defeated. He also felt nothing. All he wanted to do was lie next to Nem and fall asleep.

"Go, Ruth. Just leave."

She jerked her thumb at the flyer.

"You don't want a lift?"

Max didn't bother to answer. He turned his back on the girl and returned to the edge of the lake. The whine of dynamos filled his ears, and a shadow flitted across the water. Only afterwards did he spot the missile launcher lying on the shore. She must have left it there for him to use for protection, or had she secretly wanted him to blow her out of the sky?

It took him a day to find enough wood to build a pyre. He heaved Nem on top, putting *The Bold Knight and the Apple of Youth* into her crossed hands. He'd never realised how beautiful she was - a winter tree made human and filled with fierce intelligence and holy madness. He unscrewed a missile and emptied its contents over the wood, sparking a light from the metal casing. Watching the flames reminded him of his father's funeral all those years ago on the shores of the Forbidden Sea. He wished he had enough explosives to burn the whole body of God to ash.

Max left Nem and walked past the lake, through an archway cut in the tanzanite wall, and into the skull. Gravity told him he was on a level, thousands of miles above the singularity, but he had no idea which direction he was going - south to the eyes or sideways towards God's temples. The Skin was endless leagues away - countless lifetimes on foot.

After two days of travelling he was lucky enough to come across supplies on a plain littered with tables laid out in neat rows, as if someone had prepared a banquet for millions. Max broke open a couple of crates to find water and rations. He pulled a chair off a table, sat and munched. His mind was empty - images came and went like autumn smoke. He was the last God Talker, a cipher, nothing more. He tried to think of Abby, but as soon as he remembered her crazy hair and wicked grin he sensed his thoughts coming apart, so he pushed her away and focussed on tracing the grain on the floorboards. After finishing his meal he went through the motions of stocking up with food and a canteen, replaced the chair neatly upside down on top of the table, and set off once more.

Days came and went. One morning Max woke up to find his pack gone. Had someone stolen it, or had he dropped it and forgotten? He'd lain down at the edge of a desert to sleep, and the only tracks in the metal sand were his. What did it matter? He was going to die deep inside God's skull - why bother putting off the inevitable?

After half a day staggering up and down dunes in no particular direction he spotted a white tower rising out of a crest a couple of miles away. Old Time Scavenger curiosity gave him enough of a kick to send him in that direction. As he approached he realised it was occupied - a light shone in an upper window of the delicate spire corkscrewing into the grey sky.

Come on, you dozy bastard.

The memory of her voice caught him unawares, and he stopped. *She walked ahead of me, both hands round the butt of her pistol as we headed for the broken flyer. She wore her hair in a tight bun, with those two evil pins, one normal, one poisoned.*

"Max Ocel."

An old man in a white gown stood at the entrance to the tower, one hand raised in salute. Max staggered up the slope to find himself staring into the prison-barred eyes of a Machine Man. *I should fight.* He fell to his knees like an acolyte before his priest.

"Oh dear, oh dear, oh dear. You're in such a state. Let's get you inside."

The ground floor was fashioned from white stone covered with beautiful curves traced in the calligraphy of a forgotten language. A round table sat in the middle and the Machine Man eased Max into a chair. Unable to resist, Max let the creature peer into his eyes and take his pulse before the sage disappeared up the winding stairs. Moments later a mug of dark liquid was pushed into his hands. He drank it and energy roared through his blood. *Now what? Death? Punishment? Torture?*

"There's a giant looking for you. It won't help us mend anything until you're safe and sound," said the old man, sitting opposite and tapping his paper fingers on the wood. "You're a stubborn wretch, Max Ocel. How did you make it here?"

Max shrugged. So had Bassandis told the Machine Men he could fix things? Could he rebuild God's mind with the help of the ancient suns? To what end?

"If it means anything, Max, I think Theuderic was an idiot. Let me show you something before they turn up. I've always wanted to share this, but when I tried to they banished me here. They said I was a 'disruptive influence', like my sister Anselm. Arrogant fools."

The Machine Man pulled a book out of his robe. It was barely larger than Max's palm and the cover and pages were made of fine metal. Even so the words and pictures inside had been rubbed almost to illegibility by a billion thumbs.

"That's written in a language no-one can read, and do you know why?" The creature tapped the page. "It came from a previous universe, that's why."

Max still couldn't speak. All his words had tumbled into a pit and he looked over the edge, trying to see where they'd gone so he could use them again. He stared at the picture of a man in a tower, mouthing words at simple pentacle stars, his lacquered beard jutting from his chin like an upside-down question mark.

"Our universe is not the first. Billions upon billions of years ago it was new, and creatures came here from an older reality. One of them brought this book. No doubt that existence also had a beginning, and perhaps a portal from another dimension before it and so on and so on back into eternity. The times we live in now are merely part of an endless cycle."

The Machine Man leaned forward and put his hand on Max's, paper cold and delicate.

"If people can't pass through the God Door, new creatures like you will evolve there, or perhaps in the cosmos after that. At some point in infinity humanity shall be reborn. But not Machine Men. We are made things and our age is at an end. Theuderic is deluded. There is no place for us in the next universe, and if and when you get through, you make sure it remains that way. I and my fellows are tools created for this time. We are dusty and broken fragments to be abandoned in the shadowy corners of exhaustion. Leave the Machine Men here."

Max struggled to understand what say he'd have in the matter. He was a renegade in the hands of an enemy who would no doubt blame him for the destruction of God's mind.

"Keep the book. One day you might find someone who understands the words."

The sage cocked his head and listened.

"They've arrived. Time to go."

CHAPTER TWENTY-NINE

In three strides Crysanthe had her hand around the man's neck. She pushed him up the wall as he spluttered at her, bug-eyed and turning purple.

"Tainted ones?"

"Crys," Selva tugged at her arm. "Don't. We need him alive."

Every step we take mires us deeper in shit. The general was tired of it all. She didn't care about the man's explanation, it would just mean more hate and despair. All she wanted to do was snap his neck, if only to divert her mind temporarily from the abyss.

She let him go, and Abby pushed her gently back into the centre of the room while her captive hawked and coughed into his hands. The Time Scavenger turned, kicked the man's legs away and planted the sole of her boot on his chest, pinning him to the floor.

"One more time, bollock brain - what is this world?"

"Omega. The last realm of humanity."

"What are you on about? The singularity's the last realm."

Despite himself the man managed a bitter laugh. Selva yanked his head up by his ponytail and slapped him.

"A lie," he hissed in defiance, baring blood-stained teeth. "A lie to keep you away, to make sure that the tainted, the vile, the evil and the mad won't bring the same disease and filth that corrupted the old universe. That god you think you're making shall never be allowed near the next cosmos, and when you try to come here in your ships we'll wipe you out."

"We?" asked Crysanthe. Selva and Abby stepped back from their victim as if he'd suddenly turned venomous. The hints behind his words pointed at a monstrous truth that none them dared acknowledge.

"He means the Black Roses allied with the inhabitants of this planet," said Selva, at last. "You're from the Great White World, aren't you?"

The man sat up and wiped bloody spittle from his chin and neck. He leaned back against the wall and glared at his interrogators, shrugging at a name that was obviously meaningless to him.

"These people came here tens of thousands of years ago, from the place that's now inhabited by Aelspell's cronies." Selva carried on, stepping through the narrative. "They flew here and the Black Roses took them in."

The Lattice was a supply depot for their voyage through space. This is where they all disappeared to, leaving the giants and their worshippers to build their futile lives among the last scatterings of an entire civilisation founded on betrayal. Not just Aelspell and his peasants - we were all abandoned. A hideous rage she'd never felt before ground her heart against her ribs.

"Our forebears made the long journey in the endless night in their ships - the best of mankind, chosen to carry our legacy to the next universe," sneered their captive.

"And you left us, the discarded, to rot next to the corpse of a fake god," said the general, trying to keep her voice from trembling. "You conspired with the Black Roses against the rest of humanity. You plan to pass through the portal and leave everyone else behind."

"How many of you are there?" asked Abby. "How

many of the pure and noble ones will be allowed to travel into the new universe?"

"Half a million."

He said it like a boast. Despite herself Crysanthe laughed out loud.

"Half a million out of billions. And how long do you think you will last among the endless multitudes queueing up around you?"

The man flashed her a look of pure loathing. Selva hunkered down and inserted an elegant finger into his collar. He shuddered at her touch.

"You're not so secure, are you? Why are the Black Roses fighting each other in the sky?"

Crysanthe stared at her Companion. What had the girl found when she'd checked the rest of the building? The wretch had said the name of this place. *Observation tower 755. Observing what?*

"Ramul told me there's a war in heaven. What did she mean? Are the aliens trying to kill you as well?"

"No!" shouted the man. Abby laughed.

"Oh this is pure comedy. They hate you lot as well as us."

"They don't hate us," screamed the man. "They hate you. All the gods hate you, we all hate you, go back and die in the darkness. Vermin! Filth!"

Before anyone could stop her Crysanthe leaped forward and slammed the side of her foot into his neck. It crunched, and she felt the wall through the edge of her boot. Blood erupted from the man's mouth and nose, his tongue sticking out as if he was giving her a last raspberry. She stepped back.

"Certainly touched a nerve there," remarked Abby.

"That was unwise," said Selva.

Crysanthe stalked through the rest of the house, refusing to speak to her friends. The black anger crept in at the edge of her vision. She hefted her dagger in her hand, ready to slaughter anything that so much as twitched in this smug glass and tiled hymn to contempt.

The top floor consisted of a single circular hall ringed with instruments and boards covered in countless grids, maps, charts, schematics and plans. She saw the diamond lattice of the sky repeated in a hundred printouts and hand-annotated photographs, linked at numerous points by coloured thread. Piles of ledgers sat on a round table in the middle of the room and when she opened one she saw endless iterations of the same grid.

"Chronicles of the war," she remarked to Abby and Selva who hovered uncertainly at the top of the stairs. She tried to keep her voice indifferent and factual, but there was something in what she said and how she said it that kept her lover and her friend at bay.

She stepped outside onto a balcony that ran around the circumference, punctuated by platforms on which stood telescopes and scanners. Crysanthe hunkered down and peered through the eyepiece of a reflector the size of a dustbin. She jerked her head back in disgust at the frantic motion, as if she'd overturned a rock to find a seething heap of insects. Forcing herself to look again, she found herself staring at a knot in the lattice. Blots of darkness danced and vibrated endlessly, weaving in and out of each other like blood cells dying under a micro-scope. Once in a while a flash of white made her blink, and cleared a space in the sky that was quickly filled by more fluttering scraps of nothing.

"Now you see the truth," said Ramul.

Crysanthe rose to find the alien standing beside her with that endlessly maddening expression of patient con-cern. She looked at the valley stretching away, flanked by trees. In the hazy distance she thought she saw the edge of a lake or sea, and beyond that delicate white spires towering up into the air. She'd never seen a horizon before, and it seemed as if a porcelain bowl of exquisite design had die-cut the landscape, trapping it underneath like the contents of a snow globe. So exhilaratingly beautiful - a human world filled with people bound for the God Door. She closed her eyes and dreamed of walking down ivy-wreathed streets of cobbled marble under a bright sun with the scent of an ocean in her nostrils, one arm round Selva's waist and the girl's hand on her shoulder.

"How did you find us?"

"An easy thing to hide aboard your ship. I guessed you might try to come to this world."

"You wanted me to. That's why you showed me it on the staircase."

Ramul gave a very human shrug.

"Why did you bring me here, Ramul? To let me know that all hope for those left behind is lost?"

The alien put her hands on the rail and followed the general's gaze.

"A million years ago we took pity on humanity. We created the singularity and the wormholes so you could make a god to carry mankind into the next cosmos. Some opposed the kindness - the True and Utter Enemies - but our factions carried the day because we thought you deserved as much of a chance as any. A hundred thousand years later the first ships arrived, fleeing from the place you call the Great White World. They claimed that man was incapable of building a deity - that within a few centuries of the start of your Great Task society had splintered and turned upon itself. Heart fought Head, Hands conspired against Shoulder and Abdomen. They begged us to give them sanctuary, and to protect them from any of the wicked ones who might come after.

"And so we took counsel and created this world, Omega. The people who lived here and their descendants would accompany the Black Roses into the next cosmos. The rest would perish in the last night. All other ships would be intercepted and destroyed, and if, by chance, your god should ever wake and walk towards the door, our deity would join forces with the others to destroy him."

"That spacecraft we found - the one with all those dead people in cryogenic pods - they came later and were stopped by the acolytes of the Crystal God." She found it hard to condemn the murdered pilgrims as traitors. It took true valour to cast yourself into the unknown, at the mercy of other gods.

"Since the people from the Great White World arrived, countless other humans attempted the voyage. But this time we and the gods were vigilant and none made it through."

Crysanthe had no hate or disappointment left to turn on the alien or herself. Perhaps she should have realised the truth, pieced it together from the clues and hints, but it wouldn't have changed a thing.

"So when you talk of Utter Friends you mean the allies of this world, not those of us who've been abandoned on the singularity. None of you are on our side."

Ramul didn't reply.

"And the war in heaven? Is that between Utter Enemies and Utter Friends?"

"Precise and eternal - a contest to determine whether these people will get their chance. For aeons the stalemate in the sky has preserved Omega. As much as they try, we've always matched the enemies. Our battles are fought with exacting rituals and a meticulous attention to balance, hence they last for thousands of years."

"And all these poor humans can do is watch in fear." Crysanthe turned to face the Black Rose.

"What of us?"

"I'm sorry. I and my friends tried to save you, to plead on your behalf, but we failed."

"I never got a chance to speak."

"You did. We looked inside your mind when you climbed the stairs and saw everything."

"So we're doomed to perish in the last night while these miserable wretches go through to the next reality."

"Perhaps not even these. The war in heaven will end soon and I don't think it'll go well for the Utter Friends."

"So you have nothing for me but bitter words."

"You and your companions can take refuge here on Omega."

Crysanthe didn't even bother to reply. Ramul tapped a rhythm on the balustrade with her fingers and looked sideways at the general.

"Then I don't know what your future is, Crysanthe Uella, Empress of the Ear. We may not be the ultimate judges of your destiny after all. At the edge of these great tasks and eternal wars, these sagas of gods and giants and men, there are fragile anomalies - oddities that make us catch our breath because they show us a reality that slips beyond our easy grasp - rumours of humans making their own way into the next cosmos using nothing more than their own wits, of unborn children who can defeat titans, and of warrior women filled with ancient starlight. Maybe somewhere in all that clutter at the boundaries of perception there's hope."

"Stop. I'm sick of your hints and patronising lies. You did nothing to help us then, and you're doing nothing now," said Crysanthe, weary beyond thought.

Black shapes started to fall through the sky.

"They know you're here. You should leave. Go now or they'll destroy you. Get as far away from the gods as you can and don't return."

Ramul burst into a cloud of feathers and rose up to

meet the newcomers. Crysanthe strode back inside, gave the command to Selva and Abby and within minutes they were sprinting across the valley. Shadows crisscrossed the grass ahead of her and she thought she'd have to stand and fight it out in the shadow of the boulders, but in the end they made it to the corridor. As soon as they'd passed the threshold the floor bucked under her feet and she fell sprawling in the darkness as the Brittle Hag's ship jumped into deep space.

They drifted alongside the line of Gods, facing the column of light pouring from the door into the next universe. Despite fearing they'd alert the invaders, the Abhumans shifted the spacecraft far away from the Black Rose God. Crysanthe guessed the deity lay somewhere behind them, jostling in the queue for salvation. From the window of the main cabin she saw a woman with a skin of shining silver, swathed in a pale radiance filled with thistledown motes. Her brightness lit the armoured back of a two-headed toad creature that carried a layered wooden box a hundred thousand miles deep in its paws. How many realms and civilisations lived in each section of that monstrous carpentry? Billions? Trillions? And all humanity had was a grudging half million snivelling fools living in terror.

"It wasn't your fault," said Abby, slipping her hand into Crysanthe's. "They'd stacked the deck against mankind from the very start."

"They looked inside my mind and based their decision on what they found there."

"That's utter crap. I know what those feathery fuckers are like. Odilon was my mentor and friend for years, like a second dad. They looked in all our minds, Abhumans as well, and let's face it Neke and his mates are the best of us. If they didn't persuade the Black Rose God no-one can."

Selva's hands curved around her waist from behind, and the girl rested her chin on the general's shoulder, following her gaze towards the God Door.

"You need to rest."

Crysanthe ignored her. Everything was empty. Her mind contained nothing but light and silence. She had to will each part of her body to move. She'd even caught herself forgetting to breathe. If her heart still thumped she couldn't hear it.

"We can go back and find Max," she said eventually. Abby squeezed her fingers.

"I want to have a look at the portal first."

The Abhumans had vanished deep inside the vessel as soon as they'd dropped into normal space. The general guessed they were preparing to repel any extra-dimensional attacks that might follow the jump. That left Abby free to guide the ship towards the slab of light marking the boundary between universes.

"We could make a run for it," murmured the Time Scavenger.

"Only gods can pass through. We'd be destroyed," said Selva, though Crysanthe detected the longing in the girl's voice.

The first god in line was a blocky lump of bone and crested plates. Its arm extended towards the portal and as they grew closer Crysanthe saw that the hand had already penetrated the light. Her eyes grew accustomed to the glare, and she began to pick out details and colours beyond - threads of pale orange and green shot with fierce crimson and yellow points. *Galaxies and real stars.*

"I recognise that sky. We shagged in a meadow on a planet beneath a blue giant and looked back at this bastard's claw poking through. What I wouldn't give to slam the door and break its scabby fingers."

We could step onto its skin and reach out and touch the boundary.

Behind them the craft resonated like a bell.

"We should turn back. This is just pointless torture."

"A few more minutes," said Abby.

Maybe Crysanthe should have stayed to make sure the little idiot didn't immolate them all in a mad dash for the portal, but she was so tired and whenever she picked her thoughts up from the ashes in her head they crumbled in her hands. She left the other two and trudged back to their cabin, sitting on the edge of the bed and staring at the iron peeking out between the silk and jewelled drapes. After a while she found the box in which she'd stored mementos of the Companions. She laid the tributes to their perfections on the floor at her feet - a flask of wine, a miniature portrait, a hand bowl from an ancient world, a doll carved from a single, flawless piece of yttrium.

Selva knelt before her among the fragments and nothings and kissed her. She returned the embrace, matching passion for passion as the girl teased her clothes from her and pushed her up and back onto the sheets. It was like watching a meaningless play from a great distance. Even as she pressed her lover's head against her groin, and the Companion worked her to orgasm with her tongue, she tracked her feelings and responses with the same dispassionate calculation she'd used to plot battles. *You're doing this to show you care for me, and my failure and the end of man's hopes doesn't matter.* Eyes full of happy, loving tears stared into hers as Selva cat-curled against her in the aftermath of sex. Long after the woman had fallen asleep she still hunted for the patches of naked iron on the ceiling, as utterly empty as before.

She slipped out of bed, dressed, and wandered into the realm of the Brittle Hag's ship. The Abhuman city looked abandoned, though endless clicks, hoots and grunts poured out of the hall of maps. A tap on the shoulder and Neke stood beside her.

"Don't be sad, Empress. One day we will journey into the new universe with the help of King Max and Queen Abby."

Crysanthe didn't know what to say. To her surprise the monster hugged her and held up a sack. Inside she found fruit and a flask of water.

"I stole it from Omega," clicked the Abhuman in patient baby talk. "You'll need it for your journey."

"I'm not going on any journey."

"Yes you are. I see it in your eyes. It's always been there. Be careful, Empress. Things may still attempt to breach the ship. Even out here we sense ragged claws scraping across the boundaries of our world, trying to get in. Maybe we have toyed with reality too much, perhaps we should return to the Body of God and accept our fate."

She reached down and kissed Neke on his bread loaf head. It tasted like an old musty sofa. Crysanthe turned her back on the settlement. She took two steps and the universe rang with the tolling of a hundred bells. The ground heaved under her feet and she almost lost her balance.

"They've found us," said Neke.

The general and the Abhuman sprinted towards the hall of maps. Abby and Selva appeared at the edge of the camp.

"Crys! Look," yelled the Time Scavenger, pointing at the gulf beyond the plateau. She turned to see part of the ceiling a few miles away collapse. A black line speared after the falling wreckage, vanished below the lip of the plateau. It flexed, tightened, and the universe creaked as the harpoon's chain started to haul the ship - where? Another half dozen spears criss-crossed the sky as if the gods were trying to scribble the ship's interior out of existence. In a second Crysanthe's leaden despair switched to vicious hunger. At last - an enemy to fight.

"Weapons," she shouted to Selva and the two women turned back into the streets, leaping to keep their balance as the floor trampolined beneath them. Crys and Neke entered the hall of maps. The aftershocks died away, but the Abhumans inside the room stood plastered against the walls, staring down at the lead sheet.

"There's legions," clicked Neke and even she recognised the fearful wonder in his words.

Invisible hammers were beating the map clean. As she watched they pounded the delicate tracery flat in a seething mass of dents and circles spreading out from countless points. It looked like the surface of a pond overwhelmed by a sudden downpour.

"Which God is it?" asked Abby as the two women came in, both armed with swords and machine guns. Crysanthe stripped in a second, took the tissue armour from Selva and dropped it over her head so that it sealed to her skin, even as she checked the magazine of the carbine her lover handed to her.

"We don't know," said Neke. "We can't tell."

"It's not a god," said Goma from the other side of the room. The bells began again. The walls shook and dust fell from the ceiling.

"It has to be," clapped Neke furiously. The attack on the lead sheet increased in ferocity. It twitched and billowed as if a maid was giving it a good shake.

"It's not a god, you fat-headed moron!" replied Hama in the creatures' equivalent of a bellow.

"Then who else can it be?" asked Crysanthe.

No-one answered.

"Fuck this," said Abby and disappeared outside. Crys and Selva followed her. A crowd of Abhumans armed with steel bars, shards of metal and spanners clustered around the Time Scavenger. Together they ran to the lip of the plateau. An insane cat's cradle of black chains filled the sky beyond. The void shuddered as they tightened, fragments falling from walls and roof. Crysanthe felt a hideous twisting in her bones, as if all of creation was crunching down on itself. A thunderstorm gathered, kicked off by the attack. Dark clouds roiled and billowed, hiding the ceiling, and lightning arced between the filaments of ebony nothing.

"No hostiles," said Selva, "just chains."

"How can we fight them?"

"They'll come." Crysanthe had no doubts they'd be facing the bastards soon, whatever they were.

"Empress. Do we wait here and defend or go to them?" asked an Abhuman.

"Go to…" she started.

One more toll, this so deep that it felt as if the universe itself had been recast in bronze and struck with a hammer. The distant thunderstorm burst apart. An arrow sped towards her, growing larger and larger until it was as big as a dreadnought. It pulled a chain in its wake and gouged a black runnel in the surface of the plateau with the force of its passage, kicking up sprays of wood, plastic and metal. Selva yelled her name as the missile screamed overhead - the shock wave knocking Crysanthe onto her back. She rolled aside as the ground heaved beneath her. Debris rained from the ceiling as the harpoon slammed into a wall three miles away. Midnight coloured links dropped out of the sky but at the moment they were going to crush her the line snapped taut again and the whole of creation shuddered as the weapon's barbs bit into the other side of the iron plating. She tried to get to her knees and call out for the others but choking dust rolled over her. She heard metal plates the size of houses tumbling free under the strain and cascading onto the surrounding plateau. The floor tipped, and she didn't even have time to scream as she tumbled into the gulf.

Crysanthe lay in darkness. Although her eyes were open the blackness fell so thick it was as if someone had crammed her face into velvet. If she was at the bottom of the trench surely she'd see the room and chain above her, but there was nothing. At first she guessed she'd died, and this was her mind's last attempt to make sense before it faded, yet at the edge of hearing she detected the creaks and tolls of the ship's fabric settling.

"Is she dead?"

No. The fall didn't harm her.

Not Selva or Abby. The first voice belonged to an old woman. *Nan's ghost come to watch me die.* Yet it didn't have Caterina's imperious tones. The second was inside her head. Its rotting sweetness made her wince.

"Fantastic. Don't talk again because she won't be accustomed to hearing you, and the first time it's like having a dentist's drill in your brain. Lead me to her."

Hands touched her feet. They gently moved over her body and up to her face, fragile fingers pressing her cheeks and forehead. She ought to fight, but something made her pause.

"Noble. Beautiful. Clearly in need of a good meal. What's your name?"

Crysanthe didn't have the strength to speak. Water slopped over her lips and she gulped and spluttered.

"That's better. Now, let's see if we can get you up."

Hands plucked at her. They were weak, but with effort the general managed to struggle to her feet, resting her own palm on a bony shoulder. Three vertical rows of blue lamps drifted towards her and she heard metal steps. She made out a woman's silhouette standing beside her, upright despite her age, machine forms beyond, and at the edge of the circle a tangle of dark barbs that eddied and shifted. Once in a while she could have sworn that another figure stood among them. For some reason that vision terrified her, and she shrank away.

"There, there. You're safe. No harm will befall you, but we do need your help."

"How?" Crysanthe managed a rasping croak. The remains of her energy were coming back and with it the old careful disciplines.

"Have you ever come across a man called Maximilian Ocel?"

CHAPTER THIRTY

The Lord of the Carceral Archipelago stood on his balcony at the top of the tower with a cigar in one hand and a tin mug of beer in the other. He wanted to see Metacarpi spread out before him but these days a constant haze hid the city. As its ruler he knew he ought to walk the streets and be among his people, but for some reason he couldn't find the door leading out of the fortress, no matter how many times he searched through the empty corridors and halls of the lower levels.

So, instead, he contented himself with sitting on a chair he'd dragged from his office, or next to the fire when it rained, drinking his beer and reading a book of poems. Once in a while he wanted to talk with Max, but he was a scavenger now. The insolent boy flew the wastelands, stealing rubbish from wormhole worlds in the company of that wretched ginger-haired anarchist. What was her name? Abigail Fabrice. Her sister ran that flea pit, the Theatre of Angels. He should have closed it down years ago, but if he was honest with himself he was proud of his son's defiance - and wise enough to know the people needed to believe they could chafe at something, if only through cheap melodrama and petty acts of sabotage. All was well in the empty silence. Even if he never stumbled across the other inhabitants of the tower, his fire was always lit, the tankard always full and the verse fresh each time he read it.

Once in a while a giant visited, striding out of the distant gloom, staff in hand, to stop by the tower so his eyes were on the same level as the apartment. Today his guest was waiting when he stepped outside into the morning air.

"Hello Max."

"I'm not Max, I'm Herman. Max is my son. Have you met him on your travels?"

He thought he saw sadness in the titan's pale eyes, so he changed the subject.

"It's getting gloomier every day."

"I'm struggling, to be honest. The damage done to the Mind was greater than I thought. The ancient suns helped me keep it all together, but they've left. I told Theuderic if he kept you alive and cared for you I'd rebuild God's soul, but I don't know if I can. I'm sorry. It's just a matter of time. The darkness will grow."

"The Carceral Archipelago shall never fall."

But even as he said it he had a vague recollection of a titan putting his shoulder to these ancient stones and the four chains - *Love, Hate, Joy* and *Sorrow* - parting in clouds of screaming rust.

"This is the last of the God Talkers' Mind Palaces. All the others have disappeared, except your daughter's, but that's empty and all the energy it once held has gone."

"I don't have a daughter, I have a son. His name's Max."

That sad glance again.

"I'll keep the Machine Men at bay as long as I can. Perhaps in the end they'll give up and let you live."

He put his hat on and frowned.

"I may not be able to visit again. Take care, my friend."

A pale young man stood next to him on the balcony. He gave his visitor a hug, feeling bony shoulders under the faded jacket.

"Thank you for bringing me back," the giant said.

After the titan had gone the Lord of the Carceral Archipelago looked up at the sky to check if it was going to rain. The coals were dull, and many had fallen through the grating onto the surrounding hills. Through the gaps he thought he spotted the inside of an immense room with a table, a crib and a doll's house. Mere foolish imagination painting shapes on darkness.

He returned to his quarters and studied himself in the mirror, seeing the long jaw, sharp beard and grey eyes of Herman Ocel staring back. Satisfied he threw a few more logs on the fire and picked up his tankard.

The giant was right. Each day the darkness grew until he lost sight of all but the nearest line of hills. He wasn't too worried. The tower was an axis of moral strength, eternal and inviolate. Once two dreadnoughts had pounded the walls, and later monsters had scrabbled around its perimeter, but it still stood, chains anchoring it to the singularity.

A point of light flared in the darkness, far away, moving swiftly beneath the dead sky. He watched it with curiosity. Once in a while he'd noticed strange shapes before - creatures or shadows limping against the skyline. This was a new thing, and it illuminated a shattered landscape he hadn't seen before.

The spark grew brighter, turning all the air to fire. He flung up his arm to protect his eyes, squinting as it took on the shape of a blazing angel in silver armour. She landed light-footed on the balcony, spear in hand and red hair trailing behind her in a comet's tail. Her green-eyed gaze rolled over him from face to toes and back again. The young woman threw him a half-mocking half-worried look of petulant disbelief.

"Dad? What's with the horrible beard?"

"Who are you?" he managed to stammer. It was all he could do not to fall to his knees in front of this creature. Power he'd never experienced before roared from her, turning everything around him to insubstantial ash. Even the Carceral Archipelago trembled, on the verge of dissolving in the silver radiance.

"I'm your daughter, Rebecca. Remember?"

"I have a son. Max Ocel. I don't have a daughter."

"Charming. I come all the way back here to say goodbye and this is what I get."

"I'm Herman Ocel, Lord of the Carceral Archipelago."

Courage returned, and he got ready to face down this insolent child.

"You're Max Ocel, you dozy bastard."

"Max Ocel?"

"Max."

"Max, wake up." The woman's face filled the universe, except her green eyes had turned into shards of blue ice and instead of red hair she had an auburn razor-cut bob. He blinked, struggling to recognise her familiar beauty. Under her fringe he saw delicate verse etched into her forehead - *and stepping forth we once more beheld the stars.*

"Selva? You've grown hair."

She cradled his jaw in her hand. His head felt so heavy he could barely lift it.

"Max, listen to me. We've got you out of the cryogenic chamber but you won't be able to walk. I'm going to put a muscle suit on you. It's temporary until we can get you to the Kuraii's medical facilities."

"You've grown hair," he repeated. It was all he could think of.

She gave him a wicked grin.

"New worlds, new look."

She looked over her shoulder.

"Help me."

Slender six-limbed automatons carved from black metal and lapis lazuli appeared either side of her and eased him into the air. He glanced down and saw the body of a starving man dangling over a white tiled floor.

"This'll sting."

She slapped a disc of wet clay in the middle of his chest. It spread over his arms, legs and torso, between his thighs and up his back. When it reached the nape of his neck sharp jabs made him cry out. Strength poured through him, borne on a tide of alien chatter that filled his mind. The creatures set him down and he flexed his grey hands, marvelling at the power in his fingers. Selva stepped up and gave him a lingering kiss, nibbling his bottom lip. She stood back and laughed at the growing bulge in his crotch.

"Good. Suit's working. Welcome back."

She was dressed in skin-tight armour that shone like liquid porcelain, a silver egg helmet under her arm. This had to be the last death vision. In its destruction his flailing mind was building a fantasy of rescue and redemption. So be it, he was content to throw himself into the hallucination before the advancing clouds obliterated everything.

"Is Abby here?"

They were in the centre of a cubic room a hundred yards on all sides. The floor was covered in water flecked with ice and behind him lay a ten-foot-long shattered test tube suspended in a net of cables stretching to half a dozen steel boxes. A storm raged outside - he could hear the pounding thunder. *That's where the real me is dying.*

"Not in a fit state," answered Selva. "There'll be time enough. Right now we've got to get you to safety."

As if on cue a cherry red circle appeared in the far wall. Metal poured in smoking runnels from the hole in its centre. Two of the automatons leaped to either side of the breach, clamping themselves to the surface. Containment fields around each figure sparkled in the heat. Slender guns swung down from narrow black shoulders to pour steady pulses of yellow light back at whatever was forcing its way inside.

"Shit," said Selva. She whirled her hand in a corkscrew motion, index finger pointing upwards. "Get him back to field HQ."

A third creature grabbed Max round the waist.

"Later, Max."

Selva ran to join the others, hefting her own rifle to fire at the pale humanoids trying to wriggle through the gap. They dropped to the ground like maggots tapped out of cheese. Max's face pressed against a strip of transparent metal running down the centre of his captor's bulbous torso. He thought he caught a glimpse of a thin barrel-shaped head above a vertical line of blue lights, with triple eyes the colour and shape of olives and a downward curving gash for a mouth. What did Selva call them? Kuraii? Before he fully registered what he was seeing the being's shoulder cannon flipped upright and vaporised part of the ceiling. They shot up at the speed of a mortar shell into the middle of a firefight, the muscle suit turning into a rigid case to stop him being liquefied by the G force.

Three chains as thick as dreadnoughts angled down from a hole in sky, ending in harpoons plunged deep into the floor of the Machine Men's shelf world. A helix spiral of explosions, tracers, tumbling figures and arrowhead flyers twisted along each set of links. Clusters of fighters rose from the blue glowing atmosphere, aiming missiles and energy beams at the chains and their defenders. In reply circular discs tumbled out of the rent above his head. Each one carried a cluster of six-armed infantry firing in groups, or manning larger artillery and power beam gatlings.

In the few seconds he hung between the shattered roof of the white cube and the ragged square of nothing, Max tried to work out who was winning. Despite the firepower Theuderic's forces poured into the grapples it just splashed harmlessly. The invaders' entrance had its own shields which sparkled and coruscated with each futile impact. The ships seemed to be having better luck against the platforms, but for each one blown out of the sky, its metal insect warriors cascading to the ground, another half dozen spilled from the portal. Amid the gloriously bright resurgence of his memories he recalled how few of Theuderic's troops remained after the battle for the Mind. This war of attrition wouldn't last much longer.

And then he was in the tunnel, flipping horizontal after half a mile. His captor flew over a carpet of machines and troops. Complex skeins of light flickered intricate tactical diagrams above their heads. Moments later they landed on a metal plate beside a dozen figures clustered around a vertical map projected in the air. Max saw humans among the spindly Kuraii.

He looked for Abby, heart aching, fighting against the fear planted in his head by Selva's words. *Not in a fit state.* Was she ill? Injured? Stupid idiot would have insisted on leading an assault. What had she done to herself? The crowd centred on a woman in porcelain armour who pointed at various parts of the diagram. The creature set him down and he approached.

General Crysanthe Uella spotted Max. For the first time ever she gave him a completely innocent and happy grin of recognition, which changed into jokey dismay when she saw his beard and scrawny mud body. Even so he battled the urge to run up to her, hug her and kiss those knife-edge cheeks. She must have read his mind -

one eyebrow went up with the mocking indulgence of a queen watching the scullery boy fish a battered rose out of his trouser pocket. She clicked her fingers and three young women surrounded him.

"Come with us to where you'll be safe," said a muscular girl with lemon eyes and a white bristle cut. Max wanted to ask Crysanthe about Abby, but she'd turned back to the battle plans, issuing orders with crisp mastery.

They guided him to an open-topped flyer hovering at the edge of the disc. Judging by their jaw-dropping beauty, and the wicked hint of ascetic cruelty in their eyes, Max reckoned he was in the company of three more of Crys's Companions. The white-haired one, who told him her name was Iolitha, took him on board and steered the car away from the HQ, aiming down the colossal passageway with its black chain running a hundred yards above his head.

As they flickered past machines and flyers the enormity of what had happened began to sink in. They'd come back from the Gods to rescue him, bringing with them an army to match the Machine Men. Who were the Kuraii? What deity carried them towards the portal? Were they true allies, unlike the capricious and calculating Black Roses? He didn't know if the muscle suit was pumping him full of drugs, or its alien mind interfaced with his own. He guessed the latter - the images, ideas and feelings rattling through his head suggested it struggled with the patterns of human thought. Random memories kept overwhelming his brain as the armour took each out one of his unconscious, shook it out like a musty bed sheet and asked him if it was a priority. He fought to impose his own identity on the chaos.

Abby.

"Where's Abby. Is she alright?"

The driver's mouth twitched. He could have hit her. Without a straight answer Max started to lose his temper. *You want priorities, you alien bastard? Abby's all that matters now,* he told the suit.

"Wait here."

The woman dropped the flyer to the tunnel floor. He stepped out and before he could say anything the craft lifted into the air and sped back to the exit.

"Hey!"

His voice echoed through the empty vault. All he could see were orange lanterns spaced every twenty yards and the ever-present chain of nothing far above his head. The Abhumans had said that the harpoons were fired into the ship by extra-dimensional invaders. *The Kuraii. What are they?*

Two yellow lights like giant owl eyes drifted towards him. He tried to see past the glare to make out who drove the new machine. A shadow passed between him and the brightness.

"Max?"

There was pain and tiredness in that voice, and then arms around his neck and a soft thicket of hair enveloped his head. She kissed him, and as he bent over to tumble into a moment he thought he'd never have again, something big and round pushed at his thighs. He reached down and touched Abby's stomach.

"Alright, alright, so I've turned into the queen of sows. Don't rub it in."

The baby moved under his hand.

"Ow. Little bugger."

"Rebecca?"

"No, not Rebecca. A proper sprog. Rebecca's pissed off into wormhole land and given us our child back."

Abby poked a finger through his beard.

"You're losing that right now. What an utter state

you're in. Why are you covered in mud?"

"Selva called it a muscle suit. Theuderic put me in a test tube and I don't think he fed me much."

She held him again and even though the alien armour had sensors feeding her touch into his mind, he longed to feel the real her against his own skin.

"I need to sit down before I fall down," she grumbled. "Come on, I'll drive."

Abby waddled to the vehicle, and he sat beside her, staring at her profile as she eased the flyer into the air. She kept glancing at him, and he wanted to tell her to watch where they were going, but every time that jade gaze locked his, star shells went off in his head.

"You made it," he managed to say. "You persuaded the Black Roses to take us."

"No. They told us all to fuck off."

"The Kuraii's god?"

"They don't have one. Nobody wants us in the next universe and half the gods are getting ready to wale seven shades of shit out of ours if he ever gets anywhere near the door. Speaking of which, I'm guessing the creation of God's mind went equally well."

"The giants killed each other. The Machine Men betrayed us. Theuderic designed the titans to hate humanity, and in the end they turned their malice on themselves."

Abby whistled.

"We failed," he said.

"Oh no we didn't."

The tunnel opened into a vault. A mountain of gears, cogs, gantries and pistons sat in the middle, towering up to where the chain wrapped around a pair of spindles. A second chain stretched into an unlit passageway on the other side. Humanoids crawled over the engine, busy shadows eclipsing the sheets of flickering status lights and panels. Abby stopped at the bottom of a flight of metal steps leading up to a gantry. She was laughing to herself.

"What?"

"Nothing."

"What have you done?"

"Me?" She studied his face for an age. He sensed she was looking past the parody of the Lord of the Carceral Archipelago and seeing the Max she loved. *I'm home at last,* he realised. She leaned across and gave him an endless, suffocating kiss. "I thought you were dead. From now on all the fighting and danger are at an end."

He peeled back and looked for the jokes in her eyes, but she was serious and her cheeks were wet.

"Pregnancy does this to you," she wiped her face with her palm. "Now go up there, someone's waiting to meet you."

Max didn't want to leave Abby. He was terrified if he turned away she'd vanish and this whole dream would collapse, hurling him into the sad memories of his father, or worse, into empty death.

"Go on. I've got tits like lead melons and I'm busting for a piss every five minutes. No way I'm climbing those stairs. Don't worry, I'll still be here when you've finished."

He had to kiss her once more before he ascended the steps. As he did the machinery shuddered into life, spindles straining against the two chains. For a few seconds reality itself tightened, cosmic nails scraped across a chalkboard and he sensed space-time compressing, squeezing every atom in his body. The engine stopped, and steam and arc lightening briefly danced from valves and accumulators.

"Good. That's another fifteen miles," a woman shouted.

I know that voice.

She stood with her back to him, waving her arms as she conducted the Kuraii workers re-configuring the silver filigree circuits with star-bright flashes from their microscopic welders. Her hair was pure white and cut sharp to her shoulders, and in the flickering light he saw veined and knobbed hands flowing with the remembered skill of a retired dancer.

They paused mid-air.

"Max? Is that you?"

He had no idea who this woman was, yet she spoke with the happy anticipation of someone about to be reunited with a long-lost friend. He didn't have time for this, as fancy as that engine was. Max wanted to be back down with Abby, clinging on to the little wretch so she'd never ever leave him behind again, not stumbling through an awkward conversation with an old lady who'd mistaken him for someone else. She turned round and although he only stood a few yards away, her eyes searched the air and her fingers trembled as she groped in his direction. *You're blind.*

"We did it Max. We came back. The wormhole's open and this time it's stable."

Max felt his mouth gape, and he grabbed at the rail. This proved he was hallucinating his last in one of Theuderic's test tubes. Leontine the Steel Queen - a good fifty years older but still filled with the crazy, skittish madness that had sent him and Abby hurtling into the next cosmos.

She walked towards him and he flinched.

"Oh come on, let me touch your face."

Her fingers ran over his features.

"You've lost weight. I don't like the beard."

She cocked her head and listened to the silence.

"Yes, I stayed blind. I found I could dance the numbers

better without the distraction of sight, so I never bothered to get the Kuraii to fix my eyes."

"You were the one firing those harpoons into the Brittle Hag's ship."

"They were total sods, they really were. We knew we could use her spacecraft as an anchor point but every time we tried they cut the link, and we had no way of telling them to stop. It was only when they jumped through hyperspace close to the God Door that we managed to fire enough chains to overwhelm them."

Even the muscle suit's AI had the grace to shut up, giving him pause to work out the implications of what she was saying.

"That tunnel leads to the Body of God. So this one..." he pointed at the other entrance, "...leads to the new universe?"

"We've got it down to three hundred miles, but that's still too far to walk. I'm aiming for fifty, then we begin sending people through."

"You're going to get humanity to *walk* into the next cosmos?'

"How brilliant is that? The other gods can go boil their heads. We'll all be there long before they stumble through."

He had to grip onto the railings as he climbed down to Abby. She watched him with a foot-wide grin. Four steps from the bottom Leontine activated the engine again, curling the links of both chains around their spindles, pulling the old and new universes closer together. The squeeze in his bones threw him off balance and he fell into her, nearly pushing her over.

"Steady on, you dozy bastard."

"You went into the next universe."

She nodded with a casual shrug as if it happened every day.

"Is that what made you…" he gestured at her bump.

"Bloat up like a fat pig? Yes. Rebecca wasn't our child. There's a race of creatures who live between the universes, surfing wormholes. When we shagged just outside the first portal she latched onto our baby and took up residence, aping what she thought our daughter would be like, based on what was in here," she tapped her temple.

That's why she was turning into an even more impossible you.

"The Kuraii helped winkle her out and as soon as they did, boom - I turned into the bloated bag you see before you."

He thought of the toddler playing board games with Bassandis, of the teenager hurling Machine Men into the clouds, and the last vision of the silver angel filling all the universe with her jade gaze and tempest hair. *She came back to say goodbye.*

"Without her none of this would have happened, and I'd be dead."

"S'pose. She never bothered talking to mum again so I can't say I'm overcome with grief. Anyway, she's gone now, and I have a common or garden fidget playing with my guts on an hourly basis."

Abby took his hands.

"It's over Max, and we won. Once all this is fixed we'll start opening doors all over the singularity and inside the Body of God. We won't stop until we find every human."

Max remembered Ruth's flyer flitting between submerged statues in a hall of tanzanite. *You too. You won't escape.*

Kuraii warriors started to emerge from the tunnel, riding their platforms. Max spotted a couple of the Companions standing among the jewelled armour.

"Looks like it's finished. Crys said it wouldn't take us long to win. Let's get you to a medical facility so you can lose that chin rug and get some meat back on the bone," said Abby, thumping him playfully in the crotch. "It makes you look too much like your father. Actually..." she glanced at an open doorway in the far wall. "One more reunion and we're done."

The lead sheet had to be a mile across at the very least. Every Abhuman Max had ever seen was on its hands and knees and the din of their needles scratching the metal drowned out all other noise. In the past, whenever they'd clumped together to make changes, it had been an un-coordinated scrum of flailing grey limbs and bobbing heads. This time they worked in a perfect grid, all facing the same way, each one etching delicate tracery in its own square. The floor was a calculating engine made from a tatty rug filling the immense room, except in the very middle. A black iron sculpture resembling a woman built from coils of burnt swarf stood in an empty circle, silent-ly watching Neke and his people. The air billowed and shifted around her, and Max caught glimpses of more curving, spidery forms rippling through hidden dimen-sions.

The Brittle Hag turned her monstrous face towards him and raised her hand in a disturbingly human greet-ing.

Max sat on a rock next to the wormhole entrance, under a water-coloured sky lit by a blue sun, thumbing through the metal pages of a book older than anything. In the distance ships flitted back and forth over the Kuraii city. Beside him a steady stream of people walked out of the passageway and down the slope to the Gathering Domes. Most carried suitcases or knapsacks, some pushed their possessions on carts or in prams, and once in a while a horse pulled a wagon out of the tunnel, or a steam car came clanking on iron wheels.

At the bottom of the slope Abby and the Abhumans greeted the newcomers, embracing the tearful and frightened, exchanging cheerful back slaps with the ones who ran into this new universe shouting with joy. She kept pausing to press her hands against the small of her back, or put a hand to her stomach when the baby moved. One particularly insistent kick had her falling into the grass, only to be picked up laughing a moment later by Neke and Goma.

The corridor behind Max stretched fifty miles to the Body of God. Crys, Selva and Leontine were back in the dark end of that long night, directing the opening and closing of entrances as they flickered through the deity's corpse and across the singularity. They emptied the cities one by one, from the remnants of bright empires to the deep warrens where humanity had changed into shapes never seen before. Neither Machine Man nor alien god would ever find them, and in the last hour the paper and clockwork architects of God's soul would look around and realise they were the only ones left in that guttering, senile cosmos.

An open wagon clanked past. Max saw stacks of theatre flats and baskets full of costumes jouncing in the back.

"Well, well. The old stories play out and the beggar becomes the saviour of mankind."

That's all I need.

Rebecca Fabrice looked down at him with amusement, a black cigarette dangling from her mouth.

"The Mighty Ruler of Metacarpi," he couldn't help but say. She went *pfff*.

"Madam over there says you built a new Carceral Archipelago in your head. What in God's name were you playing at, you sad bastard?"

No matter how many times he'd faced off with this bloody woman it always ended with him at a loss for words and his ears burning. She removed the dog-end and ground it under foot.

"To be fair, you did alright, Max. Well done."

"Glad you approve."

Abby clambered up the slope towards them.

"Rebecca, is it?" her sister asked, pointing at her bump. "Excellent choice."

"Nope. She's buggered off to Dimension X. We're thinking of another name. Max thought Lucette would be nice. After his mum."

"Oh."

For the first time in his life Max had the uneasy pleasure of seeing Rebecca Fabrice on the back foot.

"Suit yourselves. We're off to prepare a bit of street theatre. Some of these poor sods have never been entertained before."

She embraced her sister, kissing her in the middle of

that absurd red thicket. Before he knew what was happening she bent down, lifted his chin with a single finger and planted one on his lips. Abby burst out laughing at his expression.

Rebecca set off down the slope, walking alongside the first theatre wagon. More followed, some with actors riding on top who shouted and waved at Abby. As the line started to clog at the bottom of the hill the convoy slowed. Max stood up and took his lover's hand. She was watching a covered dray filled with masks and props.

"I've got a lifetime of plays to write."

She tugged him to the back of the cart. Its electric tractor hummed fretfully as it waited for the queue to move again.

"Help me up."

She scrambled onto the boards, Max putting his shoulder to her bottom to give her a boost. Abby grinned down at him and patted the sack beside her. He looked at the entrance to the wormhole.

It'll call you back, Max, Crys had told him. She'd sought him out, guilt preying on her mind and anxious to talk in private, only to find out that he too in the end had set off to wander through a canvas, wood and iron wilderness looking to die. They'd clung to each other in silence like a long lost brother and sister reunited. *Survivor's guilt. The urge to return and lose yourself in the empty, sterile landscapes of the old universe will come over you like a sickness. Always one more door, always one more tunnel or staircase leading on and on. We've got to fight it, Max. Only love brings us home.*

He climbed onto the wagon and sat next to gorgeous, crazy Abby Fabrice.

"There's a part for you in every one," she said.

"Really? Hero? Villain?"

She reached up, plucked a top hat from its hook and stuck it on his head.

"The total fucking idiot of a servant."

The electric tractor's whistle drowned out his reply as the dray trundled down the slope, leaving the dying cosmos far behind.

JOHN GUY COLLICK was born in Yorkshire, England. When he was 10 years old his grandfather gave him a copy of *A Princess of Mars* by Edgar Rice Burroughs, and from then on he was hooked on science fiction and fantasy. He worked for Scotland Yard before moving to Japan for ten years to lecture in literature and philosophy. He is the author of a book on Shakespeare, essays on literature and several screenplays. *Dark Feathered Hearts* is his fourth novel and the final volume in *The Book of the Colossus* quadrilogy.

John Guy Collick lives in Hampshire, England.

Website: johnguycollick.com
Twitter: @johnguycollick